Get Your
Coventry Romances
Home Subscription NOW

And Get These
4 Best-Selling Novels
FREE:

LACEY
by Claudette Williams

THE ROMANTIC WIDOW
by Mollie Chappell

HELENE
by Leonora Blythe

THE HEARTBREAK TRIANGLE
by Nora Hampton

THREE LOVES

by

Sylvia Thorpe

FAWCETT COVENTRY • NEW YORK

THREE LOVES

Published by Fawcett Coventry Books, a unit of CBS Publications, the Consumer Publishing Division of CBS Inc.

ISBN: 0-449-50188-4

Printed in the United States of America

First Fawcett Coventry printing: June 1981

10   9   8   7   6   5   4   3   2   1

CONTENTS

THREE
LOVES

Book One

CELIA

I

Avenhurst Castle in 1751 was by no means as impressive as its name implied. Originally one of the smaller fortresses built to subdue the Welsh Marches, it had fallen into decay after playing its last military role during the Civil Wars, and now, a century later, was little more than a sprawling, irregular mound of broken walls and tumbled stone half buried in trees and undergrowth, from the midst of which reared up the scarred remains of a square keep, crumbling and ivy-covered like the rest. The lords of Avenhurst had long since forsaken the castle in favor of a mansion a mile away, and few people ever visited it, except occasionally to cart away a load of stone for building. So the young man who waited there in the pale sunlight of an early spring morning had little fear of encountering anyone except the person he had come to meet.

He half sat, half leaned on a fragment of broken wall at the outskirts of the ruins, a tall, big-boned youth somewhat too thin for his height. He wore plain, good riding clothes, and his black hair, unpowdered and simply dressed under the tricorne hat, framed a face whose boyish contours as yet gave no more than a hint of bold bone structure beneath, though there was arrogance in the line of the jaw and the high-

11

bridged nose. A face which suggested a reckless and fiery nature, with only the eyes—dark brown, long-lashed and remarkably handsome—hinting at a gentler side to his character. His name was Jocelyn Rivers. He was eighteen years old, and head over heels in love.

There was no real reason why he and Miss Celia Croyde should meet in secret. Their families were neighbors and upon friendly terms even though Jocelyn's father was Viscount Avenhurst while Celia's forebears, only two or three generations before, had been yeoman merchants. The Croydes had prospered; passed, by the acquisition of wealth and land and by judicious marriages, into the ranks of the lesser gentry and were now accepted upon equal terms by older families. Jocelyn and Celia had known each other for years, but it was only since Celia's recent emergence from the schoolroom that a romantic attachment had grown up between them. It was still new and wonderful to them both, but it was at her insistence rather than his that secret assignations were made and kept.

Somewhat belatedly kept, usually, on the lady's part, and this particular morning was no exception. Jocelyn had been foolish enough to come early to the trysting place, and as the minutes slipped away, his patience, never very great, began to slip away also, so that by the time his lady-love finally arrived, he had left his place by the wall and was pacing irritably up and down, slashing with his riding whip at the brambles thrusting out between the stones.

The instant he set eyes on her, however, annoyance fled, and with it all thought of the protest he had intended to make. She came headlong, urging her bay mare at a canter along the narrow path which emerged from the trees fifty yards away, the groom without whose attendance she was not permitted outside her father's gates following at a discreet distance. Jocelyn went quickly to meet her, catching at the mare's bridle as Celia reined in beside him.

"I'm sorry, Jocelyn! So very, very sorry!" she greeted him breathlessly. "I did not mean to keep you waiting. Indeed, I scrambled in such haste to make ready that I don't doubt I look a fright."

"You look beautiful, as you always do," he replied, and indeed she did, with her cheeks flushed from the morning air and her eyes shining. She was a dainty little creature with delicate features, a cloud of soft dark hair, and enormous

12

violet-blue eyes. Just seventeen, and as yet unspoiled by the admiration which would certainly be hers when she entered a wider world, she possessed the innocence and the confiding ways of a trusting child.

A child's heedlessness, too. Without looking to see if the groom was still out of earshot, she leaned from the saddle, hand outstretched, her radiance shadowed now. "Oh, Jocelyn, what are we to do? Papa is going to take me to London."

"To London?" he repeated blankly. "When?"

"At the end of the month. He has hired a house for the whole of April and May, and after that we are to go to Tunbridge Wells. He told me yesterday, and I had to pretend to be happy and excited, but oh, Jocelyn! I cannot bear to be parted from you."

With an effort he mastered his shock and dismay. Taking her hand and pressing it, he said softly: "Wait, love! We will talk of this directly."

He cast a wary glance round for the groom and saw that the man had dismounted some yards away and was now gazing disinterestedly up at the ivied ruins, apparently deaf and blind to the meeting taking place so close at hand. Distrusting this bland detachment, Jocelyn summoned him and handed over the mare's reins, sliding some coins into the servant's waiting palm at the same time.

"Wait here," he said briefly. "Miss Croyde will walk with me for a little while."

He held up his arms to Celia, who obediently freed her foot from the stirrup and slid down into them. Resisting the desire to hold her close, he set her on her feet—her head was barely level with his shoulder—then took her hand to lead her along a barely discernible path which wound among the massive, crumbling walls and crowding undergrowth into the heart of the castle. She set off with him willingly enough, but this was the first time she had penetrated beyond the outskirts of the ruins, and soon she found herself disliking the strangeness of the place, with its chill of ancient stone and the tangled branches shutting out the sunlight. The thorny talons of a huge bramble snatched at her skirts, and she stopped short with an exclamation of protest.

"Oh, let us go back! I do not like it here, and besides, I shall tear my habit."

"No, you will not." He dropped to one knee and carefully

13

disentangled the thorns from the fine cloth. "Look, my love! Only a few steps more and we shall be in the open again."

She saw that this was true, and reluctantly allowed him to lead her forward again. The path ended in a drop of about three feet to a level, open space at the foot of the keep, a stretch of lush green grass sprinkled with the gold of celandine. Jocelyn jumped down and once more held out his arms, and this time he did not set her down. She responded to the embrace, clasping her arms trustfully about his neck and shyly returning his kisses, though when at last he lowered her to her feet, she hid her flushed face against the front of his coat and would not look at him.

"Oh, I ought not to behave so!" she said with sigh. "It is wrong and shameless."

"Shameless? You?" He laughed gently, cradling her in his arms. "My foolish love!"

"I am," she insisted in a muffled voice. "Meeting you in secret, allowing you to bribe my servant not to betray us. No lady should even think of doing such things."

He chuckled. "I'll wager many of them do!" Then the amusement faded from his eyes, to be replaced by anxiety as he looked down at the dark curly head—her hat had fallen off onto the grass—nestling against his chest. "Celia, you did not mean what you said about going to London?"

"Yes, I did. Would I have said such a thing if it were not true?" She did look up at him now, her eyes tragic. "Papa has made all the arrangements. He says that at seventeen I am old enough to make my curtsy to society."

And old enough to find a husband, Jocelyn thought angrily, which will be easy for the beautiful only child of a rich man. If they take her to London, I shall lose her. He said urgently:

"This settles it! I must go to your father and make formal request to marry you."

The declaration of this honorable intention did not seem to afford Celia the reassurance he had hoped. She continued to stare at him, consternation now clearly mirrored in her eyes.

"Oh, Jocelyn, I wish you will not! He will be so angry."

"Angry?" The response came sharply, in a challenging, almost haughty tone. "Do you mean to tell me that your father will find such a request unacceptable?"

She disregarded the question. "He thinks we are scarcely

14

acquainted. If you ask leave to marry me, he will guess that we have been meeting and he will never forgive either of us. I shall be in *such* disgrace, and as like as not forbidden ever to see you again."

That gave him pause for a moment, for he knew how strictly she was chaperoned; more strictly by far than his own elder sister had been before her marriage. Being the only child of a man less sure of his position in the world than Rivers of Avenhurst, and consequently more anxious not to transgress the strictest rules of propriety, Celia had been watched over by nurses and governesses, as well as by her anxious parents, every day of her life. It was only by the connivance of the groom that she had been able recently to escape their vigilance, and it could not be long before these constant early-morning rides aroused suspicion.

"He is bound to learn of our meetings sooner or later," Jocelyn pointed out reasonably, "and better by far that we be honest with him than wait to be betrayed by accident or malice. I have felt all along that there is no real need for subterfuge, and now there must be an end to it."

Still she was not convinced. "Jocelyn, can you not come to London, too? Lord and Lady Avenhurst will be going soon, as they always do. Would you not be permitted to accompany them?"

Jocelyn hesitated. He knew that such permission, if he sought it, was more than likely to be granted. His father would probably be pleased by such apparent evidence that his younger and only surviving son was ready to accept the life of a man of fashion rather than the military career on which his heart had hitherto been set; but it was set now on marriage to Celia Croyde, and nothing, Jocelyn promised himself silently, would be allowed to thwart this new ambition.

"Only think of it," Celia was saying eagerly. "There will be balls and parties, we can go to the theater, to Vauxhall and Ranelagh—oh, how delightful it will be! And among such crowds of people, we can meet quite openly—!"

Her voice faltered into silence, for Jocelyn was shaking his head.

"No," he said decisively. "In London you will be watched over even more closely than you are here, and what will it avail us to meet only in some crowded ballroom or public place? I want the right to be with you, to claim you as my future wife. I shall go to your father."

"It will be not the least use," she said despairingly. "Oh, Jocelyn, do you not *see*? Papa will never believe that you have just suddenly taken it into your head to marry me. He will be suspicious and start to question me, and I shall betray everything. I always do! I have never been able to deceive Papa. And when he knows that I have behaved so shockingly, he will blame it all on you, and then nothing in the world will persuade him to forgive you. It will be the end of everything!"

There was enough truth in this to make Jocelyn stop and think. William Croyde was a man of choleric temper and extreme stubbornness, and Celia was the apple of his eye. If he became prejudiced against Jocelyn, as he certainly would if he thought his daughter had been led into impropriety, it would be impossible to make him change his mind. Clearly it was necessary to tread warily. For a minute or two Jocelyn was nonplussed, but then a solution to the problem occurred to him.

"Then I shall go instead to my own father," he said, "and make a clean breast of the whole affair. If *he* will broach the matter of our marriage, Mr. Croyde will suspect nothing. That is how most marriages are arranged."

Celia looked doubtful, and still not entirely happy. "Yes, but will Lord Avenhurst be any less shocked than my own father? If he knows how scandalously I have behaved, he may not think me a fit person to marry you."

"Very well; I'll not tell him the full, disgraceful sum of it. Just that I worship you from afar, and—!" He broke off, for Celia was looking stricken. "You goose! What harm do you suppose we have done? My father is too much a man of the world to be shocked by a few secret meetings, or—" he suited action to the words "—stolen kisses."

And far too practical, he thought with sudden cynicism, not to welcome the heiress to William Croyde's substantial fortune, even if we had gone far beyond innocent kisses. He will know how to handle Croyde, and Croyde himself is certain to be flattered by the prospect of an alliance with the Rivers family, even though I am not the heir. I shall have ample means without Celia's dowry, and we were lords of Avenhurst while Croyde's forebears were only shopkeepers.

16

Celia had thought of another possible obstacle. "Suppose Lord Avenhurst considers you too young to be married?"

Jocelyn shook his head. "No fear of that," he replied confidently. "He wishes me to make an early marriage. In fact, he commands it as my clear duty. He told me so two years ago, when my brother, John, died."

She stared at him, a frown wrinkling her brow. "But why? Your brother left a son, little Anthony."

"Yes." With an arm about her, Jocelyn led her across the grass to where a fragment of wall formed a convenient seat. "But you know that he is a sickly brat, and my stepmother has given my father no children, nor is likely to now. The future of the family, so I am told, rests with me."

There was resentment in his voice, bitterness in the set of his lips. Celia thought he looked older suddenly, and for a moment almost a stranger. She said timidly:

"It is natural, I suppose, for his lordship to be concerned."

"Perhaps!" Still that resentful note in Jocelyn's voice. "What is not natural is his obsession, for it is nothing less, with the need to exclude our cousins in the north from the succession. There is some old quarrel between them—I do not know what—and he swears that not one penny, nor one inch of land, shall fall into their hands. It is not in his power to bequeath it away from them. If he dies leaving no direct male heir, his estates and fortune, as well as the title, must inevitably pass to them. Anthony is barely nine years old, and even if he survives to manhood, it will be years before he can make the succession secure. Therefore *I* must be sacrificed."

"Sacrificed?" Celia repeated reproachfully. "Jocelyn, that is unkind!"

"I did not mean it so, believe me." He caught her hand to his lips and then kept it fast in his. "I shall obey my father gladly now, but two years ago it seemed that my only real ambition was to be denied me. I have always longed to be a soldier, and my father had promised to purchase a commission for me as soon as I was old enough, but John's death put an end to that. Father's only brother, the uncle for whom I am named, was killed fighting in Flanders before he was twenty, and he feared that a similar fate might befall me. I tried to convince him that I might just as easily die of some illness here at home, or break my neck in the hunting field, but he would not listen. My ambitions could go hang. I must bide

17

here, playing second fiddle to a puny, whining pup and safe-guarding an inheritance which is unlikely ever to be mine."

The bitter anger roughening his voice stirred Celia to vague uneasiness. She looked quickly at him, found little reassurance in the hard, unfamiliar profile, and said apprehensively, her tone pleading for a denial:

"You cannot wish the poor child to die?"

"I could wish that he had never been born, or had been born a girl, like the two who came after him." Jocelyn kicked moodily at a fragment of stone buried in the grass at his feet. "Or even that all three were sturdy boys. Then at least the succession would be secure, and I, free to follow my own destiny."

"Would you need to follow it far?" Stiving to win him out of the black mood she found so disquieting, she leaned closer, lifting her free hand to turn his face towards her. "Would you, Jocelyn?"

"No, by God!" His arm tightened about her; there was a glow in the brown eyes gazing down into hers. "Only far enough to win you, my life!"

She was crushed against him, his grip bruising her sides; his kisses became demanding in a way she had never before experienced, and, suddenly frightened, she struggled frantically to escape. Struggled in vain at first, and then abruptly he let her go, sprang to his feet and took a few hasty steps away from her.

Celia, alarmed and dismayed by the response her innocent coquetry had provoked, promptly burst into tears. Her romantic adventure had gone disastrously awry, and nothing would ever be quite the same again. She sobbed quietly, like an unhappy child, brushing the tears away with her fingertips. The sound of her weeping brought Jocelyn back to her, in command of himself now and concerned only to comfort.

"Sweetheart, forgive me! I did not mean to frighten you." He was on one knee before her, drawing her hands down from her face, tenderly drying her cheeks with a fine cambric handkerchief. "What a brute I am to use you so! I will never do so again, I swear."

"I want to go home," she said piteously.

"Yes, and I will take you," he assured her, "but not for a few minutes, love. It will not do for your groom to see you like this. Compose yourself a little. See, I will not even sit beside you, so you have no cause to be frightened."

18

He put the handkerchief into her hand and got up, walking away from her across the grass and silently cursing himself for that momentary loss of self-control. Of course she had been frightened, not only by the roughness of his kisses but by the mood which had preceded them, and by his unintentional betrayal of the resentment which had been smoldering within him for the past two years. Even now, when the early marriage his father demanded of him had suddenly become the thing he most desired, he could still feel anger at the manner in which his future had been disposed of, and the indifferent brushing aside of an ambition he had cherished since childhood. Celia could not be expected to understand these things, any more than she could, as yet, understand the strength of the feelings she aroused in him.

Celia herself, carefully drying her eyes and doing her best, as Jocelyn had urged, to compose herself, became aware of a chill, of the withdrawal of the kindly warmth of the sun. Thinking that clouds had obscured it and fearing a sudden shower, she glanced apprehensively upwards, and found that it was the shadow of the ancient keep which had imperceptibly encompassed her. Grim, jagged and roofless, it loomed menacingly above her, while the fluffy white clouds drifting by created the illusion that it was moving, was about to fall and entomb her in uncounted tons of stone. With a stifled cry she sprang to her feet, and Jocelyn turned quickly towards her.

"Oh, let us go!" she exclaimed. "This place frightens me."

Without waiting for him, she hurried back the way they had come, snatching up her hat from the ground as she passed, but the high step up to the path defeated her, and she had to pause for Jocelyn to lift her to the upper level. Jumping up beside her, he caught her hand to detain her, saying in a pleading tone:

"Celia, will you not forgive me?"

"I do forgive you, Jocelyn. Indeed I do! Do not speak of it anymore. Let us go now."

He held her back. "I shall speak to my father about our marriage as soon as I get home."

"Oh, pray do not! Remember that we are all to dine at Avenhurst Place today, and I would not be able to face his lordship, knowing that he knew. Jocelyn, promise me that you will not."

He gave the promise reluctantly. That he gave it at all

19

was due solely to the fact, of which her protest had reminded him, that there were guests at his home, and would be more later in the day. The viscount was already entertaining a certain Colonel Meriden, his wife and daughter, while various neighbors, including Celia and her parents, would be gathering there to dine.

"At the first opportunity, then." He saw that she still looked troubled, and added urgently: "Celia, you do wish to marry me, do you not? You do love me?"

She could answer the second question more readily than the first. Oh yes, she loved him. She had tumbled headlong into love at her first meeting (for one could not count an intermittent childhood acquaintance) with this dark, masterful young man who so exactly matched the hitherto shadowy hero of a schoolgirl's romantic dreams. Lord Avenhurst's son, who lived at the grand, classically-pillared mansion which was the most splendid house for miles around; who possessed a reputation for wildness which was bound to fascinate a very young lady; who, from the occasion of that momentous meeting, had courted her with reckless persistence. She had reveled in the romance of secret assignations and the heady excitement of Jocelyn's extravagant compliments and declarations of love; had, in fact, been living a fairy tale. Today, for the first time, reality had intruded, and she had retreated in instinctive alarm. She wished that everything could go on as before. She did not want her father's consent to be asked or given, for that would reduce the fairy tale to the prosaic level of every day. Most of all, she wanted to forget how violently and hungrily Jocelyn had kissed her, and the look in his face when he spoke of his frustrated ambitions. Somehow the two things were inextricably bound together in her mind, and indicated an aspect of his character which did not fit in with the idealized creation of her own romantic imagination.

"Let us wait a little," she entreated. "Only think what would happen if either of our fathers did not agree. Just a little while, Jocelyn, I beg of you."

How could he refuse her when she pleaded so prettily with that confiding air, her head tilted back so that she could look up, wide-eyed, into his face? How could he, even though his own instinct was to be done with secrecy and to claim her before all the world? He scented danger. Already at least two of his own boyhood comrades were dangling after her, and even Sir Digby Vaine, whose wealth and influence in the county were second only to Lord Avenhurst's, and who spent much of his time in the fashionable world of London and Bath, had taken to calling frequently upon the Croydes. To be sure, Sir Digby was a widower and, in Jocelyn's eyes, middle-aged (he was thirty-five), but it was possible that even his advanced years did not render him indifferent to Celia's charms. Possible, too, that his dandified dress and air of fashion might blind William Croyde to the impropriety of such a May-and-December match. It was unlikely that Celia would be forced into anything repugnant to her, but if Vaine, or anyone else, won her father's approval before Jocelyn could do so, it would make things confoundedly awkward.

"For a little while, then," he agreed reluctantly, "but only a little while. I want you betrothed to me before you go to London." He had both her hands now and held her prisoner, only half jesting as he added: "If I had my way, I would marry you tomorrow, for until we are wed I shall know no peace of mind."

"Perhaps, sir, you will know none then." She laughed, happy again, now that her fairy tale was no longer immediately threatened. "How can you tell? I may prove to be a very shrew! No"—for he had sought to draw her again into his arms—"I must make haste if I am to be home in time for breakfast. Give me my hat, which you have made me drop again upon the ground, and let us go."

He retrieved the hat, brushed it and set it carefully on her head. Her hands lifted to settle it firmly in place, were caught by and clung to his, and she let him kiss her again after all, unmindful of passing time.

"I do love you, Jocelyn, so very much," she whispered. "It is our secret, our lovely secret. Let us keep it so for a little while longer."

Hand in hand, they made their way along the twisting path to where the groom waited with their horses. Behind them, in the empty heart of the castle, the shadow of the keep lay dark and cold across the flower-starred grass.

He escorted her the short distance to her home, with the groom following always in sight, though far enough behind not to overhear a low-voiced conversation. Thus adequately chaperoned, they had covered two-thirds of the journey when, at a place where four ways met, they saw two other riders approaching along the lane on their right. Jocelyn uttered an exclamation of annoyance.

"Vaine, confound him, and young Simon!" He saw Celia's frightened look and added reassuringly: "No need for alarm, sweetheart! We met by chance, remember?"

Sir Digby Vaine, with his eldest son, fourteen-year-old Simon, a few paces behind him, drew rein at the crossroads as they all reached it. He removed his hat with a flourish, and bowed gracefully from the saddle.

"Miss Croyde, what an enchanting surprise! I never expected the pleasure of meeting you at so unseasonable an hour, but no doubt the fine weather has tempted you forth." He nodded affably to her companion. "Good morning to you, Jocelyn."

Jocelyn responded curtly, for he had never liked Vaine or felt completely at ease in his company. Vaine was a slightly built man of moderate height, but he possessed considerable presence, so that beside him Jocelyn always felt overgrown and clumsy. His thin, intelligent face was made remarkable by hazel eyes which, though usually veiled by sleepy lids, could occasionally blaze forth with disconcerting brilliance, and he dressed with an elegance which verged upon foppishness. He had been a widower for eight years, his wife having died in giving birth to their fourth child, and his neighbors had given up expecting him to marry again. Now, observing the attention he was devoting to Miss Croyde, they were beginning to wonder if they were mistaken.

"Oh, yes, indeed!" Celia said breathlessly now. "I love to ride in the early morning, when everything seems fresh and new. Particularly in the spring! It is so delightful to know that winter is over at last. When I woke to see the sun shining, how could I bear to stay indoors?"

"How, indeed?" Sir Digby's sleepy gaze rested thoughtfully upon her face and then shifted to her companion. "What of you, Jocelyn? Did the springtime sunlight tempt you also to early rising?"

There was the faintest undertone of irony in the light, bored voice. Jocelyn's hand tightened on the bridle so that his horse snorted and tossed its head, and he said shortly:

"I always rise betimes and ride before breakfast. The weather is a matter of indifference to me."

"Ah, you hardy countrymen!" Sir Digby said indulgently. "Young Simon here is the same. He has tried to hale me forth these three days past, merely to convince me that he is capable of controlling this resty young horse he wishes me to bestow upon him. Happily, I am now convinced and we are on our way home. Miss Croyde, our ways lie together. May I have the honour of escorting you to your father's house?"

She hesitated, casting an anxious, inquiring glance at Jocelyn. "That is kind of you, Sir Digby, but when we met just now, Mr. Rivers was good enough to offer to accompany me."

"Naturally, Miss Croyde, but there can be no reason, can there, why we should not all ride on together?"

Celia did not seem to know what to say. Jocelyn could think of several reasons, but for her sake could not voice them, so, inwardly seething, he watched Vaine fall in upon her other side. Simon followed with Celia's groom, and could soon be heard chatting to him about horses with an animation not echoed by two of their three companions. Celia, who regarded Sir Digby as belonging to her father's generation, was wondering apprehensively if he would mention this encounter to Mr. Croyde, while Jocelyn was too angry, and too conscious of being at a disadvantage, to bear any part in the conversation.

If Vaine noticed their lack of enthusiasm for his company, he gave no sign of it. Having inquired punctiliously after the health of their respective families and informed the unresponsive Jocelyn of the pleasure with which he was looking forward to the dinner party at Avenhurst Place that afternoon, he gave them both a considerable shock by saying pleasantly:

"No doubt, Miss Croyde, *you* are now looking forward with no small degree of anticipation to your first visit to London?"

Jocelyn started and shot him an angry, suspicious glance, while Celia, looking more dismayed than excited, colored to the roots of her hair and said, with a nervous little stammer:

"How—how did you know, sir, that I am going to London? Papa only told *me* of it yesterday."

"Very likely, my dear lady, but I have had the honor of being in his confidence for some weeks. He sought my advice regarding the acquisition of a suitable house, and it so happened that I was able to introduce him to a friend of mine who, owing to a family bereavement, will not be making use of his town residence this season and was desirous of finding a suitable tenant for it. They were able to come to a satis-

23

factory arrangement, and so I had the happiness of being of service to them both."

"Oh!" Celia was searching frantically for something to say. "We are to reside in Mount Street, I think Papa told me."

"Yes, that is correct. The house is situated almost opposite to my own, so I shall have the felicitation of being your neighbor as well as, I trust, your friend." He leaned forward a little to look past her, eyebrows inquiringly raised. "You spoke, Jocelyn, I think?"

"No," Jocelyn replied between his teeth, "I said nothing."

"Ah! Then I ask your pardon."

There was a faint smile hovering about Sir Digby's lips which Jocelyn found as infuriating as the unwelcome information he had just let fall. Unreasonable to feel that Vaine had deliberately conspired with William Croyde to part Celia from him, and equally unreasonable to be jealous of the fact that Vaine had known of the proposed visit to London while he himself was still in ignorance of it, but reason had very little to do with Jocelyn's present frame of mind. He lapsed into sulky silence while Sir Digby described to Celia some of the entertainments she might expect to enjoy during the London season.

"And what of you, Jocelyn?" Vaine inquired kindly after a few minutes. "Do you accompany Lord and Lady Avenhurst to town this summer?"

Jocelyn shrugged. "Perhaps. I spent some weeks there last year, however, with my sister and her husband."

"My dear boy!" Sir Digby was amused. "One can scarcely acquaint oneself with London society in the course of a single visit, especially at so early an age. I would have supposed that this year Avenhurst would wish you to make your bow to the Polite World under his own aegis—unless, of course, he has other plans for you. He is sending you abroad, perhaps?"

Jocelyn gritted his teeth. It was customary for any young man of rank and wealth, as soon as his formal education was completed, to be dispatched in the company of a tutor on a prolonged round of visits to the various capitals of Europe. The Grand Tour, as it was known, was considered an essential part of a gentleman's education, but though the Honourable John Rivers had made such a tour, setting out when he was Jocelyn's present age and remaining abroad for nearly two years, Lord Avenhurst had said nothing of his younger son doing the same. Jocelyn had wondered more than once if he was to be deprived of this chance to travel as well as of his military ambitions, so it was especially galling to have the matter speculated upon by someone whom he disliked as much as he disliked Sir Digby Vaine.

"I have no idea, sir," he replied in a voice of barely controlled fury. "My father has not yet seen fit to inform me of his intentions, but perhaps *you* will be so obliging as to discover them for me, as you have discovered Mr. Croyde's."

Celia, stealing a scared glance at his face, was appalled to see there the look which had frightened her a short while before in the castle ruins. In a moment, she thought distractedly, he would say something which would betray them completely, and then Sir Digby would indeed have a tale to carry to her father. She plunged frantically into speech.

"It would be delightful to have *all* my friends in London, for I will confess to feeling just a little apprehensive at the prospect of going to live in a great city where I know no one. I fear I shall be lonely."

"My dear Miss Croyde!" Vaine had been thoughtfully studying Jocelyn from beneath those sleepy lids, but now he transferred his attention, smilingly, to Celia. "You need feel no apprehension on that score. You will take London by storm, and be the toast of the town within a se'nnight."

She blushed and protested, declaring that this was nonsense, that she was nothing out of the common, but Jocelyn could see that the notion pleased her. He cursed Vaine in his thoughts for putting such an idea into her head. It was likely enough, of course, and no one would be more proud than he to see her the most acclaimed beauty in London—but only if she were safely betrothed to him.

They were not far from her home now, and the lane narrowed as it began to climb, between steep banks, towards the gates. There was not room for more than two riders to go abreast, and though Jocelyn had been fiercely determined that it was he who would remain at Celia's side, he found that somehow Vaine had outmaneuvered him. He was obliged to drop back, and his discomfiture was completed by Sir Digby glancing back over his shoulder and beckoning to his son to come up with them.

"Simon has been wishing for an opportunity to talk to you, Jocelyn," he remarked. "You have the same fencing master, who tells us that you are quite his most exceptional pupil.

25

I know that my son is hoping you will be kind enough to give him a practice bout from time to time, and the benefit of your advice."

He smiled kindly upon them both and turned back to Celia, while Jocelyn, thus ruthlessly reduced to schoolboy status, raged inwardly and paid scant attention to Simon's eager talk. He would like, he thought savagely as he glared at Sir Digby's elegant back, to have an opportunity to make use of his swordsmanship on the father rather than the son, and not with buttoned foils in a practice bout.

Avenhurst Place had originally been built during the second quarter of the previous century, but Jocelyn's grandfather, imbued with the spirit of his age, had had the old house pulled down and had built in its stead a mansion of classical design, the central block, with its immense, pillared portico, flanked by lesser wings, or pavilions, linked to the main block by curved colonnades. Jocelyn's father had extended these improvements to the gardens, replacing the old-fashioned straight walks and formal parterres with wide lawns, a lake as long and narrow and winding as a river and paths which meandered around shrubberies and through plantations in a fashionably natural manner. It was a magnificent country seat, and justifiably famous, but to Jocelyn it was simply his home, and he took its grandeur very much for granted.

By the time he returned to it that morning, his anger had cooled sufficiently for him to realize the necessity of adopting a conciliatory attitude towards his father if he was to enlist his help in approaching Mr. Croyde. The business would need to be handled tactfully, and Jocelyn admitted to himself (though he would have admitted it to no one else) that he felt certain qualms at the prospect.

The truth was that he and his father were bound neither by close ties of affection nor by common interests. Lord Avenhurst was a proud, cold, reserved man whose preoccupation was with the world of politics, with the feuds and factions of government and the subtle and sometimes devious means by which power was gained and held, while Jocelyn, until he fell in love with Celia Croyde, had yearned only for a life of action and adventure. His resentment at being denied this had gone very deep, making impossible the closer understanding which might have developed between him and his father as he grew older, for at present they were not even

26

very well acquainted. Most of the viscount's time was spent in London, and even in the country he maintained a ceremony and formality which had always kept his children at arm's length. His first wife had been a loving and devoted mother, but she had died when Jocelyn was only eight years old, and the second Lady Avenhurst, lacking children of her own, was concerned more with the fashionable world than with matters domestic. She had never made any attempt to understand Jocelyn or to alter the slight dissatisfaction with which Avenhurst was apt to regard his younger son.

Jocelyn left his horse at the stables, which were accommodated in the pavilion on the eastern side of the house, and walked through the colonnade and the corridor which traversed the main building at ground level, where it consisted entirely of domestic offices. The magnificent state apartments were on the floor above, approached by the flights of steps sweeping up to the portico, but the west wing contained smaller and less formal apartments, including a morning room, where, since only three guests were at present being entertained, breakfast would be served. This was usually eaten at about nine o'clock, and when Jocelyn entered the room, he found everyone else already at table. His father and Colonel Meriden were talking politics, while Jocelyn's widowed sister-in-law, Charlotte, was holding forth to the other ladies on the subject of some indisposition from which her youngest child, four-year-old Elizabeth, was presently suffering.

Charlotte was a thin, intense young woman whose sole passion in life was her children, and though for her late husband she had felt respect and a mild affection, the chief source of her grief at his untimely death was the fact that she was now denied the large family she so fervently desired. She could, of course, marry again, but that would mean parting with her only son, her first-born, for nothing would ever induce Lord Avenhurst to relinquish his heir. So all Charlotte's maternal devotion was lavished upon the three children she did have, and especially upon Anthony, with results which certain dispassionate observers felt to be lamentable. Lady Avenhurst, whose own childlessness was a source of constant though secret mortification to her, listened with such sympathy as she could muster to a wearisome description of Elizabeth's symptoms, but Mrs. Meriden, herself the mother of a large brood, entered into a lively discussion of the probable cause and most effective cure for the little girl's ailment.

The Meridens had been strangers to Jocelyn before this visit, and he had once or twice wondered, though without much interest, why they had been invited. The colonel, he gathered, was wealthy, with large estates in Hampshire, so probably he had influence of some kind which the viscount was anxious to enlist for political reasons. Jocelyn himself had repeatedly been called upon to entertain Miss Jane Meriden, and he soon learned that today was to be no exception, his father informing him that since Miss Meriden wished to see something more of the countryside, he had assured her that Jocelyn would be happy to act as her escort and guide.

"By all means, sir." Prompt agreement would win his lordship's approval, so necessary just now, and the hours until he would see Celia again had to be filled somehow. He turned to Jane Meriden. "I am at your service, ma'am, whenever you choose to ride out."

She nodded her thanks. "After breakfast, then," she said briskly, and he noticed for the first time that she had come to table in her riding habit. "Spring mornings like this make me feel ashamed to be indoors."

That reminded him of Celia trying to convince Sir Digby that she, too, found the spring weather irresistible, though Miss Meriden, no doubt, meant exactly what she said. No two girls could have been less alike. Jane was nineteen, a sturdy, well-built young woman with sandy-gold hair, a round, fresh-complexioned face and rather prominent blue eyes. Unlike Celia, who was always either on the heights or in the depths and flashed from one to the other in an instant, she was, one imagined, a stranger both to ecstasy and to despair; pleasant, undemanding and totally predictable.

She and Jocelyn set out immediately breakfast was over, and their expedition occupied the rest of the morning. When they arrived back at Avenhurst Place, he politely expressed the hope that Miss Meriden was not too greatly fatigued; the lady shook her head.

"Not in the least, Mr. Rivers," she replied indulgently. "I am happy to say that I can cheerfully ride all day and dance all the evening. In fact, I intend to walk in the gardens before going indoors. Lord Avenhurst has told me of the walk which is laid out around the lake."

Civility demanded that he should offer to accompany her,

28

but as they went through one of the shrubberies towards the lake, a sudden commotion arose somewhere nearby. Children began screaming, and a woman's voice, instantly recognizable as Charlotte's, was raised in agitated encouragement and warning.

"Mercy on us!" Jane exclaimed. "What can be wrong?"

Before Jocelyn could offer any suggestion, there was the sound of running feet and a young gardener raced round the bend of the path towards them. Pounding past in the direction of the stables, he flung a hasty explanation over his shoulder.

"'Tis Master Anthony, sir! Up in the great tree on the south lawn. I be after a ladder."

Both his hearers exclaimed, Jane with concern and Jocelyn with exasperation, and hurried towards the source of the uproar. What had happened was obvious. Young Anthony had taken advantage of the breezy day to fly his kite, but since in sweeping away the old gardens, Lord Avenhurst had not been sufficiently influenced by fashion to denude them entirely of trees, the toy had become entangled high in the branches of an oak which was older than the house by a century or more. Anthony had then sought to recover his plaything, but having clambered two-thirds of the distance towards it, had suddenly become paralyzed by terror and now clung there, screaming to be fetched down. At the foot of the tree, Mrs. Rivers wept and wrung her hands, while her daughter Prudence, seven years old and as intense as her mother, was rapidly working herself into a state of hysteria.

"Oh, poor little boy!" Jane exclaimed in dismay. "Mr. Rivers, what can we do?"

"Confounded little fool!" said Anthony's unsympathetic uncle. "He should know better than to attempt such a climb. He has no head for heights."

He strode towards the tree, Jane hastening at his heels, and as soon as he reached Charlotte, she cast herself into his arms, clinging to him and entreating him hysterically to save her precious boy. Jocelyn, disengaging her clutching hands, said disgustedly:

"Oh, calm yourself, Charlotte! He'll take no harm there for a few minutes, as long as he has the sense not to move." He raised his voice. "Keep still, Anthony, and stop bawling! We'll fetch you down as soon as a ladder can be brought."

"Oh, Jocelyn, go up to him, I beg of you," Charlotte pleaded frantically. "You can climb like a cat—you always could!"

29

"Well, I'm not going to climb now," he said shortly. "Good God! A fine fool I should look, swarming up a tree to rescue a screeching brat who has no one but himself to blame for the pickle he's in. Let him stay there until Gunter fetches the ladder. Perhaps it will teach him a lesson."

Charlotte recoiled. "Are you utterly heartless?" she demanded tragically. "He is your nephew, your dead brother's only son. How can you stand aside when his life is in danger?"

"For God's sake, stop behaving as though you were on the stage at Drury Lane," he retorted angrily, casting an embarrassed glance at Miss Meriden, who was stooping over Prudence and trying to comfort the little girl. "When Gunter brings the ladder—!"

He was interrupted. Anthony, silenced by Jocelyn's peremptory command, and perhaps resentful of the scorn with which it had been given, had endeavored to shift his position, with disastrous results. His foot slipped, and a moment later he was hanging by his hands from the branch on which he had previously been standing, screaming again in panic. Charlotte shrieked, Jane uttered a gasp of horror and clasped Prudence to her, hiding the child's face against her skirts, while Jocelyn, with an oath, flung his whip and gloves to the ground and swung himself into the lower boughs.

He climbed swiftly, almost by instinct, for in his not-very-distant boyhood, the branches of the oak tree had been as familiar to him as the paths below, and even as Anthony's frantically clutching fingers finally lost their grip, Jocelyn's arm reached out to seize him firmly about the waist. Panic-stricken, the child screamed and fought and struggled so that Jocelyn had difficulty in holding him, and only the fact that his other arm was clamped firmly around one of the tree's massive limbs prevented them from crashing together to the ground.

Gunter and another man came hurrying back with a ladder, which they reared against the tree. Gunter went up it, Anthony's feet were guided onto the rungs, and with the gardener supporting him, he was at last brought safely to the ground. By the time Jocelyn had followed, he was sobbing in his mother's arms.

"Oh, my dearest!" Charlotte was on her knees, mingling her tears with her child's. "My darling, precious boy! Never, never give Mama such a fright again."

"I lost my kite!" Anthony was wailing. "I want it back! Make them get it for me! Mama, I want my kite!"

"Yes, yes, my darling! Gunter will get it for you." Charlotte raised her head and gestured imperiously to the gardener, who began resignedly to mount the ladder again. "There, my love, don't cry any more. You are quite safe now, and will soon have your toy again. Let Mama dry your eyes, and then you must thank Uncle Jocelyn for bringing you down from the tree."

Anthony lifted a tear-stained face from her shoulder. He was at no time a very prepossessing child, being undersized for his age and of a sallow, unhealthy pallor; his features were sharp, and since, at that moment, his eyes were reddened by weeping, he bore, Jocelyn though unlovingly, a strong resemblance to a ferret.

Jocelyn, in fact, was in no very pleasant mood. He was hot and dishevelled; he had lost his hat and scarred the high polish of his riding boots; and during his efforts to subdue Anthony's struggles, a young branch had slashed him viciously across the face, making his eyes water and raising a long weal, flecked with tiny beads of blood, across his right cheek. He looked at his nephew with acute dislike and Anthony glared belligerently back at him.

"Say thank you to your uncle, my love," Charlotte prompted, tenderly drying her son's eyes.

"No," Master Rivers stated unequivocally, "I won't! He hurt me, holding me so tight."

"But, my precious, he had to hold you tightly to save you from falling. He did not mean to hurt you."

"I'd hurt him a damned sight more if the choice were mine," Jocelyn said wrathfully. "Don't cosset him, Charlotte! He should be thrashed for causing so much trouble."

"How can you say so?" Charlotte surged to her feet and dramatically placed herself in front of Anthony as though fearing that Jocelyn would carry out his threat. "The poor child has just looked death in the face, and you talk of thrashing him. You are utterly heartless!"

"He need not have looked death in the face, as you put it, had he obeyed me when I told him not to move," Jocelyn retorted furiously, "but he does not know what obedience means." He saw that Anthony was peering defiantly at him from behind the wide sweep of his mother's hooped skirts, and leveled a warning finger. "Mark this, my lad! If you

31

climb that or any other tree again, I'll take a whip to you myself. It's time you tasted a measure of discipline."

"I shall climb it if I want to!" Anthony's face was scarlet now; he was almost incoherent with temper. "I shall, I shall! I'll climb the castle keep if I like!"

His mother shrieked. Jocelyn gave a contemptuous snort of laughter.

"May *I* be there to see it!"

"I *shall!* You did it when you were a little boy! Papa said so!"

"Oh, be silent, you contemptible brat!" Jocelyn said disgustedly. "If there is one thing worse than a coward, it's a cowardly braggart." He turned away and so became aware of the two servants, Gunter with the kite in his hands, who were listening with obvious enjoyment. "Why are you two still gaping there? Take that ladder back to the stables."

He caught up his gloves and riding whip and strode furiously away towards the house. It occurred to Miss Meriden, a silent and somewhat shocked spectator of this family squabble, that not only had Anthony not thanked Jocelyn Rivers for saving him; Anthony's doting mother had not done so, either.

By the middle of the afternoon—Lord Avenhurst and his guests would sit down to dinner at four o'clock—even the prospect of seeing Celia could scarcely outweigh Jocelyn's reluctance to join the party, so conscious was he of the disfiguring mark across his face. The weal was darkening now into a bruise, his cheek was swollen and his eye severely bloodshot; studying his reflection in the mirror, he thought disgustedly that he looked as though he had been in a brawl. It was scarcely a face to show in the drawing room, yet to absent himself would displease his father just when it was of vital importance to stand well with him. Celia would be disappointed, and Digby Vaine, no doubt, only too pleased to force his company upon her, as he had done that morning. Mentally consigning his small nephew to the devil, Jocelyn changed his riding clothes for more formal attire and went unwilling towards the state apartments.

He thought that all the guests would have arrived, but as he crossed the vast, marble-floored entrance hall, a latecomer was just surrendering hat and cloak to one of the attendant footmen. Jocelyn saw that it was his godfather, Septimus Twigg, and with relief went forward to greet him.

Mr. Twigg was a short, stocky gentleman in early middle-age, dressed in clothes of good quality but slightly outmoded cut. He had a square, rather heavy-jawed face, ruddy as though he were used to being out of doors in all weathers, and small, shrewd, kindly eyes. More than kindly, in fact, as they regarded the tall boy coming across the hall towards him, though their expression changed to quick concern as they noticed the state of his face.

"In the name of heaven, lad," he demanded without ceremony, "what have you been about?"

"Oh, just a trifling mishap!" Jocelyn had no desire to discuss the cause of his injury. "I'm deuced glad to have encountered you, Sep. If we go in together, I may be lucky enough to escape any comment upon it."

Mr. Twigg looked skeptical, but made no objection, for he had a deeper affection for his godson than for any other living soul. Septimus, orphaned at an early age, had been the ward of Jocelyn's maternal grandfather, and he and the boy's mother, Julia, with only a year's difference between them, had grown up like brother and sister. Then Julia had been married to Viscount Avenhurst, and Septimus, when he came into his own modest inheritance, purchased a small property a few miles from Avenhurst Place. He had never married, and though devoted to all three of Julia's children, it was the youngest, Jocelyn, who held the foremost place in his affection.

In spite of nearly thirty years' disparity in their ages, they were close friends. It was Septimus who had listened to Jocelyn's childish confidences; who had sympathized with his dreams of military glory and recognized how deeply he was hurt when these were taken from him; who was the only person, apart from Celia herself, who had been entrusted with the secret of Jocelyn's first love. He hoped that this would bring his godson consolation for his lost ambitions, but was conscious of certain reservations on that score.

Together they crossed the hall and entered one of the huge, sumptuous apartments which occupied the whole of that floor of the mansion. These opened one into the other, so that when the doors were set wide, one looked along a seemingly unending vista of splendid rooms, rich in color, carving and gilding, with marble fireplaces, priceless pictures and statues

33

and furniture which had been designed as an essential part of the interior decoration of the house. It was unquestionably magnificent. It was also inconvenient and uncomfortable, or so thought Mr. Twigg, who much preferred his own old timber-framed house with its oak-paneled rooms and stone-flagged floors.

Since this was a modest gathering of no more than a score of persons, the company had assembled in one of the smaller drawing rooms, which would, however, comfortably have accommodated twice that number. Immediately he and Septimus entered, Jocelyn's glance sought and found Celia, an enchanting vision in a blue tiffany gown, though his pleasure at the sight of her was marred by the fact that Sir Digby Vaine was sitting beside her. While Mr. Twigg was greeting his hostess and apologizing for the lateness of his arrival, Sir Digby looked beyond him, met, with an expression of lazy amusement, Jocelyn's hostile glare and then allowed his gaze to linger in pointed fashion upon the boy's bruised face. His brows lifted a fraction, tolerantly, and he turned back to his companion.

Lord Avenhurst was also looking at his son, with astonishment and displeasure. "What is this, Jocelyn?" he demanded coldly. "You scarcely present an appearance proper to polite company. What has happened to your face?"

Jocelyn, who was still young enough to be self-conscious when attention was thus drawn to him, flushed darkly and grudgingly offered the same explanation he had given Mr. Twigg. The viscount was not appeased.

"You mean, I suppose, that you have been indulging in some horseplay which has resulted in your presenting to my guests the appearance of a prize-fighter. You will oblige me by making your apologies and then withdrawing."

Involuntarily Jocelyn's glance flashed to Charlotte, standing nearby with Mrs. Meriden and Mrs. Croyde. Their eyes met for an instant and then she deliberately looked away, indicating plainly that she had not yet forgiven him and had no intention of coming to his aid. Furious and humiliated but determined not to be the one to disclose what had happened, he was about to obey his father when help came from an unexpected quarter. Jane Meriden, having waited in vain for Mrs. Rivers to speak, suddenly intervened.

"Forgive me, my lord, but you are too severe."

Avenhurst, and indeed everyone else within hearing, immediately looked at her. She flushed unbecomingly to the roots of her hair but went doggedly on.

"Mr. Rivers sustained that injury when he rescued your lordship's little grandson from the tree he had been rash enough to climb. A ladder was being fetched but could not possibly have arrived in time, and only Mr. Rivers's prompt action saved the child from a fall which could have had a serious, or even fatal, result."

Lord Avenhurst, who had been regarding her with a slight frown, looked again at his son. Jocelyn shrugged and nodded, and the viscount turned back to Jane.

"Miss Meriden, I am in your debt. It seems, Jocelyn, that I owe you an apology. Your reticence does you credit, though it is to be regretted that no one saw fit to inform *me* of this accident."

The latter words were clearly intended for Charlotte, or, at all events, she took them to herself, but instead of quietly acknowledging the fault, she sought to justify it. With a spot of color burning in each thin cheek and a note of shrillness in her voice, she said angrily:

"Now that you *are* informed of it, my lord, let us have the whole truth. Let it be told how Jocelyn at first refused to help my poor, terrified child, but instead bullied him so cruelly that he almost fell from the tree in sheer fright. That he aided him at all was for fear of the consequences if he did not, never from any concern for Anthony. He even threatened to thrash him! He has no affection for him! No kindness, even!"

"If you mean I've no patience with the sniveling, disobedient brat you are turning him into, Charlotte, then you are right," Jocelyn replied flatly. "Indulge him less, and perhaps I will like him better."

"Be silent, Jocelyn," Avenhurst said sternly, and then looked at Charlotte. "Madam, you go too far! Have you forgotten that guests are present? I will hear no more of this matter."

In proof of this, he moved away and engaged some of his guests in conversation. Lady Avenhurst followed his example and the talk became general, no one else paying any particular attention to Charlotte except Mrs. Croyde, who led her to a sofa a little removed from the rest of the company and sat down beside her, patting her hand in a soothing manner.

An anxious mother herself, Mrs. Croyde was more inclined than anyone else to sympathize with the young widow.

Jocelyn, drawn like iron to a lodestone, was making his way to where Celia was still sitting with Sir Digby, and the elder man watched him approach with a glint of mockery in his veiled glance. Mr. Twigg observed this and, mistrusting Vaine's intentions, moved in the same direction, for Jocelyn, only precariously restored to his father's good opinion, could not afford so soon another fall from grace.

They arrived together, but Septimus, fractionally more prepared, was the first to speak, with a greeting for Miss Croyde and a somewhat ponderous compliment. Then, as she murmured some response, her glance already passing from him to Jocelyn, he addressed Sir Digby, endeavoring to engage Vaine's whole attention. Whether he would have succeeded was doubtful, but at that moment dinner was announced, and in the rising from seats and general stir of movement, the young couple found an opportunity for a brief exchange.

"Your poor face!" Celia whispered, a catch in her voice. "Oh, Jocelyn, you might have been killed!"

He smiled and shook his head. "There was no danger," he replied under his breath. "Celia, you look so beautiful! Will you meet me again tomorrow morning?"

Celia saw her mother's gaze upon them and hurriedly let fall her fan of ivory and painted silk. Jocelyn bent to retrieve it, and as he restored it to her, heard her say, in the tiniest breath of a voice:

"I will try." Then, more loudly: "My thanks to you, Mr. Rivers. No, I do not think it is damaged—!"

Mrs. Croyde was not the only person looking at them. From beyond Septimus Twigg's solid bulk, Sir Digby watched the fleeting encounter. He could not hear what was said, but the look the boy and girl exchanged spoke to him as clearly as words, and for a second his own eyes were no longer sleepy and hooded, but flashed upon the couple a glance so hard and menacing that Septimus, observing it, was stirred by faint disquiet. He had set no store by the gossip which linked Vaine's name with Celia Croyde's, believing the man to be indulging in no more than a mild flirtation with an exceptionally pretty girl who was, after all, nearer his son's age than his own. Now he was not so sure. The glance he had intercepted was not of mere idle fancy; it was angry, jealous, possessive; the look of a hunter who had already marked down his quarry. Then Sir Digby turned to him with a smile and a lazy jest, and Mr. Twigg was left wondering whether or not he had been the victim of his own imagination.

Dinner, to Jocelyn, seemed interminable, since Celia was seated nowhere near him, and even when the meal ended some two hours later, there was still no chance of a tête-à-tête. The ladies took one glass of wine and then retired to the drawing room, leaving the men to another two or three hours of drinking and talking. It was half past eight before the viscount led his guests back to join them, and by that time most of the older ladies were at cards, with the exception of Charlotte Rivers and Mrs. Croyde, who sat talking together a little removed from the rest of the party.

Celia, Jane Meriden and another girl of about the same age were chattering on the far side of the room, and Jocelyn, determined this time not to be outmaneuvered, went straight to join them, followed by those of his own contemporaries who were among the guests. The young ladies were by no means averse to masculine company, and a lighthearted group was soon formed. Jocelyn would have preferred to have Celia to himself, but in their present situation this was impossible, and he was given at least one cause for satisfaction. Sir Digby had hesitated, looking towards them, but apparently considered it beneath his dignity to join so youthful a party, and moved instead to the card table.

With the appearance of servants bringing in tea, cakes and coffee, the game was abandoned and conversation again became general, but, thanks largely to Jocelyn's efforts, the group of young people remained intact. Sir Digby, if he noticed this, paid no attention.

A little later a footman bearing a letter on a silver salver entered the room, and Jocelyn saw him proffer this to Colonel Meriden. With a word of excuse to his companions, the colonel broke the seals, and Jocelyn, still idly watching, saw his expression change as he read. Meriden went quickly to where his wife was sitting and bent to speak to her; in obvious dismay she snatched the letter from his hand and read it, and then, after a brief, agitated conversation in which Lady Avenhurst joined, jumped to her feet and, accompanied by the viscountess, hurried from the room.

Colonel Meriden came across to his daughter, who, sitting with her back to that part of the room, remained in ignorance of what had taken place. She looked up inquiringly as he paused beside her.

"Jane," he said quietly, "pray go to your mother. I fear we have received bad news. Your brother Gervase has suffered a serious accident." He laid a hand on her shoulder as she started to speak. "Your mother will tell you. Go to her, my child. Lady Avenhurst is with her, but will wish to return to her guests."

White-faced, Jane rose and hurried away, leaving a shocked silence behind her. Jocelyn said awkwardly to the colonel:

"I am exceedingly sorry to hear of this, sir. Is there any way in which I can be of service to you?"

Meriden shook his head. "Thank you, my boy, but there is nothing. I must make my excuses to your father. We must leave as soon as it is light."

The news the Meridens had received cast a shadow over the company, and the party broke up earlier than it would otherwise have done, the guests dispersing to their homes by the light of a newly risen moon. Jocelyn gathered from his father that Mrs. Meriden, too, had wished to set out at once, but her husband had wisely refused. A long journey lay before them, and it would be better to start at first light and travel all through the day.

Knowing that it would be expected of him, and wishing to retain his father's good opinion, Jocelyn was at hand next morning to speed the departing guests. Brief farewells were said, and then he was standing with his father at the foot of the long flights of steps, watching the coach move away from them towards the avenue of elm trees which stretched across the park to the gates half a mile away.

"A bad business," Avenhurst remarked heavily. "Meriden has five sons, but still—a bad business!" He looked at his own son, observing the whip and gloves he carried. "You are for the stables?"

"Yes, sir. I thought I would have the young chestnut out this morning."

Lord Avenhurst nodded and turned to climb the steps again, while Jocelyn strode off towards the east pavilion. The coach lumbering along the avenue had passed from his mind long before it was out of sight, as his thoughts went leaping to the trysting place by the castle ruins and the hour which might bring Celia again into his arms.

II

This was not to be. Their meeting place was deserted when he reached it, and though he lingered there until the last possible moment, Celia did not appear. He was disappointed, but returned home consoling himself with the thought that, if everything went as he hoped, the need for such clandestine meetings would soon be past.

It had been his intention to approach his father immediately after breakfast, but while they were at table, Lord Avenhurst happened to mention that he would be engaged upon business with his agent all the morning. In fact, he was engaged a good deal longer, and it was nearly two in the afternoon before Jocelyn, anxiously on the watch, saw the man come out of the library.

Trying to ignore a feeling of trepidation and hoping that his lordship was in a good humor, Jocelyn went in. Avenhurst was standing before the fire, studying a document of some kind, but he looked up as his son approached and Jocelyn saw with relief that his expression was benign.

"Ah, Jocelyn!" he greeted him. "Are you seeking me?"

"Yes, sir." Jocelyn had considered his opening words carefully. "With your permission, I would like to speak to you about the future. My future."

He thought he saw a flicker of surprise cross his father's face, but the viscount merely said pleasantly:

"An excellent idea. Let us sit down."

He laid the document on a nearby table and took a seat at one side of the fireplace, motioning Jocelyn to a chair opposite. As he sat down, Avenhurst went on:

"You are right to feel that it is time we discussed your future, and I intended to do so shortly, as soon as certain matters have been concluded. However, since you have broached the subject yourself, there is no reason why we may not speak of it now." He paused, thoughtfully regarding his son. "Has it never occurred to you, Jocelyn, to wonder why I have not arranged for you to make the Grand Tour, as your brother did?"

"Yes, sir, it has," Jocelyn replied frankly, "and I can only conclude that you do not intend me to make it."

"You are wrong. To travel upon the Continent is a necessary part of any gentleman's education, but in your case there are other and even more important considerations to be taken into account. I refer, of course, to your marriage." He lifted an admonitory hand as Jocelyn started to speak. "Bear with me a moment. You know my reason for deciding that you must marry without delay, but I would not have you suppose that because of this, you are to be deprived of anything due to a son of mine. You will make your tour of Europe immediately *after* your wedding, and your wife, naturally, will accompany you."

Jocelyn blinked, thrown completely out of his stride by this unexpected turn of events. Was it possible, he wondered, that his father had guessed the attachment between him and Celia, and already approached William Croyde? He had spoken of "certain matters" soon to be concluded, and it would be like him to set everything in train for a marriage without informing his son of it until all was settled. Dazzled, Jocelyn contemplated the prospect of enjoying the travel his restless nature craved, not encumbered with a tutor, but as a married man, with the woman he loved at his side.

"It is not usual," the viscount was saying, "and should my hope be realized and your wife find herself with child, you will, of course, return home immediately, but neither I nor your future father-in-law can see any reason why you should not travel abroad meanwhile. With a bride in your care, you will, I trust, be less likely to commit the sort of folly from the consequences of which I was obliged to rescue your brother."

So it *was* settled. All his own misgivings, all Celia's dread of being parted from him, had been needless. They would go to London betrothed; towards the end of the season, no doubt, they would be married; and after that, Paris, Rome, Vienna— all the glittering capitals of Europe as a background for their new life together.

"We had intended," Avenhurst continued, "that your formal betrothal would take place later this week, but in the circumstances, it will have to be postponed. One cannot expect a father to celebrate his daughter's forthcoming marriage while one of his sons lies gravely ill. We must hope that young Meriden's injuries are not so great that his father will be prevented from bringing Miss Jane to London."

Meriden? Jocelyn stared incredulously at his father while the bright edifice of delight his imagination had been building crashed in ruins about him. When he tried to speak, he found that he could not at first make a sound, and even when he at last recovered the power of speech, his voice was strangled, and sounded strange even to his own ears.

"You do not—you cannot—expect me to marry *Miss Meriden?*"

"Cannot expect?" Now it was his father's turn to stare. "Devil take it, boy! Why else do you suppose her parents brought her here, or why we encouraged the pair of you to spend your time in each other's company? Both Meriden and I desire the match, but we are not so indifferent to our children's feelings as to force it upon them if either held the other in aversion. You have had a week in which to become acquainted, and appear to deal together agreeably enough."

"As acquaintances, sir, yes, but not—! It is Celia—Miss Croyde—!" Jocelyn's stumbling words faded into silence before his father's look of gathering amazement.

"Celia Croyde?" Lord Avenhurst repeated blankly. There was a pause; then, as Jocelyn braced himself for an explosion of anger, incredibly he laughed. "You have a singular conceit of yourself, my son!"

"Conceit?" Jocelyn's own hasty temper flared and he sprang to his feet, discretion forgotten. "Let me tell you, sir, that Celia loves me as I love her. We are already promised to each other."

"So that is the way of it!" Still his lordship seemed amused

41

rather than angry. "That is the reason for these early morning jaunts." He chuckled again at the expression in Jocelyn's face. "Did you really suppose I knew nothing about them? You underestimate me, my dear boy! I knew, but I supposed you were tumbling some farmer's daughter, not exchanging vows of love with Miss Celia." A thought appeared to strike him, and both voice and look sharpened suddenly. "You've not seduced the girl, I trust?"

"Sir!" Jocelyn was white with anger now; his voice shook. "Say what you will of me, but do not insult my future wife."

"Here's a fine romantic high-flight!" commented Avenhurst, apparently still much diverted. "Very well, I make Miss Celia my apologies. She is a pretty little creature, and I suppose it is no wonder that you have lost your head over her. I dare say I was guilty of similar folly at your age, though I have now no recollection of it, or of the lady. But romantic fancies, my boy, have nothing to do with marriage. I have arranged a very satisfactory match for you with Jane Meriden. It is an excellent family, her father will dower her handsomely, and Miss Jane herself is a fine, healthy young woman who—"

"Good breeding stock, sir?" Jocelyn struck in savagely. "That is the only use you have for me, is it not? To sire sons to exclude our northern cousins from the succession?"

"Why, you insolent young dog!" The viscount's amusement abruptly deserted him and he, too, came to his feet, so that they confronted each other eye to eye. "It is to be hoped you *will* prove good for that, for, as I live, you are good for nothing else!"

The contempt with which the accusation was uttered, as much as the injustice of it, flicked Jocelyn on the raw. He forgot the need to be conciliatory, and lashed out with the first words to come into his head.

"Since you, sir, went back on your word and denied me the career I had been promised, it scarcely becomes you to name me good-for-nothing."

"Be silent, sir! How dare you address me in those terms?" The older man was as angry now as the younger, his temper further exacerbated by the fact that, lacking his son's height, he was obliged to look up at him. "A soldier, you? Do you imagine you would have been able to command men, when you cannot even command your own tongue? Enough of this! You will marry Jane Meriden, like it or no!"

"And if I refuse? If I say I will wed Celia, or not marry at all?"

"Refuse and be damned! Do you imagine that William Croyde will permit his heiress to throw herself away upon a younger son when his fortune can purchase a coronet for her in London? Or that a girl's silly lovesick fancy will be allowed to stand in the way of her attaining a great position? You must have even less wit that I gave you credit for."

Jocelyn stared at him with the unspoken, almost unrecognized resentment of years rising with scalding bitterness in his throat. For almost as long as he could remember, certainly ever since his mother's death, he had been made aware of his own shortcomings and inferior position, while the elder brother who was so much like their father, and then that brother's son, as heirs to the viscount, had been given every privilege, every consideration. As he grew older, he had lived for the day when he could leave Avenhurst and begin to carve his own place in the world, but first that ambition, and now this new and even dearer desire, had been snatched from him; not with malice, which would have been hard enough to bear, but with contempt, as though they, like himself, were of no account.

"Want-wit and good-for-nothing!" he said bitterly. "I marvel, sir, that you look to the likes of me to perpetuate our line."

"Had I other sons, or other grandsons, rest assured that I would not, but as it is, you know well enough where your duty lies."

"And I was prepared to do that duty, sir, even at the cost of my military career, but I expected to be given at least some choice in the matter of a bride. You cannot say that I have chosen ill. You can have no possible objection to Celia."

"Did I say that I had? I would be very happy to know there was a chance of welcoming Croyde's heiress into my family, but I know better than to subject both him and myself to the embarrassment to which such a proposal and its refusal would entail. Why, it would be an insult even to suggest it!"

"An insult?" Jocelyn's temper, which he had been struggling to subdue, leaped up again. "Am I to take it, then, that Mr. Croyde shares your lordship's own low opinion of me?"

"Heaven grant me patience!" The viscount threw up his arms in exasperation. "The insult, you obstinate young fool, would lie in the assumption that Croyde might consider mar-

43

rying his only child to a mere younger son. What he, or even I, may think of you is irrelevant."

"I see! If I were your heir, Croyde would sing a different tune. It is my sniveling brat of a nephew who stands between me and everything I most desire."

Lord Avenhurst was given no opportunity to reply. Jocelyn's angry voice must have been audible beyond the room, for he had scarcely spoken when the door was flung wide and Charlotte swept in, an avenging fury eager to do battle on her son's behalf.

"Jocelyn, how *can* you?" she cried. "How can you so malign an innocent child?"

"Innocent?" he repeated jeeringly, "That's rich! He's the worst lying, bragging, tale-bearing little brute I have ever known. The rest of us can see it if you cannot."

"Oh!" It was a cry of outrage. She swung round to face her father-in-law. "My lord, do you permit this? Is your grandson, your heir, to be spoken of in this fashion? I demand that Jocelyn take back what he has said."

"Calm yourself, madam!" Avenhurst spoke irritably, for he never had much patience with Charlotte's histrionics. "Words cannot harm the boy, and you intrude upon a matter which does not concern you."

"Anything which concerns my son concerns me," she declared dramatically. "Jocelyn hates him! He loses no opportunity of bullying and threatening him, and now he abuses him even to you. It is not the fault of my poor, fatherless child that his uncle has no hope of marrying Celia Croyde."

Avenhurst looked startled, but Jocelyn gave a scornful laugh.

"Eavesdropping again, Charlotte?" he said with a sneer. "It's easy to see where Anthony gets his underhanded ways."

"How dare you!" Charlotte's sharp features became suffused with color. "Let me tell you it is not necessary to eavesdrop when you shout your most private concerns for all to hear. I pity Miss Croyde! Be she what she may, she at least has the right to expect discretion upon your part."

"Why, you—!" Jocelyn took a threatening pace towards her and was checked by his father's outstretched arm. Avenhurst said sternly:

"Charlotte, you go too far! Whatever your differences with Jocelyn, I will not permit you to cast aspersions on Miss Celia, who has no part in the matter."

44

Charlotte tittered angrily. "I would suppose she has a very large part in it, my lord, if she has been so lost to all sense of decorum as to plight troth without her father's knowledge or consent. However, I have no quarrel with *her*. It is my own poor child I am concerned to protect. Jocelyn wishes him no good! Yesterday I had to beg and beseech him to save Anthony when his life was in danger, and even then he delayed until it was almost too late."

"Would to God I had delayed even longer!" Jocelyn, by now in a towering rage, thrust between her and his father and strode towards the door, which Charlotte's tempestuous entrance had left standing wide. "Long enough for the whelp to break his scrawny neck! I'll not be such a fool a second time, believe me!"

Ignoring Avenhurst's angry command to him to wait, he stormed out of the room, slamming the door behind him and thrusting blindly past the little knot of startled servants who had been seduced from their work by the sound of the quarrel. A few minutes later he was in the stables, shouting for his horse to be saddled and pacing furiously to and fro while this was done. He could not be still. His anger and frustration were so intense that they demanded physical expression.

When his mount was brought, he flung himself into the saddle and went clattering out of the stableyard in a manner which made those who witnessed his departure exchange significant looks. They were well accustomed to his moods, but today, as they all agreed after he had gone, Mr. Jocelyn looked ripe for murder.

Without much thought for his eventual destination, he turned his horse towards the avenue, where the broad stretch of turf bordering the carriage drive offered an opportunity for the sort of headlong gallop his present frame of mind demanded, but before he reached it, a figure emerging abruptly from a knot of trees as he passed caused the spirited animal to shy. Jocelyn cursed, and having steadied his mount, turned wrathfully upon the author of the mishap.

It was the young gardener, Gunter, who had assisted at Anthony's rescue the day before. He accepted meekly the pithy condemnation of his wits and behavior with which Jocelyn favored him, but as soon as the young man paused for breath, said hurriedly:

"Asking your pardon, Mr. Jocelyn, and I know 'twere a

fool thing to do, but I just saw Master Anthony going off, secret-like. I know Mrs. Rivers don't let him go beyond the gardens on his own—!"

"Then go tell *her*, you fool! Don't plague me with her confounded brat's comings and goings!" Jocelyn broke off, frowning. "Going where? He should be at his lessons."

"Looked to me, sir, as though him were headed for the castle," Gunter replied. "You heard what him said yesterday about climbing the old keep."

"And *you* heard what I said. That miserable puppy would not climb ten feet up those walls unless the devil were at his heels."

"Mrs. Rivers believed him'd try it, sir. I heard her tell him never to go nigh the place."

"Forbidden to go there, was he?" Jocelyn said softly. "And now he's off there as soon as his mother's back is turned, meaning, I'll wager, to come back with some lying boast of having scaled the keep." He grinned suddenly, but it did not alter the expression in his eyes. "All right, Gunter. Leave Master Anthony to me."

He let the fretting horse go and it plunged forward, careering away in the direction of the castle. Gunter, watching it go, was a prey to momentary doubt. Mr. Jocelyn was clearly in one of his black humors, and it would go hard with Master Anthony when he caught up with him. The gardener hesitated, then, remembering the numerous occasions when he had been the butt of the little boy's spiteful tricks, he shrugged and went back to his work.

Had he stayed a little longer, he would have seen the rider suddenly veer off in a different direction, for it had occurred to Jocelyn that if Anthony were indeed making his way furtively towards the castle, he would undoubtedly be scared off by the sight or sound of pursuit. Better to circle round and approach the ruins from a different direction.

His thoughts, momentarily diverted, returned to the scene in the library. "A mere younger son!" The taunt, for such it had seemed to him, burned in his memory, causing him to rage silently with almost unendurable anger and despair, for it had never occurred to him that he would be unacceptable to William Croyde. "A mere younger son!" Jocelyn had never before coveted his father's honors, but now, because to be heir to them would give him everything else he longed for, he coveted them with all his heart; and all that stood between

46

him and the granting of his dearest wish was a sickly, spoiled brat who, even if he survived to inherit, would certainly be no credit to the family.

The circuitous route Jocelyn was following brought him presently to the crossroads where he and Celia had encountered Sir Digby the previous day, and as he approached them, he heard another horse coming fast along the road on his right. A moment later the rider dashed into view, and Jocelyn recognized Celia's groom.

The man caught sight of him and reined in hard. "Mr. Rivers! Miss Croyde sent me to find you."

"Why?" Jocelyn spoke urgently, his first thought that their secret meetings had been betrayed or discovered. "What is the matter?"

"That I don't know, sir, but Miss be in a rare taking! She couldn't come herself, it not being her custom to ride at this time o' day, but her begs you to meet her in the hermitage as soon as may be. I'm to show you how to come there, and then take word to her."

Jocelyn had visited Celia's home only once, with his father and stepmother, but William Croyde, who liked to embellish his garden with curious and fashionable conceits, had insisted upon conducting them on a tour of these. The hermitage, Jocelyn remembered, was near the boundary of the gardens, almost completely surrounded by a suitably thick and gloomy wood, so it should not be difficult to reach unobserved.

"Come, then," he said curtly, and set spur to his horse, Anthony's escapade quite forgotten. Mud spattered from beneath the plunging hooves, and the two riders flew, one behind the other, along the road which led to Croyde Court.

The groom led Jocelyn to the outskirts of the wood and showed him the path which led through it. Jocelyn dropped coins into the man's hand and watched him ride off in the direction of the house, then led his horse in among the trees and tethered it. A few minutes later he entered the hermitage.

Although undeniably a safe and secluded spot for an assignation, it was by no means a cheerful place. Built against a rocky bank which formed the rear wall, it was a small hut of logs and roots, carefully constructed to give the appearance of having been rudely built. A rough-hewn table and stool were its only furnishings, and since the sunlight never penetrated the thick screen of branches which surrounded and

47

overhung it, the atmosphere within was cold and dank and earthy. The whole effect was melancholy in the extreme, and Jocelyn could not imagine Celia liking the place or even visiting it from choice, and his misgivings increased with every passing minute. Something must be very wrong indeed, to cause her to meet him in this gloomy hole.

She came at last; light footsteps outside, a shadow darkening the low doorway, a rustle of silk and waft of perfume as she flung herself into his arms. She clung to him, sobbing hysterically, her voice muffled and unintelligible against his chest.

"Celia! Sweetheart!" he said urgently. "My dearest love, don't cry! Only tell me what is wrong." She paid no heed, and he slid a hand gently beneath her chin, cupping it in his palm so that he could turn her face up towards him. "Tell me," he repeated gently.

She gazed tragically at him, her great violet-blue eyes swimming with tears, her lips trembling so that she could hardly frame the words. "Sir Digby came to call on Papa today. He wants to marry me!"

"Vaine?" Jocelyn said blankly, and then stupefaction was overwhelmed by anger and revulsion. "Damn his impudence! He is old enough to be your father."

"I know! I never thought—! I never dreamed—! When Sir Digby talked to me, I supposed he was just being kind, as Lord Avenhurst is, and Mr. Twigg. It never entered my mind that he might wish to marry me."

It had not entered Jocelyn's, either. He had resented Vaine's attentions to her, and his mockery, but with the unconscious vanity of youth, had supposed that Sir Digby was concerned more to annoy him than to indulge Celia. Now he knew better. He counted for less than nothing where Vaine was concerned, and the man's pursuit of her had been in earnest. It was outrageous, unthinkable! No wonder she was distraught.

"When Papa told me, after Sir Digby had gone, I could not believe it." Celia was more in command of herself now, but her voice still trembled piteously. "He was pleased, and so was Mama, that Sir Digby had offered for me, and they could not understand why *I* was not pleased, too. Papa says it is a very great compliment."

"Celia!" A sudden, appalling fear took Jocelyn by the throat. "He will not *compel* you to marry Vaine?"

48

"Oh, no, no! He would *like* me to accept, for Sir Digby is rich, and there is the title, and—which I think commends it to him and to Mama most of all—my home would be close by, but when I cried out that I *could* not, Papa said there was no need to be frightened. He would not command me to do anything I disliked so much."

"I should think not," Jocelyn said grimly. "A man of Vaine's age, with a family! Why, young Simon is less than three years younger than you are."

The shock of what she had told him was passing now, and his worst fear, of seeing her forced into an immediate betrothal, had not been confirmed. He felt calmer, more able to soothe and comfort her; but Celia would not be comforted.

"Jocelyn, you do not understand," she said tearfully. "I did not dare to tell Papa about you, but when he spoke of my disliking the thought of marrying Sir Digby, I *did* venture to say that I would prefer to marry someone like you."

"Well?" Jocelyn prompted hopefully as she hesitated. "What said he to that?"

"He—he laughed," Celia confided tragically. "He laughed and patted my hand and—and said, 'Someone *like* young Rivers, perhaps, but certainly not a younger son. We can do better for you than that.'" She saw his expression change, and gave a little gasp of fright. "Jocelyn, do not look like that! Papa did not mean—! But you see how hopeless it is."

"Yes, I see!" he said savagely. "I see that I am of no more account to your father than I am to my own. He, too, laughed at the notion of 'a mere younger son' aspiring to the hand of an heiress."

"You told him?" Celia sounded apprehensive. "Oh, Jocelyn, was he very angry?"

"Angry? Oh, no!" Jocelyn's voice was bitter. "He was too greatly amused to be angry. A match between us would delight him, he said, but he would not insult your father by proposing such a thing."

"Insult?" she exclaimed indignantly. "Oh, how could he be so cruel! What does it matter that you are a younger son? I love you. I do not care about a title."

"My sweet love!"

He caught her close, kissing her lips, her throat, her tear-wet cheeks, and she clung tightly to him, cut to the heart by the hurt he had suffered. This was no longer a fairy tale. It was high tragedy, and they, two fated lovers sundered by cruel, unfeeling parents; true to each other in defiance of all the world.

Her second state of mind was as far removed from reality as the first, but she did not realize this. It was her nature to see things always as extremes; to dramatize every possible aspect of life and to ignore the rest. Yesterday she had not even been sure that she wanted to marry Jocelyn. Now, faced by the prospect of some other bridegroom, she wanted it more than anything in the world.

"I do not think I can bear it," she said tearfully, when he permitted her to speak at all. "I shall never, never love anyone but you, but Papa will never give his consent, and in the end he will lose patience and *make* me marry someone else. I know he will!"

Jocelyn knew it, too, however hard he tried to thrust the knowledge from him. William Croyde would not let his beautiful daughter dwindle into spinsterhood simply because she loved a man whom he considered unsuitable. He would indulge her at first, no doubt, but the time would certainly come when he decided to exert his parental authority.

"We must not abandon hope," he said urgently. "Not yet! Nothing will happen immediately, and we may yet find a way. You must be strong, my love, and firm in your refusal of any other match suggested to you."

"I will try," she replied miserably, "but I have never yet defied Papa about anything. I cannot bear for anyone to be angry with me."

"Sweetheart, he will not be angry. Has he not assured you he will not compel you to any marriage you dislike?"

"Yes, but as yet I have refused only Sir Digby, and even Papa admits I have some reason for doing that," said Celia, who knew her father better than Jocelyn did. "If I refuse other proposals, he will soon lose patience." She saw that he was frowning, and added desperately: "Jocelyn, you cannot understand! It is different for a man, and besides, *your* father is not trying to arrange a marriage for you."

"Is he not?" Jocelyn said grimly. "He informed me just now that Miss Meriden is *my* chosen bride."

"Jocelyn!" She stared at him in horror, and then her tears brimmed over again. "Oh, our love is doomed indeed! Too much stands between us."

"Only one thing stands between us," he retorted bitterly.

"The fact that I am not my father's heir. If I were, Mr. Croyde would agree at once to our marriage."

"I know, but you are *not* the heir, and he will never consent," she said hopelessly. "Oh, Jocelyn, dearest Jocelyn, better that we part now. I shall always love you, but I cannot bear the pain of meeting you like this, knowing that we have no hope of happiness. Kiss me farewell and go! It is the only way."

"No!" he said vehemently. "There *is* another way—there must be! I will find it if I have to go to the devil himself for counsel." He gripped her by the shoulders, looking compellingly down into her eyes. "Celia, trust me! I *will* find a way, because I must. I love you, and I will not give you up."

His vehemence convinced her against all reason, the more easily because she desperately wanted to be convinced. His masterfulness, which was one of the things about him which had first attracted her, was not to be denied, and she was too young and inexperienced to recognize that in this instance it sprang from a despair almost as great as her own. When he spoke with such authority, how could she doubt him? She could see no solution to their difficulties, but if one existed, she was confident that Jocelyn would find it.

Jocelyn himself had spoken the simple truth. To lose Celia was unthinkable, and therefore a way to win her must be found; or created, if it did not exist. After he had sent her, somewhat comforted, back to the house, he mounted his horse again and for hours rode by the loneliest and least frequented ways he knew, seeking solitude in which to wrestle—vainly, as it proved—with the problem.

The afternoon was waning by the time he approached Avenhurst again, and a tremendous sunset was flaring above the Welsh hills, great towers and pinnacles of dark cloud shot through with shafts of golden light which slowly deepened in color as the sun sank lower. Passing close to the castle, Jocelyn saw the jagged outline of the keep rearing black and sinister against that splendid, stormy sky, and for the first time since receiving Celia's message, he remembered Anthony and his furtive visit to the ruins. The brat was fortunate to have escaped a well-deserved thrashing, but his uncle must be prepared to keep a tight rein on his temper if he heard him boasting of having climbed the keep.

The sunset light was concentrated now upon one great

51

gash in the clouds, through which poured a fiery light that bathed the whole landscape for a minute or two in an unearthly blood-red glow. Then, with the abruptness of a candle being snuffed out, the uncanny light was gone, and Jocelyn crossed the park in the fading afterglow, and clattered into the shadowy stableyard.

It seemed strangely quiet and deserted, and though at his shout a groom came running to take charge of his horse, there was something odd in the man's manner, and in the sidelong, half-fearful glance he bestowed on Jocelyn as he led the animal away. Jocelyn frowned, then shrugged and made his way towards the house, his footsteps echoing with a lonely sound along the colonnade.

From the corridor, an inner staircase led up to the entrance hall, and as Jocelyn emerged into the huge apartment, his father's chaplain, the Reverend Edward Holt, appeared at the doorway of the library. His face was grave.

"Mr. Jocelyn," he announced, "his lordship desires that you attend him immediately."

He stepped aside, indicating with a gesture that Lord Avenhurst was within, and Jocelyn, conscious of a pang of uneasiness, crossed the hall and went past him into the library, the chaplain following but pausing to close the doors.

The viscount was standing by the fireplace, resting one hand on the mantelpiece as he stared down at the fire, but as Jocelyn came across the room towards him, he raised his head to watch his son's approach in the marble-framed mirror above. Not until the boy paused close to him did he turn, his face pale and stern in the candlelight, to say abruptly:

"Where have you been?"

The question had almost the sound of an accusation. Jocelyn's first thought was that his meeting with Celia was suspected; his first reaction was to protect her. He said curtly:

"Riding, sir."

"Riding where?"

Now the note of accusation was more pronounced. Jocelyn resented it, and the effort of disguising this made his voice sound sullen as he replied.

"Nowhere in particular. I went as far as Hangman's Wood."

"Not to the castle? Yet you told one of the gardeners that was your intention, when he informed you that he had seen

Anthony going in that direction. It was also your intention, I am told, to punish the boy for his disobedience."

So that was it. Whatever trouble had been brewed for him in his absence, Anthony—and that meant Charlotte, too—was at the bottom of it.

"I changed my mind," he said angrily, "and if that lying whelp says otherwise—!"

"Anthony is dead."

The brief cold statement, uttered with unnatural restraint, cut through Jocelyn's protest with the brutal finality of an executioner's ax. He stared at his father, numb with shock, and Avenhurst stared back with a look of bleak and bitter anger. At last, after what seemed an endless silence, Jocelyn found a strangled remnant of his voice.

"How, in God's name?"

"He fell." Still that icy, unnatural calm. "Fell from the keep which *you* maintained he lacked the courage to attempt to climb. Which you could have prevented him from climbing if you had followed him as you said you would."

Beside them, the chaplain made an involuntary gesture of protest. Jocelyn stared blankly at his father.

"My God! Of what are you accusing me?"

"I accuse you of nothing." There was sudden weariness in Avenhurst's voice; his shoulders sagged a little beneath his velvet coat. "Surely, though, you realize how invidious your position is? You virtually threatened Anthony's life a few hours ago. Now he is dead, and he would not be, had you followed him and brought him back. I insist that you tell me why you did not."

"I *have* told you, sir. I changed my mind." Impossible to disclose that all thought of Anthony had been driven out of his head by a summons from Celia; that he had gone to a secret assignation with her. "I was in no humor to deal gently with him, and upon reflection, it seemed better not to court a temptation I might be unable to resist." He realized how damaging this sounded, and added quickly: "To thrash him, I mean. I swear I never intended more than that."

"And instead of going to the castle, you rode to Hangman's Wood. You could scarcely have chosen a more deserted place."

Jocelyn's eyes met his unwaveringly. "I was in no mood for company, sir. You will appreciate why."

A slight inclination of his father's head acknowledged the justice of this, but he said coldly: "It is unfortunate, to say

53

the least. Better for all of us if you had spent the afternoon among other people."

"And better still if I had brought Anthony home from the castle." Not all Jocelyn's efforts could quite erase the resentment from his voice. "It should not be necessary, sir, for me to assure you that I would have done so had I the least suspicion that he would try to make good his boast."

"He did not go far towards doing so, poor little fellow," the viscount said heavily. "Those who found him say that he must have fallen when he tried to cross the first gap in the stair. A great mound of broken stone lies below, and he fell upon that. His back was broken."

Jocelyn sat down rather suddenly, elbows on knees and head on hands. He felt slightly sick. It was a horrible way for a child to die, alone and terrified in those frowning ruins, for how could anyone be certain that the fall had killed him instantly? That was a thought which must surely haunt them all henceforth.

There was silence for a few minutes, and then the viscount sighed and spoke in a tone of weary resignation.

"Go to your room, Jocelyn. I have many matters to attend to. We will talk of this tomorrow."

Jocelyn nodded and got up. Bidding his father and the chaplain good night, he went slowly out of the library, across the hall and up the wide, gracefully curving marble staircase. He still could not fully accept what had happened. It seemed incredible that one short afternoon could have wrought so great a change in life at Avenhurst.

Not until he had reached his own room and was standing, staring from the window across the darkening gardens, did the full magnitude of the change dawn upon him, and when it did, the shock of realization was as great, in its way, as the news of the tragedy had been. Anthony was dead. He, Jocelyn, was now heir to Avenhurst.

It was the second day after the accident. In accordance with custom, the dead boy lay in state, so that his grandfather's neighbors, tenants and dependents might pay their last respects, marking their sorrow for a young life so suddenly and terribly cut short, and their sympathy for the bereaved. In one of the state bedchambers, the small corpse seemed pathetically tiny in a vast four-poster draped and covered in white, the color of mourning for a child. Anthony had not endeared himself to many people, but even those who had found him most trying in life could not fail to be moved by the poignancy of his death.

In the adjoining room Lord and Lady Avenhurst received the condolences of their friends and acquaintances. It was a harrowing duty, and one in which Charlotte, prostrate with shock and grief, was not able to take part, but though Jocelyn, too, would have evaded it if he could, he had no choice but to obey his father's stern command to be present.

His state of mind was chaotic. Plagued though he was by a nagging sense of guilt, he could not, try as he would, completely banish all thought of what Anthony's death meant to him. Whenever the knowledge forced itself to the forefront of his mind, he thrust it away with shame and self-reproach, for it seemed almost sinful to acknowledge, even to himself, that the tragedy had made possible all his own dreams and desires. To feign a grief he did not feel was sheer hypocrisy, yet, if he did not, might it not be supposed that he was exulting over the change in his fortunes?

His dilemma was not made any easier when he found himself confronting Sir Digby Vaine, making his formal visit of condolence. Vaine's manner was faultless, his expressions of sympathy sincerely spoken, but Jocelyn, encountering one of those singularly penetrating glances, felt certain that behind that polished facade, very different emotions were stirring. Whether or not anyone else was pondering the change in Jocelyn's prospects, Sir Digby was undoubtedly doing so, and must be wondering, too, how it would affect his own hopes.

Septimus Twigg arrived hard upon Vaine's heels, and though Mr. and Mrs. Croyde had already come and gone (Celia being excluded by her careful parents from so distressing an errand), several other members of the local gentry were present. The low voices within the room, and the muted footsteps passing through the adjacent bedchamber, scarcely disturbed the silence, and so it was doubly shocking when that reverent hush was shattered by a woman's wail of grief. The wild cry rang out from the direction of the bedchamber, and after an instant's stunned silence, Lady Avenhurst exclaimed in dismay:

"Charlotte!"

She got up and went quickly to the double doors between the two rooms, flinging them open. Charlotte, clad in deepest mourning, was on her knees beside the great bed, her head down on the satin coverlet and her arms outstretched towards her dead child; she was weeping hysterically, with great, tearing sobs that shook her whole thin body, while her clenched fists beat with futile despair upon the bed. Her personal maid, a dour, uncompromising woman also dressed in unrelieved black, stood impassively behind her, while on the far side of the room, a group of country folk in their best clothes stared with pity and dismay, none of them knowing what to do.

"Charlotte!" Lady Avenhurst went quickly forward and laid a hand on the shuddering shoulder. "My dear, this will not do! Let me take you back to your room."

"Anthony!" Charlotte's voice rose to a shriek. "Oh, my son! My darling, precious boy!"

Her ladyship, vainly trying to raise her, cast an angry glance over her shoulder at the maid.

"Help me," she said peremptorily. "Your mistress will do herself harm if she is allowed to give way to her grief in this fashion."

After a moment's hesitation the woman obeyed, and between them they got Charlotte to her feet. She stood swaying, head thrown back and eyes closed, tears streaming down her cheeks; then, as they tried to lead her away, she suddenly opened her eyes and looked straight through the doorway into the next room, where the viscount and his companions stood staring in the same shocked helplessness as the villagers behind her. Her tear-reddened eyes, sunken in her ravaged countenance, singled out Jocelyn; one trembling hand rose, pointing an accusing finger.

"You did this!" she cried wildly. "You murdered my innocent child! He stood in your way and you killed him!"

There was a gasp from the onlookers, a little ripple of sound which, though startled and horrified, yet held a faint undercurrent of excitement. Jocelyn himself stood, rigid with disbelief, staring blankly at his sister-in-law, for though he had dreaded her bitter and endless reproaches, he had not expected an outright accusation.

"You do not deny it!" Charlotte's voice was rising again; she paid no heed to Lady Avenhurst's attempt to quiet her. "You cannot! You were jealous of Anthony! He was the heir and you hated him for it."

"Charlotte, control yourself!" The viscount, recovering

from his momentary stupor of shock, moved forward. "You do not know what you are saying."

"Do I not, my lord? Do I not? When he has abused my son openly, and even wished the poor mite dead? You and I were not the only ones who heard him say that!"

"Be silent, madam!" There was dismay as well as anger now in the viscount's voice, a fact which was not lost upon some, at least, of those who heard him. "You shame us all by such wild talk. There has been a tragic accident, but though I feel for your grief, I will not permit an outburst such as this."

"I will not be silent! My dead child's blood cries out for vengeance! Jocelyn killed him! He murdered Anthony because he is wild to marry Celia Croyde, and his only hope of winning her was to become your heir."

This time the murmur from her audience was distinctly audible, and, perhaps encouraged by this, she wrenched herself suddenly from Lady Avenhurst's hold and, the maid making no attempt to restrain her, sprang towards Jocelyn with hands outstretched and fingers curved like claws. The viscount caught her by the wrists and for a moment or two she struggled frantically to free herself, her voice a demented scream as she continued to hurl her accusations.

"He killed my son! He goaded him into going to the castle and then flung him down from the keep. He hated and envied him because Anthony stood between Jocelyn and Avenhurst, between him and Celia Croyde. They have plighted troth but her father will not consent—!"

Avenhurst let go one wrist and slapped her sharply across the cheek. Her tirade ceased abruptly; she collapsed, sobbing, and would have fallen had he not been supporting her. Without waiting even to summon a servant, he lifted her in his arms and strode through the bedchamber, past the bed where her dead son lay, past the staring, gaping country folk and through the open door beyond. After an instant's hesitation his wife followed, but the maid came forward to the doorway between the rooms. For a moment she paused there, her grim gaze passing over each of them in turn and resting finally, with undisguised malevolence, upon Jocelyn. Then she withdrew, closing the double doors and shutting off the view of the room beyond.

Instinctively all eyes turned towards Jocelyn, who still stood as he had done when Charlotte first accused him. He was deathly pale, so that the ugly bruise across his cheek seemed darker by contrast, and there was a stunned look in his eyes. He seemed unaware of his companions until Septimus Twigg laid a hand on his arm, and then he said in a stunned voice:

"She is mad! She must be! The shock has turned her brain."

"To be sure!" Unexpectedly it was Digby Vaine who spoke, his voice calmly bridging the awkward silence, and only Jocelyn and Septimus failed to see the significant look which accompanied the words. "Poor lady, we must hope that she will soon be restored. My friends, let us go! Lord and Lady Avenhurst will forgive the incivility of our not taking leave of them, for they will know that we are prompted by consideration for their feelings."

There was a murmur of agreement and relief, and with brief farewells, he and the others withdrew, until only Septimus remained. Jocelyn drew a shuddering breath and sat down, bowing his head on his hands, while Twigg, after studying him for a moment in a troubled way, came to stand beside him.

"Jocelyn," he said quietly. "My dear boy, do not take this too much to heart. That poor woman does not know what she is saying."

"No?" Jocelyn lifted a white, drawn face towards him. "Sep, you do not know the half of it!" He gave a brief account of the quarrel with his father and Charlotte which had preceded his leaving the house, and the summons from Celia which had driven every other thought from his head. "Nothing will persuade me to disclose where I went, for you know what Charlotte is for spite. She would not care about harming Celia as long as it meant striking at me."

Septimus listened with a sinking heart. Jocelyn's concern for Celia was blinding him to any need for misgivings on his own behalf, but his godfather was less sanguine. The scene which had just taken place, combined with the events of the preceding days, could well brew up a scandal-broth which, to a greater or lesser degree, would scald them all.

III

During the days which followed, Mr. Twigg watched with dismay his vague misgivings being fully justified. Rumor and conjecture flared through the countryside, and gradually a disturbing element crept in. More and more frequently Celia Croyde's name was mentioned, and with less and less respect; knowing looks and sniggers were exchanged, and what had been an innocent romance took on instead the air of a shameless intrigue.

Nothing, Septimus knew, could be more surely calculated to drive Jocelyn into headlong and disastrous action, and so, not without some qualms, he took it upon himself to inform his godson of what was being said. As he had expected, Jocelyn was furious, and it took all the persuasion of which Mr. Twigg was capable to convince him that any action on his part could only make matters worse, most of all for Celia herself.

"But what the devil am I to do?" Jocelyn demanded, pacing restlessly up and down the pleasant, oak-paneled room in Mr. Twigg's house where the conversation was taking place. "I cannot speak to her father while our family is so newly in mourning, for you know what a stickler for propriety he is. I've not seen Celia herself since the day of the accident, and for all I know, Croyde may have heard this damned gossip and forbidden her to leave the house."

"You will have to be patient," Mr. Twigg replied. "Yes, I know you think that is easier for me to say than for you to do, but you have no choice, my boy! For Miss Celia's sake, you *must* be circumspect."

"That's all very well, Sep, but in a week or two she will be going to London, and who knows what may happen then? If she receives an offer her father thinks she should accept, how can I be sure that she will be able to hold out against him if I am not there to give her support?"

Mr. Twigg could find no answer to this. He was by no means convinced that Celia Croyde was the right bride for Jocelyn, but he knew that to voice his doubts would do no good and might even result in an estrangement from the boy who meant so much to him.

He sighed, his glance turning involuntarily to the picture which held pride of place in this, his favorite room. It was a head-and-shoulders portrait of a young girl, brown-haired and sweet-faced, with eyes which were a painted replica of the eyes now moodily regarding him across the room. Julia, Jocelyn's mother, at the age of sixteen; Julia, whom Septimus had loved steadfastly and without hope, and for whose sake, as much as for his own, he now loved the son who most closely resembled her.

"I wish I knew the source of these confounded rumors," Jocelyn said after a minute or two. "It cannot be only what Charlotte said that day."

"Gossip feeds upon itself, lad," Septimus pointed out. "Miss Celia can scarcely have enemies, and who but Mrs. Rivers wishes *you* ill?"

"Vaine does," Jocelyn replied promptly. "He hopes to marry Celia himself."

"Then it cannot be he," Septimus said with finality. "No man would traduce the woman he wished to make his wife."

After a moment's reflection, Jocelyn agreed, yet, had he but known it, his idle suggestion had hit upon the truth, for Digby Vaine was a man to whom the attainment of a desired end justified any means. He had suspected all along a romantic attachment between Celia and Jocelyn, and because he was a jealous as well as a devious man, he had bitterly resented it, for to his own surprise and exasperation, he had fallen passionately in love with this child only half his age, and was maddened by the thought of a more favored rival. He had had no fear of Jocelyn being acceptable to William Croyde, but when Anthony's death made Jocelyn Avenhurst's heir, Vaine perceived at once that here was the greatest danger to his own pretensions.

To him, Charlotte Rivers's dramatic accusations offered a heaven-sent weapon, and the scandal they provoked he assiduously nourished. Setting himself up as Jocelyn's advocate, he contrived, even while protesting the boy's innocence, subtly to suggest the opposite, while as for Miss Croyde, he defended her good name with such vigor that his very vehemence led his hearers to suspect the worst.

Inevitably echoes of the gossip reached William Croyde, and, just as inevitably, when Celia was challenged, she broke down and confessed. Mr. Croyde was furious. Ambitious though he was for his daughter, he had no intention of allowing her to marry a young man who had involved her in so ugly a scandal, viscount's heir though he might now be. She would be lucky, he told her grimly, to find a husband at all, now that she had been so careless of her reputation.

He half believed this himself. He was not familiar with London society, and had no means of knowing whether or not Celia's matrimonial chances could be damaged by what had happened. Other girls from the neighborhood would be spending the season in town, and the parents of these less-well-endowed young ladies might not be above spreading the sort of malicious rumors which were at present rife here at home. It was a relief to share his worries with Sir Digby, when that adroit gentleman came to call.

Sir Digby was less reassuring than Mr. Croyde had hoped. He admitted reluctantly that in London the destruction of reputations was as much a pastime as dancing or cards, indulged in for the slightest cause or even for no cause at all. If anyone were spiteful enough to circulate there the sort of gossip which at present so undeservedly tarnished Miss Croyde's fair name, irreparable harm would be done. He let this sink in, and then reminded the now desperately worried father that there was, of course, one sure way of scotching the rumors once and for all. Mr. Croyde knew what Sir Digby's feelings were with regard to Miss Celia, and those sentiments remained wholly unchanged....

The news of Celia Croyde's betrothal to Sir Digby Vaine spread rapidly through the district, provoking astonishment and conjecture. When Jocelyn heard it he was at first incredulous, and then furiously angry, his anger being directed almost equally against Vaine himself and William Croyde, who had obviously bullied his daughter into submission.

It was imperative, Jocelyn decided, that he should see Celia without delay, so that he could comfort and reassure her and let her know that he would rescue her from this iniquitous betrothal. Surreptitiously seeking out her groom, and generously greasing the fellow's palm, he persuaded him to convey to his mistress the information that Jocelyn would meet her in the hermitage next morning at eleven o'clock.

He was at the rendezvous betimes, but he waited in vain. Some twenty minutes past the hour, the groom appeared with a note which, crumpled and tear-stained, said simply that she could not come. Jocelyn must go away and never try to see her again.

Jocelyn read it and then crushed it in his hand. He looked at the groom.

"Is Miss Croyde confined to the house?"

The man stared. "Oh no, sir! Her came to the stable to see the mare and slip me that note, and as I was bringing it, I saw her walking in the garden."

Jocelyn's hand clenched even harder on the scrap of paper, and he said with dangerous quietness:

"Then go back and tell her that I shall await her until noon. If she has not come by then, I shall come looking for her, to the house itself, if need be."

The servant started to say something, thought better of it and turned away, not even waiting to see if further largesse was forthcoming. He hoped very much that Miss Celia would go to the hermitage. Young Mr. Rivers meant what he said, not a doubt of it, and there would be the devil to pay if he carried out his threat.

Apparently Celia was of the same opinion, for it still wanted some ten minutes to noon when she entered the hermitage. Jocelyn, who had been prowling up and down the little hut rather in the manner of a caged wild animal, sprang forward to take her in his arms, but she fended him off with both hands.

"Oh, Jocelyn, you should not have come, and I should not be here. Sir Digby—!"

"Damn Sir Digby!" said Jocelyn violently, and pulled her into his arms.

In the grip of the pent-up emotions of the past two weeks, he was in no mood to be gentle, and her struggles merely inflamed him more, so that by the time it dawned upon him that these struggles were more than a mere token, and he did let her go, she was tearful and dishevelled, her hair ruffled and the lace on her bodice disordered. Wrenching herself from his slackened grip and retreating as far as the confines of the hut permitted, she said in a breaking voice:

"Oh, you are rough and hateful! Go away and leave me alone!"

"Am I mad, or are you?" Jocelyn stared at her, too stunned even for anger. "My love, if I frightened you, forgive me! I should have been more gentle, but I have been in hell since last we met—!"

"And so have I!" she broke in tearfully. "Did you suppose it could be otherwise?"

"Forgive me!" he said again. "Sweetheart, I know it has been hard for you. This damned scandal! If I knew who had set these tales about, I would cut his heart out. And now they have bullied you into this devilish betrothal, but listen, Celia! I have thought of a way. When you go to London, I will follow. There are places there where we can be married with no questions asked, and once it is done—!"

"No!" The single syllable, high and clear, stabbed like a dagger into his hurried words, then, as he stared blankly at her, she said again, more quietly this time: "No! I will not marry you. How *could* you think I would—now?"

"You will not?" He was bewildered, fumbling blindly after her meaning. "Because of Vaine? But if you were compelled to accept him—?"

He broke off, leaving the words echoing like a question between them, but Celia, still backed against the farthest wall of the hut, stared back at him without replying. Yes, she had been compelled to accept Sir Digby. This time her father had given her no choice, and that had seemed to be just one more blow to add to the others under which she was reeling. For the first time in her life she was in deep disgrace with her parents, made to endure endless recriminations and reproaches, and she had expected much the same from Sir Digby himself; but Vaine was too clever for that, just as he was too clever to make any demands upon her at present. He had been gentle and reassuring, a kind friend who promised that her troubles would soon pass, that he would look after her and shield her from anything unpleasant, and she had responded thankfully, finding here the comfort no one else had offered. Her parents were angry and disappointed, while Jocelyn—! She had been trying not to think of Jocelyn, not to remember what he had said, what he had done. She wanted never to see him again. Would not have come to him now had she not been afraid of what he might do if she refused.

"Please go away," she said piteously. "It is over. There is nothing left. Oh, do you not understand?"

"No," he said slowly, "I understand nothing. Only two weeks since, in this very place, you swore you loved me, that you would marry me if we could contrive it. Yet now that I have found the way—!"

"Oh!" It was a cry of repudiation. "When you said that, I never dreamed—! That poor little boy! How dare you suppose I would still be willing to marry you?"

For the space of perhaps ten seconds Jocelyn stared at her, while the meaning of her words sank slowly into his mind, into his heart, carrying with them the bitterness of disillusion and the coldness of death. Death of hope, death of love, death of the faith in each other he had thought they shared.

"You believe that?" he said at last in a low voice. "You believe me capable of such infamy, even for your sake? My God! And you said you loved me!"

Something in his voice, something more than anger or even pain, flicked her like a whiplash. It seemed to imply a criticism, a suggestion that she who had been deceived and made to suffer was not altogether blameless. Her own image of herself as the innocent and tragic victim of undeserved disgrace, an image skillfully fostered by Sir Digby, was somehow blurred and cheapened by the way Jocelyn spoke, by the way he was looking at her.

"What right have you to reproach me? Have you forgotten what you said—that the only obstacle between us was the fact that you were not your father's heir? That you would find a way even if it meant going to the devil for counsel—?"

She broke off, frightened by the look on his face, and aware suddenly of how secluded the hermitage was, how far from the house and her father and the servants. She could retreat no farther; her back was to the wall, and Jocelyn stood between her and the door. She gave a little whimper of fear and stretched her hands out before her as though to hold him off.

64

"Don't come near me," she said fearfully. "Don't touch me again."

He did not move. For a second or two he looked at her, every trace of boyishness gone from his face, and then he said, in a tone which invested the words with the finality of an epitaph:

"I shall not, be sure of that. It is my hope that I never set eyes on you again."

He turned and went out, with never a backward glance, and left her standing there alone in the chill dampness of the little hut.

Three weeks had gone by. The Croyde family and Sir Digby Vaine had left for London, and so had those other neighbors who intended to pass the summer in the capital and then at one of the spas. The scandal which had rocked the district at the time of Anthony Rivers's death still simmered, bubbling up again from time to time when some small incident provoked it, and so thoroughly had Sir Digby done his work that only Lord and Lady Avenhurst and Septimus Twigg still declared their total conviction that Jocelyn had been guilty of nothing more than thoughtlessness.

Jocelyn himself was living in a curious, unhappy limbo. The shock of Celia's desertion, and her belief in his guilt, had been so complete, so overwhelming, that his very emotions seemed numbed. Robbed of his ambitions, abandoned by his love, his life had now no direction, no purpose. Indifferent and morose, he spent his days riding alone about the countryside, in much the same way as Charlotte was drifting, like a restless, black-clad ghost, through the splendid rooms of Avenhurst Place, weeping for her dead son. It was whispered among servants and country folk that Mrs. Rivers was mad, driven out of her mind by her bereavement, but no one suggested that Mr. Jocelyn was similarly afflicted. It was remorse that was driving him, they said, and an uneasy conscience.

One evening, when Jocelyn returned from his solitary ride, he was greeted by the information that his lordship desired to see him immediately, and was to be found in the library. He shrugged and nodded and made his way there without even troubling to lay aside his riding whip. Lord Avenhurst watched him come down the long, beautiful room towards him, and frowned his displeasure at the dusty boots and clothes. He said acidly:

"Is it necessary to come into my presence as though into the stables?"

This time Jocelyn did not shrug—even in his present frame of mind he knew better than to do that—but his look and tone implied it.

"I was told, sir, that you wanted to see me at once. However, if it is your wish that I first change my clothes—?"

"No, no," his father interrupted testily. "Now that you are here, I will say what I have to say, and be done with it." He paused, laying his hand on a letter on the inlaid writing-desk at which he was seated. "I have been in correspondence with Colonel Meriden, and we have come to a decision. Young Gervase mends apace, but his parents intend to remain in Hampshire this summer. Next week you and your stepmother and I will travel there. You and Miss Jane will be married in a private ceremony—our bereavement will make that unremarkable—and then you will go abroad. The present situation is intolerable, but even the most poisonous scandal dies when it has nothing left to feed upon, and by the time you and your wife return, these rumors will be forgotten."

"Will they?" Jocelyn's brows lifted. "I would I had your confidence, sir, but if I know Charlotte, it will need more than my absence to silence her tongue."

There was a pause, then: "Charlotte is a sick woman," Lord Avenhurst said in an expressionless voice. "Always unstable, her mind has been wholly overset by grief. If her delusions do not soon abate, I fear it will be necessary to remove the two little girls from her care."

Jocelyn did not pretend to misunderstand him. This, then, was to be the price of Charlotte's obedience, for the threat of being deprived of her two remaining children would undoubtedly be enough to prevent her from stirring up any further trouble. Whether or not the trouble she had already stirred up would be as readily forgotten as Avenhurst supposed, seemed to Jocelyn less certain.

He turned away and stood staring down at the logs which glowed in the marble fireplace, for the evening was chilly. It would be a relief, he admitted to himself, to get away from Avenhurst, away from bitter memories, from the awkwardness of meeting those he had thought were his friends, and from the constant reminders of how he was now regarded in the community where he had grown up. As for the proposed marriage, he supposed he owed it to his father to agree to that, out of gratitude for Avenhurst's steadfast belief in him and his outspoken repudiation of Charlotte's accusations. To marry, to provide heirs, this was a duty now as it had not been while Anthony was alive, and as well marry Jane Meriden as any other, even though he could scarcely recall what she looked like. He was resigned to it, and yet the latent antagonism between him and his father would not let him admit this.

"Well?" Avenhurst prompted impatiently at last. "Have you nothing more to say?"

Jocelyn turned again to face him. "What is there for me to say, sir? What point in saying it if there were? It would not be attended to, any more than it was when last we spoke of this matter."

The viscount frowned. "I am astonished that you have the temerity to refer to that. It does not mean, I trust, that you are still hankering after Celia Croyde?"

"No!" Jocelyn's voice had hardened; bitterness sounded in it. "That folly is over and done with. I suppose I should be grateful that Miss Meriden is still willing to marry me—though no doubt the prospect of being the next Viscountess Avenhurst outweighs the fact that I am branded a child-murderer."

The impatience in Avenhurst's face deepened to anger. "Enough! I will listen to no more in that vein. What right have you to mock at Miss Meriden in this fashion?"

A sneer twisted Jocelyn's lips. "Does your lordship suppose my altered circumstances mean nothing to her?"

"I hope they mean a great deal, and I wish I could be as confident that you will uphold the dignity of *your* rank as I am that she will uphold the dignity of hers."

"I am flattered, sir, to know that your opinion of me remains unchanged."

"By God! Is there no end to your insolence?" The viscount sprang to his feet, his chair sliding back across the polished floor; his voice was low, but savage with anger and contempt. "Do you dare expect me to show you in private the face which necessity compels me to wear before the world? To forgive what you have done, as well as seek to repair the harm and shield you from the consequences?"

Jocelyn stared at him, aware of a coldness spreading

67

through all his being, of a shock greater even than that of Celia's desertion. He said in a voice scarcely louder than a whisper:

"God help me! You believe I *was* responsible for the boy's death. All your defense of me has been a sham."

"You are my heir," Avenhurst said bitterly, and even in his shock and pain Jocelyn noticed that he did not say "my son." "If you were not—!" He checked himself, and then went on: "What happened that day must forever lie between you and your conscience, but what is done, is done, and I must look to the future. Avenhurst will be yours! You have chosen to take up that responsibility, and by God! I will see that you do your duty by it."

Septimus Twigg woke with a start and lay wondering what had disturbed him. All was silent now, but some noise had jerked him awake. Then, as he puzzled over it, it came again, a sudden pattering, as of rain against the window. Yet the weather was fine and clear, and the sound was too sharp to be made by raindrops. Mr. Twigg sat up and pulled aside the bed-curtain.

The first gray light of day was seeping into the room, enough to show him the familiar outlines of the furniture; enough to reveal, when he reached the window, a tall, cloaked figure standing on the flagged path below, one hand lifting to toss another handful of earth against the glass. At sight of movement within, the action changed to a gesture enjoining silence, and then to point imperatively to the front door. Before Mr. Twigg could thrust open the casement, the intruder had turned, taken half a dozen stealthy strides, and vanished into the deep stone porch which sheltered the entrance to the house.

With profound misgivings, Septimus fumbled his way into slippers and dressing gown and kindled a light. Then, moving softly and giving thanks that his servants had their quarters at the back of the house, he went down to unbar the door. Pulling it open, he said in a whisper which somehow contrived to be muted and explosive at the same time:

"Jocelyn! What the devil are you about?"

Jocelyn, slipping past him into the house, did not reply, but the candlelight revealed a look in his face which prevented Mr. Twigg from immediately repeating the question. Instead he shut the door, took his godson by the arm and led him into the room where Julia's portrait gazed serenely down from the wall. That door, too, he closed; then, setting down the candle, said quietly:

"Now, lad, tell me."

Above the candle flame, Jocelyn's eyes met his, somberly.

"I am leaving, Sep," he said in a low voice. "Forgive me for rousing you at this hour, but I could not go without bidding you farewell."

"Go?" Septimus repeated. "Go where? No," he added quickly, "leave that for the present. What has happened?"

"I have discovered the truth!" Jocelyn's voice was bleak. "My father believes, along with everyone else in this damned neighborhood, that I deliberately caused Anthony's death. He regards me with contempt and disgust, but seeks to crush the scandal because there is no one else to inherit Avenhurst except our cousins in the north. To exclude them, he is prepared even to condone the murder of his grandson."

Septimus was staring incredulously at him. "You must be mistaken. You have misconstrued something your father said."

"Oh, no! There is no mistake. He told me last night, in plain terms which even a numbskull like myself could not misinterpret. I have chosen, he said, to take on the responsibility of inheritance and must be prepared to do my duty—which appears, at present, to be to marry Jane Meriden immediately and father a son with the least possible delay."

Mr. Twigg regarded him with a troubled frown. "I can understand that you find the prospect of marriage repugnant just at present, but I fancy that Miss Meriden will make an excellent wife."

"Very likely, and the irony is that I was prepared to be dutiful. I owed my father that, I thought, if only out of gratitude for his faith in me. His faith—hell, that's rich!"

The angry, bitter young voice paused, but Mr. Twigg, more completely at a loss than ever before in his life, could find nothing to say. He was angry and alarmed. Avenhurst was a fool. If he had ever taken the trouble to know his younger son, he would have known, too, that he was incapable of the deed now attributed to him. To believe otherwise was unforgivable, and Jocelyn would not forgive. Septimus, at least, knew that.

"So I am going away," Jocelyn resumed after a moment. "Bad enough to be a puppet manipulated by another, even though that other be my own father, but to be a despised puppet, used because there is none better—no, that I will not endure. I would come to despise myself, and that would be the worst of all."

Septimus still looked troubled. "If you go, Jocelyn, it will be taken as a confession of guilt. You will convict yourself."

"I am already convicted, in the eyes of everyone here. It does not matter. I shall never return."

Mr. Twigg's anxious frown deepened. "Where do you mean to go?"

Jocelyn shrugged. "My first thought was naturally to join the army, but my father's influence spreads wide, and it might be that even in the ranks, under an assumed name, he would still find me. So I am bound for Portsmouth."

"The fleet?" Anger and dismay made the other man's voice harsh. "Good God, boy! Are you mad? You cannot volunteer as a common sailor!"

"Why not?"

"Why not? Have you no idea what life aboard a man-o'-war is like? Harsh enough for the officers, but hell on earth for the ordinary seaman. Why, do you suppose, are press gangs needed to keep the fleet up to strength? Because even convicted criminals prefer to rot in jail than serve in a King's ship. I will not let you do it!"

Jocelyn shook his head. "You cannot prevent me. Unless you think you can overcome me by force and put me under lock and key?" Mr. Twigg, knowing very well that it was beyond his power to do anything of the kind, made an angry gesture of repudiation. "No, and I do not think you will betray me to my father, either."

"I ought to," Septimus said roughly. "I ought to warn him at once so that he may come after you."

"My dear Sep, you do not imagine, surely, that his lordship would so demean himself?" Jocelyn spoke with bitter mockery. "I should be haled back in disgrace by his lackeys like some errant schoolboy. Not for my own sake, you understand, but simply so that I may play stallion to the brood-mare he has selected for me."

Yes, thought Mr. Twigg, I understand. I understand the hurt you have suffered, the resentment and the shame you feel. I even understand and sympathize with your determination to be rid of us all, but I cannot let you do it. I cannot let you commit suicide, for that is what this crazy notion amounts to. Yet how am I to dissuade you from it?

In his agitation he had been walking about the room, and now found himself beside the bureau where he had been writing a letter before he went to bed. The letter itself, sealed, ready for dispatch, still lay there, and as he stared at the superscription, unseeingly at first and then with quickening attention, an idea occurred to him. He turned to face his companion.

"Jocelyn," he said abruptly, "do you recall my mentioning to you a man named Thaddeus Loring?"

"What?" Jocelyn, too, had been lost in thought, and stared blankly at him for a moment. "Loring? Yes, I believe so. Was he not a boyhood friend of yours who settled in one of the colonies?"

Septimus nodded. "In Jamaica. We have corresponded at intervals ever since he left England. This"—he picked up the bulky packet from the bureau—"is my most recent letter to him. I intended to send Thomas off with it in the morning to Bristol, to the ship which lately brought Loring's letter to me. She is due to set sail for the West Indies in a few days' time." He paused, then added meaningly: "You could take the letter for me, instead."

"I? To Bristol?" Jocelyn frowned at him, and then suddenly he understood. "Sep, are you suggesting that *I* go to Jamaica?"

"Why not, since your purpose is to get as far away from here as possible? I will give you a letter of introduction to Loring. He is a merchant and ship owner—the vessel at Bristol belongs to him—and he will help you to establish yourself. You seek a new life. I offer you one where, if you are to prosper, it must be by your own ability and effort. A challenge, Jocelyn! It is what you need."

He paused, and for a while there was silence in the shadowy room. Jocelyn stood staring at the candle flame and trying to come to grips with the proposal Septimus had laid before him. In the wretched hours since the interview with his father, he had thought only of escape, of cutting adrift from this place where he was despised and distrusted, and losing himself in anonymity; it was still his foremost, his only, concern. The thought of Jamaica appealed to him solely because he knew it would never occur to Avenhurst to seek him there. The viscount knew nothing of Sep's friend, Thaddeus Loring, for he had never taken the smallest interest in

71

Mr. Twigg's personal concerns, treating him always with the distant courtesy he used towards all those who were unlikely ever to be of use to him. If Jocelyn rode now for Bristol instead of Portsmouth, and if Septimus would agree to cover his tracks....

Mr. Twigg was intently watching his godson, willing him with all his strength to agree. If he had to lose him, this boy who was so dear, he wanted him to have at least a chance of building a new life in place of the one he was casting aside; to have, for it amounted to nothing less, a chance of survival.

"Very well," Jocelyn said at last, in a tone of decision. "I will do as you suggest, Sep—upon one condition. That you give me your solemn oath never to disclose my whereabouts to anyone, for any reason at all. That you disclaim all knowledge of me, even of the fact that I have gone, until you hear of it from others."

"That last is not likely to be believed," Septimus pointed out, "least of all by your father, but I am willing to prevaricate on that point. For the rest, you have my word. I cannot like what you are doing, but I swear by your mother's memory that no one shall ever learn from me where you have gone or anything else concerning you. Here's my hand on it!"

Their hands met in a hard grip which said a great deal they could not put into words. There was silence for a moment, a silence taut with emotion, but then Septimus became brisk again.

"Now, to business! Did you leave any word at all at the Place?"

Jocelyn shook his head. "I want it to be supposed that I have simply ridden out as I do every day. Even the fact that I left before anyone else was awake will not arouse suspicion, for it's not the first time I have done it. I have been sleeping badly, and prefer to be abroad rather than lie tossing in bed."

"And your horse?"

"Tethered in the spinney by the road."

Septimus nodded. "Good! Now, this is what you must do. You will still have to make for Gloucester, since that is the nearest place where you can cross the Severn. Halt there to bait, and make a point of inquiring which road you must take for Portsmouth. Set out in that direction, and then circle back across country to the Bristol road, so that when his lordship sends in search of you, his messengers may, if we are lucky, follow a false trail."

"God send they do! I have no mind to be dragged back here like a criminal. I shall have a good start, at least, for it will be hours before anyone realizes that I do not mean to return."

Septimus picked up the candle and took it across the bureau. "I will write the letter for you to give to Loring, commending to him my young friend—!" He broke off, turning again to Jocelyn. "My young friend—who? You will need another name."

"Yes." Jocelyn thought for a moment, and then looked at the portrait of his mother. "Julian! I will call myself Julian, after her. And in place of Rivers?" A wry smile touched his lips for a second. "Why not 'Severn'? Yes, that will serve! Julian Severn."

Septimus took up his pen, and for several minutes the scratching of the quill across the paper was the only sound to break the silence, while Jocelyn stood looking about the familiar room with the sadness of farewell, knowing that he would never see it again. He had passed unmoved and uncaring through the magnificence of Avenhurst Place as he left it for the last time, but this simple room, with its dark old paneling and homely furniture, and the youthful portrait of his mother above the hearth, embodied for him the happiest aspect of his boyhood. In the same way, Septimus Twigg, an equally homely and at present slightly comical figure in nightshirt and dressing gown, his nightcap flopping forward over one eye as he bent over the bureau, inspired an affection in Jocelyn which he had never felt for his own aloof and imperious parent. With a sudden, piercing sense of loss he realized how lonely he would have been without Septimus; how lonely they would both be from this day on.

The letter was finished; sanded, folded and sealed; the name and direction of Thaddeus Loring written upon it. Septimus scribbled another, much shorter, note and then took them both up, together with the letter he had written earlier, and held them out to Jocelyn.

"I have described you to Loring as a young man without family and of very limited means who desires to make his way in the world. What details you add to that bare outline is for you to choose. You can inform me of them when you send me word of how Julian Severn is faring. The other note is to Captain Fuller of the *Lucilla,* requesting him to give you passage to Jamaica. Now, you will need money—!"

73

"No!" Jocelyn spoke quickly. "Sep, there is no need! I still have my quarter's allowance barely touched."

"You will need money," Mr. Twigg repeated, ignoring the interruption. "Oh, as a loan, my dear boy, if that will ease your pride! You can repay it to me through Loring when you are able, though why I cannot give my godson a present is more than I can understand. Wait here! I will be only a few minutes."

He lit another candle from the first and went softly out of the room. Jocelyn looked at the letters in his hand, two of them inscribed with the name of a man he did not know, in a town on an island on the other side of the world, and the full impact of what he was doing struck him for the first time. With a stifled sound which was neither a groan nor a sob, but a broken mingling of both, he dropped into a chair by the table and buried his face in his arms, and remained so until the stealthy rattle of the latch heralded Mr. Twigg's return. When the other man entered the room, he was standing with his back to the door, putting the letters carefully away in his pocket.

"You must make haste." Septimus spoke gruffly, as though he, too, had difficulty in controlling his emotion. "The servants will soon be stirring. Take this."

He held out a well-filled purse and Jocelyn turned to face him, but they did not look at each other as the money changed hands and was stowed away; as Jocelyn spoke his thanks and said that he would repay the loan, and as Septimus said again that there was no need. Then they walked in silence to the front door, and Septimus opened it to reveal a world into which color was already creeping to dispel the predawn grayness, and where the rose-tinted eastern sky spoke of sunrise not far off.

In the porch they turned silently to face each other, the stocky, middle-aged man in the nightcap and the tall boy with the drawn face and haunted eyes. In silence they again clasped hands, and then Mr. Twigg released his grip and instead clasped his godson in a quick, hard embrace.

"Goodbye, my dear lad," he said huskily. "God bless you."

He let him go. Jocelyn's hands rested on his shoulders for a moment, gripping hard, and then he turned and strode quickly away. Septimus watched until he disappeared through a gap in the thick yew hedge which bounded that part of the garden, and then he went back into the house, closed and barred the door with exaggerated care and returned to the room where the candles still burned.

For a few minutes he stood with bowed head, and then slowly he looked up until his tear-moist eyes met the painted eyes of the portrait. He raised both arms in a gesture which seemed at the same time to seek comfort and to ask forgiveness, and then he blew out the candles and, walking like an old man, went slowly up the stairs to his bedroom.

Book Two

ALATHEA

I

Thaddeus Loring lived at Kingston, in a large white house on the outskirts of the town, but he conducted his business from a countinghouse adjacent to his warehouses behind the wharves of nearby Port Royal. He was not often to be found there, for he was a rich man now and could afford to employ others to carry on the day-to-day conduct of his many interests, but the safe arrival of one of his ships could always be counted upon to bring him down to the harbor. It was understood that he must be informed at once, and so as soon as the *Lucilla* was sighted, the most junior of his clerks was sent off with the news; by the time the ship had come to her anchorage and started to unload, Mr. Loring's coach was threading its way through the throng to the wharf, and a boat was waiting to carry him out to her.

Captain Fuller was waiting to greet him when he came aboard, a greeting more friendly than formal, for they had known each other for many years. It had been a fair voyage, the captain informed him; the ship and the crew were in good heart. Mr. Loring expressed his satisfaction and asked one or two questions, and then, glancing towards a tall, unfamiliar figure glimpsed on the poop above, he remarked:

"I see you bring a passenger, Captain."

"Aye, sir. Mr. Severn. He came to me in Bristol just before we sailed, with a request from your friend, Mr. Twigg, that I should give him passage to Jamaica. I assumed that you would wish me to do so."

"A friend of Septimus Twigg? You did right to take him aboard, Fuller, and I look forward to making his acquaintance. Invite him to take a glass of wine with us."

Captain Fuller dispatched one of his men with the message and led the way to the main cabin astern. It was not long before the passenger joined them, and Loring's first reaction was surprise that he was so young. The name of Septimus Twigg had led him to expect someone of his own generation, but this was a mere boy. As Fuller presented him, Mr. Loring studied him curiously, seeing a lanky, black-haired youth in good clothes which were far too heavy for that tropical climate; an aquiline face tanned by the long weeks at sea and yet strangely haggard, with lips which seemed too sternly set for his age and brown eyes which, though remarkably handsome, were totally unrevealing. There was courtliness in the bow he made, the easy grace of one trained from childhood in the polite ceremonies of life, and Loring's curiosity deepened. It was to remain unsatisfied for many years.

"Captain Fuller tells me, Mr. Severn, that you are a protégé of my old friend Septimus Twigg," he said kindly. "How fares he?"

"Well, sir, when last I saw him." The answer came composedly, and Thaddeus Loring never suspected the stab of homesickness, the sudden wrench of loneliness provoked by the memory the words conjured up. "He was kind enough to give me a letter of introduction to you."

He proffered it. Loring broke the seal and, having read the letter, looked up with a smile.

"So you have come to Jamaica, Mr. Severn, in the hope of making your fortune," he remarked. "Well, well, so did I, five-and-twenty years ago, and there are still opportunities here for those with the will and the ability to seize them. You must tell me in which direction your ambitions lie, and meanwhile, pray do me the honor of being my guest."

Julian Severn was startled. "You are too kind, sir. I have no wish to impose upon your hospitality."

"You do not, be sure of that." Loring spoke with finality. "A visitor fresh from England is an all-too-rare occurrence, and my wife, I know, will be eager to welcome you to our home."

There was no more to be said, and Julian could only express his gratitude and wait until Mr. Loring found it convenient to go ashore. He felt profoundly relieved. This was a new world, and his first taste of it would be a good deal more palatable as a guest in Thaddeus Loring's house than if he were left to fend for himself at an inn.

He felt curiously adrift and in sore need of a firm anchorage, something to which he could hold until he could take the measure of life in this unknown land. The voyage had been an interlude, timeless, divorced from both past and future, and though he had brooded endlessly over the one, the other had seemed vague and formless; impossible to imagine, even if he had felt any inclination to do so, because his knowledge of the West Indies was almost nonexistent. Now, face to face with reality, he found himself unprepared for it.

Mr. Loring did not stay long aboard the *Lucilla*. Later he would go more thoroughly into the details of the voyage with Captain Fuller, but his present visit was simply one of welcome, and to receive the eagerly awaited letters and goods which had been sent from England, so within an hour Julian Severn was setting foot on Jamaican soil for the first time.

His first impressions were chaotic. The hurly-burly on the waterfront at Port Royal was typical of seaports the world over, but to a newcomer fresh from England, the blazing sunshine, the predominance of brown and black faces over white, the sound of English spoken in accents which rendered it almost a foreign tongue, were overwhelming. It was a relief to climb into Thaddeus Loring's coach, to be granted a brief respite from the impact of new experiences.

Loring, remembering perhaps his own arrival in the New World, gave him time to collect his thoughts and recover a little from his bewilderment, and instead of making conversation, occupied himself with the long letter he had received from Septimus Twigg. He expected to find in it further information regarding young Mr. Severn, and was surprised and puzzled that there was none. Coming to the end, he sat pondering for a little while, and then remarked:

"I take it that your decision to leave England was a sudden one, Mr. Severn?" Julian turned a startled, almost dismayed, face towards him, and he added, tapping the letter with his forefinger: "Our friend Twigg makes no mention of it here."

"Oh!" The hesitation was no more than momentary. "As to that, sir, Mr. Twigg had already written that letter when I arrived at his house to seek his advice concerning my future, and it was the fact that he intended sending it to you by means of the *Lucilla* which gave him the idea of suggesting that I, too, should seek passage aboard her. He has always been kind enough to take an interest in my welfare, and he believed that you would be willing to advise me once I arrived here. It seemed to me a chance too good to be missed."

"You are a man of decision, I see." Mr. Loring seemed amused. "There cannot be many either willing or able to uproot themselves at a moment's notice and travel to the other side of the world. Twigg mentions that you have no family?"

There was a note of interrogation in the latter words. Julian Severn shook his head; there was an almost imperceptible hardening of his expression.

"No, sir, none," he said with the utmost finality. "I am entirely alone in the world, with neither obligations nor encumbrances."

The elder man looked at him rather hard but made no comment upon this, asking instead: "And what of your ambitions, Mr. Severn?"

"To tell truth, sir, I am not sure where those now lie. Had the choice been mine, I would have elected to serve in the army, but unless one has the means to purchase a commission, that is out of the question."

"If you settle in Jamaica, you will be required to serve in the militia, as are all white men of military age, but it is doubtful whether that would satisfy your military ambitions. You might do better at sea. However, time enough for that! Look about you for a little; learn what opportunities offer themselves here in the colonies. You may depend upon me for whatever help or advice I am able to give."

"You are very kind, Mr. Loring. Believe me, I am exceedingly grateful."

It was said with obvious sincerity, but Loring observed that there was no real lightening of the speaker's expression, no warmth in the brown eyes. Julian Severn's formal courtesy enveloped him like armor, and Thaddeus found himself wondering if the guard would ever be lowered.

*　　*　　*

To English eyes, the Loring house presented a somewhat curious appearance, for though very spacious, it consisted of only one storey—a precaution, Julian discovered later, against the ravages of earthquakes and hurricanes. Since Thaddeus Loring himself had had it built, it was in many respects an English house, approached through tall iron gates leading to a short avenue, and with gardens before and about it. Yet the servants who appeared as the coach drew up before the front door were, like the coachman and footman, Negro slaves, and the gardens, though laid out in the formal fashion which Mr. Loring must have known during his boyhood in England, were filled with trees and flowers which, to Julian, seemed exotic and unfamiliar. Inside the house the rooms were large and handsome, floored and paneled with mahogany, the furniture also of native hardwood. Strangeness and familiarity seemed oddly mingled, adding to Julian's sense of unreality.

Mrs. Loring was considerably younger than her husband, almost young enough, in fact, to be his daughter; a plump, pretty woman in a modish silk gown frosted with fine lace, her chestnut-colored hair dressed close under a frivolous little cap of lace and ribbon. She seemed delighted to receive her husband's guest and greeted him with a warmth which was soon explained, for when he somewhat hesitantly apologized for the inconvenience which he feared his unexpected arrival must cause, she brushed this airily aside.

"Not in the least, Mr. Severn, I assure you. It is a rare treat for us to entertain a guest newly arrived from England, and you must indulge us with news of what is happening there. I was fortunate enough to spend a year there when I was a girl, and so such news is of special interest to me."

"What you mean, my dear," her husband put in with some amusement, "is that you would like to know about the latest fashions, the newest plays and the scandals of London society, but I doubt whether these are matters which greatly interest Mr. Severn."

"They are matters, sir, of which I fear I have very little knowledge. I spent a short time in London last year, but that is all."

"Last year!" Margaret Loring repeated. "My dear sir, to us that is but yesterday. Presently you must tell me—!"

She was interrupted. There was the sound of pattering footsteps, and into the room burst the most beautiful child

Julian had ever seen. Her face was a perfect oval, the features classically perfect and the complexion exquisite, while the hair which tumbled in a mass of glossy curls over her shoulders was a glowing auburn. Casting herself upon Mrs. Loring and clutching at her wide, hooped skirts, she cried excitedly:

"Mama, Mama, the boxes from England have come! Oh, pray open them quickly so that I may have my present!"

"Yes, my love, in a moment, but you forget your manners. Papa has a guest. Make your curtsy to Mr. Severn." She glanced at Julian with the complacency of a parent certain that her offspring cannot fail to be admired. "My daughter Lucilla, sir."

Lucilla bestowed upon him an indifferent glance from long-lashed eyes of greenish gray and dropped a perfunctory curtsy, but returned at once to the matter of more immediate importance. Turning to her father and clasping one of his hands in both her own, she looked up at him with a pretty air of cajolery.

"*You* will open the boxes, won't you, Papa? Do you know which one my present is in?"

Mr. Loring looked fondly down at her and pinched her cheek. "Yes, you rogue, I know. In the smallest of the three. Tell Samuel to uncord it and bring it to me, and we will see what can be done."

Lucilla darted away, almost colliding in the doorway with another, slightly older girl who was just coming in, and who was obliged to fall back to let her pass. Mrs. Loring beckoned the newcomer forward, smilingly but, Julian noticed, without the look of doting pride she had bestowed upon the younger child.

"And this is Lucilla's elder sister, Mr. Severn." Even the form of introduction seemed to relegate the other girl to second place. "Her name is Serena."

Serena Loring curtsied sedately. Considered alone, she was an attractive child, gray-eyed and chestnut-haired, with a broad brow, straight nose and wide, grave mouth, but she could not compete with her little sister's striking beauty. It was plain that Lucilla was the favorite, and this discovery struck a chord of sympathy among Julian's own childhood memories. He bowed to Serena with as much ceremony as he had bowed to her mother, and after an instant's astonishment, she rewarded him with a sudden smile of piercing sweetness

84

and charm. The effect was almost startling, as though a light had been unexpectedly kindled in a shadowy place.

Lucilla could be heard outside, issuing shrill, imperious commands to the butler, until, apparently satisfied that these were being obeyed, she came skipping into the room again. Pausing before Julian, she demanded:

"Did you come from England, too, aboard the *Lucilla?*"

He admitted it, and she went on: "Papa named her after *me*, you know. Can you guess why?"

He shook his head, refusing to pander to her childish vanity, but she was in no way abashed. Pirouetting before him, she looked up at him over her shoulder, fluttering those incredibly long, dark lashes—even at seven years old, Lucilla Loring was a coquette.

"Because she is his best and most beautiful ship, of course," she declared mischievously. "That is so, isn't it, Papa?"

Thaddeus Loring chuckled, reaching out an arm to draw her close to his side. "To be sure it is, puss! What other reason could there be?"

"Lucilla, my love, you have lost your cap *again*," her mother put in, with more resignation than displeasure. "Come here to me and let me tidy your hair."

Lucilla came obediently but stated, as Mrs. Loring sought to restore some order to the tumble of curls, that it would only come down again, and she had no idea where her cap might be. Then Samuel came in, carrying a small, sturdy wooden chest, and she broke away again, dancing with excitement and impatience, while this was set down on a stool and the lid lifted. Beneath this a folded cloth had been placed to protect the contents, and when, at a nod from Mr. Loring, Samuel removed it, two dolls were revealed, lying side by side.

They were of much the same size, but while one was clad, country-fashion, in flowered dimity and a wide straw hat, the other was in full ball-dress—a satin gown with panniers and lace, powdered hair and a pearl necklace. Lucilla never hesitated. With a cry of delight she snatched up the more elaborate toy, hugging it to her and then holding it at arm's length to admire it, flinging her free arm round her father's neck in gratitude and then flying to her mother to show off the beauties of her new acquisition.

Mr. Loring picked up the other doll and gave it to Serena, who all this while had remained quietly by her mother's chair, and though she thanked him prettily and cradled it in her arms, Julian noticed how her gaze went longingly to the beautiful, elaborate plaything which her younger sister had so promptly and confidently appropriated. It was a small incident, but it told him as much about the Loring family as he could have learned in a month's acquaintance.

He was to have that month's acquaintance, and a great deal more, for having once welcomed him to their house, Thaddeus and Margaret would not hear of him leaving it. Looking back in later years, he always marveled at their kindness and forbearance, for he realized then, though he was incapable of realizing it at the time, that he was a far from easy guest.

He was still in that curious frame of mind, rootless and indifferent. The past haunted him. The ruin of his hopes; his undeserved disgrace; the knowledge that both the girl he had loved and his own father believed him guilty. Even the memory of Septimus Twigg's staunch friendship and unswerving faith was spoiled and tarnished by the memories which obsessed his mind.

If he could have spoken of it, poured out to a sympathetic listener his bitterness and anger, his self-doubts and vain regret, he might have found a measure of relief, but since the time of his parting from Septimus, these emotions had been driven back upon themselves, so that by the time he arrived in Jamaica, they festered like some hidden sore, poisoning his whole outlook and cutting him off from all but the most superficial relationships. New experiences—and they were many in this new, strange land—washed over him and left him unmoved. New friendships offered were met only with that formal courtesy which had been so instilled in him that it was now second nature, for he was incapable of any warmer response.

He knew that he was at fault. He had been granted a respite, and should be making use of it to establish himself in some occupation which would support him when his little store of money ran out, but he could not overcome the lethargy which possessed him. The experiences he had passed through had set a lasting mark upon him, a burden which he felt incapable of casting aside.

The days slid by until, some six weeks after his arrival in the New World, he fell victim to one of the deadly fevers which afflicted all the inhabitants of the islands, but to which newcomers were particularly susceptible. The attack was a violent one, and for days, sheer physical misery overwhelmed every other thought and feeling. He believed he was going to die, and did not much care if he did. For a time the Lorings feared so, too, but in the end his youth and excellent constitution asserted themselves, and the fever abated.

He was very weak. A major effort was required to lift a hand from the coverlet, or his head from the pillow, but lying there, drained and exhausted, he made a curious discovery. The past with its burden of bitterness and disillusion no longer possessed him. He had not forgotten it, and the scars of its wounds would never completely fade, but it was as though his close approach to death had purged him of it. He felt empty of all feeling, empty as a seashell which had been scoured through and through by the tides; liberated from the past, but with nothing to put in its place.

Into that emptiness, so quietly and gradually that he was scarcely aware of it happening, came the child Serena. Following her mother on one of Margaret's visits to the sickroom, she stood at the foot of Julian's bed, gazing at him with wide, grave eyes. He was so weak that even to smile at her was almost too great an effort, but he made it, and won the response of her own blindingly sweet smile in return. Though he drifted almost immediately into exhausted sleep, the memory of her stayed with him, threading through his dreams and lingering pleasantly in his mind when he woke.

Next day she came again, diffidently, as though fearing a rebuff. When this did not come she grew more confident, and after that her visits were frequent. He would wake to find her sitting beside his bed, stitching laboriously at a sampler, or she would help the servant who brought him food and drink, walking delicately with her hands clasped carefully about bowl or glass and her face serious and intent with the importance of her task.

Later, as his strength increased, they would talk. Or rather, Serena would talk and Julian listen, prompting her now and then with a question, intrigued and fascinated by the aspects of her character thus revealed. She was a lonely child, not neglected, but very much aware that Lucilla was the favored one, and it was perhaps this very loneliness which forged the first link between her and Julian. Each instinctively recognized the other's need, and though it was an odd friendship, between the nine-year-old girl and the young man some ten years her senior, it was a friendship nonetheless, and one which grew increasingly important to them both.

Thaddeus and Margaret, seeing their shy little daughter succeed where everyone else had failed, were as much astonished as delighted, not realizing that just as Serena had found her way into the heart of the aloof young stranger from England, so he had discovered the key to the child's personality.

Serena, to Julian, was an endless delight. Behind her quietness and reserve lay charm and a lively imagination, with, occasionally, an odd maturity which was both enchanting and endearing, and Julian reflected indignantly that if the Lorings were less besotted with the showy perfections of their younger child, they might learn to value the elder as she deserved. It was some time before he realized that Serena had revealed more of herself to him in a few short weeks than she had ever done to her parents, but when he did, he resolved with a rush of mingled pride and protectiveness that this trust in him must never be betrayed.

By the time he was strong enough to leave his room, he had come to a decision regarding his future. He knew now that his original purpose in coming to Jamaica had been, not to seek a new life, but merely to escape from the old, and that he had wasted months wallowing in self-pity and fruitless regrets. He had been robbed of everything he had once hoped and yearned for. Very well. He would find a new purpose in life, and new ambitions to replace the old. The important thing was not to admit defeat, but to seize the future and mould it into something in which a man could take pride. To take up the challenge which life—and Septimus Twigg—had cast at his feet.

As his convalescence progressed, he had long talks with Thaddeus Loring, who, encouraged by the change in Julian's outlook, spared no pains to instruct him. Loring had a finger in many pies, and to understand the ramifications of his business it was necessary to understand also something of the past history and present political situation of the Indies. Julian's imagination was caught, and soon he was as eager to learn as Loring was to teach.

By this time he had been adopted completely into the Loring family. His illness had broken down the barriers of formality, and now he was Julian to them all, even the little girls, while the slaves treated him as though he were a son of the house. It was a pleasant novelty, for he had never experienced real family life. Even when his mother was alive, the demands of her social position had kept her apart from her children for long periods; they had been cared for by nurses, governesses and tutors, and later the boys were sent away to school, while always the ceremony of life at Avenhurst Place precluded the sort of affectionate informality which existed in the Loring establishment. Thaddeus treated him like a son; Margaret behaved as she might have done to a younger brother; and even Lucilla, once she had absorbed the fact that here was one person upon whom her blandishments had no effect, accepted him as a matter of course. He was grateful, and soon became sincerely attached to them all, but it was Serena who held a special place in his heart.

When Julian was well enough, he accompanied Mr. Loring to the counting house in Port Royal, where the most senior of the clerks, who had worked for Loring for more than twenty years, took over the task of instruction begun by Thaddeus himself. Julian, his interest already caught and his determination to prosper growing stronger every day, found a whole new world opening before him, a world of trade and commerce which he had scarcely known existed. It fascinated him, and, eager to learn all he could as quickly as possible, he was soon spending as many hours at the counting house as the clerks themselves.

Thaddeus was very well pleased. He had an occupation in mind for young Mr. Severn which would, he thought, appeal to the boy as well as being of real service to himself. His business interests were not confined to Jamaica, but spread among the other English colonies, and at one time he had traveled frequently between the islands. Now his health, originally undermined by privations suffered during his early years in the New World, was deteriorating, and he could no longer face the prospect of such voyaging. Julian, he decided, should be his deputy.

Julian himself, when the proposition was finally laid before him, assented eagerly. The experiences he had passed through had matured him and cured him of much of his youthful wildness but had not curbed his restlessness, and the prospect of traveling among the other colonies appealed to him more than it had ever done to Loring.

About this time Julian struck up a friendship with Michael

Langdale, the captain of another of Loring's ships, the *Merry Venture*. Langdale was in his middle twenties, a lean, bronzed, active fellow with bright blue eyes and a ready laugh, and he and Julian took to each other at their first meeting. From this a friendship developed which was to survive, unchanged by their variously changing fortunes, for the rest of their lives. It was Julian's first experience of such a friendship, and it played its part, along with all the other influences in this new life, in shaping the character of Julian Severn.

Langdale was soon to embark on another voyage, and on the day before he sailed, invited Julian to dine with him at the town's principal inn. They lingered over the meal, so that evening was approaching when they emerged, and while they stood talking before going their separate ways, an extraordinary group of riders came clattering along the street.

It was led by an enormous man on a great black horse, richly, almost extravagantly dressed. Behind him came two stalwart Negro grooms in livery of green and gold, well mounted and well armed; then two more, each leading a laden packhorse, while a second pair of armed outriders brought up the rear. It was Julian's first glimpse of a man who was to have a profound effect upon his life, and as he stared in astonishment he heard Michael say with a chuckle:

"Now there's a sight Kingston is not privileged to see more than once or twice in a twelvemonth. Take a good look, Julian! They say he's the richest man in Jamaica."

"Who the devil is he?" Julian spoke without turning his head, his fascinated gaze still on the approaching cavalcade.

Michael chuckled again. "His name is Jethro Verwood. He's a planter who lives just about as far from civilization as it's possible to go. His plantation is one of the old Spanish places, and was falling into decay when he bought it, but they say he spent a fortune clearing land and extending the fields, until it is one of the largest in the island. He rules over it like a feudal monarch—in fact, everyone refers to it as Verwood's Kingdom."

The riders halted before the inn and Jethro Verwood dismounted, tossing the reins to one of his attendants. Seen thus at close quarters, and on foot, his size was overpowering, for he topped even Julian's lanky height by four or five inches and was correspondingly broad, with huge shoulders and a thickness about the waist which on a man of average stature would have amounted to corpulence, but which on him looked insignificant. His face, too, was impressive, large featured, heavy-jawed and deeply lined, with a great beak of a nose. He wore no wig, only a silk kerchief bound about his head beneath the braided tricorne hat, and his skin was so darkly tanned that Julian wondered if he were a mulatto.

"Not that I know of," Michael said in answer to this question when Verwood had disappeared into the inn, "but there's little enough anyone knows about him, even though he has lived here for fifteen years. It's not even known whence he came."

"Is he not English, then?"

"Oh, yes, he's English, right enough, but it was not from England he had come when he arrived here. My father remembers it well. The ship that brought him carried no passengers other than Verwood and his wife, a few free servants and all their household slaves, and stayed only long enough for them to disembark. It was assumed that Verwood had bribed the master not to linger so that no one should discover where he had come from. He hired a house at Spanish Town to live in until he purchased the plantation, but no one outside his own household ever saw Mrs. Verwood."

Julian stared. "What, not in fifteen years?"

"Oh, she died long ago. There is a daughter, so it's said, but she never leaves the plantation. Verwood himself only leaves it once or twice a year, and then just for a few days, but all his business dealings are with Mr. Loring, so it is quite likely that you may meet him."

Julian was intrigued by the story and later was gratified to learn that Jethro Verwood was to dine with them the following day. The planter's huge presence dwarfed even the spacious rooms of the Loring house; he towered over his host's spare figure and made plump Margaret seem dainty and doll-like by comparison; and, when Julian was presented, regarded him with keen interest.

"So you are lately from England, Mr. Severn?" he remarked in the rumbling bass voice which matched his enormous physique. "Have you come to settle here, or do you mean to return to home and family when you have made your fortune in the New World?"

The question was half jocular and no doubt kindly meant, but Julian felt himself stiffen. He said evenly:

"I have no family, sir, and my home is in Jamaica now."

"Good! Good!" Verwood said approvingly. "The colony can use young men of your stamp. No family, eh? No sweetheart either? No fair maid pining for you to return and wed her?"

This was intolerable. The fellow might be Jamaica's richest citizen, but he was an ill-bred lout nonetheless. Julian looked up at the big, dark face, framed now by the stiff curls of a powdered wig, and his own face wore an expression of disdain. At that moment he looked as haughty as Lord Avenhurst himself had ever done. He said with icy courtesy— for Verwood was, after all, a much older man and Thaddeus Loring's guest:

"If there were such a lady, sir, it would be unbecoming in me to make free with her name, especially upon so slight an acquaintance with you."

Thaddeus made haste to intervene, but Verwood seemed more pleased then otherwise by the rejoinder. He allowed himself to be diverted, but more than once during his visit Julian caught the big man's gaze upon him, thoughtful and oddly speculative. He found himself resenting it, and the resentment irritated him.

As usual when a visitor was present, the Lorings could not resist the temptation to show off their adored Lucilla, and the little girls were summoned to the drawing room to make their curtsy to Verwood. In their best gowns of stiff silk, simpler versions of the style their mother was wearing, with their hair dressed close under little lace caps, they made an enchanting picture, and he beamed upon them with obvious pleasure, admiring their pretty dresses and remarking how much they had grown since last he saw them. Lucilla responded as she always did to admiration—she basked in it, Julian often thought, like a pampered kitten. She went confidently to Verwood, smiling roguishly up into his face, squealing with delight when he scooped her up with one mighty hand and set her on his knee, but Serena held back, and then, as soon as she was certain that Lucilla was the center of attention, retreated quietly to Julian's side, where he stood a little part from the others, and slipped her hand into his. Her fingers felt cold, and when he glanced down at her he saw that she was still watching Verwood, her face pale and troubled. Julian was surprised, for though at first the giant must seem overwhelming to a child, Serena had obviously met the man on previous occasions. He bent towards her.

"Don't be scared," he whispered jestingly. "Verwood is no ogre, I give you my word, even if he does look like one."

She looked quickly up at him, but without the smile he had expected his words to evoke. Her eyes, of that changeful gray expressive of every mood, were dark as though with foreboding, and her lips were trembling. Perturbed, he moved to the nearest chair and sat down, thus bringing himself closer to Serena's level, and put his arm round her to draw her to him.

"What is it, sweetheart?" he asked softly. "You are not really frightened of Verwood, are you?"

"No." Her whispered reply came, hesitant and uncertain. "Not—not *frightened*, precisely, just—just unhappy. As though something dreadful were going to happen."

Julian was concerned but took care not to show it, and gave her a reassuring hug.

"Nothing dreadful is going to happen," he promised her, "Verwood or no Verwood. I'll not allow it. But if you show him that downcast face he may try to cheer you up, and then what shall we do?"

That did make her smile, rather tremulously, but she stayed close within the circle of his arm until it was time to go back to the schoolroom, when she made her curtsy again with downcast eyes, and shied away like a startled colt when Verwood chucked her under the chin. Then, meeting her mother's reproving frown, she flushed to the roots of her hair and fled from the room in scarlet-cheeked distress, which made Julian long to comfort her and increased his distaste for the big planter to a quite unwarrantable degree.

II

It was Serena's fifteenth birthday. She had a new gown in honor of the occasion, and to mark her approach to womanhood, it was made to be worn over a hoop. She stood in front of the pier glass in the bedroom she shared with Lucilla and studied her reflection with grave, considering eyes. She had grown suddenly much taller during the past year or so but remained childishly slim—Lucilla, barely thirteen, already possessed a more womanly figure—but the new dignity of the spreading skirt, and the gauze fichu draped round her neck and tucked into the low neckline of the bodice did much to disguise this. The dress was of pale yellow silk, the skirt open at the front to show the petticoat of quilted, light green satin, and there were flat bows of green satin, diminishing in size, down the front of the stiff, tapering bodice. The scrap of lace which formed her cap was trimmed with a cluster of tiny roses of yellow silk with green satin leaves, and she was holding a fan with ivory sticks which her father had given her that morning.

"You look very nice." Her sister was regarding her critically from the window seat. It was one of Lucilla's more likable attributes that, calmly confident of her own perfection, she never grudged praise where it was due. "Different, of course, but very nice." She smiled mischievously. "Wait until Peter Standish sees you in that dress."

Serena blushed. "Oh, Lucy, don't be silly! Peter is only a boy, and I have known him since we were both in the nursery."

"He is a year older than you are," Lucilla pointed out. "More than a year, in fact, because he is almost seventeen. I expect he will call today. He knows it is your birthday." She jumped up from the seat and performed a pirouette, arms gracefully outstretched. "Oh, how glad I shall be when *I* am fifteen and can wear a hoop and have young men coming to call on me. Crowds of young men, all vying for my favors! I wonder if any of them will fight a duel over me? Wouldn't *you* like to have a duel fought in your honor, Serena—?"

Serena moved to the window and stood looking out, letting Lucilla's chatter wash over her. Lucy seldom paused for an answer, anyway, especially when picturing that longed-for day when she would be a young lady, with scores of men fighting for her attention. As she undoubtedly would have; that was why she did not grudge her elder sister the tongue-tied, transparent admiration of their old playfellow.

Serena stroked her skirt and felt the stiff silk cool and smooth under her fingers. It was a beautiful dress and it was her birthday and she was almost grown up—and everything was as dust and ashes because the most important person in her world was not there to share the occasion with her. This was the first time in the six years since he came to Jamaica that Julian would not be at home on her birthday, but she could have accepted that with resignation, had his absence been planned or even expected, but it was not. He had sailed with Captain Langdale aboard the *Merry Venture*, and their return had been long expected and hoped for.

She was no stranger to Julian's absences at sea. He was Papa's partner now, and the business was known as Loring and Severn, but this present venture was no ordinary trading cruise. England was at war with France—formally at war, not just the semipiratical skirmishes which were always happening between the various nationalities in the Caribbean—and the *Merry Venture* had sailed under letters of marque as a privateer. It had been Julian's idea; Papa had been dubious, and now he was growing more worried every day. She had heard him say so to Mama, and Mama had frowned him into

96

silence, with a quick sidelong glance at Serena to see if she had heard.

Mama need not have bothered, Serena thought wretchedly, staring out unseeingly across the blaze of color in the garden. She knew very well what dangers threatened Julian. They had lurked at the back of her mind all the time he was away, and lately had occupied all her thoughts by day and haunted her dreams at night. Suppose—but she would not suppose it. Would not even admit the possibility, because to admit it might make it more likely to happen.

It must not happen, for a world without Julian in it was unthinkable. Ever since she had sat at his bedside when he was recovering from that first bout of fever, he had been the center of her life, the inner life of the imagination and the spirit; she could talk to him as to no one else, reveal her most secret hopes and dreams and fears, secure in the knowledge that he would understand. He filled a need, an aching void in her life, and she knew, without altogether understanding, that she filled a similar need in his. Without Julian, Serena thought wildly, her fingers clenching hard on her silken skirts, she would never be whole, never be a complete person again.

To check the feeling of panic rising within her, she turned back to where Lucilla was posing in front of the mirror with the fan which Serena had laid aside. She flirted it in the way Mama had taught them, opening it with an easy flick of the wrist and holding it before her face to cast a languishing glance above its edge at her own reflection in the glass. When Lucilla achieved grown-up status, she would be ready for it....

"Do stop prinking, Lucy, and give me my fan!"

Serena spoke sharply out of the nagging misery within her, but though Lucilla pulled a face, she handed over the trinket without argument and tripped in front of her sister, out of the room and along the wide corridor to the drawing-room. The spoiled darling of fortune, she could afford to dance through life untroubled by the whims of less favored mortals.

In the drawing room Thaddeus Loring regarded his elder daughter with surprise, approval and just the smallest pang of sadness. The children were growing up. Serena seemed to have become a young woman overnight, and soon it would be Lucilla's turn. Lucilla, his darling, his pride and delight, growing up, growing away from him, moving into a world where he was no longer the only or the most important man in her life. Thaddeus sighed, suddenly aware of the weight of his fifty-seven years and the gradual but remorseless deterioration of his health.

"Why do you not play for us, my love?" Margaret said gently, seeing Serena's small, dutiful smile and the shadows in the gray eyes, and knowing very well why she was fretting. "Papa has not yet heard the new piece you have learned."

Serena assented passively and went to seat herself at the harpsichord. Music filled the room and muffled the sound of hoofbeats in the avenue, so that when Samuel opened the door with a flourish, it took them all by surprise. He beamed at them, teeth very white in his broad black face.

"Message from Port Royal, suh," he announced, and stood aside to let one of the clerks from the counting house enter.

The music faltered and died. Serena sat with her hands resting on the keys, so still that she scarcely seemed to breathe. The clerk was smiling, too. It *must* be good news. The tiny pause before he spoke seemed to her to go on forever.

"The *Merry Venture* has been sighted, sir," he said, and there was excitement and triumph in his voice. "She is putting into harbor now."

"Thank God!" Thaddeus said fervently, and they all knew that he was not thinking only of a ship and a valuable cargo safely home. "Samuel, have the coach brought round—and fetch me my hat."

"Papa!" Serena spoke tautly from her seat at the harpsichord. "May I go with you?"

"To the ship?" He was startled, and cast a doubtful, questioning glance at his wife. "I do not think—?"

"If you go out with Papa in the boat," Lucilla put in practically, "you will spoil your dress."

"I can wait in the coach," Serena said desperately. "Oh, Papa, *please!*"

"I see no reason why she should not drive with you as far as the wharf," Mrs. Loring said placidly to her husband. "You are not likely to be long aboard, and Japhet and Joel will be there to look after her while you are gone. Go and put on your hat, Serena, but mind! You are not to get out of the coach."

"No, Mama, and thank you. Thank you!"

Serena sped across the room and along the corridor. She felt as though her feet were not upon the ground; as though

98

the force of her joy and her relief was bearing her along above it. Julian was safe; he was home; in a little while she would see him.

When her father alighted from the coach at the end of the wharf, she leaned eagerly forward, scanning the harbor for a glimpse of the *Merry Venture*. Mr. Loring pointed out the ship and then, with a word to Japhet, the coachman, walked away along the wharf. The coach had been drawn up in a patch of shade cast by one of the buildings, and the servants took up positions, one by each door, with Japhet facing the harbor, and folded their arms, prepared to stand there indefinitely to guard their charge.

There followed a long wait. Serena grew tired of watching the activity in the blazing sunshine on the wharf and drew back into the shadow. It was hot in the coach. She unfurled the ivory fan and waved it gently, leaning back against the soft leather squabs behind her, drowsy with contentment. Julian had come home.

"Missy!" Japhet's ebony face and flashing grin appeared in the opening where the glass window had been let down. "Mistuh Severn coming now."

Serena started up as he opened the door and lowered the step. Julian was coming alone along the wharf, taller than most of the men about him but no longer the lanky boy who had first arrived in Jamaica. His big frame had filled out, and was now wide-shouldered and narrow-waisted in a well-cut suit of cream linen, his face lean and brown above the lace at his breast, his black hair touched at the temples with the silver which had first appeared there when he nearly died of the fever. Serena stepped down from the coach just as he reached it, and he halted with a comical look of surprise, his startled glance taking in the fashionable gown with its spreading hoop and the wide straw hat with yellow ribbons. Then he swept off his own hat and made her a magnificent bow, there in the noisy, dusty street.

"Miss Loring! What an enchanting surprise!"

Rising to the occasion, Serena curtsied gracefully; Julian took her hand to raise her and lifted it formally to his lips. They looked at each other for a second, and then with a little sound which was halfway between a laugh and a sob, she flung herself into his arms and was caught in a hard, satisfying hug. Emerging breathless and with her hat awry, she said guiltily:

"Mama said I was not to get out of the coach."

"In with you, then!" He handed her in, paused for a word of greeting to the beaming slaves and then followed. "Let me look at you. I cannot get over this. I left a little girl and come home to find a young lady."

"You have come home. That is all that matters," she said unsteadily, holding tightly to his hand. "Oh, Julian, I have been so worried!"

"Sweetheart, I know! We suffered some damage and had to put into port for repairs, but of course there was no way of sending word to you. I told Langdale that if I was not home in time for your birthday, I would call him out. I have a special gift for you. Hold out your hand."

She obeyed; he took from his pocket some small object wrapped in a piece of silk and tipped it from its covering into Serena's outstretched hand. She felt the smooth hardness, saw an iridescent gleam and gasped.

"Pearls!" she whispered. "Oh, Julian!"

The silk floated to the floor as she held the necklace up with both hands; two rows of small but perfectly matched pearls, just long enough to rest around the base of her slim throat. For a little she gazed at it in breathless rapture and then tried to put it on, but her fingers were shaking and fumbled at the fastening.

"Let me do it." Julian reached out and took the necklace from her, adding with a laugh: "I thought you could keep it until you were old enough to wear such things, but I see now there is no need to wait. Turn around."

She did so, bending her head, and an odd little shiver went through her as she felt his fingers brush the back of her neck. Then the necklace was in place, smooth and cool against her skin, and she was facing him again with flushed cheeks and shining eyes.

"It is beautiful, Julian," she said breathlessly. "The loveliest present I ever had! Thank you!"

He laughed, patting her cheek in a careless, affectionate caress, and asked what had been happening at home while he was away. They slipped easily into the old, easy comradeship and understanding, but in her secret heart Serena knew that what she had said was not absolutely true. The loveliest gift of all was Julian's safe return.

* * *

Thaddeus, frowning over a letter which had just been brought to him, glanced up from it as Julian came into the room. The younger man also carried a letter, and looked even more perplexed than his friend.

"This has just come for me from Jethro Verwood," he said abruptly. "He wants me to visit him." He took in the lack of surprise in Loring's face, the paper in his hand and added blankly: "You, too?"

"I have received no invitation," Thaddeus replied drily, "but he mentions that he has requested *you* to come. There are some documents requiring his signature, which he hopes that you will carry to him."

"His own messenger could do that. He has always done so in the past."

"The documents, I gather, are incidental to your visit rather than the reason for it," Loring informed him. "What does he say here? Ah, yes—'perhaps Mr. Severn will be so obliging as to bring the necessary papers when he comes to visit me.' He has no doubt, it seems, that you will accept his invitation."

"Invitation? It reads more like a royal command." Julian dropped the letter on the table in front of Loring. "Why the devil should he want *me* to visit him and, as I understand it, to remain for several days? From what I have heard, no outsider has ever set foot in Verwood's Kingdom."

"Verwood himself has not been to Kingston for nearly a year," Thaddeus said thoughtfully. "It may be that he is ill, or has met with some accident, and is unable to make the journey himself. Perhaps he has some proposition to set before us which he is unwilling to commit to paper." He looked curiously at Julian. "Do you not wish to go? Most people in these parts would be only too eager to satisfy their curiosity."

Julian considered this. He had met Jethro Verwood on numerous occasions, and his first dislike of the big planter had given place to a tolerant acceptance of his eccentricities and a very real respect for his business acumen. He found now that he, too, was exceedingly curious, and a little flattered to have been singled out by an invitation to the Verwood plantation.

"I am quite happy to accept his invitation," he said at length. He nodded towards the letter. "At my earliest convenience, he says, and his messenger will act as my guide. When will the documents be ready?"

101

"They are ready now, for I have been awaiting his instructions. You can set forward tomorrow, if you wish."

Julian shrugged. "Why not? There is no point in delay. I will leave in the morning."

When the rest of the family learned of the proposed visit, Margaret and Lucilla were agog with curiosity, but Serena took no part in their excited speculation. She became very quiet, and later drew Julian aside to say earnestly:

"Please don't go! No one ever visits Verwood's Kingdom."

"Why, what's this?" He smiled down at her, affectionate and indulgent. "I thought you had forgotten your old dread of the ogre."

She turned her head away, unresponsive to the jesting note in his voice. "Don't tease me, Julian! I am not a baby."

"Then tell me why you think I should not go."

"I cannot tell you. I do not know myself. I simply feel that no good will come of it."

"And no harm, either." He threw an arm round her shoulders and gave her a quick brotherly hug. "It may be known as Verwood's Kingdom, but it is only an ordinary plantation, not an enchanted castle guarded by evil spirits or fire-breathing dragons. I shall be home again in a few days."

She saw that it was useless to persist, for her feeling of impending disaster was so tenuous that she could scarcely justify it even to herself. The truth was that the old sense of unease and foreboding with which she had always regarded Jethro Verwood had not, as even Julian supposed, entirely left her, though she was old enough now to be ashamed of it. She did not know why she felt as she did. Mr. Verwood had always been kindly, and one grew accustomed to his size and his great, rumbling voice. Perhaps it was the mystery surrounding him which made her feel there was something sinister about this summons to his remote, forbidden plantation, which Julian had received so soon after his return to Jamaica. It was as though Jethro Verwood had been waiting for him, yet how could he have known that Julian was back? Why did he wish to know? And why did she feel that Julian himself was about to embark upon another perilous voyage which might take him away from her forever? She could not tell. She could only try to hide her fears, and to pray that they were without foundation.

Julian, riding towards Verwood's Kingdom next day with Jethro Verwood's taciturn servant, secretly acknowledged a sense of anticipation of which he felt faintly ashamed. What did he expect? It would be the same as any other estate he had visited since coming to Jamaica. The planter's big house, built strongly to withstand equally the certain violence of nature and the possible violence of a slave rebellion; the slave cabins with their little garden plots; the sugar works and mill; the spreading acres of cane. The reputed splendor of the place was probably no more than idle gossip, and in any case was unlikely to impress one who had grown up amid the Palladian magnificence of Avenhurst Place.

His journey took him farther than ever before towards the island's wild interior of mountain and jungle, for Verwood's was the most outlying of all the plantations, and when they finally reached it, Julian was staggered by its sheer size. From its boundary they seemed to ride for miles through a green sea of sugar cane before they even came in sight of the house, and that, too, was far larger than he had expected. Set on a slight rise and built in the Spanish style of a hollow square, it presented an almost blank face to the outside world. The fields of cane reached to the foot of the slope below its white walls, so that the whole place seemed to rise like an island from a green, undulating sea, and though he discovered later that on the far side lay farm and stables, and between these and the slave cabins, a stretch of cultivated and meadow land, that first impression remained fixed in his mind. The green knoll rising above the endless cane fields, crowned by the stronghold of the ruler of Verwood's Kingdom.

The impression was heightened when he drew rein before massive, iron-studded doors which would not have been out of place in a castle. The building looked impregnable, but as he dismounted, the doors swung ponderously wide, each leaf hauled open by a slave in the green-and-gold Verwood livery, while a third Negro, elderly and dignified, bowed him into the house.

He found himself in a dim, cool hall, sparsely furnished with a few massive pieces of furniture in dark wood which looked as though they might have come from a church, and with antique armor and weapons decorating its whitewashed walls. At the far end, another door stood wide open to a shady piazza, and beyond the pillars of this showed the luxuriant foliage and brilliant flower colors of the garden around which the house was built.

Preceded by the elderly butler, and followed by one of the

underlings carrying his saddlebags, Julian was conducted through the hall and along the piazza, onto which, in this style of house, all the principle rooms opened. House and garden lay wrapped in a silence broken only by the sound of their footsteps and the musical plash of a fountain out of sight somewhere amid the greenery, and Julian remembered suddenly how he had told Serena that he was going to visit an ordinary plantation, and not an enchanted castle. Perhaps he had been wrong. There was some strange and eerie quality about this silent house with its dim, cool rooms and the green garden at its heart.

The room allotted to him was paneled, and handsomely furnished in the style of the previous century. The butler, having cast a critical glance around it, informed Julian that Mr. Verwood would be pleased to receive him when he was ready, and then withdrew, while the footman who had brought the saddlebags unpacked them and deftly bestowed the contents in chest and cupboard, rolling a curious eye at the visitor as he did so. A young female slave in a green cotton gown with a white fichu and apron and a white mobcap with a green ribbon, brought a can of hot water; she was smiling and deferential, but as blatantly curious as the man. Julian, feigning indifference, was thankful when they left the room.

A short time later, however, when he stepped out again into the piazza, the footman immediately appeared from somewhere, ready to conduct him to the master of the house. Julian, surprised to find in this outlandish spot a quality of service his own father would not have scorned, followed him along the gallery until he paused at an open door to announce:

"Mistuh Severn, suh!"

He stood aside and Julian went forward into a handsome library, only to halt again as abruptly as though he had walked into a wall. He felt rather as though he had done so, so violent was the impact of the shock he received as he set eyes on Jethro Verwood for the first time in a twelvemonth. The man was almost unrecognizable, a gaunt and suffering shadow of his former self. On his huge frame the clothes hung in the same grotesque folds as the skin of face and throat, where the flesh had wasted away; his eyes seemed to have receded into purplish sockets as cavernous as those of a skull, and the dark complexion was underlaid now by a livid, grayish pallor. He sat hunched among cushions in a great carved chair, and did not move as his guest entered the room.

"Welcome to my house, Mr. Severn." Even the voice had changed; each word seemed to require a separate, painful effort. "Forgive me for not rising to greet you."

Julian moved forward again and took the outstretched hand. It was like grasping the fingers of a skeleton.

"Mr. Verwood!" He stood looking down at the elder man with pity and concern. "We had no idea, sir, that you were ill. Your messengers have said nothing of it."

"My servants know better than to gossip when they are sent upon errands to Kingston or Port Royal."

"To gossip—no! But to tell your friends that you are ill cannot be regarded so. I could have brought a physician with me—!"

Verwood was slowly shaking his head. "There is no need, Mr. Severn. I am well aware what ails me, and no doctor can cure it." The sunken eyes fixed themselves upon Julian's face with curious intensity. "You speak of my friends. How many do you suppose I have?"

"Whatever their number, sir," Julian replied quietly, "I trust that I am numbered among them."

"I hope so, too," Verwood said unexpectedly, but did not pursue the matter, asking instead: "What news of Loring and his wife? How fare they?"

"Thaddeus, I think, is as well as he can ever hope to be. Mrs. Loring enjoys excellent health."

"And the little girls?"

Julian smiled. "The little girls are growing up. Serena is fifteen now, and seems already a young woman. It makes me begin to feel the weight of my own years."

"No great burden yet, I fancy. How old *are* you, Mr. Severn?"

"I was twenty-five last month, sir." Julian was too well accustomed by now to Verwood's ways to resent the question as he might have done the first time they met.

"Twenty-five!" Verwood repeated, and sighed. "A good age, Mr. Severn! An excellent age! Youthful folly left behind, but ambitions still to be fulfilled, goals to be striven for. Are you an ambitious man?"

Julian considered this. "I believe so, sir. At all events, I could not endure to waste my life in idleness."

Verwood seemed obscurely pleased by the reply, but before

he could make any comment upon it, they were interrupted by the sound of a door opening on the other side of the room. Julian glanced round—and the whole world seemed to come to a stop.

A girl was standing there, though in that first, dazzled instant she seemed less a mortal woman than a statue of ivory and gold. Golden hair that seemed to gleam and glint with a life of its own, piled in a great mass of waves upon a proudly-carried head; face and throat the creamy pallor of ivory, and a gown of shimmering satin which echoed the gold of that wonderful hair.

"Alathea!" he heard Jethro Verwood say, and the golden statue stirred and came slowly towards them. "I present Mr. Julian Severn. My daughter, sir."

Alathea Verwood did not curtsy, and for once in his life, Julian forgot to bow. Dazedly he took the hand she extended to him, and then stood gazing at her, drinking in the details of her remarkable beauty. Her face, with large, heavy-lidded eyes of velvety brown and red lips full and enticingly curved; the seductive lines of her perfect figure, clad in a gown which owed nothing to the hooped and whaleboned dictates of fashion but hugged her body like a second, gleaming skin. A gown as simple as that worn by the black slave girl, and differing from the slave's only in that it was made of satin, with a fichu of lace so fine that the smooth curves of shoulder and breast could be glimpsed beneath it. About her throat a necklace of rubies glowed like great drops of blood, and in that shaded room she seemed to gather to herself all the light there was, to shine with a radiance which blinded him to everything else. Fragments of classical mythology, forgotten since his schooldays, spun dizzily through his mind. Helen of Troy. Venus rising from the sea. The enchanted castle enshrined, not an elfin princess, but a goddess.

"I am happy to make your acquaintance, sir." The voice was rich and vibrant, but the words and manner were those of a carefully-schooled child, and the contrast was oddly appealing, making the goddess approachable and human. "Father told me that you were coming to visit us."

He made some reply which sounded idiotic to his own ears, for he was in the grip of emotions which robbed him of all his usual self-possession. He realized that he was still clasping her hand, and bent to kiss the white fingers with a warmth which had nothing to do with mere ceremony. They

106

were not withdrawn, and when he came reluctantly erect again, Alathea was studying him with candid curiosity, as though she had never before seen anyone quite like him. Meeting his bemused gaze, she smiled with unaffected pleasure, while from the chair beside them, the human wreckage which was Jethro Verwood watched their meeting with sunken, brooding eyes.

For Julian, the rest of that day passed like a dream, through which he moved mechanically, conscious of only one reality, the alluring, infinitely desirable reality which was Alathea. He found it almost impossible to tear his gaze away, for no matter how often he looked elsewhere, it was drawn irresistibly back to her as though to a magnet. Simply to watch her walk across a room was a delight. She was tall for a woman, and moved with the perfect, sinuous grace of a cat, the supple folds of her satin skirts flowing in fluid lines about her. Later, when candles were lit, the light gleamed in the living gold of her hair with every turn of her head, while the blood-red jewels at her throat flashed baleful fire. By the time they parted that night, he was lost, desperate with desire, enmeshed beyond hope in the toils of that flawless golden beauty.

They were to ride together in the morning. Verwood himself suggested it, regretting that he was unable to conduct his guest personally around the plantation—for, having finally admitted an outsider to his kingdom, he seemed determined that he should see every aspect of it.

"Alathea will guide you," he concluded, "for she knows every inch of the place as well as I do myself. I shall rest tomorrow. This demon which is devouring me will exact payment for the manner in which I have indulged myself today."

That was just before he retired for the night, hoisted from his chair by the two brawny slaves without whose aid he now found it impossible to move about. Alathea went to him, reaching up to kiss his cheek, and Julian wondered whether she was aware of the hopelessness of her father's condition. Verwood was so plainly a dying man.

He hoped that she might linger, but when he turned from closing the door through which Mr. Verwood and his attendants had passed, he found that a Negress had appeared silently in the doorway leading to the piazza. She was very old, a tall woman stooping beneath the burden of her years,

107

her face an incredible network of wrinkles; like the other female slaves, she wore the green dress and white apron, but instead of a cap, her head was swathed in a complicated headdress of dark, patterned cotton. She stood impassively, hands clasped in front of her and eyes downcast, and yet there was something peculiarly compelling about her implacable, waiting presence.

Alathea seemed to feel it, too. "I am coming, Mehitabel," she said quickly, and held out her hand to Julian. "Goodnight, Mr. Severn. I am looking forward to our ride in the morning."

She could not, Julian thought later as he lay wakeful and restless, be looking forward to it with half the eagerness that he was. He slept at last, dreamed confused and tantalizing dreams, and woke with a sense of eager anticipation such as he had not known for years.

He was in the entrance hall when Alathea joined him, presenting herself to his startled gaze, not in the conventional long-skirted riding habit, but in close-fitting breeches and boots of soft and supple leather that reached to the thigh. Above this she wore a long waistcoat of richly embroidered linen and a silk shirt that was open at the throat and had wide sleeves gathered tightly to the wrist. Her hair was down today, tied back like his own with a black queue-ribbon, and falling in a gleaming cascade to below her waist, crowned by a wide-brimmed straw hat secured beneath her chin with a leather thong. It was an outrageously becoming attire, its very boyishness emphasizing her femininity.

She greeted him gaily, apparently unaware of the effect her presence had upon him, and led the way out to where a groom waited with their horses, Julian's handsome bay gelding and a spirited gray which he would have supposed to be far too fiery for a woman to ride.

He was soon undeceived. Alathea rode like a centaur. Once astride the gray, she seemed to become one with the horse, and Julian, accomplished horseman though he was, was hard put to it to catch her as she flashed away from him down the slope and along one of the broad, straight avenues which intersected the fields of sugar cane. Neck and neck the two horses raced along, and when at last their riders drew rein, Alathea's cheeks were flushed and her eyes sparkling. There was a look almost of wildness about her, and she seemed a totally different being from the languorous beauty who had bewitched him the day before. Not Venus, this morning, but Diana.

"By God, Miss Verwood, but you can ride!" he said impetuously. "I have never seen a woman ride so well."

She laughed. "Perhaps you have never seen one ride astride. Father says that elsewhere one must wear a skirt and sit sidesaddle. I should hate that." She looked mischievous. "Does my costume shock you, Mr. Severn?"

"Not in the least." He studied her with admiration. "I would never have believed that mere masculine attire could be so transformed simply by being worn by a beautiful woman."

Alathea urged her horse forward again, at walking pace this time. "Mehitabel was right, then!" She sounded pleased. "She said this costume would not displease you."

"The old woman I saw last night? Is she your maid?"

"My maid now, my nurse when I was a child, my friend always. As she was to my mother, and to *her* mother, too."

"She must be very old."

"No one knows how old, not even Mehitabel herself. She was already a grown woman when she was brought from Africa, and that was more than sixty years ago. My great-grandfather bought her and had her trained to look after his little girl. When *she* grew up and married, Mehitabel went with her to her new home, and the same thing happened when my mother married Father. Mehitabel is the chief of all our household slaves, but she will allow no one else to take care of me."

"Who could blame her for that? Had *I* that inestimable privilege, Miss Verwood, I, too, would share it with no one."

She looked puzzled for a moment, and then understanding dawned and she smiled delightedly. "Would you not? I am so glad! I would like you to take care of me." Then, while his mind was still reeling with astonishment: "But don't call me Miss Verwood. No one has ever done so before, and it sounds so strange."

"Miss Alathea, you honor me—!" He was stammering like a schoolboy, completely at a loss, and she checked him with a quick shake of her head.

"No, no! Just Alathea—and *I* shall call *you* Julian." They had reached an intersection of the avenues, and she gestured towards the right. "Let us gallop again. We'll go that way, past the mill."

The gray was off again at a stretching gallop, and Julian followed, utterly bewildered, but more fascinated than ever by this girl with the looks of a pagan goddess and the ways of an artless child. Alathea must be nineteen or twenty, yet even Lucilla Loring, just thirteen, was infinitely more worldly, and more mature in her behavior.

Yet Alathea was conscientious, too. In obedience to her father's wishes, she conducted Julian painstakingly around the plantation, showing him the sugar works, the farm which supplied the needs of the estate, the slave cabins as numerous as the cottages in an English village. There were decent, solid-looking houses for the overseers, and even a small school for their children. Julian was astonished by the extent of the place; and when he remembered the many other business ventures in which Jethro Verwood owned a profitable share, he knew that rumor had not lied about the man's wealth. It must be enormous.

A further surprise was in store for him. When they returned to the house, they were told that Mr. Verwood intended to keep to his bed that day, and begged Mr. Severn to excuse him. Alathea went off at once to see her father, and Julian wandered into the library.

This time he noticed details about it to which Alathea's presence had hitherto blinded him, and he discovered with amazement that his host must be a man of formidable learning, for there were books on many subjects and in almost every European language, all with a well-used look about them which showed that they were not mere ornaments. This presented Verwood in a new and even more perplexing guise. What had prompted the man, Julian wondered curiously, to live almost the life of a recluse, when his interests were so wide and his abilities so great? He was no miser, living frugally and gloating over hoarded gold; there was a degree of luxury here which equalled anything Julian had seen in Jamaica, and the plantation appeared to be worked by the most up-to-date methods, yet no one was ever invited here, either upon business or pleasure. He himself would probably never have been summoned had Verwood not been physically incapable of making the journey to Kingston; and why *had* he been summoned? Why should he be the only stranger ever to enter Verwood's Kingdom? Ever to see Alathea?

That, of course, was the heart of the matter, the real reason for all this speculation. He had seen Alathea, and nothing could ever be quite the same again. Even if he were compelled to leave now and never set eyes on her again, the memory of her would tantalize him for the rest of his life. He ought to leave now, while some remnants of sanity still remained; before the madness which had come upon him possessed him utterly.

He ought to leave but he knew that he would not. He would stay here, roaming restlessly about the silent house and the green garden, wasting the endless minutes until he saw her again, and then savoring each moment in her presence with no thought for the future.

When eventually she rejoined him, she had changed her clothes, and was dressed as she had been at their first meeting, except that her gown now was of shimmering silk which mysteriously changed from green to blue as she moved; and instead of the rubies, she wore about her neck a twisted golden chain studded with emeralds. He stood looking at her, his eyes frankly worshipping her beauty, and said in a low voice:

"Each time I see you I think it cannot be possible for you to look more lovely, and each time you prove me wrong."

"*Am* I beautiful, Julian?" There was no coquetry in the question, only simple curiosity. "Father says I am, and so does Mehitabel. Now you tell me so."

"And does your mirror not tell you the same when you look into it?"

A little frown wrinkled her brow. "It tells me that I am not unpleasing to look at, but as for beauty—!" She shrugged, and then added with a simplicity which he somehow found shocking: "I have never seen another woman of my own race, so I cannot judge."

"Never?" he repeated incredulously.

She shook her head. "My mother died when I was a baby, and I do not remember her."

"But your father's free servants, the overseers and so forth. Surely some of them have wives and daughters?"

"Oh, yes, but they are all of mixed blood. There are no white people here except Father and me."

Another oddity to add to Jethro Verwood's ever-growing list of eccentricities. Julian said slowly:

"So you have no companions, had no playmates even when you were a child. Are you never lonely?"

"No, for I have Father and Mehitabel." Alathea paused,

111

a puzzled look coming into her face. "At least, I never *knew* I was lonely, until you came."

The admission implicit in the guileless words made his pulses quicken, and once again the questions spinning through his mind seemed of less importance then the gold of Alathea's hair, the warmth in her eyes, the sheer intoxication of her presence. He had stepped into a realm of fantasy, where a girl could grow to beautiful womanhood surrounded by luxury, waited upon by deft, soft-footed slaves, and yet denied all contact with the world beyond the bounds of her father's domain. There was a strange excitement in the thought that he was the first man to meet her upon equal terms, to ride with her through the cane fields and to sit with her at table; the first to tell her that she was beautiful.

The day unfolded like some delightful dream. They walked in the garden, among flowers as bright as butterflies and butterflies like living flowers; at dinner they toasted each other in wine glowing jewel-like in glasses of exquisite fragility; afterwards they played cards, and Julian was constantly the loser because he was thinking less of the game than of the turn of Alathea's wrist as she dealt the cards or the tilt of her head as she pondered those in her hand.

At last she laughingly declared that they would play no more, that he must be allowing her to win, which was a thing her father never did. Julian shook his head.

"How can I win when the odds are weighted so unfairly against me? When I cannot see the cards because *you* dazzle my eyes?"

She smiled radiantly at him. "Do I really? You say such pretty things, Julian!" She pushed back her chair and got up. "Let us leave the cards, and walk in the garden instead. I love it there at night."

Julian looked towards the piazza. Darkness had fallen and the garden was a place of mystery, of moonlight and starlight, of fireflies flickering among the leaves. In the far recesses of his mind, the fading voice of reason told him that to walk there with Alathea would be madness, that they ought to stay here where candlelight maintained some sort of barrier between them, but she had already taken his assent for granted and stepped out through the doorway. He hesitated for only a moment, and then followed her.

She moved ahead of him along the path, and then the pale blur of her figure vanished suddenly as she stepped into a patch of dense shadow. He had the absurd impression that he had lost her, that she had been absorbed into the darkness, and he quickened his pace in response to that illogical alarm. Next moment he was beside her again, in the open space where the fountain glimmered and splashed in its marble basin, but that fleeting instant of panic was his undoing. As she turned towards him he caught her in his arms and captured her lips with his.

For one startled moment she was rigid and unresponsive, but then slowly she relaxed and one arm crept up around his neck. He could feel the supple warmth of her body through her thin garments, and pressed her still closer against him while his lips explored her face, her throat, the smooth curves of her breasts from which with unsteady fingers he had drawn aside the folds of filmy lace. She seemed to melt into his embrace, giving herself willingly to his caresses, and it was this complete surrender, this innocent delight in a hitherto unknown pleasure, which stabbed him with the knowledge of her total inexperience. Reared in seclusion, denied even the most formal acquaintance with any man, what defense had she against the response his own passion was awakening in her? And what manner of man was he, to take such base advantage of her innocence?

It was the hardest thing he had ever done in his life, but slowly his hold upon her slackened; he drew her upright and then let her go, very gently unclasping her clinging arms. Bewildered, a little hurt, she stared at him in the moonlight.

"Julian?" she said uncertainly, and stretched out a pleading hand.

He did not dare to take it, did not dare to touch her again. The moonlight washed over her, silvering her shining hair and making the white flesh of shoulder and bosom gleam like marble, and he knew he would not be able to dam the flood a second time.

"Go back to the house, my love," he said huskily. "We shall see each other tomorrow."

She hesitated, and he found himself praying that she would go while he still had the strength to resist temptation. Yet when she did as he asked, when he saw her walking slowly and reluctantly away from him, it needed an actual physical effort to remain where he was and not follow to take her again in his arms. From the torrent of conflicting emotion which had him in its grip, one thought, one resolve, stood out like a rock amid turbulent water. Today had been passed in a fool's paradise. Tomorrow, if the fool were not to become the knave, he must conclude his business with Jethro Verwood and return to Kingston, and sanity.

In the morning he asked the slave who attended him to find out whether Mr. Verwood was well enough to receive him, and after a little while the planter's elderly body-servant arrived to conduct Julian to his master. As they reached the door of Verwood's room, this was opened from within and Mehitabel emerged, carrying an empty glass on a salver. She acknowledged Julian's presence only with one upward glance, but, meeting her eyes for the first time, he was left with such an impression of vitality and power that he paused to watch her as she walked away along the piazza. Almost unbelievingly he saw her stooped figure and hobbling, old woman's gait, for these were utterly belied by those dark, ageless eyes. Sixty years a slave, he thought, and yet there smolders still a spark which has not been quenched. He found it oddly disturbing.

"Come in, Mr. Severn!" Jethro Verwood's voice spoke from inside the room. "Forgive me for receiving you here, but I am told that your business is urgent."

Was it his own uneasy conscience which suggested a note of accusation in the labored voice? Julian walked forward to the bed, where Verwood was propped against a mound of pillows, a dressing gown about his shoulders and his hairless skull covered by a turban-shaped cap of crimson silk. He was freshly shaven, but the livid pallor of his skin seemed more marked than ever.

"The urgency, sir, lies only in the fact that our business is yet to be concluded." Julian kept his voice deliberately impersonal. "There are certain documents here which await your signature, and I must remind you that the matter cannot go forward until this is done."

He laid the papers on the coverlet, and after another searching look at him, Verwood picked them up and began to read. Julian waited, thinking of Alathea and wondering if she had expected him to ride with her again that morning. Heaven grant it did not occur to her to come seeking him here!

Mr. Verwood laid down the last of the papers and glanced towards the slave waiting patiently in the background.

114

"Pen, Micah, and ink."

Micah brought them, handing the quill to his master and standing beside him to hold the inkwell while Verwood dipped the pen and wrote and dipped again. When the last shaky signature was written, he returned the pen and nodded dismissal.

"Leave us."

Micah restored pen and ink to their place and silently withdrew, while his master handed the documents back to Julian.

"So you are impatient to leave us, Mr. Severn? Is there no inducement I can offer which would persuade you to stay?"

Julian stiffened. What was the man driving at? Did he suspect what had happened last night, or—of course, Mehitabel! She was Alathea's constant attendant, and would have seen her when she returned to the house with her hair and lace in disarray. Perhaps Alathea had even innocently confided in her. Now Mehitabel had carried the tale to her master, but what did Verwood want, or expect? Damn him, Julian thought furiously. Damn him for bringing me here, letting me meet her, leaving us so long alone in each other's company.

"I am flattered, sir," he said coldly, "just as I am flattered, to have been invited into your home, but since this matter—" he indicated the papers he held—"has now been dealt with, there is no reason for me to linger. Unless, of course, there is some other proposition you wish to put to us? Mr. Loring thought there might be, since you wished me to come here instead of sending these documents by your messenger."

"Loring is right, save that the proposition concerns you alone." Verwood's sunken eyes fixed their gaze with sudden, burning intensity on the tall young man standing beside his bed. "I asked you to come here, Julian Severn, so that I might suggest to you that you marry my daughter."

Julian stared blankly at him, overwhelmed, incredulous, literally incapable of making an immediate response. The silence seemed to drag on interminably, until Verwood added drily:

"I take you by surprise, it seems."

"Surprise?" Julian said uncertainly. "You take my breath away, sir! Why in God's name should you wish *me* to marry Miss Verwood?"

"Believe me, my choice has not been suddenly or lightly

115

made," Verwood assured him. "Alathea is more dear to me than anything on earth, but I long since faced the fact that a day would come when I must give her into the keeping of some other man, one whom I could trust to cherish her as I have done. I believe you are that man."

"I—I am honored, sir, more than I can say, but why? You know nothing of me! Who I am, why I came to Jamaica—!"

The turbaned head moved fractionally against the pillow; Verwood said with finality:

"Set your mind at rest! I ask no questions, for I know all I need to know, from my own observation and from trustworthy reports of you." He saw Julian's startled expression and the faint travesty of a smile touched the corners of his mouth. "Oh, yes, I have watched you! More closely than you knew, ever since you first came to Jamaica as an inexperienced boy thrust into a totally strange world. I have watched you become Thaddeus Loring's partner in business as well as his close and trusted friend. I know that your voyages with young Langdale have been not without incident, and that you have acquitted yourself well. In short, you are a man of decision and enterprise, and one, moreover, of whom it is well known that his word, once given, is never broken. I tell you this, not to flatter you, but to explain why I want you to marry my girl." He paused, his haggard gaze still holding Julian's. "No need to tell you why I broach the matter to you so abruptly. I have no time left for diplomacy."

This was so self-evident that Julian did not insult him by contradicting it or by mouthing platitudes of hope or encouragement. Verwood went on:

"My daughter's husband will inherit all that is mine, and that, too, I willingly entrust to you, for it is not, I think, of greater importance to you than Alathea herself. Yet you will use it wisely, for her sake."

Julian looked doubtfully at him. "Mr. Verwood, I know nothing of working a plantation."

"That does not matter. My head overseer, Ira Yatton, will do that for you, as he does for me. His family has served mine for three generations. All other aspects of my interests, you are more than capable of handling. I have no fears on that score."

He paused, but to Julian the whole situation seemed so fantastic that he could find nothing to say. As though in a dream, he walked across to the door and stood staring out

116

into the green depths of the garden, bewildered and uncertain. In spite of what Verwood had said, still the question nagged—why me? There must be many more eligible men in Jamaica, sons of old Creole families who would be eager to marry the heiress of Verwood's Kingdom even if she were not the loveliest thing to walk the earth. . . .

Jethro Verwood lay back against his pillows, thankful for a brief respite from the sustained effort he was being obliged to make, for a chance to rally the remnants of a strength sapped to its last reserves by months of savage suffering. Fate—he had long ago ceased to believe in God—had singled him out for a slow and agonizing death, but the worst anguish of all during these last endless weeks, when it had seemed possible that Julian Severn might never return, had been the dread that he would not now be able to make for Alathea the provision he had resolved upon. Now at last his plans were coming to fruition. From what Mehitabel had seen last night, Julian was already so mad for Alathea that to possess her, he would accept the condition which must be imposed, give the promise which must be exacted; and his word, once given, would be binding unto death. . . .

"Well, my friend," he prompted at length, "what is your answer? Will you let me see my daughter safely married to you before I die? I have never in my life begged anything from any man, but I am doing so now."

"Begging?" Julian exclaimed, turning to face him. "You offer me paradise and think you must beg me to accept it? Ever since the first moment I saw her—!" He broke off, a doubt assailing him. "But Alathea? Will she—?"

"Be willing to marry you?" Verwood put in as he hesitated; the faintly mordant note was in his voice again. "You have, I believe, good reason to know that she will not refuse." He paused for a moment, sardonically observing Julian's discomfiture. "No matter! That is as I hoped. Oh, she would marry you without question if I commanded it, but this was the better way."

"Was it, sir?" Julian came slowly back to the bedside and stood looking at Verwood in a troubled way. "For me, perhaps! I had only to see her to forget every other woman I have ever known, but in some ways Alathea seems still a child. She has lived in such sheltered seclusion here—!"

"And must continue to do so," Verwood broke in. "Let this be clearly understood. I offer you my daughter and all my

117

worldly possessions, but in return I must have your word that Alathea will never leave the plantation."

"Never?" Julian was incredulous. "But surely—?"

"Never!" Verwood repeated emphatically. "This is her home, her kingdom." The travesty of a smile crossed his ravaged features at the look on Julian's face. "Verwood's Kingdom! Did you suppose I did not know? It is true. This is the kingdom I have created for Alathea, and you must never take her from it." Impatience darkened his face as he saw the gathering doubt in Julian's eyes. "Do you think I do not know what is best for her? You cannot judge her by ordinary standards, for she knows nothing of the outside world, nor wishes to. She is happy here. Happy and safe!" He moved uneasily against his pillows, and there were beads of sweat on his face. "Give me your word—or go back to Kingston now and never see her again!"

Julian hesitated, conscience insisting that he had no right to make such a promise, but the alternative he could not face. Never see Alathea again? Never again hold her in his arms, never possess that golden loveliness? Her father loved her dearly. He would never demand the promise unless he knew it was for her good.

"You have my word, sir," he said in a low voice. "I swear by everything I hold most sacred that I will never take Alathea away from here."

"My thanks...to you." Verwood closed his eyes, relief at having achieved his purpose fading as the serpent of agony always coiled within him began to stir. Mehitabel's witch-brew could keep it quiescent for a while, but the blessed periods of relief were growing shorter, his need for the potion more frequent. "One thing more. Mehitabel brought Alathea into the world and has cared for her as her own. Trust her! Always! Trust Mehitabel."

Mehitabel, bent and wrinkled, old as time; the implacable, watching presence with smoldering fires in her eyes. Trust her? Questions formed in Julian's mind, but Verwood's body was braced and rigid, his hands clenched hard on the coverlet, and he seemed oblivious of everything except the need to finish what he had to say.

"There must be no delay. I have very little time. Go back to Kingston today. Fetch the parson—and my lawyer. There will be work for him to do. Presently I will give you letters to them, but leave me now. I must rest for a time."

118

Julian, shocked by the change which had come over him, turned to go, then paused and looked again at the sick man.

"With your permission, sir," he said, "I would like Thaddeus Loring and his wife and daughters to return with me." Verwood's eyes opened, and, reading refusal in them, Julian added firmly: "They are the only family I have, and I would like them to be present at my wedding."

The searing coils of pain were tightening their grip, and all that mattered was to obtain release. Verwood nodded.

"As you wish. Go now...and find Alathea. Tell her that she is to be your wife." The younger man hesitated, and he added peremptorily: "Go! We will talk again later."

Julian sketched a bow and went out. His footsteps were still echoing along the piazza as Jethro Verwood reached out a hand for the silver bell which stood beside him, to summon Micah and Mehitabel and a brief surcease of pain.

III

"Serena! Serena, what do you think?" Lucilla burst into the room where her sister sat reading. "Julian is back, and—!"

"Julian has come home?" Serena looked up, delight flooding into her face. "When? Where is he?"

"In the drawing room, with Mama and Papa. Serena, poor Mr. Verwood is dying, and Julian is going to marry his daughter!"

It seemed to Serena that the whole world came to a sudden stop, was petrified for a fraction of time into utter stillness. She stared, white-faced, at Lucilla, and said between stiff lips:

"I don't believe it!"

"Believe it or not, it's true!" Lucilla retorted. "I saw Samuel taking Julian's saddlebags to his room, and I asked where he was, because I wanted to find out what Verwood's Kingdom was really like, but when I got to the drawing room door, I heard Julian telling Mama and Papa about Mr. Verwood, so I thought I had better not go in at once. *Then* I heard him say—!"

"You were eavesdropping," Serena said accusingly. "Lucy, how could you?"

"I was not! I just *happened* to hear what they were saying, and I thought you would like to know, so I came to tell you. Oh, Serena, isn't it exciting? We are all to go to Verwood's Kingdom for the wedding."

"But it is absurd!" Serena protested, arguing with her own dismay as much as with Lucilla. "Julian has only been away three days! How *could* he have arranged in that short time to marry Miss Verwood when he had never even met her before? You are mistaken, Lucy, or you are making it up. It cannot be true!"

Only it *was* true. Mama herself came presently to tell them, trying to mask her own bewilderment with a matter-of-fact briskness which deceived no one. She explained that Mr. Verwood had always had a very high regard for Julian and wanted to arrange a marriage between him and Miss Verwood, but because, poor man, he was very, very ill, it all had to be done in a great hurry. Yes, Lucilla, they *were* all invited to the wedding, and no, there would not be time to have a new dress made, and with or without a hoop...

Margaret, dealing with her younger daughter's eager questions and demands, still had time for an anxious study of the elder. The news had hit Serena hard, as she had known it would, and though the child was saying very little, her eyes betrayed the shock and the hurt she had sustained. Serena cared so much for Julian. From the very first there had been a rapport between them, an understanding which seemed to exclude the rest of the world. It had been of benefit to them both, for the boy who had come into their lives six years ago had been bruised in spirit, and Serena's undemanding, unquestioning devotion had provided a balm no adult could have offered, while, under his influence, the little girl's personality had developed until she was no longer always eclipsed by her younger sister's brilliance of beauty and vivacity, but became a person in her own right. Watching this happen, Margaret and Thaddeus had been glad, and lately had begun to hope that the bond of affection and understanding would, in a year or two, provide the foundation of an exceptionally happy marriage; though, mercifully, no suspicion of that hope had ever entered Serena's mind. The match between Julian and Alathea Verwood might have been of her father's contriving, but one had only to exchange a dozen words with him to realize that it was no mere marriage of convenience.

Serena, though stunned by the news, did not need to be

122

told that nothing would ever be the same again. Home, to Julian, would no longer be here, but the plantation house at Verwood's Kingdom; the room he had occupied for six years would be empty again, emptier than it had ever been while he was away at sea, for now it would not be awaiting his return. No use to go there, as she had gone so often during his absences, just to sit quietly among his possessions, conversing with him in imagination, feeling his presence all about her. Serena was not jealous of the unknown Miss Verwood. She just felt desolate, bereft, incomplete.

It was a little while before she saw Julian, for, having broken his news, he was off again to Kingston to make arrangements with the parson and to carry Jethro Verwood's summons to his lawyer. She was glad of the respite. It gave her time to begin constructing the mask she would have to wear from now on, even with Julian. Most of all with Julian.

Perhaps, if he had not been utterly possessed by thoughts of Alathea, he would not have been deceived, but for once he did not see below the surface, and on the surface Serena by that time had herself gallantly in hand. She listened with composure and even an appearance of enthusiasm while he told her about Alathea and her strange, lonely life at Verwood's Kingdom; while he spoke of visits which Serena would make there and prophesied that she and Alathea would become friends. She could not tell him that this was no consolation, that nothing could replace the precious comradeship of the past six years. She knew that the time had come for her to step aside, that henceforth Alathea, and not she, would be the center of his life. She knew, too, just as certainly, that Julian would always be the heart of hers, and in accepting that fact with courage and resolution, Serena, without realizing it, put childhood irrevocably behind her. A week ago the immediate future had seemed to beckon, bright with promise, for Julian had come safely home and she herself was poised on the threshold of the adult world, certain that he would be there, strong and understanding and kind, to guide her first tentative steps into it. Now she would have to take those steps alone. It was all over, the confidences, the comforting of sorrows, the shared jests which were meaningless to anyone else. As meaningless as her own life seemed suddenly to have become.

"Serena," Lucilla said suddenly as the two girls settled down in bed that night, "I have just thought of something.

123

They say, don't they, that Mr. Verwood is the richest man in Jamaica?"

"Yes, I believe so," Serena replied indifferently. "Why?"

"Well, when Julian marries Miss Verwood, and her father dies, everything will be his. *He* will be the richest man here. Isn't he lucky?"

"You should not think so much about being rich," Serena rebuked her. "I do not understand you, Lucy! It is not as though we were poor now."

"No, but I would like to be very, very rich," Lucilla said candidly. "I would like to live in a huge house like a palace, with marble floors and painted ceilings and priceless pictures and statues, and ride in a coach with a crest on the door." She yawned and snuggled deeper into the pillow, adding sleepily: "And I will, one day. Just wait and see."

She probably would, Serena reflected, for Lucilla always seemed to get what she wanted, and if Mama could persuade Papa to take them to England in a few years' time, as Serena knew that she hoped to do, even those highly-colored ambitions might be fulfilled. How lucky Lucilla was, to want something which might well be hers one day.

Serena, too, cherished a dream of the house she would like to live in. She did not know where it was, except that it was not here in Jamaica, but she knew exactly what it was like. Not a great palace of a house such as Lucilla spoke of, but a gracious one, with rooms full of light, and green lawns, tree-shaded, which sloped down to a river; where the summer air would be sweet with the scent of roses, and in winter, firelight would flicker and curtains be drawn to enclose a world of warmth and happiness and peace.

It was a dream she had cherished ever since she was a little girl, and which she had confided to no one except Julian. He would come to call upon her there, he had said, joining in the make-believe, but as time passed, whenever she imagined her house, Julian was somehow there all the time, just as he was here at home. Now, she reminded herself bleakly, he would be at home no more, and even if she found her lovely house one day, he would be here in Jamaica with his wife, and would never see it.

Lucilla had fallen asleep at once, curled up like a kitten at her sister's side, but Serena lay staring desolately into the darkness, dry-eyed, but weeping in her heart for all that could never be again. She was going to be very lonely.

124

The journey to Verwood's Kingdom was the longest the Loring sisters had ever made, and Lucilla, at least, was agog with the excitement of it. They traveled with their parents in one coach, while the parson and the lawyer followed in another, with Julian's luggage piled on the roof. Julian himself rode beside the Loring coach until the boundary of the plantation was reached, then spurred ahead to carry word, he said, to the house of their approach. Serena, aware of his barely curbed impatience, knew it was because he could wait no longer to see Alathea again.

Thaddeus and Margaret were as astonished as Julian had been by the size of Jethro Verwood's estate, by the stretching acres of the cane fields and the countless slaves who worked there, pausing now in their labor to gape at the unheard-of sight of two coaches lumbering by, but Serena was not interested in the plantation. She was waiting, with a mixture of eagerness and trepidation, to see the house Julian had described, its white walls raised upon an island in this ocean of sugar cane. The house which would be his home henceforth.

Her first thought was that it looked forbidding; forbidding and secretive, as though it turned its back upon the world. As the coach lurched to a halt, she saw the huge doors of the house swing wide, saw slaves in green-and-gold livery, and then Julian himself stepped out into the sunshine. He came forward to hand Mrs. Loring down from the coach, and as Serena followed her mother, she heard him say:

"Mr. Verwood sends his apologies, and me as his deputy to greet you. He is not well enough today to welcome you himself."

He offered his arm to escort Margaret into the house, the girls following with their father. Alathea, with Mehitabel standing a couple of paces behind her, was waiting in the hall, and Serena experienced a little shock compounded of astonishment and admiration and dismay. Julian's bride was the most beautiful woman she had ever seen, but the aged Negress seemed to hover at her shoulder like some dark guardian spirit. Serena shivered, and tried to tell herself it was because of the coolness of the hall after the stifling heat of the coach.

Alathea made a formal little speech of welcome which sounded as though she had learned it by heart, and when the appropriate responses had been made, seemed to have nothing left to say, but just stood looking curiously at Mrs. Loring and her daughters. After a moment or two, Mehitabel came forward and asked leave to conduct the ladies to the rooms which had been prepared for them.

Margaret thankfully agreed, for she found Alathea's silence and her wide-eyed gaze disconcerting. Of course, from what Julian had told them, the girl had been taught no social graces, but surely she need not stare so? And her dress—those clinging folds of silk which so blatantly revealed her shape! Margaret was profoundly shocked, and almost wished she had not allowed the girls to come.

Mehitabel was hobbling towards the inner door, and Mrs. Loring followed, shepherding her daughters before her. Alathea accompanied them. Margaret had seen the old slave woman speak softly to her as she passed, and assumed that she was reminding the girl of her duties as hostess.

Alathea did not speak again until they reached the room prepared for Mr. and Mrs. Loring. Then, still studying Margaret's gown, with its wide hoop and the whaleboned bodice which rigidly encased her body above it, she said in a puzzled tone:

"Is not that dress very uncomfortable?"

"Not in the least!" Margaret was affronted. "It is the accepted mode."

Alathea reached out to touch the swaying hoop, stroked her hand across the stiff bodice and shook her head.

"*I* would not wear a dress so cumbersome and stiff. I would not be able to breathe in it, or move."

"Miss Thea!" Mehitabel spoke with a nice blending of deference and reproof. "Why don't you show the young ladies *their* room? Mistus Loring'll likely want to rest for a spell."

Alathea nodded, smiled at the two girls and beckoned to them to follow her. In the adjoining room she looked from one to the other and then said to Serena:

"You must be Serena. Julian told me about you. He hopes that we shall be friends."

"I hope so, too," Serena agreed politely, but though she infused into her voice all the warmth she could, she found it impossible to picture herself upon terms of close friendship with this strange girl. For Julian's sake she would try, but it seemed unlikely that they would find anything in common.

It was an uncomfortable evening. An excellent meal was served to them by well-trained slaves under Mehitabel's

126

watchful eye, and Julian, deputizing for their host, did his courteous best to put the guests at their ease, but they all felt like intruders in this house which for more than twenty years had offered hospitality to no one. The thought of its ailing master was like a tangible alien presence, and they were all glad when the time came to retire to their rooms. With relief they wished each other good night, hoping that there would be less constraint among them on the morrow.

Looking back afterwards to Julian's wedding day, Serena found that she retained only fragments of memory, a series of vivid, disjointed pictures which it was difficult to blend into a coherent whole. Waking for the first time in her life in an unfamiliar room, with a strange slave to wait on her; a brief, startling glimpse of Alathea in her boyish riding costume, being urged towards her room by a scolding Mehitabel; Mehitabel herself, ubiquitous and deferential, the embodiment of a faithful old family servant—until one looked into her eyes; the shock of seeing Jethro Verwood, remembered as a vigorous, overpowering giant, shambling, gray-faced, between his two supporting Negroes.

The wedding ceremony took place in the late afternoon. Alathea chose to wear the gown of gold-colored satin in which Julian had first seen her, with the ruby necklace flashing blood-red about her throat, and by contrast with the delicate colors worn by Margaret and the girls, there was an insolence about her beauty, a barbaric quality which seemed more in accord with the primitive music from the slave cabins (for in honor of the marriage, the field hands had been given a day's leisure and extra rations) than with the words of the Christian marriage service.

As the parson pronounced the couple man and wife, Jethro Verwood relaxed a little, allowing the tide of relief to flood over him. He had achieved his purpose. Alathea would be safe now, for, come what might, Julian would never break his word, neither the sacred vows which had just been exchanged nor the other, earlier promise which had been a condition of the marriage.

Now there was just the evening to get through; the meal to which, as host, he must entertain the company and the toast he must propose to the bridal couple. Today Mehitabel had made her potion stronger, and perhaps he would be able to endure until he could with decency bid his guests good

127

night. Tomorrow they would be gone, and Verwood's Kingdom be inviolate again.

That night, although Serena felt exhausted, she could not sleep. Time crawled by, and still she lay tense and wakeful while Lucilla slumbered peacefully beside her. It was then that she heard the drums. Not from the slave cabins this time, but from another direction, and sounding somehow different, a savage, insistent rhythm that went on and on until it seemed to be beating inside her head. She shuddered, pressing her hands over her ears and burying her head in the pillow, but she could not shut out that terrible, throbbing summons; and now behind the darkness of her own closed lids, she seemed to be looking into the eyes of Mehitabel. Eyes of the night. Ageless eyes, with somber fires smoldering in their unfathomable depths, and wise with an ancient, evil wisdom.

She fell asleep at last just as dawn was breaking, and when she woke to full daylight, the drums and the eyes seemed no more than the lingering memory of nightmare. Yet even the memory was disquieting, and she knew she would be glad to leave Verwood's Kingdom.

Ten days after his daughter's wedding, Jethro Verwood died. He suffered greatly, and towards the end Julian more than once saw him writhing in such agony that his attendant slaves were obliged to hold him down upon his bed, but he possessed a will of iron and scarcely a sound passed his lips. Julian soon realized that this was for Alathea's sake. She was permitted now to visit her father only once a day, and never unless he sent for her, which he did only in those brief intervals when Mehitabel's powerful medicines had afforded him a brief respite. Yet he was deteriorating visibly, and though Julian was thankful that Alathea did not perceive this, he was puzzled, too. She seemed to have no idea that her father was dying.

His own foreknowledge cast a shadow, the only shadow, over that halcyon time, that brief period of ecstasy when he was dazzled and drugged by the beauty of Alathea, by the willingness of her surrender and the vein of wildness in her nature which met and matched the demands of his desire. Uninhibited by the conventions of a society of which she knew nothing, she abandoned herself to pleasure as naturally as the wind blew from the sea or the flowers bloomed in the jungle, and bloomed herself with a new radiance which made her, if possible, even more beautiful than before.

When, on the tenth day, they were summoned to Jethro Verwood's deathbed, Julian awaited with dread the effect this would have upon Alathea, but to his astonishment and relief, she remained perfectly calm. The end was peaceful, for Verwood was already almost unconscious from the mercifully deadening effect of Mehitabel's potions, but even when all was over and the old slave woman drew the sheet up over the still face, Alathea did not weep. Julian feared that the full impact of her loss had not yet struck her, and waited apprehensively for realization of it to dawn, but the breakdown he dreaded did not come. Even on the morrow, when Verwood was laid to rest in the tree-shaded plot where his wife was buried, she remained composed.

In any other woman Julian would have assumed this to be a deliberate, courageous dissembling of sorrow, but he had already learned that Alathea knew nothing of self-restraint. Her behavior was governed always by the emotion of the moment, and so her reaction to her father's death was all the more unexpected. Some time was to pass before he could accept that bereavement had not touched her very deeply, but though the realization brought perplexity and the first faint flicker of disquiet, this was soon forgotten in the heady delights of those early days of their marriage, and in the challenge offered by the responsibilities he had inherited.

Where the working of the plantation was concerned, he had to rely completely, as Verwood had advised him to do, on the head overseer. Ira Yatton was an octoroon, a tall, lean man in his late forties, and at first he seemed a trifle wary of his new master. Julian, seeing this, went to some trouble to allay his uneasiness, for he knew that it was essential to win the man's loyalty and cooperation. Summoning him to the room in the domestic wing of the house which served as an office for the business of the estate, he motioned him to a seat and then said frankly:

"Yatton, I need your help. Mr. Verwood told me that he left the working of the plantation entirely to you?"

"Yes, sir, he did," Yatton admitted. "He never took much interest himself in the growing of the crop, but my father was head overseer in his time, and *his* father before that, so I was reared to it, you might say."

"The Verwoods have been planters, then, for generations?"

Yatton nodded. "That's so, sir, but Mr. Jethro being the younger son, and always more interested in book-learning, his father let him go to university in England. After that he traveled—all over Europe, so I've heard—and never came home but once in twenty years. He inherited the family plantation when his brother died, and came back then to settle in the Indies."

"But not, I believe, in Jamaica?"

"No, Mr. Severn," Yatton agreed, meeting Julian's eyes squarely, "but by your leave, I'll not tell you where. When we left, Mr. Jethro made all of us swear we'd never mention where we came from, and I'll not break my word to him dead any more than I would have done while he lived."

"Nor would I ask it of you." Julian's curiosity was overwhelming, but he knew that if he were to win the overseer's respect, it must remain unsatisfied. "Well, Ira Yatton, *I* was not even raised upon a sugar plantation, so I shall depend upon you even more than Mr. Verwood did. He did me the honor of believing that his interests would be safe in my hands, but I cannot fulfill his trust unless I have your help."

"You'll have it, Mr. Severn, I give you my word," Yatton replied emphatically, "and not mine alone. Mr. Jethro chose you to follow him, and that's good enough for us. He was a good master. Even the field hands mourn him."

Julian, remembering the wild chant of pagan sorrow which had echoed from the slave cabins the whole night through, knew that this was true. He had learned already that the brutality and torture which were common on many plantations were unknown at Verwood's Kingdom; punishment for transgression was hard but it was always just, and the slaves were adequately fed and housed. Verwood's death must have sent a ripple of dread through the whole plantation, dread that a change of master might mean a change for the worse in lives which already were bleak enough.

"There will be no changes here of my making," he said quietly. "Let that be known, so that it may allay any misgivings."

He nodded dismissal and Yatton got up.

"I'll do that, sir, for I'll not deny we wondered—!" He hesitated, turning his hat awkwardly between his hands, as though he wished to say something more but did not know quite how to put it. "Mr. Jethro knew that he could trust us, and I'll make bold to tell you, Mr. Severn, you can do the same—if the time ever comes."

He went quickly out of the room, as though afraid of being asked to elaborate upon this. It seemed a curious thing to say. Julian puzzled over it then, and for several days afterwards the memory of it recurred at intervals to mystify him, until gradually it receded to the back of his mind and was buried beneath matters of more immediate interest. Many months were to pass before he thought of it again.

It took some time for him to accustom himself to being the master of a great fortune and a large estate, for though he had prospered during his years in Jamaica, he had never, until that fateful summons to Verwood's Kingdom, intended to remain there for the rest of his life. Now his future was bound irrevocably to the island by the promise he had made to Jethro Verwood, and he was content that it should be so.

In Alathea he found constant delight, and though they quarreled from time to time—she had a temper which sometimes startled him by its violence—their disagreements were as brief as they were fierce, and were followed by ardent reconciliations. Life, to Julian, was very good, and if he looked back at all to the memory of a boy named Jocelyn, who had once believed that life could never again hold happiness or purpose, he did so with amazement, and wry amusement at the follies of his youth.

By the time Serena's birthday came round again, Margaret Loring had convinced herself that her elder daughter's childish dependence upon Julian had been outgrown, but she could not have been more grievously mistaken. In thought and imagination Serena still conversed with him, shared laughter or sought comfort, consulted his judgment on any matter of moment. Lived a secret inner life which no one suspected.

In reality she had had very little contact with him since his marriage, but though she missed him desperately, there were many times when she was thankful that he was far away in the fastness of Verwood's Kingdom, for as soon as the news of his marriage leaked out, every speculation and rumor which had ever been rife concerning Jethro Verwood was immediately resurrected, accompanied now by a flood of gossip about Julian and his bride. It was said that he had been bribed into the marriage by the Verwood fortune because Miss Verwood was hideously ugly; was crippled or de-

131

formed; was the child of a wild Negress straight from the jungles of Africa's slave coast whom Jethro Verwood had been tricked into marrying during a drunken frolic. That, said the scandal mongers, was why she and her daughter had been kept hidden away. Even though those who had been present at Julian's wedding indignantly refuted this nonsense, it persisted, for it had its roots in envy. Jamaican society might have disliked and distrusted Jethro Verwood, but it could not forgive him for having bestowed his fortune upon a comparative newcomer to the colony.

Julian, Serena hoped, remained in ignorance of the gossip. Since marrying, he had made only one or two brief, essential visits to Kingston, and of late even these had ceased. Alathea was expecting a child. He had told them that on his last visit, months ago, and it seemed unlikely now that he would leave the plantation again until after the baby had been born. The most that Serena could hope for this year was a letter on her birthday.

The letter came, and one for her parents, too, and later Serena was summoned to the drawing room. Her mother was there alone.

"My love," Margaret said without preamble, "you are invited to visit Julian and his wife. Would you like to go?"

"Why—yes, of course!" She paused, puzzled. "I alone?"

Mrs. Loring nodded. "As you know, Alathea is shortly to be confined. I gather from Julian's letter that she is in low spirits, and he hopes that your company will divert her. If you are willing to go, and your father and I agree, he will come himself to fetch you."

So it was for Alathea's sake she was invited. No matter. She would see Julian, too, and have him to herself on the journey. Little enough, but better than nothing.

"I would like very much to go," she said firmly, "if you and Papa will permit it."

Thus, a few days later, she came to be riding with Julian along the road she had first traveled almost exactly a year ago. The journey was to be made on horseback because there was no coach at Verwood's Kingdom, and they had set out as soon as it was light. Julian had arranged for them to halt during the hottest part of the day at the house of an acquaintance and they would probably not reach their destination before nightfall, but since they were attended by armed and mounted servants, this caused Thaddeus and Margaret no anxiety.

Serena was happier than she had been for a long time. She had half feared some constraint between herself and Julian, but they had slipped immediately into the old, easy companionship, able to talk or to be silent together as the mood prompted, so that for a few hours she could pretend that everything was as it had always been.

The pretense did not survive their arrival at Verwood's Kingdom. It was dark by the time they reached the plantation house and Althea had already retired, so only Mehitabel was waiting to greet them. Once again Serena met the gaze of those inimical dark eyes, and once again a little tremor of disquiet flickered along all her nerves. No one could have found fault with the old woman's manner, with her respectful greeting or her solicitude for the guest's comfort, and yet Serena could not rid herself of the feeling that, as far as Mehitabel was concerned, she was an unwanted and deeply resented intruder.

Next morning she found herself breakfasting alone with Julian, for Alathea, once accustomed to being abroad as soon as the sun was up, now lay abed far into the morning. At last she wandered into the room, clad in a loose gown of drifting, shimmering silk the color of sea water, and still beautiful even now that she was big with child. She seemed pleased to see Serena, and accepted with naive delight the gifts she had brought for the expected infant—two robes of fine lawn exquisitely stitched and embroidered by Serena and her mother, while Lucilla (under constraint) had contributed a little lace-trimmed cap.

This sunny mood, however, was not of long duration, and Serena soon discovered that Alathea bitterly resented the physical restrictions imposed by her pregnancy. She had little learning, and no aptitude for sewing or embroidery, while domestic matters interested her not at all, since the whole household ran smoothly under Mehitabel's expert governance and even the most trivial and personal tasks were performed by the deft black hands of the innumerable slaves. Boredom made the time hang heavily; she was moody and restless, and before long Serena decided that Julian's invitation must have been prompted by sheer desperation. For his sake she did her best to please and amuse Alathea, but it was like trying to entertain a capricious child. She could be diverted for a little while, but all too soon any occupation would pall, and she would either become sullen and withdrawn or fly into a rage of almost frightening intensity which even Julian seemed unable to soothe. At such times Mehitabel alone had the power to calm her, and Serena noticed that the old slave woman was now never far from her mistress's side.

Between Alathea's tantrums and Mehitabel's constant watchfulness, Serena felt as the long days passed that she would soon be at the end of her endurance. She could not be easy at Verwood's Kingdom, for it seemed to her that sinister undercurrents stirred beneath its placid surface. They were in the very atmosphere of the place; in its isolation on the edge of the jungle, with the wild mountains towering close at hand; in the claustrophobic feeling of a small enclosed community having scarcely any contact with the outside world; in the savage drumming which on more than one night she heard faintly from somewhere near the slave cabins, a sound which seemed to conjure mysterious, primitive forces out of the darkness. Not even the delight of seeing Julian every day could entirely outweigh the malefic influences she felt all about her.

Aware of Alathea's frustration at being unable to go beyond the house and the garden, Serena resisted for a long time the temptation to accept Julian's repeated invitations to ride with him sometimes about the estate. Eventually, however, a day came when she felt that she could no longer endure her virtual imprisonment. Alathea was resting; Mehitabel was within call; there seemed no reason in the world why she should not for once indulge herself.

They were away from the house for less than two hours, but on their return found Alathea in a mood of sullen resentment which persisted for the rest of the day. All efforts to win her out of it met with no success, and eventually they gave up in despair and, after they had dined, settled down to a game of chess. This was one of Julian's favorite pastimes and he had taught Serena to play when she was barely ten years old, but though he had tried to teach Alathea, too, the subtleties of the game were beyond her comprehension.

That evening, reclining among piles of cushions on an old-fashioned daybed, one hand behind her head, she lay staring towards the table where the two players sat. Both were totally absorbed. The light from the half-dozen candles in the heavy silver holder beside them shone on their intent faces, casting a glow over Serena's clear, pale skin and glinting on the streaks of silver in the blackness of Julian's hair. He was waiting for her to make her move, watching her with lazy affection, the faintest of smiles on his lips, while she, with a tiny frown between her brows, gravely pondered the position of the pieces on the board between them. Neither was aware of the sudden change in Alathea's expression or noticed her heave herself upright and swing her feet to the floor.

Serena's hand hovered above the board, hesitated, and then moved. She looked up with one of her rare, sweet smiles to meet her opponent's look of amused dismay.

"Checkmate," she said mischievously. "You are sadly out of practice, Julian!"

Before he could reply, Alathea was beside them and with a sweep of her arm, sent not only the board and chessmen, but the candles, too, crashing to the floor. Serena cried out and both players sprang to their feet. Some of the candles had been extinguished by the fall, but the remaining flames were licking dangerously at the covering of the cushion which had fallen from Serena's chair, and Julian's first reaction was to snatch up the holder and stamp on the smoldering stuff.

Alathea, with incoherent cries of fury, was trampling on the board and the scattered pieces, and Serena, aghast at seeing Julian's cherished chessmen so wantonly damaged, caught her by the arm.

"Oh, Alathea, pray do not! You must—!"

She broke off with a cry as the other girl turned upon her, striking her in the face with a force which sent her staggering back, and would have repeated the blow had not Julian swung round and caught her upraised arm. She struck at him with the other hand, but he grabbed her wrist and held her prisoner, while, sobbing with rage, she struggled wildly to be free.

Suddenly, silently, Mehitabel was in the room. She hobbled quickly forward and took Alathea by the arm. The girl tried to shake her off, but there was unsuspected strength in the bony old fingers.

"Shame on you, Miss Thea!" the old woman said sharply. "Come now! Come with Mehitabel!" To Julian she added: "Just help me get her to her room, suh! I'll look after her."

Between them Julian and the old Negress urged their struggling, sobbing prisoner out of the room, and for what seemed a long time, Serena stayed where she was, crouched in a chair with her hand pressed to her smarting, throbbing cheek, trembling in every limb and too shaken by that unprovoked outburst of violence to move. At length, however, looking at the scattered chessmen, she dragged herself out of her seat and began to gather them up. Many of them were broken, and she was still kneeling on the floor with the fragments helplessly cupped in her hands when Julian came back into the room.

"Serena, what can I say?" He came quickly across to her, hand outstretched to help her up; then, as she lifted her face towards him and he saw the darkening bruise on her cheekbone and the little smear of blood where one of Alathea's rings had torn the skin, his voice changed. "Oh, my dear, I did not realize—"

He bent swiftly and lifted her to her feet, and she stood passively while he turned her face to the light of the remaining candles and very gently wiped away the blood with his handkerchief.

"Sweetheart, I'm sorry!" he said contritely. "I would not for the world have had this happen! God knows what possesses her to behave so!"

"Julian, do not be angry with her!" Serena spoke shakily, with trembling lips. "Her situation—!"

"Her situation is one common to most women at some time or other, but they do not all behave as though they were demented."

"But Alathea so hates being heavy and clumsy—! It was thoughtless of me to come riding with you when she cannot, and then to play chess, which we both know she dislikes." She looked anxiously up at him. "As long as she has done herself no harm! Is she quiet now?"

"Yes. Mehitabel can always handle her." He took the broken chessmen from her unresisting hands and laid them on the table, adding with some difficulty: "Serena, if you wish to stay here no longer, tell me, and I will take you home tomorrow."

"No, Julian," she said quickly, her heart wrenched by the worry in his face and voice. "No great harm was done, and you must not be away from the plantation when Alathea is likely to be confined at any moment. I will not hear of it."

As it happened, the question did not arise. Alathea was brought to bed during the night, and after a short and easy

136

labor, gave birth to a daughter. Mehitabel, who had acted as midwife, as she had at Alathea's own birth, and that of her mother, brought the news to the library, where Julian and Serena had been keeping anxious vigil, and Serena, seeing joy and relief flood into his face, was conscious, even in the midst of her own gladness, of a new sense of desolation. He had his own family now; was part of a close-knit circle of which she, no matter how dearly valued as a friend, could never be a part.

Later that day he took her to see mother and child. Alathea, pale and beautiful, her face bent tenderly above the swaddled infant in the crook of her arm, looked up with a smile as Serena came to the bedside, but her expression changed as she caught sight of the purple bruise spreading around the cut on the girl's cheekbone.

"Oh, you have hurt yourself!" she exclaimed. "How did that happen?"

It was clear that she remembered nothing of her own actions the previous evening. Serena was taken aback but managed to rise to the occasion.

"It is nothing. I tripped and fell. Do let me look at the baby."

Proudly Alathea put back the wrappings from the baby's face, and then, as Serena bent admiringly over the child, lifted her own face to smile radiantly at her husband.

"Julian, we must name her Anabel, after my mother. Father will be so pleased and proud...and how surprised he will be, when he comes home, to find that he has a granddaughter!"

Alathea's reference to her father, which had been so great a shock to Julian and Serena, was not repeated; she did not speak of him again, and there was no way of telling whether or not the delusion persisted. Physically her recovery was rapid and the baby thrived, but Serena, watching them together, was irresistibly reminded of a small girl with a doll. At times Alathea could not bear to be parted from her daughter, but then without warning her mood would change, she would thrust the infant into Serena's arms or those of Rachel, the black nurse appointed by Mehitabel, and apparently lose all interest in her. Serena was troubled, but shrank from mentioning her misgivings to Julian. Perhaps, she thought,

137

such erratic behavior was typical of a new young mother; she had no previous experience by which to judge.

She remained at Verwood's Kingdom for the full month of Alathea's lying-in, but when the time came for Julian to take her back to Kingston, she was glad to go. She knew now that she could never make a friend of Julian's wife, and though Julian himself was as dear to her as ever, their ways lay now apart. Somehow, she thought sadly, being familiar with the routine of his life here at the plantation made him seem more remote, less a part of the happy remembered days at her father's house.

Julian spent two days with the Lorings, discussing business with Thaddeus, going with him to the countinghouse and alone to Port Royal for an hour or two with Michael Langdale aboard the *Merry Venture*, which chanced to be in port at that time. Later, riding home to Verwood's Kingdom, he was conscious, for the first time since his marriage, of certain small regrets. He realized that he missed the normal social contacts of everyday life, while the brief time he had spent aboard the *Merry Venture* had aroused an unexpected hankering for the heave of a deck beneath his feet and the space and emptiness and fierce challenge of the sea. One day, he thought, he would make another voyage with Michael.

Yet for the next few months life flowed by pleasantly enough. He was still bewitched by Alathea, and they were almost as happy now as they had been when they were first married; almost, but not quite, for now there hovered always upon the horizon the small cloud of Alathea's unpredictable behavior. The odd whims and childish tantrums; her attitude to the baby, which veered wildly from the fiercely maternal to the totally indifferent; the turbulent moods which sometimes sent the boyish figure on the big gray horse careering madly through the cane fields as though pursued by furies. Julian tried to convince himself—and very nearly succeeded—that all these were the result of her strange, lonely upbringing, yet always there lingered in the far recesses of his mind a question to which he dared not seek an answer. The question of why Jethro Verwood had chosen to live as he did.

Before another year was out, that question was to be terribly and irrevocably answered. One evening, when little Anabel was some seven months old, Julian was in the estate room with Ira Yatton, discussing the purchase of some new

138

field hands, when, somewhere not far off, a woman began to scream on a high-pitched note of sheer terror. He recognized Alathea's voice and, springing to his feet, raced out of the room and across the garden, while the terrible, heart-stopping screams went on and on.

They were coming from the nursery. Julian, dreading what he might find, reached the door and flung it open and was inside the dimly lit room before he realized that, apart from Alathea and the baby, it was empty. She crouched on the floor in a corner, her body hunched protectively over the wailing child, which she was clutching to her breast with one arm while the other was raised as though to fend off some attack.

"Alathea!" Julian strode forward and gripped the upraised arm. "In God's name, what is it? What has frightened you?"

She stopped screaming, but the face she lifted towards him was pallid and distorted, rigid with fear, the eyes so distended that the whites could be seen all around the iris.

"A *loupgarou!*" she cried hysterically. "A loupgarou! Do you not see it? There!"

She wrenched her arm free and flung out a wildly pointing hand towards the far corner of the room, but when Julian swung round to look in the same direction, expecting to see some hitherto unknown (to him) animal or reptile, the corner was empty.

Others were coming into the room now. Rachel thrust past him to snatch the screaming baby from her mother's arms and cradle her against her own ample bosom, and as Julian, shaken and still mystified, lifted his wife to her feet, he found Mehitabel beside them. Alathea clutched at the old woman's arm.

"A loupgarou!" she insisted frantically. "Mehitabel, help me!"

"There, child, it's gone now," Mehitabel assured her, patting her hand, "and Rachel got the baby safe. You come with me." In a whispered aside to Julian, she added, "Leave her to me, suh. I know what to do."

She led Alathea away, an arm round the girl's shoulders, leaving Julian standing alone and bewildered, still not quite sure what had happened. He looked at Rachel, rocking the whimpering child, but she refused to meet his eyes. Micah, who had been at Mehitabel's heels, had turned away and was going sadly out of the room, shaking his head; one or two of the other slaves, who had been peering in at the open door, scuttled off, whispering fearfully among themselves. Only Ira Yatton remained, waiting uneasily on the piazza at the edge of the patch of light from the nursery.

Julian joined him, closing the nursery door, and beckoned the man to accompany him, which he did reluctantly. Leading the way to the library, Julian summoned a slave and told him to fetch brandy and two glasses. Then he turned to Yatton.

"What," he asked, "is a loupgarou?"

The overseer shifted uncomfortably and did not reply. Julian's expression hardened.

"Well?" he prompted impatiently. "Come, man, you must have heard what my wife said, and you were born and reared in the Indies. What is a loupgarou?"

"It's a word the blacks use, sir," Yatton explained unwillingly. "It means a—a monster, a demon. They believe a loupgarou will get through the thatch into a hut and suck a child's blood."

Julian was listening with gathering wrath. "Confound it, Yatton! My wife is not some ignorant, superstitious slave."

"No, sir!" Yatton looked acutely uncomfortable. "But she has always been cared for by slaves, and must have heard tales of the loupgarous in her nursery."

"We were all terrified by some kind of ghost or goblin when we were children, but we do not carry such beliefs into adult life," Julian retorted angrily. "Besides, this was more than mere fancy. She really believed she could see the damned thing!"

The overseer made no reply to this, standing silent and uncomfortable while Julian paced the length of the room and back, pausing at last by the table where candles burned. Yatton, watching him, thought that his own presence had been for the moment forgotten; he wished that he dared stealthily to withdraw, but though Mr. Severn was pleasant and reasonable, there was something about him which precluded the taking of any liberties. In the present circumstances Yatton felt exceedingly sorry for him, but even more sorry for himself. This was a situation he had dreaded and hoped to avoid.

The slave, coming back into the room with decanter and glasses on a silver tray, looked apprehensively from one man to the other. He poured the brandy, carried one glass to his master and the other to the overseer and then beat a hasty retreat. Yatton, envying him, swallowed a generous mouthful, hoping that it might help him through the hideously difficult minutes ahead.

Julian, who had accepted his glass of brandy as though unaware of what he was doing, set it down untasted on the table and spoke with sudden resolution.

"Yatton, I have had enough of secrecy and evasion. You told me once that Jethro Verwood made you swear never to disclose whence he came. I do not ask you to break that oath, but I want to know *why* he left that place and settled in Jamaica."

"Don't ask me that, Mr. Severn," Yatton said wretchedly. "I beg of you, don't ask me!"

"Damn it, man! Who else am I to ask?" Anxiety made Julian's voice harsh and threatening. "Are you suggesting that I, of all men, have no right to know?"

Obviously there was to be no reprieve. Yatton recklessly swallowed the rest of his brandy, hoping that it would give him Dutch courage, and faced his employer with a kind of resigned despair.

"Very well, sir. It goes back to the time Mr. Jethro came home after his brother died. There was another plantation adjoining the Verwood estate. A small one, badly run to seed because the old gentleman who owned it had drunk away all his money. He lived there with his granddaughter, Miss Anabel, and a handful of slaves—Mehitabel was one of them—and barely managed to scrape a living out of the place. Miss Anabel was beautiful—Mrs. Severn looks just like her— and Mr. Jethro no sooner saw her than he made up his mind to marry her, even though he was twice her age. No one could believe it when the old gentleman refused him point-blank, Mr. Jethro being so rich and important, and them so poor."

"What happened, then? Did he elope with her?"

"No, sir. I'm not saying he wouldn't have done, but then the old gentleman died very suddenly, and, Miss Anabel having no other family, Mr. Jethro married her straight away."

Yatton paused, twisting his empty glass nervously between his hands. So far the story had been easy enough to tell, but he shrank from telling the rest, which, no matter how he worded it, was going to deal a mortal blow to a man he liked and respected. Julian, seeing his reluctance to continue, silently picked up the decanter and refilled his glass.

141

Then, motioning Yatton to a seat and sitting down facing him, prompted him with another question.

"I take it Miss Anabel was willing?"

"Oh, yes, sir. They were happy enough at first, but then we began to hear bits of gossip from the house slaves, how Mrs. Verwood was acting strange, saying things that didn't make sense, hearing things no one else could hear." Yatton hesitated, took another pull at his brandy and then added in a low voice: "Reckon it was then Mr. Jethro realized why her old granddad had been so set against her marrying."

Again he paused, but this time Julian did not speak. He could not, for although his mind rejected the implication of what Yatton was saying, a cold hand was tightening relentlessly upon his heart. After a moment he heard the overseer say:

"Mr. Jethro wanted to keep it secret, because by that time Mrs. Verwood was with child. So he sold the plantation and most of the slaves and came here to Jamaica, where no one knew him, bringing just a few of us with him, them he knew he could trust. He bought this place because it was so far from all the other plantations. He wanted no neighbors to pry into what didn't concern them. Miss Thea was born here, and she has never been beyond the boundaries."

Alathea must never leave the plantation. The meaning of the promise demanded by Jethro Verwood was becoming hideously plain. Julian thought of Mehitabel always in close attendance on her mistress, of Micah near to tears tonight and Yatton so reluctant to speak. They were all seeing the beginning of a pattern they had known before, a pattern as tragic as it was inevitable.

"No!" he said violently in answer to that latter thought, and sprang to his feet, his chair scraping backwards across the polished floor. "No! My God, it cannot be true!"

Yatton said nothing and would not meet his eyes. Julian strode round the table and gripped him by the shoulder, making him wince.

"You're lying!" he said, but it was less an accusation than a plea for reassurance, a reassurance the other man could not give. He sat motionless, with bowed head, his hands gripped tightly together between his knees, and slowly Julian's grip relaxed. His hand dropped to his side and he said dully: "You are telling me that my wife's mother was mad and that Alathea herself is going the same way?"

Wretchedly Yatton nodded. Julian turned away, dropped into his chair again and buried his face in his hands. He was numb with shock, and yet he knew, with a relentless inner certainty which could not be denied, that everything Yatton had told him was true. It explained so much that had always puzzled him, confirmed his own secret, unacknowledged fears, answered so many of the questions he had brushed aside because of his passion for Alathea.

"He knew?" he said suddenly, lifting a ravaged face. "Verwood knew it would happen?"

Yatton was watching him with sorrow and compassion. "He feared it, sir. I know that. It's the reason he lived as he did, even after Mrs. Verwood died."

"My wife told me she never knew her mother?"

"That's true, sir. Miss Thea was less than a year old when Mrs. Verwood died." He saw the question in Julian's eyes and shook his head. "It was the fever, sir. Mehitabel reared the baby. She'd been Mrs. Verwood's nurse, and *her* mother's, too."

"Was the grandmother—?" Julian could not bring himself to frame the question, but Yatton understood.

"I don't know, sir, though I've often wondered. You'd have to ask Mehitabel."

Trust Mehitabel! Jethro Verwood's words echoed in Julian's memory with a new and sinister significance. Mehitabel, guardian of a terrible secret through two, perhaps even three, generations, and now—? But that was a thought he could not even begin to contemplate. He looked again at the overseer.

"You can go, Yatton," he said wearily; then, as the other man got up but hesitated, added harshly: "Leave me! There is nothing you can do."

Nothing that anyone can do, he thought. Jethro Verwood had done all that was possible when he created this strange, isolated little kingdom for the wife who had not lived and the child who had; a kingdom where they would be safe and indulged and protected, their affliction a secret known to no one. He had shut them away from the world, and himself with them, and when death approached he had found someone to take his place, handed on the responsibility to a man who did not even know he was accepting it. And there, Julian thought bitterly, is the difference between us. Verwood made

143

the choice of his own free will; I have had it thrust upon me. I love Alathea and our child, but do I love them enough?

The knowledge that he could even ask himself such a question filled him with a self-disgust too great to be borne. If that was the direction in which thought was leading him, then thought must be blotted out. He reached for his untouched glass of brandy, swallowed it at a draught and filled the glass again. When, some time later, Micah summoned up the courage to peep into the room, the decanter was empty and Julian, his head buried in his arms outstretched upon the table, had found the oblivion he sought.

It was a long while before he could bring himself to visit Kingston again, and when he did, Serena was quick to sense the change in him. This was not easy to define, for superficially his manner was as it had always been; he listened to news of what had been happening during his absence, inquired after friends and acquaintances, laughed at the amusing anecdotes she had been saving to tell him. Only when the conversation turned towards his own affairs, when he was asked for news of Alathea and little Anabel, did Serena become aware of a certain withdrawal, a reserve which had never been there before. Yes, Alathea was well and sent her compliments and good wishes. The baby was thriving, and grew more captivating every day. He recounted several incidents in proof of this, but Serena was left with the impression that he had, in fact, told them nothing. It seemed, she thought unhappily, as though he was becoming like Jethro Verwood, who had so rarely left his plantation and, when he did, never talked of it or of his daughter. Perhaps this was the effect that the brooding isolation of Verwood's Kingdom had upon those who lived there.

Yet in one respect, at least, she found as the months went by, Julian did not follow his father-in-law's example, for his visits to Kingston became more and more frequent and less hurried. He involved himself closely again in the business affairs of Loring and Severn, persuading Thaddeus to increase and extend these, combining with them the various interests he had inherited from Verwood. He was the driving force now in all their mutual concerns; his was the vision and the enterprise, while Thaddeus, nearing sixty and in feeble health, left more and more of the decisions to him. Ironically Julian prospered, for if one venture failed, another would soon turn his losses into profit. Kingston society watched his progress with envy and malice, while Serena, deeply uneasy, tried without success to understand the change in him.

She was not the only person to notice it. On one occasion, when Julian had taken an obviously reluctant leave of them and set out for home at the end of a week's stay, her mother said to her with a sigh:

"Poor Julian! I fear he is learning the truth of the adage that to marry in haste is to repent at leisure."

Serena looked anxiously at her. "Do you think he regrets his marriage, Mama?"

"I am certain of it, my love, and not in the least surprised. I know it brought him a great fortune, but—!"

"Mama!" Serena was indignant. "You cannot believe that was the reason!"

"No, my dear, though it might perhaps have been better for him if it were. As it is, he married Alathea Verwood because he was utterly infatuated with her, and now he realizes that mere beauty is not everything. I feared this would happen! A girl with little education and no social graces whatsoever, whom he cannot even present to his acquaintances—that is no sort of wife for a man like Julian."

"I do not think Alathea wants to be presented, Mama. She seems quite content to remain always at the plantation."

"Well, for that we may be thankful!" Margaret retorted with asperity. "We should be obliged to entertain her here, and I can well imagine the kind of scandal she would provoke. There is quite enough spiteful gossip about Julian as it is."

Serena knew that this was true. Although nearly three years had passed since Julian's marriage, the rumors and speculation this had provoked had never been allowed to subside. Since he had never introduced his wife to local society or invited any guests to Verwood's Kingdom, curiosity, unsatisfied, fed upon itself. At first those who had been present at the wedding were eagerly questioned, and when all proved reticent—the Lorings out of affection for Julian, the lawyer and the parson by virtue of their respective callings—it was taken as further proof that some mystery did exist. Lately it had been remarked that Julian now spent more and more time in Kingston; knowing looks were exchanged and fresh rumors murmured behind a fan or over a glass of wine.

Serena was distressed and worried, though less by the

145

gossip than by the change in Julian himself and the certainty that he was no longer happy. He seemed driven by a need to fill his time and his thoughts with matters as far as possible removed from Verwood's Kingdom, and yet he was unwilling to leave the island. Michael Langdale had tried to persuade his friend to sail with him again, but though Serena felt convinced that Julian longed to agree, he remained adamant in his refusal. Another inexplicable contradiction; he seemed full of them these days.

She kept her anxiety to herself. To have discussed it with anyone, even her parents, would somehow have been a betrayal of the precious bond which still existed between her and Julian, and yet that very closeness prevented her from trying to force his confidence. If he wanted her to know what was wrong, he would tell her. She could not bring herself to question him.

IV

Julian had promised to be in Kingston for Serena's eighteenth birthday, but when the day came he had neither arrived nor sent any word. The lack of a message encouraged her to hope that he was on his way, but the hours went by and the guests who had been invited to dine had already assembled before Samuel came softly to tell her, with an air of fatherly indulgence, that Mr. Severn had just arrived and gone straight to his room. Serena excused herself to her companions, withdrew as unobtrusively as she could and hurried happily to knock on the familiar door. His voice bade her enter, and she went in.

Ezra, his body-servant, was already laying out on the bed the silk coat and breeches and embroidered waistcoat his master intended to put on—Julian was so often in the house now that many of his possessions had found their way back there—but Julian himself stood staring from the window, though Serena knew immediately that he was not watching anything outside. His face, glimpsed in profile in the instant before he turned towards her, was set in lines of such bitterness that she felt a rush of sympathy and dismay as sharp as physical pain, and though the expression vanished as he smiled in greeting, the memory of it haunted her for the rest of the day.

"Serena!" He came quickly to meet her, taking her out-stretched hands and stooping from his fine height to kiss her cheek. "Did you think I had forgotten my promise to be here today?"

She shook her head. "No, I knew there must have been some last-minute delay, for if you had not been coming at all, you would have sent word. Julian, is anything wrong? Alathea is not ill? Or Anabel?"

"No, nothing of that kind. There was a trifling mishap at the mill which meant I could not leave until this morning, and even then I was later setting out than I intended."

It was a lie, and he hated lying to Serena. She was looking anxiously up at him, her clear gaze searching his face, and he forced himself to add lightly:

"I had no idea that the house would be full of guests."

She made a little grimace. "That was Lucy's notion, not mine. I would have preferred to spend the evening quietly on our own, but you see, until she is sixteen Mama will not let her go into company, but when we entertain at home she is allowed to join us."

And of course, he thought angrily, it was Lucilla's wishes that prevailed. Will Thaddeus and Margaret never cease to indulge her selfishness? Aloud he said:

"We'll spend the whole day quietly together tomorrow. Now I had better make myself fit to be seen, for your mother will not thank me for causing dinner to be delayed. Go back and pave the way for me to make my peace with her."

She laughed and shook her head at him, knowing as well as he did that there was no need for her to do anything of the kind, but as she returned to the drawing room, her gladness that he had come was clouded by recollection of the expression she had glimpsed in his face. What could have happened to make him look like that?

A little later, when he joined the company and made his way across the room in response to Margaret's affectionate greeting, Serena reflected with pride that he was by far the most distinguished-looking man present. It was not merely because of his exceptional height or the quiet elegance of his dress; there was a courtliness about him, an assured ease of bearing, which always set him a little apart from the rest of the men she knew. Once, long ago, she had heard her mother

148

say that Julian had an air of the great world about him, and though she had not understood at the time, she remembered it suddenly and thought that it was an apt description.

They went in to dinner almost immediately, and she had no opportunity to talk to him again until the gentlemen rejoined the ladies in the drawing room some hours later. She had been playing to entertain the guests and was still seated at the harpsichord when the men came in. Julian went across to her, but they had barely exchanged a dozen words before he was addressed by one of the other ladies, a handsome, dark-eyed, rather plump young woman in a low-cut, tightly-laced gown of rose-colored satin and rather too many jewels.

"Mr. Severn, you compel your friends to take you to task for sparing them not one word of greeting. I am not at all sure that I shall forgive you."

Julian turned courteously towards the speaker, but his glance was wary. Four years before, when Mary Carndon was still Mary Standish, she had made determined but futile efforts to capture his interest, and though for the past three years she had been married to a wealthy planter who doted on her, she had never forgiven Julian for his indifference. Now it was her habit, pretending amiability, to loose spiteful little verbal darts at him whenever they met.

"Then I can only hope, madam, that your kind heart will prevail, and accept that the only reason for my neglect was the lateness of my arrival."

"You condemn yourself, sir!" She shook her head at him with apparent playfulness, but malice sparkled in her eyes. "Shame on you for such tardiness! I am sure that this poor child"—she smiled with false sweetness at Serena—"was convinced you did not mean to come at all. Upon her birthday, too!"

"Oh, I think not, ma'am," he countered coolly. "*Serena*, you see, is so well acquainted with me that she knows if I were unable to come, I would send to tell her so."

"To be sure!" Mrs. Carndon colored angrily but passed with scarcely a pause to another form of attack. "And when are we to have the pleasure of welcoming *Mrs*. Severn to Kingston? It is a pleasure we have awaited with eager expectation for far too long."

A sudden hush fell upon those in the immediate vicinity. There was probably no one else present who was bold enough to put that question to him, but it was one which they had

149

all been asking themselves and each other for nearly three years, and no one wanted to miss the reply.

A moment passed before it came, a moment which to Serena, sitting frozen with dismay at the harpsichord, seemed to last interminably. Julian's expression had scarcely altered, but she was aware of a sudden tension in his tall figure, the clenching of the hand resting on the polished wood of the instrument, and her heart began to beat fast with apprehension.

"Then it is an expectation, Mrs. Carndon, which I regret will never be fulfilled," he replied in the same cool tone. "My wife chooses to live retired. She has done so all her life, and would be confused and ill at ease in a gathering such as this."

She looked archly at him. "Why then, sir, *you* are to be rebuked for not encouraging her to grow accustomed to company in her own home. I am sure that any of us would be delighted to make the journey to Verwood's Kingdom—!"

She broke off, warned, perhaps, by the look in his face that this time she had gone too far. With a rather forced laugh and a shrug of her plump shoulders, she turned away, but avenged her discomfiture by saying in a deliberately carrying undervoice to those nearest to her:

"So Mrs. Severn *chooses* to live retired! No doubt we should congratulate our friend on having acquired a rich wife who can be kept so conveniently out of sight."

There was a snigger, hastily stifled, and then several people began to talk at once. Serena, her frightened gaze on Julian's face, saw it rigid with anger and humiliation and something more, something which reminded her of the look she had seen earlier. She feared that he was going to walk straight out of the room, and in desperation she began to play again, willing him to listen, to look at her, to turn the pages of music for her as he usually did. And somehow she succeeded; somehow her sympathy and concern and fierce loyalty reached out to him, penetrating the fog of helpless fury and frustration and making him aware of the aid she was offering. He accepted it, moving a little closer to her, half turning his back on their companions as he waited for her to reach the bottom of the page of music. As he leaned forward to turn it for her, she heard him say, so softly that no one else could hear:

"My dear little friend! What would I ever do without you?"

* * *

150

Serena slept badly that night. She dozed and woke and dozed again, her troubled thoughts mingling with frightening half-waking dreams. Then, suddenly, she found herself wide awake, certain that some sound had startled her into full consciousness. Lucilla, who always slept like the dead, still slumbered peacefully beside her, but Serena, after listening intently and to no avail, slid cautiously out of bed and reached for robe and slippers.

The bedroom door opened noiselessly under her careful fingers and she stepped out into the corridor. Still no sound, but when she tiptoed towards the front of the house, she saw that a thin line of light showed around the edges of the dining room door. Without hesitation she stole forward, for some instinct told her, even before she gently pushed open the door, who she would find in the room.

Julian did not immediately become aware of her presence, and for a few moments she stood in the doorway, watching him with deepening disquiet. He had not been to bed, for he still wore the silk breeches and stockings and silver-buckled shoes he had put on earlier, though he had discarded coat and waistcoat and close-fitting stock and his ruffled shirt was open at the throat. He sat in the little circle of light cast by a single candle at one end of the long table, his chair half turned from it and his right arm resting along the polished mahogany, the hand curved loosely round a glass of brandy. His chin was sunk on his chest, and the candlelight threw harsh shadows across his face, deepening the lines which lately had etched themselves there, and showed that there was now more gray than black in his hair. In his whole attitude, in his face and in every line of his body, there was such utter dejection that Serena felt tears prick her eyes.

She moved forward, closing the door gently behind her, and the tiny sound it made brought his head up with a jerk. He sat staring at her as she crossed the big room towards him, but as she came into the light he said with forced cheerfulness:

"Did I disturb you, Serena? Forgive me! I thought no one would hear me, but now you have caught me red-handed, filching your father's brandy."

She brushed this aside. "I was awake anyway. Julian, what is wrong?"

"Why should anything be wrong?" He twirled the stem of his glass to and fro between finger and thumb, watching the

151

amber liquid in it instead of meeting her eyes. "Just because I could not sleep—!"

"Oh, Julian, do not try to pretend! I have known for a long time that you are troubled about something, and today—!" She hesitated, not knowing quite how to frame the question. "Is it anything to do with what Mary Carndon said this evening?"

He shrugged, still not looking at her. "Mrs. Carndon's gibes are not so important to me that I am likely to lose any sleep over them. I was angry at the time, I admit, but she was only saying to my face what most people whisper behind my back."

So he did know about the gossip! Serena, sinking down into a chair facing his across the corner of the table, said with muted indignation:

"They talk a great deal of nonsense, and should be ashamed of having nothing better to do than to pry into matters which do not concern them."

"Human nature, my dear!" There was a faintly derisive note in Julian's voice. "People will always speculate about matters which arouse their curiosity, and invent their own explanations when none are offered. The good people of Kingston have been gossiping about Verwood's Kingdom for a quarter of a century, and are not likely to stop now. Do not let it disturb you."

No, she thought, but it disturbed you today, deny it as you will. When Mary Carndon sneered at you, you were angry and humiliated and something more, something I cannot quite define. Whatever it was, it is only part of the greater trouble, of the change in you, of the fact that you cannot rest, but sit here in the middle of the night, staring at nothing, with a glass of brandy in your hand. Aloud she said:

"I do not like to hear spiteful gossip about you, or to be asked impertinent questions because I am the only person who has ever been to visit you and Alathea. I know it is because they envy you, but—!"

"Envy me?" The low-voiced question, spoken with indescribable bitterness, checked the words on her lips; turned her cold with alarm and dismay and the overpowering certainty that whatever tormented him was worse even than the most lurid imagination had yet surmised. "Envy *me?* Dear God!"

He rose abruptly from his chair and went to stand by the

window with his back to the room, his hands gripping the window frame on either side. Serena, too dismayed to speak or to move, thought that with head bowed and arms outstretched, he looked as though he had been crucified.

So people envy me, Julian was thinking. They envy the fortune I married and the success of my business ventures, not knowing that I pursue success so relentlessly because I must have some goal if my life is to hold any meaning at all. I know I have no one but myself to blame. Jethro Verwood trapped me but I was a willing dupe, so wild to possess the jewel he dazzled me with that I never paused to wonder why it was kept in so strange a setting, to ask myself whether it might be fatally flawed. I cannot condemn him, but neither can I forgive him for the prison in which he has confined me.

For Julian knew now, irrevocably and beyond all doubt, that Alathea was incurably insane. At first, even after what Ira Yatton had told him, there had seemed reason to hope, for there were intervals, sometimes lasting for weeks at a time, when she was once again the happy, loving, passionate woman he had married. Life had swung for a time between the extremes of heaven and hell, but her deterioration was appallingly rapid. The periods of lucidity became shorter and less frequent; more and more she passed beyond his reach into a dark world peopled by beings only she could see or hear, beings which were occasionally benign but more often horrors which sent her screaming into hiding or fleeing in blind panic through house and garden to beat frantically upon doors which now must be kept always locked and barred.

When he could endure uncertainty no more, Julian, desperate for any kind of reassurance, brought himself at last to question Mehitabel, but the old woman, speaking sorrowfully and with downcast eyes, had no comfort to offer. This was the third time, she told him, that she had had to watch this happen, for not only his wife's mother, but her grandmother, too, had died insane. Sick at heart, Julian turned away and, seeing his baby daughter golden and beautiful in her nurse's arms, realized despairingly that he was faced with the same terrible responsibility as had rested upon Jethro Verwood. That one day he, too, would have to make the same decision.

That was a week ago, and the final abandoning of hope had been as shattering in its way as the first discovery of Alathea's affliction. This time he had not sought the conso-

lation of the bottle, but only recollection of his promise to
Serena had brought him to Kingston at all, after a conflict
of feeling which left him still uncertain whether he yet had
sufficient command of himself to hide his despair.

And he had not hidden it, at least not from Serena's grave,
perceptive gaze and loving heart. It would be an immeas-
urable relief to confide in her, to tell her the truth and accept
the balm of her compassion and her unquestioning affection,
but he must not do it. As he stood at the window he could
see, reflected in the glass as in a mirror, the little patch of
lighted room behind him. Serena had risen from her chair
and now stood beside it with one hand resting on its back,
and her face, framed by the lappets of the muslin cap tied
beneath her chin, turned anxiously towards him; her silk
robe fell straight and simple from shoulder to foot, and without her hoop she was still childishly slim and touchingly,
heart-rendingly young. He could not burden that sweet innocence with the tragedy which had engulfed his own life,
or let the dark influence of Verwood's Kingdom lay its shadow
on her.

"Julian?" Her low voice, questioning and a little frightened, came to strengthen his resolve. "Julian, why will you
not tell me what is wrong?"

He made himself turn to face her. "Because nothing is,
sweetheart. Nothing of any importance," he lied. "You must
allow me a black mood from time to time, you know, and not
tease yourself over the cause of it. Now, back to bed with you,
or you will have shadows about your eyes in the morning and
I shall feel guilty because of it."

He had moved back to the table as he spoke, and for something to do, so that he could avoid looking at her, he picked
up the glass and drank the brandy. Setting it down empty,
he was aware of her uneasy glance at it and then at the
decanter which stood close by. He shook his head.

"I don't intend to drink myself insensible, if that is what
you are thinking. I give you my word not to touch another
drop tonight, so you may go back to bed, and to sleep, and
not worry your head over trifles. There is no need."

Certain that he was not telling her the truth, she was
sorely tempted to challenge him. Words formed themselves
in her mind. "Julian, trust me! Don't shut me out of your life!
You treat me still as a child, but why can you not see that

154

I am a child no longer? I am a grown woman, and I love you—!"

Her thoughts halted there, stumbling upon a realization so unexpected, so shattering, that dizziness assailed her and she was obliged to cling to the chair for support, staring at Julian as at a stranger, as though she were seeing him for the first time—which, in a sense, she was. Of course she loved him. Not with a child's love now, but utterly, completely, in every way a woman could love a man. Hopelessly, because he was married to Alathea.

Julian had picked up the decanter and was replacing it on the silver tray on the sideboard. His back was towards her, and by the time he turned to face her again, she had withdrawn a little from the vicinity of the candle into the kindly shadows. Somehow she must disguise the emotional cataclysm which had just engulfed her. She said in a low voice:

"Good night, then, Julian," and without waiting for a reply, fled softly from the room to the sanctuary of her bedchamber.

Discarding robe and slippers, she slid into bed beside Lucilla, who sighed and turned over and then sank again into sleep, while her elder sister lay staring into the darkness and trying to come to terms with her new self-knowledge.

Love had taken her unawares, developing so naturally out of her childish devotion that it was full-grown before she recognized it, but as it had been slow to flower, so it would endure. She knew that instinctively, without having consciously to think about it. She had always felt that somehow she belonged to Julian, but now she realized, and accepted with a maturity beyond her years, that she could never know complete happiness or fulfillment without him; that whatever the future held for her could never be more than second best.

One thing it must never hold was betrayal of the truth, for that would be to lose even what she had. Somehow she must keep her secret, seem content with his friendship and affection, never allow him to suspect that she yearned for so much more. If she could do that, she thought, if she could keep the truth from Julian, she need not fear she would betray it to anyone else. Her family was so accustomed to him coming first with her that none of them would look any further than that.

*   *   *

Serena had just received, and refused, her second proposal of marriage. It was not, perhaps, a very impressive total of offers for a good-looking, well-dowered girl of nineteen, but there was an aloofness about this quiet, self-contained young woman with the grave gray eyes which most men of her own age found a little daunting. She was always pleasant to them, but had a habit of regarding them with a sort of kindly indulgence which made no concession to masculine vanity.

Of her two suitors, the first had been an officer from one of the Royal Navy ships stationed at Jamaica, a needy young aristocrat on the lookout for a rich wife, and she had felt no regret when her father sent him about his business. The second was Peter Standish, the childhood playmate who, inexplicably indifferent to Lucilla's dazzling charms, had been Serena's devoted admirer ever since he was a schoolboy.

It was more difficult to refuse Peter, knowing that the match would have met with almost universal approval. Their families had been friends for years and he was heir to a prosperous plantation, a completely eligible suitor in every way, and, conscious of this, he did not accept his dismissal with very good grace. In fact, he refused to accept it at all; argued, with the familiarity of lifelong acquaintance; and finally announced his intention of repeating his proposal as often as was necessary to persuade her to change her mind. When she assured him that this would be useless, he became pugnacious, and what had begun as a romantic interlude descended almost to the level of a schoolroom squabble, ending with him stalking out of the room in a rage, leaving Serena to hope, not very optimistically, that this would be the end of the matter.

The door had scarcely closed behind him when it opened again and Julian came in. He looked surprised and a little amused.

"I met young Standish on the doorstep," he remarked, "in such an ill humor that he could scarcely bring himself to be civil. What in the world have you been saying to him?"

"I said 'no,'" Serena replied flatly. "He asked me to marry him."

"To marry—?" Julian's amusement abruptly evaporated. "The damned impertinent young puppy!"

She could not help smiling. "Julian, Peter is twenty! Only nine years younger than you."

"The devil he is!" A faint bitterness underlaid the aston-

156

ishment in Julian's voice. "I was forgetting that. Probably because I feel almost old enough to be his father."

And look almost old enough, too, Serena thought sadly, for had a stranger been invited to guess Julian's age, he would probably have supposed it to be nearer forty than thirty. His hair was completely gray now, and the lines had deepened in the lean, brown face with its arrogant features. His mouth looked stern, and though his eyes were as handsome as ever, it seemed to Serena that the emotions they mirrored were merely on the surface; that beneath amusement or surprise or anger there lay always a bleak and bitter despair.

"What does your father think of Peter Standish's pretensions?" Julian's voice broke in upon her thoughts. "Or does he not know of them?"

"Of course he knows. Peter sought his permission to speak to me. Papa would be glad if I agreed, and for a little while I was afraid he might insist upon it, but he did not. I believe Mama persuaded him against it."

He cast her a comprehending glance. "Your mother is still hoping for that visit to England?"

Serena nodded. "Now more than ever. Mama is anxious for Lucilla to have greater opportunities than offer here, and you must admit, Julian, she is so lovely that it does seem a shame to deny her the chance of making a brilliant marriage."

"Particularly since Lucilla herself is so determined upon it."

There was a sardonic note in his voice which made her look quickly at him. "Don't you believe she could do it?"

"My dear, I don't doubt for a moment that she could do it. Her looks, the dowry your father will give her, and above all, Lucilla's own single-minded ambition, make it inevitable once she is given the opportunity. The only thing which puzzles me is your father's reluctance to indulge her. It is the only time to my knowledge that he has ever denied her anything."

"Yes, but don't you see?" Serena was matter of fact, for it had long since ceased to trouble her that Lucilla was their parents' favorite. "If we went on a visit to England and Lucy did make this brilliant marriage, she would have to stay there. Papa could not bear to have her so far away."

This was obvious, now that Serena pointed it out to him, and Julian was selfish enough to be thankful for it. The Loring household was his sanctuary now even more than it had been during his first bewildered days in Jamaica; a haven of peace and normality to which he could retreat when life at Verwood's Kingdom became unendurable. He was accepted here without comment as a member of the family, and if they wondered, as they surely must, why he never spoke of his wife and child except to give the most brief and formal replies to inquiries after them, they never questioned him. He could relax a little here, take part in the ordinary events and contacts of everyday life, and so gather enough strength to take up again his almost intolerable burden.

For during the past dreadful year Julian had found the answer to the agonized question he had asked himself on the night he learned the truth about Alathea. He did not love her and their child enough. Not as Jethro Verwood had loved his doomed, demented womenfolk. Not enough to accept without resentment or rebellion the sacrifice he was called upon to make, the sacrifice of his freedom and any hope of happiness.

Perhaps for Verwood it had been different; he had been an older, experienced, much-traveled man, a scholar who could find in his books some solace for the lonely life he was compelled to lead. Julian had no such consolation. He was a young man still, a man whose inclinations had always led him towards a life of action but who now found himself condemned by duty to a future of virtual imprisonment upon his remote plantation.

Imprisonment which had to be shared with a madwoman. Alathea had only fleeting moments of sanity now, and though she was still allowed the freedom of house and garden, Julian knew with dread that the time was approaching when she would have to be more closely confined. Even now she had to be constantly watched and guarded, and he remembered with fury and despair the golden goddess on the great gray horse, flying through the cane fields with bright hair streaming.

Her physical beauty was as yet scarcely impaired. Her women kept her as richly gowned and jeweled as she had been when he first saw her, and as often as she disordered her garments or her hair, these were lovingly and patiently restored, but the only feeling she aroused in Julian now was pity. The golden loveliness was no more than a shell, as meaningless to him as he now was to her. The phantoms of her madness were more real to her than the living people about

158

her—with one exception. Mehitabel she still knew, and clung to as she had no doubt clung in childhood; and Mehitabel alone could control her. No matter how wild Alathea's behavior, how lost she was to all reality, the aged Negress seemed able to communicate with her. When Julian was obliged to exert all his strength to restrain his wife by force, Mehitabel would grip her hands and look into her eyes and murmur to her in a strange tongue; and Alathea would become docile, and let her one-time nurse lead her away to her room, where she would stay peaceably for hours with only the old slave-woman beside her. Julian accepted this with relief, but also with misgiving. Mehitabel was invaluable, but she was old, incredibly old, and what would become of Alathea when Mehitabel died? And of Anabel, still a happy, normal infant but bearing the dread seed of madness within her? Julian felt for his little daughter a despairing tenderness mingled with savage regret that she had ever been born. He loved the child but could see her only as one more link in the chains which bound him.

Serena, watching him, saw that he had forgotten their conversation and retreated into one of the dark moods of introspection which so often seemed to take possession of him, but she dare not, as she would once have done, try to win him out of it. Too many dangers lay along that road.

For Serena, too, had learned some hard lessons during the past year. Her resolution had not faltered, but it had cost her part of the small consolation she had depended upon—the consolation of her comradeship with Julian. To keep her secret, she had been obliged to withdraw a little, to deny herself the old, spontaneous gestures of affection and the impulsive confidences of earlier years. To hold aloof, when every instinct was urging her to offer whatever comfort she could to his wretchedness and torment.

The strength of her love for him frightened her a little, and so did the darker passions which seemed inseparable from it. The jealousy, almost hatred, she felt for Alathea; the fierce, secret rebellion against the circumstances which condemned both Julian and herself to suffer; the almost overpowering desire to cast discretion aside and tell him what she really felt, reckless of where such a declaration might lead. If he wanted her, she often thought with exultation and shame, no consideration on earth would keep her from him.

Yet no hint of these tumultuous emotions was visible now in her face, except in the expressive gray eyes as she watched him, and since he was not looking at her, he did not read the message so clearly written there. When at last she spoke and he turned towards her, her head was bent and she was engaged in rearranging the little posy of flowers at her breast.

"Did you see Captain Langdale?" she asked, for Julian had just come back from Port Royal. "When does he expect to sail?"

The war with France which had begun in 1756 still dragged on, and Michael Langdale was soon to put to sea on another privateering cruise. He had made several since that first enterprise from which he and Julian had returned on Serena's fifteenth birthday, and though Julian had never accompanied him again, the *Merry Venture,* which in those days had been owned jointly by him and Thaddeus Loring, was now Julian's own property. During the past three months he had spent lavishly on having her rearmed and refitted for her next voyage, so that she was now one of the best-equipped privateers to sail from Port Royal.

"Yes, I saw him. He will put to sea two days from now. Serena"—he turned more fully to face her—"I shall go back to the plantation tomorrow."

"So soon?" She heard the blank dismay in her own voice, and added hurriedly, hoping to disguise it: "Surely you will wait to wish him Godspeed?"

"No," he said shortly, and then, after a tiny pause, added wryly: "The truth is, I dare not! Michael is trying to persuade me to sail with him, and I am so sorely tempted that I had best put myself beyond that temptation before I yield to it."

"Is it really not possible for you to go, if you want to so much?" Perhaps, she thought, a voyage with his friend would dispel some of those haunted shadows from behind his eyes. "You have told me more than once that Mr. Yatton runs the plantation, and you know that Papa would look after any other business for you."

Julian shook his head, crushing down the longing to agree. God! To be away from Jamaica, free for a time from the demon-haunted atmosphere of Verwood's Kingdom, breathing the salty air and knowing once more the simple, uncomplicated challenge of storm or battle. He longed for it as any prisoner longed for liberty, but he knew that even such brief escape as that was beyond his reach. Regret and resentment and black despair might tear him apart, but Alathea was his wife, whom he had sworn before God and man to love and to cherish, and though he no longer loved her—if, indeed, the blind desire which had swept him headlong into his disastrous marriage could be dignified by that name—he could not turn his back upon the duty he owed her. She, poor soul, was entirely innocent, and entitled to his loyalty and protection, if to nothing else.

"It is quite out of the question," he said with finality, "but Michael is very persuasive, and, unless I am mistaken, you are about to add your voice to his. I am not sure I can withstand such an onslaught, and so I shall play the craven and go home in the morning."

In spite of the forced lightness with which he spoke, something in his voice warned her not to pursue the subject. After a pause, she asked in a low voice:

"When will you come again?"

"In a week or so, I expect. There are still some matters for me to attend to here, but they must wait now until the *Merry Venture* is safely at sea."

Because of various trifling delays, Julian left Kingston the next day considerably later than he had intended. He was well armed but accompanied only by Ezra, for he had long since dispensed with the sort of escort Jethro Verwood had favored. They maintained a brisk pace, but night had fallen by the time they reached the boundary of Verwood's Kingdom and began to cross the cane fields towards the house.

Rising out of the darkness before them, this showed no light in all its spreading bulk, though since all the rooms faced inward to the piazza and the garden, this was in no way remarkable. Neither was the fact that the two ornate lanterns flanking the great double doors were unlit, for the master of the house had not been expected home and no visitor ever came there. Julian reined in and beckoned Ezra up to him.

"We will go straight to the stables," he told him, "and go in that way. No need to rouse the whole house."

In the moonlight he saw Ezra roll his eyes uneasily towards the dark building, and as they rode on, it occurred to Julian that the man had seemed ill at ease ever since they left Kingston. Then they turned the last corner of the house, and a sound of which for some time he had been vaguely

161

aware suddenly increased in volume, jerking his mind into full awareness of it. The throbbing of drums from somewhere beyond the slave cabins. He had heard such drumming many times before, but always from within the house, so that the sound was blurred and muffled by the thick stone walls. Now, hearing it plainly for the first time, he found the primeval rhythm deeply disturbing.

Ira Yatton had told him that this drumming, and the dancing which accompanied it, was permitted by Mr. Verwood because he held the somewhat unorthodox view that the slaves worked more willingly if they were allowed to amuse themselves in their own fashion when the day's labor was over. Julian had never questioned this, just as he had never tried to interfere in the working of the fields, but now, feeling the savage rhythm of the drums vibrate along his nerves, he doubted for a moment the wisdom of Verwood's belief.

In the yard between the stables and the house, they dismounted, and Julian, leaving Ezra to summon a groom to attend to the horses, went to the door giving onto the passage which traversed the domestic wing. His hand was already outstretched towards the bell chain hanging beside it when he realized the door itself was standing wide.

Angry and a little uneasy, for all the house slaves were well aware that no outer door must ever be left open and unguarded, he went quickly along the dimly-lit passage. Everything was silent as he crossed the garden, and he trod softly along the piazza to his wife's room and very quietly opened the door, wondering, with the sick apprehension he always felt on returning home after an absence, in what state he would find her. Many candles burned there, as her terrors demanded they did from dusk till dawn, and these showed him that the bed was empty, its sheets and pillows smooth and unruffled. The truckle bed on which Mehitabel slept was untouched, too, and somehow the deserted, lighted room struck him with a sudden sense of foreboding.

Snatching up a branch of candles, he went quickly, and with no regard now for quietness, to the library and then to the other living rooms, but all were empty and dark. With deepening disquiet he hurried next to the nursery, for there, at least, he was bound to find Rachel and the child. A dim light burned there; Anabel slept soundly in her narrow bed, while on a stool beside her crouched, not Rachel, but a black girl-child about twelve years old.

She had heard his footsteps echoing along the piazza, and when he came in was staring, terror-stricken, towards the door. The sight of him did not seem to reassure her. Her mouth gaped open, her eyes rolled frantically as though in search of escape, and as he approached she cowered back with upflung arm in expectation of a blow.

"What are you doing here?" Julian kept his voice low for fear of waking Anabel, but his anger and alarm sounded fiercely in it. "Where is Rachel? Mehitabel?"

The girl's lips moved but no sound emerged. She was incapable of speech or even of coherent thought, and, when he gripped her by the shoulder and shook her, only whimpered like a frightened animal. With an exasperated exclamation he let her go and strode out again onto the piazza.

The stillness of the house was all about him, and he knew, with a certainty which admitted of no doubt, that he and the little black girl and the sleeping child were its only occupants. It was deserted, an empty shell. The house slaves, like the field hands, had answered the throbbing summons of the drums, but where was Alathea?

Fury and fear were rising together in him. Fury at the slaves for abandoning their duty, and fear of what might have befallen the mistress they had deserted. Had she wandered out by way of that carelessly unbarred door, and if she had, where might she not be by now? Out in the cane fields, fleeing before the phantom furies of her madness, or swallowed up already by the dark jungle which waited beyond the borders of the cultivated land?

To go in search of her alone would be worse than useless. He hastened back through the echoing silence of the house, out across the stableyard and along the track which led to the village of slave cabins. Here, too, all seemed deserted, and if any of the occupants remained there, they were staying out of sight within their huts. The track ended there, and beyond the last row of cabins and their little gardens lay a rough meadow across which passing feet had worn a narrow path which straggled towards a grove of trees where torch or firelight flickered, and from whence spoke the pounding voices of the drums.

The grove was the largest of several clumps of trees which had been left standing near the house when the land was originally cleared, but Julian had never before had occasion to enter it. The lights flared red among the leaves, and the pulsing urgency of the drums reached out to engulf him; it possessed the night, so that the very air throbbed and quivered with its savage message; it was no longer an external sound, it beat in his brain, in his blood, dazing him and drawing him on.

In the midst of the grove an open space had been made, lit now by torches tied to poles stuck in the ground, from a mound in the middle of which reared up a single tree larger than all the rest, a forest giant which must have been old before the Spaniards came. On either side of this the drummers squatted, the great drums gripped between their knees, and between them, at the very foot of the tree, stood a barbaric figure which for a moment Julian had difficulty in recognizing as Mehitabel. Gone was the neat green gown and white apron, and in its place she wore a long white robe and countless strings of beads, while with one upraised hand she shook a sort of rattle formed from a gourd decorated with beads and tiny bones; her head was thrown back, and her wrinkled face, uplifted in the flickering torchlight, was rapt with a sort of ecstasy. Clearly she was presiding over whatever primitive rite was being performed, and the spark of something savage and untamed which smoldered always within her now burned fierce and strong, so that there emanated from her a strange sense of malevolent power.

All around her, lit by the encircling torches, was a scene which might well have served for a medieval vision of hell. The field hands usually went all but naked, and tonight the house slaves, too, had abandoned the trappings of civilization, so that the red light gleamed on black bodies and lithe limbs swaying and gyrating to the pounding of the drums, whirling insanely or coming together in unbridled lust. It was a strange and fearful glimpse into another world, another time, and for a minute or two Julian forgot even his anxiety and his anger as he stood, hidden in the shadows of the trees, repelled yet fascinated by what he saw. Then a shift in the writhing, stamping figures gave him a plainer view towards the center of the clearing, and with a rush of horrified disbelief he saw, among the swaying ebony figures at the foot of the tree, the ruddy torchlight flaring on white flesh and streaming hair of living gold.

The shock was so great that for an instant the whole scene spun and wavered before his eyes while nausea rose scalding in his throat. Then weakness ebbed and white-hot fury took its place. His pistols he had left for Ezra to carry into the house, but the sword he had put on for the journey was still at his side, and, dragging it from the scabbard, he took a step forward into the clearing.

One step, and no more, for even as he moved, strong arms seized him from behind, a hand was clapped over his mouth and Ira Yatton's voice spoke urgently in his ear.

"Mr. Severn! For the love of Christ, sir, no!"

He was dragged back among the trees, the sword dropping from his hand as he fought furiously to free himself. He sensed that two men were trying to overpower him, but with the strength of madness he wrenched himself away. He spun round to face his assailants, his spurred heel caught in a tree root, he felt himself falling and then his head struck something with stunning force and he plunged into total oblivion.

Consciousness returned painfully, with giddiness and throbbing head. He lay upon cushions, and someone was holding a wet cloth to his brow. He opened his eyes to candlelight too bright to be borne, hurriedly closed them again and tried to recall what had happened to him.

Memory returned all too soon. He opened his eyes once more, found the overseer's anxious face bending over him, and said weakly:

"Damn you, Yatton! Who in hell's name gave you the right to manhandle me?"

The other man shook his head. "I'm sorry for that, sir, and sorrier still you knocked yourself senseless, but I had to stop you. As well toss a lighted candle into a keg of gunpowder as go among the blacks when they've whipped themselves into that sort of frenzy. They'd have torn you to pieces."

Julian looked past Yatton and found that he was lying on Alathea's daybed in the drawing room of the plantation house. Alathea! The memory of what he had seen in the clearing rushed back at him. Had Yatton seen her, too? He looked at the man's face, met his eyes and knew that he had.

"What brought *you* there?" Anything to delay admitting what they both knew.

"Ezra. When he heard the drumming he knew you'd find none of the house slaves here and was afraid you would go looking for them. I was on my way here to warn you when I saw you crossing the meadow."

Julian tried to sit up, managed it, with Yatton's help,

swung his feet to the floor and rested his head on his hands. The room was spinning round him and he felt sick again.

He heard Yatton go out of the room, but between physical discomfort and mental agony was beyond caring why. Minutes passed. The overseer returned, bringing him a glass of brandy. The spirit helped to steady him, and he began to wonder how he came to be in the house.

"You did not carry me here on your own?"

"No, sir, my son Benjamin was with me. I sent him home once we had brought you here." A pause, then, meaningly: "You can trust him, Mr. Severn."

Trust him to say nothing of what he, too, must have seen in the clearing. Inwardly writhing, Julian forced himself to ask:

"Did *you* know that sort of obscenity was being practiced here? Obeah—that's what they call it, isn't it?"

"Yes, sir, in Jamaica. In other parts it's known as voodoo."

"Call it what you like, it is still a heathen abomination! And you have not answered my question."

"Yes, Mr. Severn, I knew," the overseer admitted uncomfortably, "but there was nothing *I* could do to stop it. Even Mr. Jethro couldn't—or wouldn't!"

"*He* knew?"

Yatton nodded unhappily. "It's been going on a long time, sir. Ever since he married Miss Anabel." He hesitated and then added hurriedly, as though anxious to have it said before his courage failed him, "But I'd stake my life he never suspected *Miss Thea* would ever—!"

Involuntarily Julian shut his eyes, and the scene in the grove flared again behind his closed lids. Alathea, naked among the naked slaves, abandoning herself to their disgusting rites. Mehitabel, priestess of the horrible cult, triumphant beneath the great tree, flanked by the drummers in the smoky torchlight. Mehitabel! Was this how, through long years of slavery, she had taken her revenge? Trust Mehitabel! Merciful God, if Verwood had only known!

"That damned hell-hag!" Julian sprang to his feet but the floor seemed to slip sideways beneath him, and only Yatton's quickness saved him from falling. He allowed himself to be lowered to the daybed again, but continued no less forcefully: "This is all her doing! By God, I'll have her hanged!"

He fell back against the cushions, willing his surroundings

to stop spinning dizzily before his eyes. When they had and he could see more clearly, he found that his companion looked profoundly uneasy.

"By your leave, sir, that's more than we dare do! Hang Mehitabel, and the slaves will rise. They outnumber us by more than ten to one, and we'd all be wiped out before anyone outside the plantation knew what was happening. It might even start a rising that would set the whole island ablaze."

Reluctantly Julian acknowledged the truth of this. The fear of a servile uprising was a nightmare which haunted every West Indian colony; it was the reason why the big plantation houses were as solid as castles, and why the smallest rebellion by a slave was punished with immediate and brutal severity. He said angrily:

"You expect me to let the old witch live?"

"I don't think you have any choice, sir! To do anything else would be to sign all our death warrants—and we have *our* families to think of, too, Mr. Severn."

It was true. Jethro Verwood had bequeathed responsibilities and obligations as well as his great fortune, and Julian knew he could not endanger the lives of loyal servants out of a blind desire to avenge his own betrayal. He bowed his aching head on his hands again.

"Go home, Yatton," he said wearily. "My thanks for your help, but leave me now."

Yatton hesitated, studying him with anxiety and doubt.

"Let me help you to bed first, sir."

"No, I'll rest here for a time. Do as I bid you—and my thanks once more."

He lay back again upon the heaped-up cushions and closed his eyes. The overseer lingered for a few moments, worriedly watching him, then extinguished all but one of the candles and went quietly away.

Julian heard his footsteps receding, and after that there was no sound but the distant throbbing of the voodoo drums. The scene he had witnessed in the grove was as vivid in his mind as though he still stood watching it, and the same sick revulsion had him in its grip. Hideous specters mocked him while horrifying questions screamed in his mind. When had Mehitabel first drawn her charge into the power of her devil's cult? Was this the first time Alathea had taken part in those bestial rites, or had she—God forbid!—been already abandoned to them when he married her? What now of the hapless, helpless innocent out of duty to whom he had been prepared to sacrifice his entire future?

He pressed his hands to his temples, for a savage pain was beating now behind his eyes. The walls of the room seemed to be closing in upon him, and beyond them was the house, turning its blind, blank face to the outside world, looking always inward upon itself and upon the terrible secrets it concealed. He felt as though he were entombed within it, buried and stifling like a prisoner in some forgotten dungeon; and all the while the drums beat on and on.

It was unendurable. He had to get away. He could not bear to look at Alathea, even to be near her, after what he had just seen; could not encounter Mehitabel without giving way to the murderous hatred he now felt towards her. If she came within his reach, he knew he would kill her.

He dragged himself up and, staggering a little but driven by an overmastering need, took up the candle and went along the piazza to his room. His pistols and saddlebags lay on the bed where Ezra had dropped them before hurrying to summon Ira Yatton. Julian picked them up—the sword he had dropped in the grove had been restored to its scabbard and still hung at his side—and went out across the garden and through the stables.

Ezra must have returned and attended to the horses they had ridden from Kingston, for these were back in their stalls, but he was now nowhere to be seen. Julian saddled a fresh mount and before long was riding again through the cane-fields, back the way he had come an hour or two earlier.

Throughout the night he rode, guided by instinct and driven by the demon of memory. Day broke, blinding him with its brilliance, seeming to stab at his eyes with white-hot daggers, so that he rode blindly in a daze of pain, scarcely knowing what road he followed. Only when he found himself at last on the waterfront at Port Royal and saw in the harbor the bustle of departure around the *Merry Venture*, did he know why he had come.

He summoned one idler to take his horse to the nearest inn, and another to row him out to the ship. Michael Langdale, who had seen the approaching boat and recognized its passenger, met him as he came aboard.

"What the devil brings you here?" he greeted him cheerily. "I thought you were going home yesterday." He broke off as he noticed for the first time his friend's haggard look, the livid pallor and unnaturally bright eyes, and then added in a quite different tone: "Julian, what in God's name is wrong?"

With an enormous effort Julian focused his gaze on Michael's face, which seemed to be advancing and receding in a disconcerting way in the midst of a swirling mist. He said, enunciating the words with the utmost care:

"I am coming with you," and pitched forward, unconscious, onto the scrubbed planking of the deck.

Book Three

SERENA

I

It was more than four months before the *Merry Venture* made landfall again at Jamaica. When she had come to her anchorage and while the business of unloading her cargo got under way, her captain stood anxiously scanning the harbor. Surely Thaddeus Loring would come? To be sure, he was no longer owner of the ship, but after the manner of Julian's departure, described by Langdale in the hasty, scribbled note he had sent ashore just before weighing anchor, word would have been sent to him of her return?

At last, among the small craft of all descriptions which dotted the harbor between the larger vessels, Michael caught sight of one bearing the man he was hoping to see—and not Thaddeus Loring alone. There was a woman beside him, and as the boat drew nearer, Langdale recognized Serena. She was in riding dress. That meant they had come in haste....

He was waiting to greet them when they came aboard, and after the barest civilities had been exchanged, Serena asked the anxious question he was expecting.

"Captain Langdale, where is Julian?"

"He is below, ma'am. I will take you to him." Michael hesitated for a moment. "To tell truth, Miss Loring, I am exceedingly glad you have come. Julian was wounded in our last brush with the French—no, not seriously," he added quickly as alarm leapt into her eyes, "but he does not mend as he should. I am worried about him, and feel that he ought to stay in Kingston for a time rather than go back to that remote plantation. Perhaps you will be able to persuade him."

"I do not know." Her troubled gaze met his frankly. "Something has happened—! Captain, *why* did Julian decide so suddenly to go with you?"

"I wish I knew." Langdale's worried glance went from her to her father. "He came aboard just as we were about to weigh anchor—half out of his mind, or so it seemed to me—and insisted upon sailing with us. What could I do? He is not only my friend, he is the owner of my ship, and I could not turn him off her. All I could do was to send you a message, for I'd a suspicion he'd said nothing to anyone."

"No," Thaddeus agreed rather grimly, "he had not. His overseer came looking for him later that day."

"Some devil is riding him," Michael said with conviction, "and has been for a long time." He paused, looked from one pale, strained face to the other, and added, stating an obvious fact: "Now you bring him bad news?"

"The worst," Serena agreed in a low voice. "Captain Langdale—?"

"Of course, ma'am! Forgive me. I will take you to him."

Julian was in the main cabin, half sitting, half lying on the cushioned seat below the big, sloping windows astern. He was in shirt and breeches, the shirt open to the waist and draped awkwardly over his left arm which, swathed from wrist to shoulder in bandages, rested in a sling. Thin to the point of gauntness, his face lined with pain and with the telltale flush of fever along the cheekbones, he turned his head listlessly to see who entered.

"Serena!" Slight animation returned to his face and he rose unsteadily to his feet, but she went quickly forward and pressed him gently back onto the seat.

"Don't get up, Julian!" She forced herself to speak calmly, dissembling her dismay at seeing him look so ill, resisting an almost overmastering desire to put her arms around him. "I am sorry to find you like this."

He smiled faintly and gripped her hand but made no reply. Thaddeus, still by the door, said quietly to Langdale:

"I think you had better stay, captain. He will have need of his friends." He went forward without waiting for a reply

174

and held out his hand to Julian. "We are glad to see you safely home."

Julian released Serena's hand to grasp her father's. "It's good to see you, Thaddeus—and good of you both to come so speedily to greet me. Or"—with a forced attempt at lightness—"is it to take me to task for the manner of my departure?"

"No doubt you had some good reason for that." Loring's voice was strained, and he glanced uneasily at his daughter. "Julian, I fear we bring bad news."

"Bad news?" Julian's voice sharpened. "Why, what has happened?" Loring hesitated, searching for words, and he added urgently: "Thaddeus, what is it?"

"Would to God there were some way—some kindlier way—of breaking it to you," Loring said pityingly, "but I can find none. My dear boy, I have to tell you that your wife, and your child, are both dead."

Serena, her anxious gaze fixed on Julian's face, saw him take the news like a physical blow. Saw the stunned disbelief slowly give way to rising horror and heard him say hoarsely:

"How?"

"It happened more than six weeks ago." Her father was trying to evade the question, but she knew that he was, at best, merely delaying the need to answer it. "Ira Yatton brought us the news—there was nothing we could do...."

"How did it happen?" Julian was on his feet again, swaying, speaking harshly: "In God's name, Thaddeus, what are you trying to keep from me?"

Serena stepped forward past her father and took Julian's sound hand in both her own, gripping it hard, pressed against her breast. Looking up into his eyes, holding his gaze with her own, she said in a low voice:

"Julian, Alathea killed herself and Anabel. She smothered the little one and then cut her own throat."

Julian's fingers closed convulsively on hers. That, and the steady, compassionate gaze of the gray eyes, were his only protection, the only thing which saved him from plunging headlong into the roaring chaos which had suddenly engulfed the world. He was unaware that he reeled, that both Thaddeus and Michael started forward to steady him or that they guided him back to the seat. It was Serena alone who supported him, who enabled him to retain some contact with reality.

175

Someone thrust a glass against his lips; he tried to protest, and in doing so, swallowed a generous portion of the brandy it contained. It made him choke, but after a few moments the darkness ebbed away and his surroundings swam back into focus. He was sitting on the locker again, and now Serena was seated beside him, half turned towards him, his hand still held fast between her own. Her father and Michael Langdale stood nearby, and in the faces of all three, in the pity and the sorrow he read there, was confirmation of the terrible thing Serena had told him. He uttered a groan and slumped forward, burying his face against her shoulder.

Above his bowed figure Serena's eyes signaled a clear message to her companions, and in obedience to it they went quietly out of the cabin. There was nothing more they could do. If any comfort at all could be given, it would have to come from her.

"Julian!" Now she could yield to the longing to hold him close, to smoothe the thick hair which, even after these few short months, had lightened from iron-gray to silver. "Julian, no one else knows how they died. No one outside the plantation, and Mr. Yatton will make sure that the truth is never betrayed from there. We let it be thought that a fever took them." A long shudder shook him, and she added, still softly but with a little more insistence: "My dear, do you understand me? No one need ever know what really happened."

"*I* know!" The words seemed wrung from him, anguished as the confession of a man upon the rack. "And I know that I am to blame. May God forgive me, for I shall never forgive myself!"

This was what Serena had most feared. Whatever the reason for Julian's abrupt departure, that departure which savored almost of flight, and whatever the true state of affairs between him and Alathea, she felt certain that he would hold himself responsible for the terrible tragedy which had occurred in his absence. She had tried to think of some way to comfort him, but being ignorant of the circumstances, was afraid to try in case she unwittingly made matters worse. Now, too, another thought was prodding at her mind. He had asked *how* his wife and child had died, but, when the dreadful truth was told, he had not once asked, "Why?" Could he guess, then, what last resort of terror or despair had driven Alathea to such an act?

"I must go back!" He dragged himself upright again and

looked at her with haggard eyes. "I will come ashore with you now, and—!"

"No!" Serena spoke gently but very firmly, for here, at least, she was sure of her ground. "You will come ashore, but you are coming home with us. You are not well enough to travel all the way to the plantation." He shook his head, and she added compassionately: "Oh, my dear, there is nothing that you can do there."

He was too ill, and too shattered by the news she had given him, to offer much argument. It was a relief, in a way, not to have to make any decisions, take any action, have anything to distract him from contemplation of the awful burden of guilt which weighed upon him. He was scarcely aware of the journey to Kingston, alone with Serena in a hired carriage, for Mr. Loring had ridden ahead to warn his household to expect a sick man. Margaret greeted Julian with tears in her eyes; his old room had been made ready; and big Samuel, his broad black face creased with sympathy, was waiting to help him to bed. He was dimly aware of all these things, but they seemed to be happening to someone else; his only reality was the physical pain which for many days had been his constant companion, and now the bleak horror of what had happened at Verwood's Kingdom.

The wound in his arm, just above the elbow, had been caused by a flying fragment of wood when a shot from the French ship crashed into the timbers of the *Merry Venture*. It was not serious in itself, but the torn flesh had become infected and now was foul and suppurating, the arm swollen and inflamed for the whole of its length. The surgeon who dressed it looked grave, and spoke of the possibility of amputation, only to find himself confronted by a pale, determined, gray-eyed young woman who would admit no such possibility and demanded to be shown what must be done to avert it. He told her, privately doubting both her ability and her fortitude but soon learning that he had underestimated her.

By nightfall Julian was in a raging fever. It had been agreed that one of the female slaves would tend him during the night, but when Serena went to his room about ten o'clock and heard him muttering in delirium, she sent the woman away and took her place. This naturally brought Mrs. Loring in to remonstrate with her; Serena listened patiently and then shook her head.

177

"Mama, we *must* nurse Julian ourselves until his fever breaks. He is delirious, speaking of Alathea and—and what happened at the plantation. Our girls are trustworthy up to a point, but you know how they love to gossip. We dare not take the risk of them finding out."

Margaret listened for a moment or two to the broken mutterings from the shadows of the bed, and realized that her daughter was right. It needed a little more persuasion to convince her that it would be best if Serena took her share of the nursing during the night, but she yielded in the end and went reluctantly away.

Julian was aware of neither the argument nor its outcome, nor even of Serena's presence. He was lost in a fever-nightmare where drums throbbed and torches flared and Mehitabel's wrinkled face, lit with malevolent glee, peered through the drifting smoke; where Alathea stood before him all ivory and gold, with blood-red jewels at her throat which, the next moment, had become a gaping wound from which her lifeblood flowed in a scarlet tide. One minute he was aboard the *Merry Venture,* at grips with a French ship, and the next in the silent, secretive house among the cane fields, hearing his wife's demented screams echoing down the long piazzas.

Throughout the night Serena tended him, cleaning and dressing the festering wound, bathing his face, giving him water when he begged for it and listening with pity and with horror to the confused mutterings which made so little sense and yet hinted at the dark and terrible secret of Verwood's Kingdom. Through it all ran one constant thread, a theme of rebellion and guilt and desperate remorse, an echo of that anguished cry, "I am to blame," with which he had answered her attempt to reassure him. Moved to tears by pity and tenderness, she began to comprehend a little of the burden he had carried for the past few years.

It was three days before the fever abated and before they were certain that his arm could be saved. Serena nursed him almost constantly, driving herself to the limit, able at last to give practical expression to her love for him, allowing nothing to deflect her from her purpose. Only when the crisis was past would she agree to hand over the nursing to Margaret and the maids and take the rest of which by now she stood in desperate need. By the time she saw him again he was in full possession of his senses, and though still very weak, had started along the road to recovery.

"They tell me that I owe you my arm, and possibly my life," he said, looking up at her as she stood beside his bed. "I do not need to tell you, my dear, how grateful I am."

Are you? she thought with a sudden pang, looking into his eyes and seeing there, curbed now and under control but no less desperate, the same pain and guilt and remorse which had echoed through his delirium. Are you not thinking that life now is a burden you would have been thankful to cast aside? Aloud she said, trying for a rallying note:

"If that is so, Julian, you must prove it to me by getting well as fast as you can. There is very little now that *I* can do to help you to recovery."

"But there is," he said in a low voice, and his right hand came out waveringly towards her. "Be with me, Serena, whenever you can. Help me to keep the ghosts at bay. Will you do that?"

"Of course, Julian." She put her hand into his and felt the weak fingers close upon it. "Whenever you need me..."

Serena sat by the window of the drawing room, where Lucilla, under their mother's indulgent chaperonage, was amusing herself by playing off one admirer against another. Lucilla, now seventeen, had more than fulfilled her early promise of beauty, and there were nearly always several besotted youths dallying around her. She treated them abominably, flirting with them one day and frowning on them the next, so that they never knew what she really thought of them. Serena knew. Lucy cared for none of them; she was merely practicing, trying out her powers in preparation for the time when she would use them to attain the place in the world she had always wanted. As Julian had once said, Lucilla was single-minded in her ambition.

Always Serena's thoughts returned to Julian. She was tense with anxiety now because today Ira Yatton had come from Verwood's Kingdom to see him, and she knew that Julian had agreed to the meeting with reluctance and awaited it with dread. Now he would have to face the full horror of the death of his wife and child, hear of it first-hand from the man who must have been one of the first upon the scene when the tragedy was discovered.

She had told the servants to let her know immediately Yatton left Julian's room, and when at last one of them came to her with a soft-voiced message, her heart gave a great lurch of mingled relief and apprehension. She withdrew quietly and hastened to him.

He was strong enough now to leave his bed and sit in an armchair near the window, and it was there that she found him, staring blindly out with eyes which saw nothing of the scene beyond. He did not look round when she entered, but, even in profile, she could see how white and drawn his face was. Going quickly forward, she laid a gentle hand on his shoulder, and his own came up to cover it, gripping her fingers hard.

"Julian!" Suddenly the barriers which had grown between them no longer seemed insuperable; suddenly, because of his need and the wordless cry for help implicit in his grip upon her hand, she could speak of matters which had been forbidden before. "Tell me about Verwood's Kingdom. About Alathea."

He gave a brief, curt shake of his hand, still not looking at her, but she freed her hand and with one swift, graceful movement knelt beside him, sinking in a billow of flower-sprigged silken skirts to the floor beside his chair.

"Julian, look at me! All these years I have turned to you for comfort and understanding, and you have never failed me. Now that *you* are in need, do not shut me out. How can I help to drive away your ghosts, if I do not know what they are?"

Now, at last, he did look at her; really look at her for the first time for years, his gaze searching her upturned face. With a startling sense of discovery he realized that Serena was no longer the dear, defenseless child he had cherished and protected, but a woman whose gentleness was underlaid by a core of quiet strength, and a serenity which matched her name. The bond of affection between them endured, but now they could meet upon equal terms. The tragedy of Verwood's Kingdom might shock and sadden her, but she would face it unafraid.

So at last the story was told, in a low voice and difficult, halting phrases, from the first dazzled moment of setting eyes on Alathea to the disillusion and disgust of seeing her participate in the obeah ceremonies.

"I knew that the poor, crazed creature she had become could not be blamed," he concluded wretchedly. "The horror lay in the thought that this might not be the first time, that she might have been practicing that abomination for years, even before I married her. My wife—sharing those revolting orgies with the slaves. It so sickened me that I could not bear even to be in the same house with her. Somehow I had to escape. So I abandoned her, her and our child, and the blame for their death is mine."

"No!" Serena spoke forcefully. "Julian, that is not true! You did not abandon them. You left them, as you thought, safe and well-guarded in their own home."

"Safe?" he repeated harshly. "In the care of that hell-hag?"

"Mehitabel had looked after Alathea all her life," Serena reminded him, "and her mother and grandmother, too. Mr. Verwood trusted her." She broke off, her eyes widening in dismay as she realized the direction his thoughts were taking. "You do not—you cannot believe that she was responsible for their madness?"

"How can I tell? How could anyone? I only know that those three unfortunate women, mother, daughter and grand-daughter, were in her care from infancy, and all three died insane. That when Verwood first courted Miss Anabel, her grandfather forbade the marriage, and that when he died 'very suddenly,' Mehitabel came with her mistress from poverty to all the luxury Verwood could provide. That, according to Yatton, obeah has been practiced by Verwood's slaves ever since that time." He paused, his somber gaze holding hers. "Are you thinking that I, too, am a little mad? Believe me, Serena, if you had seen the old witch as I did that night, you might share my doubts. She seemed like evil personified."

"I do believe you," she said in a low voice. "I have always been a little afraid of her. Those strange eyes—!" She hesitated, anxiously regarding him. "Julian, what are you going to do? If you try to have her punished, the whole story will come out."

He shook his head. "She is beyond man's punishment now. Mehitabel died peacefully of old age"—there was bitter irony in his voice—"only a few days before Alathea killed herself. That is another reason why I wonder—! She could always control Alathea, even at her most violent. She seemed to have some kind of power over her, and as soon as that power was withdrawn—!" He sighed. "So many questions, Serena, which can never be answered. They buzz in my mind like hornets."

"You have been very ill, Julian," she said gently, racked by pity for him, "and talking to Mr. Yatton has made greater demands upon you than you realize. Try to rest now. You will find it easier to bear these thoughts when you are stronger."

"Will I?" He leaned his head wearily against the cushion behind it. "I wonder?" He reached for her hand again. "I am glad you know the truth, my dear, but those ghosts you spoke of cannot be easily laid to rest. Not even you can do that for me. I alone can vanquish them—if they *can* be vanquished."

"They can!" She was kneeling upright now, facing him, her eyes almost level with his own. "Never doubt that, Julian! Mr. Verwood deceived you but you have kept faith, and you are *not* to blame. It was a terrible and tragic thing, but they are at peace now, Alathea and your little girl. Grieve for them, but do not poison your whole life with needless self-reproach."

He knew that she was right. He also knew that it would not be easy, but somehow Serena's shining faith and courage convinced him that it could be done; that someday the dreadful burden of guilt and remorse which weighed him down would oppress him no longer.

The first, and most difficult, step would be a return to Verwood's Kingdom, but as soon as he was strong enough he steeled himself to take it. The ordeal was even worse than he had anticipated.

The great house, as Ira Yatton had already warned him, stood shuttered and deserted, for the Negroes had fled from it on the day of Alathea's death and refused to return, believing that the duppies, or spirits, of her and her murdered child still dwelt there. It would be impossible to live there again, even had he wished to, but Julian had decided weeks before that he would never do so. Now, lodging in Yatton's house while, with the help of Ira and his family, the plantation mansion was stripped of its books and silver and other articles of value, the thought took shape in his mind that now he would leave Jamaica. Many of the plantations belonged to men who did not live in the colony, and in Yatton he had an ideal deputy.

It was no more than an idle thought at first, but after his return to Kingston, the prospect grew increasingly beguiling. Facile sympathy was expressed for his double bereavement, but he knew that behind it seethed still the curiosity and speculation, the envy and malice which had dogged him ever since his marriage, and he was plagued by a morbid fear that by some accident the whole story might become known. More and more his inclinations were urging him to leave the island; the question which remained unanswered was where to go.

He had no intention of returning to England. Ever since his arrival in Jamaica he had maintained a correspondence with Septimus Twigg, and three years ago he had received news of his father's death. Julian himself was now Viscount Avenhurst, and Mr. Twigg had urged him repeatedly, and in the strongest terms, to return and claim his inheritance, but even if he had been free to do so, Julian knew that he would have refused. He wanted no part in it. As far as he was concerned, Jocelyn Rivers had been dead and buried ever since the day Julian Severn stepped aboard the *Lucilla* in Bristol harbor. Septimus was bound to silence by his parting promise, and since it was known that Lord Avenhurst himself had, until the day of his death, made tireless but unsuccessful efforts to trace his missing son, Jocelyn was eventually presumed to be dead. Now the title and the broad estates had passed to a youthful member of the northern branch of the family.

Not England, then. Europe, perhaps? Make the Grand Tour he had been denied in his boyhood? For a little while the thought intrigued him, but inevitably the question came—what then? A man might spend two or three years, even five, tasting the pleasures of great and famous cities, but a time was bound to come when even traveling would pall. He was thirty now. Youth was behind him, and yet his life seemed to have no more direction or purpose than when he had fled from England as a penniless lad of eighteen. He had the means now to travel anywhere in the world, and he could not even decide where to go.

In the end, chance—or fate—decided for him. Because he could not endure being idle, with too much time to brood, he had taken to going often to Port Royal, to the countinghouse and the warehouses, taking an active part again in the business of Loring and Severn. Thus he made the acquaintance of the master of a ship trading out of Yorktown in Virginia; friendship grew between them, and in the end Julian was persuaded to visit the other colony when his new acquaintance sailed home again.

When he broke the news to Serena, she stifled her own dismay and applauded his decision, for he would never, she thought, come to terms with what had happened as long as he remained in Jamaica. The reminders there were too many and too constant. So she wished him Godspeed with smiling lips and eyes and the ache of tears in her throat, and resigned herself yet again to months of patient waiting.

Julian had fallen in love with the land of Virginia. Arriving at Yorktown, he spent a week there as the guest of his seafaring friend and then moved on to Williamsburg, a dozen miles or so up the James River. Williamsburg was the capital, a pleasant, prosperous town of white-painted or red brick houses set amid fragrant gardens, with a handsome capitol where the Assembly met, an equally handsome residence for the Governor, a fine college and a theatre. Julian took a room at the Raleigh Tavern, and since his friend the captain had numerous acquaintances in the town, he was soon drawn into the social life of the place.

He found the Virginians friendly, generous and amazingly hospitable to the stranger in their midst. They made him welcome, invited him into their homes, both in Williamsburg itself and at the plantations—tobacco, here, instead of sugar—along the river, and the more Julian saw of Virginia, the more he liked it. Jamaica had been to him in turn refuge, paradise and prison, but never had he looked upon it as home. Not, he knew now, as he could come to regard this other colony, this land of forest and mountain where opportunity was as boundless as the land itself, the vast wilderness to westward where the frontier crept slowly forward year by year; where the people were people he would be glad to live among.

His health had improved enormously since leaving Jamaica, and with returning strength came, as Serena had foretold, some lifting of the burden which weighed upon his spirits. The experiences of the past five years had left a mark which would never completely fade, but the ghosts were receding a little. He could grieve for his dead now without the bitterness of guilt, and even begin to contemplate the future. This was a land of the future. Here, God willing, he could start afresh, casting aside old griefs and disappointments; here, perhaps, he could at last find contentment and peace and a real purpose.

He let it be known that he was interested in acquiring a property, and, like a good omen for the future, heard of a plantation, nostalgically named Meadowsweet, which was

184

about to be sold. The owner had recently died, and his child-
less widow intended to sell the estate and come to live with
a bachelor brother in Williamsburg.

Julian went to inspect the property and found that it was
in excellent order and well worth the price which was being
asked, but it was not until he was in the plantation mansion
itself that he finally reached a decision. It was a gracious
house of rose-red brick, its rooms full of light even on this
autumn day, and with a subtle atmosphere about them which
spoke of home. He stood at one of the windows of the white-
and-gold drawing room and looked across wide, tree-scat-
tered lawns that sloped to the broad river; there were many
rose bushes in the garden, with a few late blossoms left to
hint at the glory they must have had in the summer. He was
groping after an elusive sensation of familiarity. He felt that
he recognized this place, even though it was impossible that
he had ever seen it before.

Suddenly it hit him. This was Serena's house, the house
of her childhood dream, almost exactly as she had described
it to him years ago. Memory brought the moment back to
him. He could see again the sweet, serious little face, hear
her voice as she shared with him a precious secret known to
no one else; and Serena cherished that dream still, he was
certain.

A curious excitement gripped him. He would buy Meadowsweet and then go back to Jamaica and tell her that her
dream was a reality; that the house she had longed for existed, was here in Virginia, waiting for its mistress; waiting
for her presence to transform it into a home.

He checked there, stunned by the revelation which had
suddenly dawned upon him. This was the certainty towards
which his whole life had been leading, the knowledge which
should have come long ago; would have come, he realized
now, if his blind infatuation for Alathea had not intervened.
Serena, whose childish trust and affection had filled a void
in his life and rescued him from bitterness and disillusion;
with whom he shared an understanding so complete that it
transcended time and distance and changing fortunes. Serena, a child no longer, but a warm, generous, courageous
woman whom he needed, and wanted, and loved in every
conceivable way. Without whom life was barren and empty
and incomplete.

Filled now with an overmastering sense of urgency, he

plunged into the business of making the plantation his own, buying the slaves along with it and arranging for the white men now in charge of them to remain in his employ. He left the lawyers breathless with the speed and certainty of his decisions, and almost before they could recover, was aboard ship again, Jamaica-bound.

Impatience and anxiety were now his constant companions. What if he came too late? Serena was nearly twenty—*was* twenty now, for her birthday had come and gone while he was in Virginia, and though she had so far shown no inclination to marry, it was just possible that she might have changed her mind. Or Thaddeus might have decided that to have a daughter unmarried at that age reflected unfavorably upon him, and compelled her to accept a proposal from that impertinent puppy Peter Standish.

The voyage seemed endless, and when at last he set foot again on Jamaican soil, he did not linger even to visit the premises of Loring and Severn, but hired a horse and rode headlong to the Loring house at Kingston.

Samuel opened the door to him, surprise and relief chasing each other in quick succession across his face. "Mistuh Severn, suh! Mistus Loring shore be glad to see you home again, suh!"

"Where's Miss Serena, Samuel?" Julian asked, but before the servant could reply a nearby door was flung open and not Serena, but Margaret, came running forward to fling herself into his arms.

"Julian! Oh, thank heaven you are back at last!" She clung to him, almost crying with relief. "I was so afraid you would not come home in time."

"In time for what?" Alarm clutched at him, making him speak more abruptly than he intended. "Margaret, what is it? What is going on?"

"It's Thaddeus!" She choked back her emotion and did her best to speak calmly. "He has been ill, Julian. So dreadfully ill! We all thought he was going to die. He *will* die if he suffers another such attack, and it is certain he will if he stays any longer in this climate. So we are going home, back to England. For good!"

Thaddeus Loring had become an old man. Propped up with cushions in a big armchair, wearing clothes grown too big for his wasted frame, he seemed to have aged ten years in

186

the few months Julian had been away. Shocked and dismayed, Julian went forward to grasp his hand.

"Thank God!" Loring said simply. "I do not know what I would have done, Julian, had you not come home."

"I am only sorry I was not here when I was most needed," Julian said remorsefully. "You have done so much for me, Thaddeus, time and again, that it irks me to know that when I might have done something to repay the debt, I was not here to do it."

"There *is* no debt," Loring replied fretfully, "and it is now that you are needed, my boy! Margaret seems to think we can set out for England on the first ship that sails. She has no conception of what is involved. The sale of this house, the business—I could not make her understand that, since you and I are partners, nothing can be done without consulting you."

"Well, now you *can* consult me," Julian said reassuringly. "In fact, you can leave everything to me. Just let me know what you wish to do. To tell truth, Thaddeus, I have returned to Jamaica only to settle my affairs here. I have bought a property in Virginia, and intend to settle there."

"I am glad to hear that," Loring said unexpectedly. "A new life in a new land! It is what you need, Julian, for Jamaica holds too many sad memories for you ever to find peace of mind here." He paused, his anxious gaze searching the younger man's face. "I wonder, though, whether that makes it more or less difficult for me to ask of you the favor I have in mind."

"Good God, Thaddeus, do not speak of favors! You know that anything in my power I will gladly do for you. What is it?"

"Come with us to England!" Loring's thin hand came out to clutch Julian's sleeve. "Only I know how precarious is my present grip on life, and if I should not survive the voyage, what will become of Margaret and the girls? They know no one in England, for I cut myself off from such relatives as I had there more than thirty years ago. There is Septimus Twigg, of course, but they could not communicate with him until they arrived in England, and to find themselves unprotected in a strange land—!"

"Calm yourself, my friend! Of course I will come with you." A return to England was the last thing he wanted, but it

187

never occurred to him to refuse. "As soon as we can settle our affairs here."

Later, alone in his own room, Julian took stock of the situation. He had not yet seen Serena, for she had gone with Lucilla to some social event which the younger girl had refused to miss but could not attend alone, and now he was not sure what he should say to her. The fact that he had committed himself to returning to England cast a very different light upon the future.

Standing in front of the mirror, he tried to study his reflection dispassionately, to see himself through the eyes of those who had once known Jocelyn Rivers. Would they recognize him, Septimus or Celia or Charlotte? He did not think so. He looked older than his thirty years. His face was lean now, with the arrogant jut of nose and jaw, and the stern line of the lips, robbing it of any semblance of youthfulness, while Jocelyn's pale complexion had been darkened to swarthiness by years of exposure to the tropic sun and the salt sea-winds; and the illness following his last return to Jamaica had left his hair pure white. He did not even resemble his father, having inherited his cast of countenance from his mother's family. Septimus might recognize him on that account, but not, he thought, anyone else.

Yet he could not be sure, and if he *were* recognized, what a furore would ensue. The lost heir of Avenhurst, back from the dead; the younger son who had caused his small nephew's death in order to inherit, and then turned coward and fled from the condemnation his crime provoked. Even if he made no claim to his birthright, the succession would be thrown into confusion, and he might become involved in months or even years of legal wrangling before the matter was settled.

He could not take the risk of exposing Serena to that sort of scandal. If all went well and no one suspected who he was, he would have the right, once the Lorings were established in England, to tell her he loved her and ask her to come with him to Virginia, but until that time he must somehow contrive to behave towards her exactly as he had always done. Somehow!...

It was fortunate for his resolve that when the two girls arrived home, Samuel broke the news of Julian's return as they entered the house, so that Serena, too, had time to command her feelings before they met. This was in the drawing room just before dinner, and outwardly it was no different from any other reunion of recent years. She came to him smiling, with outstretched hands, and he took them in his own and bent to kiss her cheek, so that neither guessed the other was longing for a greeting of a very different kind. Lucilla was there, bubbling over with excited chatter about the proposed removal to England, and so the perilous moment passed.

"Julian is coming to England with us," Thaddeus announced, and Serena sent Julian a look of thankfulness and gratitude, for she, at least, had grave misgivings about her father's fitness to make such a journey.

"To England?" Lucilla spoke from her seat on a low stool by Loring's chair; she sounded surprised and not altogether pleased. "To live?"

"No, not to live." Julian addressed himself, ironically, to Lucilla. It was safer to do that than to look at Serena. "I'm sorry to disappoint you, Lucy, but after I have indulged myself with a brief visit to London, I intend to settle in Virginia. I have bought a tobacco plantation there."

Margaret, to whom this was as much a surprise as it was to her daughters, exclaimed at it, and at once began to question him about his intended home, and even Lucilla displayed some curiosity, but Serena sat with bent head, apparently intent on trying to smooth a small crease from her gown. If she looked up, she thought, her face would most certainly betray her.

She felt suddenly very tired, for during the past few months her emotions had swung constantly from one extreme to the other. There had been the sadness of Julian's departure, followed by the faint beginning of hope, of which at first she was almost ashamed, that now he was free, he might in time turn to her. He recognized at last that she was no longer a child, for he would not have shared with a child the secret of Verwood's Kingdom, and surely it was not possible to love someone as much as she loved him without winning some kind of response.

Then had come her father's sudden, serious illness, the fear that he would not recover and the relief when he did; the decision to remove to England; her dread that they would be gone before Julian returned. Today had brought the overwhelming joy of his homecoming and of the news that he would go to England with them, and now this fresh blow. She scarcely heard what he was telling them about Williamsburg and the country around it, about a plantation called Meadowsweet. All she could think of was that Virginia and England were thousands of miles apart.

After Julian's return the preparations for departure went smoothly forward. The business was disposed of and a purchaser found for the house. Margaret engaged free white servants, a valet for Thaddeus and maids for herself and the girls, and Julian announced his intention of purchasing all the Loring house slaves and sending them north in Michael Langdale's charge to staff the house at Meadowsweet. Samuel's eldest son, Reuben, was already his body-servant in place of Ezra—he wanted no reminder of Verwood's Kingdom—and when the other slaves learned that they were not to be separated, the melancholy which had pervaded their quarters was transformed into rejoicing.

It was a busy time, a period of upheaval with little leisure for any exchange of confidences, but gradually Serena became convinced that Julian did not really want to go to England. There was nothing at which she could point in what he said or did, but she found herself remembering that he had never talked, even to her, of the land of his birth; that he had always turned aside any question, however innocent, about his early life. Now, too, she sensed in him a new reserve, and inevitably, wondered whether this, and his intention to settle in Virginia, had anything to do with someone he had met there.

The possibility completed her sense of desolation. It seemed that everything familiar and beloved was slipping from her grasp along with the life they were leaving, and, unlike her mother and sister, she could find no consolation in anticipating delights to come.

II

The rain which had been threatening London since morning had at last begun gently to fall, silvering the roofs and pattering lightly on the young leaves in the Green Park. People of fashion whom it had caught walking abroad, scattered hastily in search of shelter, but the short, stout, elderly gentleman who was walking slowly along Piccadilly from the direction of Leicester Fields did not quicken his pace. Even though the raindrops darkened the shoulders of his coat of countrified cut and clung glistening to his hat and his brown tie-wig, his footsteps, as he turned left into Arlington Street, slowed even more; almost they seemed to drag.

The fact was that Septimus Twigg, within minutes of the meeting which was the purpose of his present visit to London, found himself increasingly reluctant to arrive at it. He had been overjoyed when Julian's letter arrived, announcing that he, and the Loring family, were in England; he had set out for London immediately, without even writing a reply, but now he was beset by doubts. He remembered so vividly the boy to whom he had said goodbye that now he was afraid to face the changes which the difficult, intervening years must have wrought.

He was within a dozen yards of the house he sought, silently berating himself for cowardice, when a carriage passed him and halted before it. A servant sprang from the box and ran to let down the steps, and then a man alighted and, turning, offered his hand to a lady. His back was towards Mr. Twigg, who could see only that he was very tall, with wide shoulders beneath a perfectly cut coat of dark-blue velvet, his heavily powdered hair confined in a black solitaire, but as his companion emerged from the coach, she paused for a moment on the step, her hand in his, and lifted her face as though enjoying the soft caress of the rain upon it. A young face, with broad brow and wide, grave mouth. Then the man said something in a low voice, and she looked down at him with a smile of startling sweetness. She stepped onto the footway and went quickly into the house.

Mr. Twigg had paused, deciding with craven relief that it would be better to postpone his own visit until no other callers were present, but as the tall man started to follow the girl indoors, he glanced casually towards him, his attention caught by the odd sight of an elderly gentleman standing motionless in rain which was now rapidly increasing to a downpour. Mr. Twigg received a fleeting impression of a lean dark face framed by the powdered hair, and then in an instant the stranger was striding towards him.

"Sep! Septimus Twigg, as I live!" Mr. Twigg's hand was caught in a crushing grip, and he looked up incredulously into familiar dark brown eyes; Julia's eyes. "I had no idea you had arrived in London!"

Utterly bemused, Septimus found himself swept into the house, where, in the hall, the girl had paused to wait for them. Julian, his hand still tightly clasping his godfather's arm, said to her:

"Serena, this is Septimus Twigg, of whom you have heard so much. Miss Loring, Sep."

Mr. Twigg bowed in an abstracted way. Serena curtsied, and gave him her hand and another glimpse of her enchanting smile.

"Yes, indeed! I am happy to meet you, sir, for I have heard you spoken of with warm affection ever since I can remember. Papa will be so happy to see you again at last."

Mr. Twigg pulled himself together. "And I to see him, my dear young lady. I was deeply distressed to learn of his illness."

"Yes, but he has seemed a little stronger just lately, and

192

we hope that now he is in England, his health will continue to improve." She looked from one to the other. "You and Julian will have a great deal to talk about and so I will leave you. I will tell Papa that you are here, sir, and no doubt Julian will bring you to him presently."

She sketched another curtsy and went away up the stairs, while Julian led Mr. Twigg to a parlor at the rear of the house. Closing the door, he turned to face the elder man, gripping him by the shoulders and smiling down into his face.

"Septimus!" he said in a tone of deep satisfaction. "I swear you have scarcely changed at all. A little stouter and more grizzled, but I would have known you anywhere."

Mr. Twigg, returning that searching regard, was unable to say the same, for there was almost nothing left of the boy he remembered in this assured man, his strong, dark features in such striking contrast to the thick, formally-dressed hair which, as Septimus realized with a sense of shock, was not powdered as he had thought, but snow-white. It was the face of a man who had put youth behind him, who had passed through some personal time of trial and had finally come to terms with life and with himself.

"I would not have known *you*, my boy," Septimus confessed sadly, "except, perhaps, by your eyes. Otherwise, you could have passed me by in the street and I would not have recognized you."

"You reassure me, Sep," Julian replied lightly. "That I may be recognized is my constant dread."

Mr. Twigg looked sharply at him, but he had already turned away to a small table where a silver tray bore decanters and glasses. He continued in the same light tone:

"Sit down, Sep, and let us take a glass of wine. Thaddeus will be resting at present—it is his custom for an hour or so before we dine—and it will be a little while before the family is ready to receive you."

Mr. Twigg took the chair he had indicated. "What *is* the state of his health, Julian?"

"I fear it has been permanently impaired. He *is* considerably stronger than when we left Jamaica, but he cannot hope to be anything other than an invalid for the rest of his life."

"A bad business!" Septimus shook his head, and shot a questioning glace at Julian as he accepted a glass of wine. "Does he know that?"

"He knows, and I believe is resigned to it. His health has been deteriorating for years, and I think he is glad to be rid at last of all the responsibilities of business." Julian took up his own glass and raised it, adding quietly: "To you, my friend! It warms my heart to see you again."

"And to you, my boy," Septimus responded. "May the future deal more kindly with you than the past."

Julian inclined his head, his expression enigmatic, but made no other response, and Septimus found himself fighting the feeling of unreality. He had known there would be changes, but this man seemed a total stranger, and the years yawned between them like a gulf too wide to be bridged.

Julian had taken up a position by the fireplace, an elbow on the mantelpiece, one foot in its silver-buckled shoe resting on the hearth. The blue velvet coat hung open over a waistcoat of primrose silk embroidered with silver, and black satin breeches with white silk stockings gartered over them; there was a fall of fine lace at his breast, and half covering the long brown hands. Yet the foppishly elegant garments clothed a powerful frame which looked as though there was not an ounce of superfluous flesh upon it, and which conveyed a disturbing impression of physical toughness. Tempered steel, Mr. Twigg thought suddenly, and decided that, in whatever situation he happened to find himself, Mr. Julian Severn was likely to prove a force to be reckoned with.

"Your letter told me very little," he complained after a pause. "Have you disposed of *all* your interests in Jamaica?"

"All those I held in partnership with Thaddeus. I still own my ship, the *Merry Venture*, and the plantation I inherited from my father-in-law."

He spoke briefly, almost curtly, for though he had learned to live with the past, the shadow of Verwood's Kingdom still had the power to lay a chill finger on his spirit. Septimus assumed that the brusqueness was prompted by the memory of his bereavement, and said gruffly:

"I cannot tell you, my dear boy, how grieved and shocked I was by your letter telling me of your sad loss. To be robbed of both wife and child—!" He broke off, shaking his head. "Tragic! Tragic!"

Julian made no reply. He had told Septimus that Alathea and Anabel had died of fever, for the fewer to know the truth, the better. Only Serena and her parents knew what had really happened; even Lucilla had been kept in ignorance of it.

194

Mr. Twigg, who had reasons other than simple curiosity for wishing to know what Julian's plans were, found his silence daunting. He drank a little more of his wine, and then set the glass down with an air of resolution.

"I have kept faith with you, my boy," he said deliberately. "Since the day of your departure I have denied all knowledge of you. I even forced myself to think of you as Julian Severn. Yet when your father died, I would have given a great deal to be freed from my promise, for I believed—I still believe—that you have both a right and a duty to claim what is yours."

"A right, perhaps!" Julian's voice had hardened. "But what duty, in God's name, do I owe to those who crucified me and cast me out? I have been Julian Severn for twelve years, and intend to remain so until I die."

"But the succession—!"

"The succession is not in dispute. I have been pronounced dead, and Avenhurst has passed to the next heir."

"Yes! To that branch of the family your father hated and despised."

"True! I find in that a certain justice."

"Justice?" Septimus repeated dryly. "Or revenge?"

"That, too, perhaps," Julian conceded calmly, "if one may be revenged upon a dead man, yet even that fails really to move me. The truth is that Avenhurst means nothing to me. That chapter of my life is long since closed."

"Yet you have come back to England."

"I came because Thaddeus asked it of me. That is where my duty lies, Sep, as well as my affection. With Thaddeus and his family, who over the years have come to mean far more to me than my own kin ever did."

"And have you no duty to yourself?"

"If I have, it does not prompt me to stir up a hornets' nest of scandal for the sake of a fortune I do not need and a title I do not want. I shall remain in England as long as Thaddeus and Margaret need me, but as soon as they are comfortably established—well, there is a home waiting for me in Virginia. It is a land I have come to love, and its people are those among whom I shall be happy to spend the rest of my days."

Briefly he recounted his visit to Williamsburg and his purchase of Meadowsweet, and as he talked, Mr. Twigg was visited (he thought) by a revelation. There was something about the way Julian was speaking, about the way he looked—! Of course, Septimus thought triumphantly. While

195

he was in Virginia Julian had found a woman he could love, who could fill the void left in his life by the death of his wife and little daughter. That was why he did not intend to remain in England.

It was enough. Not for the world would Septimus have sought to deny Julian a chance of happiness, so, not knowing that his assumption was only partly correct, he abandoned the subject of Avenhurst and inquired instead about the Lorings' future plans.

"For the present they are my guests—I have hired this house for three months—but Thaddeus intends to purchase a small estate. I cannot in conscience abandon him until the matter is concluded, but the devil of it is that he has no idea yet in which part of the country he wishes to live. That depends on Lucilla."

"Lucilla?" Mr. Twigg was puzzled. "The younger daughter?"

"Upon whom she marries. Thaddeus and Margaret so dote upon her that they will not consider acquiring a house until they know in which part of the country her home will be after she is married. Therefore, to find a husband for Lucilla is a matter of paramount importance."

"Will that be so difficult? Is she nothing like her sister?"

"No," Julian stated unequivocally. "Lucilla is exceedingly beautiful, and can be captivating, but she is also spoiled and utterly selfish, with a single-minded determination to become a great lady."

"Well, as long as she is clever enough to disguise her less admirable characteristics, she should do well enough," Septimus remarked with unexpected cynicism. "Presumably Loring can afford to dower his daughters respectably?"

"Say 'handsomely' and you will come nearer to the mark. They are also joint heiresses to everything he owns. There is one difficulty, though. Both Lucilla and her mother are determined upon a title for her, and that, when one lacks the entrée to polite society, is almost impossible to achieve."

Mr. Twigg nodded his comprehension, but said modestly that perhaps he could be of assistance in that respect.

Julian grinned at him. "Sep, you astonish me! You were not used to be a leader of fashion."

"Nor am I now, confound your impudence!" Septimus retorted good-humoredly. "It has plainly escaped your memory, however, that I am related to someone who is. My cousin, Augusta Selford."

"Old Lady Selford?" Julian said incredulously. "Never tell me that *she* is still a force to be reckoned with?"

Septimus laughed. "The world will be obliged to reckon with Augusta to her dying day, and probably beyond."

"That I can believe. I saw her only once in my life, when I was about ten years old. She scared me out of my wits, but I have never forgotten her."

"Very few people do forget Augusta, and none disregard her. If she will lend countenance to the young ladies, every door will open to them."

Julian's brows lifted. "Is there any reason why she should?"

"She has a kindness for me," Mr. Twigg replied mildly. "I believe I am the only relation with whom she has not quarreled. I'll call upon her tomorrow."

"That's good of you, Sep, but in the name of pity say nothing to the Lorings until her ladyship has consented, for Lucilla is already mightily put out that she has been in London more than a week and not yet penetrated the world of fashion. She has been noticed, of course, but that is not at all the same thing." He glanced at the clock. "Come, let us go up to the drawing room. Loring should be there by now."

Mr. Twigg's visit to Lady Selford achieved its purpose, even if it was not an unqualified success from his own point of view, since her ladyship, being thus apprised of his presence in town, first took him to task for what she called his antiquated appearance, and then bullied him out of his comfortable little inn to become a guest in her own imposing mansion in Hanover Square. This was not at all to Mr. Twigg's taste, but at least he had the satisfaction of sending a note round to Arlington Street informing Julian that her ladyship had consented to call there the following afternoon. It might be as well, he added cautiously, to impress Mrs. Loring and the young ladies with the importance of winning her approval.

Augusta Selford, arriving with Septimus in attendance, was certainly an impressive figure. Though nearly eighty, she was still active and erect, a tall, thin old lady with the face of an aristocratic bird of prey. An elaborate powdered wig, surmounted by a lace cap and a black silk hood, framed her patched and painted features; her gown of rich violet silk spread over an enormously wide hoop; her wrap was lined with sable and her hands thrust into a large sable muff. When Julian came forward to welcome her, she raised a lorgnette and studied him with shrewd, faded eyes, approving his height and bearing, the quiet elegance of his suit of fine mulberry-colored cloth, the arresting quality of his lean brown face and pure white hair. Augusta Selford, as she would have been the first to admit, still had an eye for a personable man.

Julian was given a gnarled, jeweled hand to kiss, and permitted to lead her ladyship to a chair and to present his good friends, the Lorings. Lady Selford was pleased to be gracious. She sympathized with Thaddeus over his ill-health, instructed him which physicians to consult and prescribed one or two infallible remedies of her own; complimented Margaret on the charming appearance of her daughters and had a few kind words for the girls themselves. Then, having held court for approximately half an hour, she departed, promising to send cards for a rout party which she was giving two days later.

Mr. Twigg, who in spite of his confident words to Julian, had not been altogether certain of the outcome, was delighted by his autocratic relative's reaction. Her approval of his friends was further confirmed as they drove away from Arlington Street in her ladyship's luxurious town carriage.

"I agree with you, Septimus. They are unexceptionable, even though they do come from the colonies. Those girls should have no difficulty in establishing themselves. I like the elder sister. There's rare quality there. The younger is a designing baggage, but with that face and figure and a handsome marriage-portion, she will be able to call herself 'my lady' soon enough. Let her but make her curtsy to society and she will become the rage of London."

Mr. Twigg agreed, but ventured to predict that Serena, too, would enjoy considerable success.

"Oh, without doubt, and not the sisters only. Your Mr. Severn will break hearts, if I know my own sex at all. I presume he is a bachelor?"

"A widower," Septimus replied briefly. "His wife and baby daughter died within a few days of each other about a year ago."

"Romantic looks, a large fortune and a tragic history," her ladyship remarked cynically. "Oh, he will cause a flutter in the dovecotes, devil a doubt! I believe I must be grateful to you, Septimus. Your friends from Jamaica promise to afford me no small degree of entertainment during the next few weeks." Without a pause she added a sudden question, sharp as a sword thrust. "Septimus, who *is* Julian Severn?"

Taken by surprise, her kinsman started guiltily and stumbled a little over his reply. "I told you yesterday, cousin. He is the son of an old friend, now deceased. As a boy, Julian found himself alone in the world with his own way to make. He came to me for advice, and since he was anxious to try his fortune in the colonies, I gave him a letter of introduction to Thaddeus Loring, in Jamaica."

"The name of Loring I can recall, but I have never before heard that of Severn."

"It *is* just possible, cousin," Septimus retorted, "that you are not familiar with the names of all my friends."

"Perhaps, but I have never heard this name anywhere." She withdrew her hand from her muff, lifted her lorgnette and surveyed him with some suspicion. "Which county?"

"Northumberland," he replied recklessly, choosing the most remote he could think of, "and it is scarcely surprising that you do not know the name. Julian is the last surviving member of his family."

"H'm!" For a few seconds longer the lorgnette remained unnervingly leveled, and then she let it fall and tucked her hand back into her muff. "I can see that you mean to tell me no more, and it is not my custom to waste effort when there is plainly no hope of success." Mr. Twigg drew an audible breath of relief, and she added maliciously: "But do not flatter yourself you have convinced me there is no more to tell."

On the morning of the rout party, Mr. Twigg arrived early in Arlington Street; so early, in fact, that the Loring family were still abed, and Julian out trying the paces of a new horse. Septimus insisted upon waiting for him, and was shown into the back parlor which was apparently Julian's particular sanctum. After about twenty minutes he heard brisk footsteps outside and his godson entered, a soldierly figure in buckskins, top boots and a riding coat of scarlet cloth.

"You choose devilish early hours for your morning calls, Sep," he greeted him. "Had I known you would be abroad at

199

this hour, we might have had a mount out of the stable for you and ridden together. That gray I bought is a capital beast."

"Very likely, but I did not come to talk of horses," Mr. Twigg retorted. "Julian, are you still determined to conceal your real identity?"

"Did you rise early just to ask me that?" Julian strolled forward and perched on the edge of the table, regarding Mr Twigg with some amusement. "Yes, I am so determined. Is there any reason for you to suppose I had changed my mind?"

"You may be obliged to," Septimus retorted grimly. "I have been talking to Augusta, and it seems that most of the people who knew Jocelyn Rivers well are coming to her confounded party this evening."

Julian frowned. "Who, precisely?"

"Your stepmother, for one. She is chaperoning John's elder daughter, Prudence, through her first London season. The girl should have made her curtsy two years ago, but her mother kept putting it off, saying her health was not equal to it." There was a sardonic note in Mr. Twigg's voice, for he had never had any sympathy with Charlotte. "Prudence will not know you, of course, but what about Lady Avenhurst?"

"My dear Septimus, her ladyship and I were never more than acquaintances! I was away at school most of the time, and when I *was* at Avenhurst, she and my father were very rarely there. If *you* did not recognize me, even though you knew I was in London and were expecting to see me, it is highly unlikely that she will suspect who I am."

"No, perhaps not," Septimus agreed; he hesitated a little, casting a searching glance at Julian from beneath bushy brows, "but Sir Digby and Lady Vaine are also among the guests."

"The devil they are!" This time Julian did sound slightly taken aback. "I thought you told me in one of your letters that Vaine had been crippled in an accident?"

"I did," Septimus assented briefly. "His leg was badly crushed when his coach overturned, and now he can only walk with a crutch, but he has not permitted his infirmity to alter his way of life. I've never liked the man, but one cannot but admire his fortitude."

"I'll admit I never expected him to be in London," Julian admitted, "but he is even less of a danger than my stepmother. He hardly knew me. He and my father were political allies, but I believe Vaine only became aware of my existence during those last few months."

"Precisely! Which brings us to the gravest threat of all. Lady Vaine."

There was a pause. Julian was not looking at Septimus now, but thoughtfully regarding the toe of the highly polished riding boot he was idly swinging to and fro. His face was unreadable, and Septimus could not tell whether the prospect of encountering again the woman who had been his first love brought anticipation or regret or merely apprehension that his secret might be discovered.

"And remember, my boy," Septimus resumed at length, "that if she does recognize you, she is not likely to do it discreetly. One cry of 'Jocelyn' when she sees you, and the truth will be out."

Julian shrugged. "That is a risk I shall have to take. I cannot let Margaret and the girls attend the rout unescorted, and since I am bound to encounter Vaine and Celia and my stepmother eventually, I would prefer to do it at once. It is to my advantage that they all believe me to be dead. One scarcely expects to meet one's deceased relatives at an evening party."

More than that he could not say, and Septimus was left wondering whether that ironic indifference was sincere, or simply a mask for the sort of uncertainty and anxiety he himself was feeling. He could not tell then, and he could not tell that evening, when they met again in Hanover Square.

As always when Augusta Selford entertained, her house was thronged with people of fashion, and as Julian led Margaret forward to greet their hostess and the two girls followed, Lucilla looked triumphantly about her. This was London as she had always imagined it would be, where she would find at last admirers really worthy of her.

Find them she did, quickly enough to satisfy even her expectations, for in a gown of white tiffany over palest pink satin, with pink roses in her powdered hair, her eyes sparkling and her cheeks faintly flushed with excitement, her beauty was breathtaking. Other young ladies might look resentful and their mothers disapproving, but that did not worry Lucilla when two-thirds of the men in the room were vying for her attention.

"Bees about the honey pot!" Lady Selford remarked drily to

Julian. "I trust you are aware, Mr. Severn, that that young woman's suitors will henceforth be besieging your house."

"An unnerving prospect, ma'am," he replied, "but Lucilla's suitors, I thank God, are her father's concern, not mine."

"Then it is to be hoped he chooses wisely among them."

Julian laughed. "Madam, the choice will be made by Lucilla herself, for her father has never yet denied her her own way in anything. I can assure you, though, that it will be made by her head rather than her heart."

She gave her rather harsh chuckle. "So you may believe, sir, and so, for that matter, may she, but old heads do not grow on young shoulders. Offer Miss Lucilla a choice between a handsome young ne'er-do-well and an eligible but aging *parti,* and see which way the wind blows then."

"I would not presume to contradict your ladyship, but, knowing Lucilla as I do, I think it more than likely that she will contrive to have the best of both worlds. Who, for example, is the young man sitting beside her now?"

Lady Selford leveled her lorgnette towards the spot where Lucilla was holding court, with her mother and Serena, as it were, in attendance. A good-looking young man had drawn his chair daringly close to hers and was leaning forward to murmur in her ear. Lucilla sat with her eyes modestly downcast, but the smile curving her lips suggested that what she heard was very much to her liking. Her ladyship chuckled again.

"You may be right, Mr. Severn. If she can catch *that* bird in her net, she will have had a triumph indeed. That is Avenhurst." She added the explanation she supposed to be necessary. "Viscount Avenhurst. Probably the biggest matrimonial prize in London at present."

Startled, and more than a little curious, Julian studied the man who had unknowingly usurped his birthright. The viscount appeared to be only in his early twenties, and though very much the exquisite, dressed all in shades of blue with a foam of costly lace at breast and wrist, he was no effeminate fop, and would, Julian thought, look equally at home in the hunting field as in the drawing room. He was obviously much taken with Lucilla, and she, as Julian could tell from her expression, was very well pleased.

"A paragon indeed," he remarked lightly. "Is *nothing* known to his discredit, ma'am?"

"No more than is known of any other young man with the same opportunities to make a fool of himself," Lady Selford replied trenchantly. "Less than some, in fact! I believe there is no real harm in him. Don't worry, Mr. Severn! Between us, we will have Miss Lucilla *and* her sister creditably established before the season ends."

She was looking at him as she spoke, and though the change in his expression was almost imperceptible, her shrewd old eyes discerned and correctly interpreted it. She glanced at Serena, who, though not rivaling her sister's success, had two attentive gentlemen hovering near her, and then looked again at Julian. Yes, she was right! Miss Serena Loring's future was of far more immediate and personal interest to him than Miss Lucilla's.

She had to admit, though, that he did not wear his heart on his sleeve, for after only the tiniest pause he said with a smile:

"Lady Selford, I become more convinced each moment of our great good fortune in finding you our friend. *We* know nothing of the world of fashion, but I have a shrewd suspicion that it dances to a tune of your piping."

"A great part of it does," she agreed complacently. "You see, Mr. Severn, although I am very old, I am still in possession of all my faculties, including an excellent memory, and could, if I chose, recount to you every major scandal, and a good many minor ones, of the past fifty years. That makes people wary of offending me." She raised the lorgnette again as Mr. Twigg, stiff and uncomfortable in his seldom worn, somewhat outmoded formal dress, wandered up to them. "'Fore Gad, Septimus! You might at least try to look as though you are enjoying yourself." She nodded to Julian. "I despair of him, Mr. Severn! Perhaps *you* can raise his spirits."

She moved away to talk to some other guests before Septimus could think of a suitable retort. Julian looked humorously down at him.

"Well, Sep, *can* I raise your spirits? A glass of wine, perhaps? A hand of cards?"

Mr. Twigg glared at him. "Confound it, my boy, don't try to humor me. I am not yet in my dotage."

"No, but you are in a cursed testy humor," Julian said frankly. "What's the matter?"

"That, for one thing!" Mr. Twigg nodded towards the viscount, still murmuring compliments into Lucilla's receptive ear. "Are you aware that that affected puppy is the present Viscount Avenhurst?"

Julian nodded. "So Lady Selford informed me. Lucilla has made a notable conquest."

"Never mind Lucilla." Septimus glanced round and lowered his voice. "Does it not trouble you to know that *he* stands in your rightful place?"

"Not in the least. I wish you would believe me, Sep, when I tell you it means nothing to me. I do not grudge the boy his inheritance, and if he offers for Lucilla, I shall be in his debt. Besides, what have you against him? Even Lady Selford says there is no real harm in him."

"Augusta does not know everything, even though she thinks she does," Septimus said darkly, and let his affronted gaze wander disparagingly over Julian's coat of deep-rose-colored brocade, and cream satin waistcoat embroidered with rose and gold. "No wonder *you* can find no fault with that overdressed popinjay! For sheer peacock finery there's little to choose between you."

"Sep!" Julian was laughing at him. "If you can find no greater cause for disapproval than my fine clothes—!"

"I can find plenty, I have no doubt!" Mr. Twigg was now thoroughly out of temper, but then his glance went beyond Julian and his expression abruptly changed. Julian himself had just an instant's warning, just the sudden alarm and dismay in the other man's face, and then a woman's voice spoke almost beside him.

"Mr. Twigg, what must you think of me? L caught a glimpse of you when I arrived, and meant to come at once to speak with you, but first one detained me, and then another—! Will you forgive me?"

Celia came past him, her hand extended in an appealing gesture to Septimus Twigg, and because Julian was so much taller than she, he was aware at first only of the perfume she was wearing, of a blue dress and powdered hair, and a little collaret of lace and pearls about her throat. Septimus, bowing over her hand, made some civil response which Julian did not hear, and then she turned and looked inquiringly at him.

The huge violet-blue eyes were as lovely as ever, and she still had that little childlike trick of tilting her face up towards anyone taller than herself, but Julian was shocked to see how thin she was, how frail-looking. Daintiness had become a fine-drawn delicacy; there was a faint tracery of lines about eyes and mouth, and hollows in her throat which the ruffle of lace could not hide. She looked—his mind groped after and found the word; she looked brittle, as though gaiety and assurance were only a fragile shell protecting—what? He could not guess, for he felt that he was looking at a stranger. It was all so long ago, that old rapture and old heartbreak; another life, another name; it had nothing at all to do with Julian Severn.

She did not know him. There had been no look of startled recognition, no gasping of a half-forgotten name, although as their eyes met for the first time, he had seen a faint look of puzzlement in hers. Septimus, doing his best to disguise uneasiness, gruffly introduced "Mr. Severn, from Jamaica." Julian bowed. Celia, inclining her head in acknowledgment, said uncertainly:

"Is this your first visit to England, sir?"

"Yes, Lady Vaine, it is." That was true, up to a point, and he was still wary of her. "I arrived in London barely two weeks ago."

She colored faintly under the rouge. "Acquit me of idle curiosity, sir, I beg. I asked because I have the oddest feeling of familiarity, as though we had met before."

From the corner of his eye Julian saw Mr. Twigg's tiny movement of dismay, but though Celia's words shook his confidence, he managed to dissemble.

"A not uncommon illusion, my lady. I, too, have occasionally experienced it when meeting someone for the first time."

"I suppose so." The perplexity still lingered in her eyes, but she seemed convinced by the finality with which he had spoken, and merely added in a rallying tone: "Perhaps, Mr. Severn, it is an indication that we are to become better acquainted in the future."

He bowed slightly. "I would be happy, madam, to believe that it is."

Before she could reply, another voice spoke unexpectedly beside them. A light, bored voice with an undertone of irony.

"You may rest assured, sir, that it is, if Lady Vaine wills it so."

Celia gasped, and Julian turned quickly to confront the speaker. The talk and laughter and movement all around them had masked the sound of a crutch on the polished floor, allowing Sir Digby to approach them unobserved.

He had changed remarkably little. His thin face was more

deeply lined, but he still regarded the world with an air of boredom from beneath sleepy lids. He was as foppishly elegant as ever, tonight in pearl-gray velvet with a waistcoat of darker gray, and supported himself on a crutch of polished ebony banded with silver. His left leg, though faultlessly hosed and shod, hung wasted and deformed, the toe of the grotesquely twisted foot barely touching the floor, and Julian remembered suddenly that as a girl, Celia had had a horror of any kind of physical infirmity.

"Digby!" She spoke breathlessly, in a high, nervous tone. "I did not see you there. Mr. Severn, allow me to present you to my husband, Sir Digby Vaine."

Julian bowed. Sir Digby inclined his head.

"From Jamaica, I believe, Mr. Severn? I have already had the privilege of being presented to the charming ladies who are in your care. Mrs. Loring, is it not, and her daughters?" He turned to Septimus. "Well, Twigg, what is this? Do not tell me that you, of all men, have succumbed to the lure of town life?"

"For a short while only, sir." Septimus spoke briefly, for he was profoundly uneasy. "I came to renew acquaintance with a very old friend. Thaddeus Loring and I were boys together."

"And, of course, Lady Selford is your cousin," Vaine added lightly. "I see it is you, Twigg, whom we have to thank for the advent of the new beauty." He turned to his wife. "Miss Lucilla is quite astonishingly lovely, is she not, my dear? I see that our young friend Avenhurst is already her devoted admirer."

"Has that boy of yours returned to London yet, Sir Digby?" Septimus broke in abruptly before Celia could make any reply. "I was surprised to see him in the village just before I left, but I gather he had come to attend to some matter of business concerning the estate."

"Had he told you he had seized upon the flimsiest of excuses to escape from town for a few days, it would have been closer to the truth," Vaine replied acidly. "I will confess to you, Twigg, that Simon is a sad disappointment to me. He thinks of nothing but new-fangled methods of farming, and it was only with the greatest difficulty that I persuaded him to come to London at all this summer."

"Yet I am told," Septimus continued doggedly, "that some

of his experiments have produced quite remarkable results. You should be proud of him."

"My dear sir, I find no cause for pride in an eldest son whose interests are those of a ploughboy!"

"Simon is my stepson, Mr. Severn," Celia explained brightly. "My own children are still in the nursery."

"Madam, who could doubt that?" he replied courteously. "The young gentleman is obviously of an age to please himself, and it is inconceivable that *you* could be the mother of a grown son."

Vaine's watchful, ironic glance rested for a moment on his wife's face and then shifted to Julian's, but Mr. Twigg, anxiously watching, could detect no trace of recognition. No reason why there should be, he told himself. It was not suspicion of Julian's identity which had prompted Vaine to intervene, but merely the sight of his wife in conversation with the stranger whose dark, arrogant face, among the pale English complexions, patched and painted, of the men around him, stood out like a challenge. Vaine's jealousy was notorious, and Mr. Twigg was not in the least surprised when he found some pretext to lead Celia away. His relief was short-lived, however, for a moment later Lady Selford appeared again beside them.

"Mr. Severn, if Septimus will forgo your company for a few minutes"—Mr. Twigg knew very well that this was a mere formality; he was not going to be given any choice—"I would like to present you to Lady Avenhurst."

"Lady Avenhurst?" There was nothing but perplexed inquiry in Julian's voice, and Septimus could only admire such self-command, for his own heart had given another unpleasant lurch of alarm. "Ah! Your ladyship means the mother of the young viscount?"

"No, Mr. Severn, I do not. The family connection is far less straightforward than that." She explained it briefly, adding in conclusion: "Her ladyship has expressed a desire to make your acquaintance."

"I am flattered, Lady Selford." Julian offered her his arm. "Though I cannot imagine why Lady Avenhurst should so honor me."

Augusta laughed shortly as she laid her hand on the rose brocade sleeve, but offered no explanation. She and Julian moved away, and Septimus, murmuring that he, too, ought to pay his respects, trailed after them. He did not know what

207

he could do if Julian were recognized, but felt that he must be there to lend his support.

There was no glimmer of recognition, however, in the Dowager's eyes as she studied, with interest and approval, the tall, white-haired man bowing before her. She smiled at him with the utmost affability and extended a plump, be-ringed hand.

"I am delighted to meet you, Mr. Severn, and, if it is not presumptuous of me, to welcome you to London."

He murmured some conventional response, thinking that she had changed more than anyone and that he would have had some difficulty in recognizing her. She had grown very stout, and was so heavily painted that her face had almost the appearance of a mask. Nothing, however, could have exceeded her amiability, while her eagerness to make Julian's acquaintance was explained when, after a brief exchange of platitudes, she beckoned to a girl who made one of a group of young ladies nearby.

"Prudence, my love," she said to her, "I wish to make Mr. Severn known to you. My granddaughter, Miss Rivers, sir."

Julian bowed again, reflecting that in this case, at least, no introduction was needful, for Prudence looked exactly as her mother had done at nineteen. Thin, sharp-featured, rather sallow, with the same dramatic intensity of look and gesture. Like her brother, she had not been an attractive child; she was not an attractive young woman. She did her best, however, to profit from the opportunity the Dowager had procured for her, to be one of the first girls to be presented to the striking stranger who was Lady Selford's protégé, though not even Lady Avenhurst could convince herself that Prudence made any great impression on him. He was courteous but distant, and, making his escape as soon as he decently could, went to join Mrs. Loring and her daughters. The Dowager sighed, and reflected with some irritation that since Mr. Severn apparently stood *in loco parentis* to the sisters, he might have been expected to spare some attention for less fortunate young ladies.

Within twenty-four hours Lady Selford's prophecy concerning Lucilla's suitors had been amply fulfilled, Lord Avenhurst showing considerable address and stealing a march on his rivals by having an enormous bouquet of roses delivered at the house in Arlington Street early on the morning after the rout party, so that they were waiting for Lucilla when she woke. She was enchanted.

"He must have given orders to his people last night," she said to Serena. "I *do* like a man to be enterprising."

Later that day the viscount came to pay his respects, and she thanked him prettily for his charming gesture.

"Such a delightful surprise, my lord! Your bouquet was the first thing I saw when I opened my eyes this morning."

"Oh, happy flowers!" he murmured, his blue eyes smiling audaciously into hers. "I never expected to be envious of a mere rose."

"My lord!" Lucilla made a great play of hiding her blushes behind a fan of delicately-painted chicken skin. "I fear I must reprove you."

"If you *fear* it, madam, there must be hope that you will forgive me."

She was far too accomplished a coquette to deny any suitor the excitement of the chase, and merely shook her head at him before turning to talk to another of her admirers, for there were callers coming and going in Arlington Street for most of that day. Having been vouched for by Lady Selford (who had also dropped one or two discreet hints regarding the Loring fortune), the two sisters from Jamaica had overnight become the most sought-after young ladies in London.

Nor was it only the Loring girls who created a sensation, for inevitably Julian also became an object of interest to the fashionable world. His looks compelled attention, and after a few days, rumors began to circulate of his great wealth. For this, servants' gossip was originally responsible, for Reuben, himself an object of some curiosity to his fellow menials, did not hesitate to brag about his master, and his stories were corroborated by the Lorings' personal attendants, all natives of Kingston who were familiar with the events of Julian's life in the colony. From below-stairs, the rumors drifted up to drawing room and boudoir; were discreetly inquired into and confirmed; and it dawned upon the fashionable mothers of marriageable daughters that a new and glittering matrimonial prospect had appeared upon the London scene. To be sure, nothing was known of his antecedents, but he possessed an air of breeding as unmistakable as it was instantly recognizable in the circles among which he now moved, and besides, he was a favorite of that arbiter of taste and fashion, Lady Selford.

Julian, cynically amused, remained as maddeningly indifferent to the blandishments of nubile misses as he did to the discreet invitation implicit in the attitude towards him of certain fashionable young matrons. He had no desire to enter into an intrigue à la mode, but was waiting with ever-growing impatience for Lucilla to choose among her many suitors; for Thaddeus to decide in which part of England he meant to spend the rest of his life; for the time to come when he could ask Serena to come with him to Virginia. He was finding it more and more difficult not to throw caution to the winds and declare himself, but always to restrain him, when temptation seemed almost irresistible, would come the fear that he might yet be recognized. If he were, the ensuing scandal would be hideously complicated by Lucilla's growing involvement with the supposed viscount, and he could not risk exposing Serena to such a conflict of loyalties.

No, the danger could not be disregarded, no matter how little chance there appeared to be of it materializing. Celia, who had to be regarded as the greatest threat, seemed to have no suspicion of past acquaintance, and any fleeting sense of familiarity which she had felt at their first meeting had apparently been forgotten. Sir Digby, Julian had never really feared; their paths had crossed only briefly, during that fateful springtime twelve years before, and no doubt, Julian reflected with a touch of bitterness, Vaine had erased Jocelyn Rivers from his memory as soon as Jocelyn ceased to be an obstacle between him and Celia.

There remained the Dowager Lady Avenhurst, though she had proved to be more of an embarrassment than a danger. After their first encounter, when she had so pointedly and unavailingly introduced Prudence to his notice, she had adopted a different strategy, cultivating Mrs. Loring's acquaintance and encouraging Prudence to strike up a friendship with the girls. There had been several invitations in which Julian had been included, and from which he had found it impossible to extricate himself, and since these had to be reciprocated, he found himself seeing rather more of his relatives than he liked. He had been surprised to discover that Lady Avenhurst was apparently on cordial terms with the young viscount, but when he commented upon this to Septimus Twigg, the latter said drily:

"Her ladyship is a practical woman. When your father died, Mrs. Rivers made a great drama of refusing to stay anywhere near Avenhurst, and took herself off to Bath, where she has lived ever since, playing at being an invalid, but Lady Avenhurst simply moved into the Dower House. When young Godfrey Rivers and his mother and sisters came to Avenhurst Place, she put herself out to be pleasant and helpful. I fancy she had some notion of contriving a match between Godfrey and Miss Prudence, for she had the girl to stay with her last summer and did her best to throw them together, but nothing came of it. *My lord's* thoughts were not running in that direction."

He spoke contemptuously, but in this instance Julian's sympathy was with the viscount. Prudence was too much like her mother, though no doubt breeding and an ample marriage-portion would eventually achieve a respectable alliance for her. He said lightly:

"So now her ladyship is trying to throw Prudence in *my* direction. It's damned embarrassing, but at least it proves she has no suspicion that I am the girl's uncle."

Septimus looked sharply at him. "Do you think *anyone* has?"

"I believe not, but I shall not be really easy in my mind as long as I remain in England. It was against my better judgment that I ever came back here at all."

Lord Avenhurst was entertaining a party at Ranelagh Gardens, to take supper and to hear one of the concerts of music for which the gardens were justly famous. He and his guests—Mrs. Loring and her two daughters, Julian Severn and Septimus Twigg—had traveled to Ranelagh by river, entertained on the way by a group of musicians his lordship had hired to accompany them in another boat, and were now strolling among the fashionable throng below the great dome of the Rotunda.

Avenhurst himself was, of course, at Lucilla's side, and no efforts of his rivals, several of whom had deserted their own parties to pay homage to the Beauty, had succeeded in dislodging him. Julian, walking with Serena a short way behind, watched the maneuvers with growing irritation. What the devil was the girl playing at? All she had ever wanted was hers for the taking, for among her numerous suitors were two of even higher rank than Avenhurst and of equal or greater wealth. Julian had supposed, when a marquis started to pay her serious attentions, that the matter

211

was as good as settled, for surely even Lucilla could look no higher than that? He was disappointed. The marquis was treated like the rest, kindly and coldly by turns, and was still no more certain than his rivals how the object of his courtship really regarded him.

Serena, walking silently at Julian's side and, as always, acutely attuned to his feelings, was aware of his impatience with Lucilla, just as she was aware of the restlessness which lay beneath his apparent enjoyment of the life of a wealthy man of fashion. He was not contented in England. He had come for their sake and he stayed out of a sense of duty towards them, for they all depended too heavily upon him. Mama and Lucy, though wholly taken up with the latter's successes, were comfortably if almost unconsciously aware of his protective presence. Papa, growing a little stronger but still so enfeebled that he could not face the responsibility of finding a home for his family, yet would not allow Julian to do so while Lucy's future was still undetermined. It was not right, it was not fair to him to keep him here any longer, though it seemed she was the only one who could see that, even though it would break her heart to let him go.

The Rotunda at Ranelagh, however, was not a place where one might for long indulge in introspection, for it was a favorite haunt of the fashionable world and one could always depend upon meeting friends and acquaintances there. It was not long before the disposition of their group was altered by such interruptions, and Serena, who had her own share of admirers, found herself walking with her mother and one of them, while Julian dropped back to accompany Mr. Twigg. Thus it was that the two men had an excellent view of Lady Vaine, escorted by a young man of somewhat serious aspect, making her way slowly but obviously of set purpose towards Avenhurst and his party. Even so, Julian would have thought little of this had not Septimus uttered an exclamation compounded almost equally of astonishment and disapproval.

Julian glanced curiously down at him. "What's the matter, Sep? I'll own it is unusual to see her ladyship unaccompanied by Sir Digby, but one would scarcely expect to find *him* walking round and round this infernally dull edifice. Besides, unless I am much mistaken, the young man with her is Simon Vaine."

"No, you're not mistaken. Young Simon must have been prevailed upon to come back to town at last." Mr. Twigg seemed to be regretting his outburst and gave Julian no chance to pursue any inquiries. "In any event, Vaine *is* here. I saw him just now, sitting in one of the boxes. Upon my soul, I cannot understand why he takes so unkindly a view of his son's interest in agriculture, and insists upon dragging him to London season after season."

"Ah, but you are a countryman yourself, Sep! Vaine, as I recall, spends no more time on his estates than is absolutely necessary. Moreover, in this instance I suspect that, as a prudent father, he wishes his son to make a try for the Loring fortune, for you see that Celia is now presenting him to Margaret—though much good it may do him!"

They paused, watching the group a little way ahead of them. Simon Vaine bowed gravely to Mrs. Loring, to Serena and to Lucilla, at whom he stared with the bemused expression common to most men seeing her for the first time. A few words were exchanged, and then the whole party walked on together, but it was plain that Lucilla, escorted on the one hand by Avenhurst and on the other by the marquis, had no attention to spare for an untitled gentleman, particularly one with so little address. She turned her back on him, and since his stepmother was now engaged in conversation with Mrs. Loring, he walked behind them in uncomfortable silence until Serena, evidently taking pity on him, drew him into conversation with her.

"Yet another luckless admirer to pander to Lucilla's vanity," Julian remarked drily. "Sep, we have now encircled this confounded amphitheater half a dozen times, and for my part I am heartily tired of it. For God's sake, let us go out and walk in the gardens for a change!"

Septimus agreed with relief. On their way out they passed the box where Sir Digby Vaine was sitting, the ebony crutch propped against the back of his chair, his hooded eyes inscrutably surveying the shifting scene before him. He saw them and nodded a greeting; Julian, returning it, said idly to his companion:

"Someone should point out to Simon Vaine that the simplest way to avoid his father's importunities would be to marry some suitable lady who shares his preference for country life. I wonder that so obvious a solution has not already occurred to him."

He was to remember those casual words with deepening uneasiness during the next two or three weeks, for, contrary

213

to his expectations, Simon's stunned admiration of Lucilla's beauty did not survive their first fleeting encounter. On that same occasion, Serena had led him, with tact and sympathy, to talk about his ruling passion, and had listened intelligently to a long dissertation on the benefits of crop rotation. Simon, utterly overwhelmed by at last meeting a young woman—and an attractive, sought-after one, at that—who was not patently bored by the only subject upon which he could talk with fluency, promptly lost his heart to her. Thereafter he courted her as assiduously, if less entertainingly, as the viscount was courting her sister, until even Lucilla stopped teasing and seemed tacitly to accept that Serena was simply waiting for Simon to decide the time was ripe to approach their father for leave to propose to her.

Serena did not attempt denials which would probably not have been believed. She liked Simon Vaine, and felt more at ease with him than with any other man she had met since coming to London. He had neither liking nor aptitude for dalliance, and so did not pester her with gallantries which annoyed and embarrassed her. She had never suffered such before, but the aloofness which had served her so well in Kingston was seen by the bolder London beaux as a challenge, a defense to be breached and overcome. With Simon she did not feel the need to be constantly on her guard, and so favored him more and more often with her company.

It did not occur to her that Julian might fall into the same error as Lucilla, but he did, and suffered agonies of jealousy and anxiety. Confound Lucilla! Why could she not make up her mind? Thaddeus, he knew, had already received five offers for her hand, including one from the marquis, but Lucilla had refused them all.

Julian said something of this to Lady Selford on one occasion. Her ladyship chuckled harshly.

"She is waiting for Avenhurst. *She* knows he will propose to her and *he* knows that she will accept, but they are both enjoying the chase too much to bring it to an end just yet." She met Julian's dubious look and chuckled again. "You were right, Mr. Severn! Miss Lucilla has found the best of both worlds, for her heart is involved now as well as her head."

"*Lucilla*'s heart?" He was incredulous. "I have seen no evidence of it."

"Then you must take *my* word that it is so. Oh, the feeling does not go deep! I doubt whether either of them is capable of that, but for the present they have succeeded in convincing themselves that they are in love with each other. A charming romance, worthy of the theater!"

There was a mordant note in her voice, but Julian looked across the ballroom where their conversation was taking place and watched Lucilla and Lord Avenhurst going together through the last stately steps of a minuet. Her hand in his, she was smiling up at him with an expression Julian had never before seen on her face, and he realized that Lady Selford was right. Of course, he thought with exasperation, for Lucilla everything must be perfect, even if that perfection did not last.

"What is more," her ladyship continued, and Julian, still watching Lucilla, was unaware that the shrewd, faded eyes were now intent upon him, "it appears that the story is to be rounded off as neatly as any dramatist could contrive. Miss Lucilla will marry Avenhurst, and Miss Serena, unless I am much mistaken, will take young Vaine. So the sisters will be neighbors, and it will only remain for their father to find a property close by. Upon my soul, I cannot recall ever having heard of an affair coming to so tidy a conclusion!"

By a tremendous effort of will Julian forced himself to remain outwardly unperturbed, to go on watching Lucilla and Godfrey, not to react in any way to Lady Selford's remark until he was certain he could control both his expression and his voice. Then, in command of himself at last, he turned to face her.

"I do not know, Lady Selford, whether to be disappointed or flattered that you do not include me in your *dramatis personae*. Is there no part for me in the play?"

"I wonder." The lorgnette was raised now as she studied him appraisingly, and he could not see the expression in her eyes. "You, my dear sir, are the unknown quantity. I cannot tell whether you would make the piece, or mar it."

III

Serena, returning from a prolonged shopping expedition with her mother and sister, was informed that Mr. Loring wished to see her. She found him in the drawing room on the first floor, immersed in the *Gentleman's Magazine,* but he looked up with a smile and beckoned her to a chair facing his own across the empty fireplace. He was stronger now, and able to go about the town a little, though he still preferred receiving visitors to paying calls.

"Sit down, my dear," he greeted his elder daughter, and eyed her approvingly as she obeyed. "That is a very becoming gown."

"Thank you, Papa." Serena arranged the folds of blue tabby silk elegantly about her. "I was told you wished to see me."

"Yes." Thaddeus laid aside the paper and took off his spectacles. "While you were out, I received a visit from Mr. Vaine. He has asked my permission to marry you." He paused expectantly, but Serena made no response and merely stared at him with a sort of frozen stillness. A look of faint impatience came into Loring's face, and he added deliberately: "I wish you to accept him."

So the blow had fallen at last; the thing she most dreaded had happened. Serena moistened her lips and said faintly:

"Why, Papa?"

"Why?" Impatience was rapidly becoming exasperation. "Bless my soul, girl, do you need to ask? It is an excellent match! The Vaines are an old and wealthy family, and young Simon will inherit his father's title some day. Moreover, I believe it is now tolerably certain that your sister will marry Avenhurst, and it will be agreeable for her to have you living nearby. Needless to say, I, too, would endeavor to purchase a property in the same neighborhood."

She ought to have foreseen this, Serena thought with despair. It would have been easy enough at the outset to treat Simon Vaine with indifference, but she had been blind to the danger, forgetful of the fact that, in their father's eyes, Lucilla's pleasure and convenience must always take precedence over every other consideration. Instead she had blundered into the trap, and now it was closing about her.

"Papa, I don't *want* to marry Mr. Vaine," she said desperately.

"What?" He was not pleased, but then a thought appeared to strike him. "You mean you have some other suitor whom you prefer? Well, well, it would not be so much to *my* liking, but if the young man is eligible, I will consider it. *Is* there such a man?"

Oh, yes! she thought wretchedly. There is only one man in the world I shall ever want to marry, but it is foolish to go on hoping that he may some day turn to me. Aloud she said in a subdued voice:

"No, Papa. I meant that I would rather not marry at all."

"Upon my word!" Thaddeus was really angry now. "I never expected such missish qualms from you. You are not a child! You are twenty years old and it is high time you had a husband. I have given Simon Vaine leave to propose to you, and when he does, you will oblige me by accepting him. There is no more to be said."

In proof of this, he replaced his spectacles and picked up the newspaper again. Serena could see that his hands were shaking, and remembered with a sudden stab of conscience that it was bad for him to be upset. Yet for her own sake she must make one more bid to escape.

"Papa, you have said more than once that you would never compel either Lucy or me to marry anyone we disliked."

"True!" He lowered the paper a little and looked at her over the top of his spectacles. "But if you dislike Simon Vaine, my girl, you have a very odd way of showing it.".

It was no use. There was some justice in what her father had said, for she did not dislike Simon, but there was no way of making Papa understand unless she told him the truth, and anything, she thought, would be preferable to that.

Dismissed from the drawing room, and feeling that she could not for the moment endure the company of her mother and sister, she went as if by instinct to the back parlor, which was regarded as Julian's alone. He was not there, but the room already bore the imprint of his personality. Letters and cards of invitation littered the escritoire; a book he had been reading lay on the table beside his favorite chair, together with his pipe and tobacco jar, for he had acquired the habit of smoking while he was in Virginia, even though in public he would still take snuff as gracefully as any man.

Serena sat down in the chair, remembering how, as a child, she used to go to his room while he was away and somehow feel closer to him in spirit. She would always belong to him, she thought sadly, even if she married Simon Vaine; even when he was far away on the other side of the world.

For a little while she wondered whether Julian would be able to persuade her father to change his mind, but then she asked herself, to what purpose? Julian himself did not love her. There had been times, especially during the long voyage to England, when she had thought that perhaps he did, but she had been deluding herself. If he did love her, if he wanted to marry her, he would have told her so by now, for it was more than a year since Alathea's death, and by even the strictest code of propriety he was free to speak.

No, the time had come to abandon hope, to face the fact that she must accept second best. Simon Vaine was a serious and responsible young man, and if she agreed to marry him, she could no doubt persuade him to shoulder the responsibilities towards her family which were keeping Julian in England. That was the only thing she could do now for the man she loved; give him the freedom to bid her farewell, to return to whoever was waiting for him in Virginia.

She began drearily to enumerate to herself the advantages of being obedient, since she was not going to be allowed to remain unmarried. She liked Simon Vaine well enough; she would be mistress of a country house, and not have to spend most of her time in the endless pursuit of pleasure which seemed to be the sole purpose in life of people of fashion, and which, now that the first novelty had passed, was already beginning to pall. She could be a dutiful wife, sympathetic to her husband's interests, and perhaps, as time passed, liking would deepen into affection.

So profoundly was she sunk in troubled thought that the sound of Julian's familiar footsteps approaching the door took her unawares, so that she did not even have time to rise from the chair before he came in. He looked angry and disturbed.

"I'm sorry," she stammered, getting hastily to her feet. "I did not expect—!"

"My dear girl, there is no need to apologize," he said impatiently. "Sit down again, for Heaven's sake."

Confused and embarrassed, afraid that the surge of gladness she always felt at sight of him might have shown in her face, Serena sank back into the chair. Julian, who was carrying a letter which must have been handed to him when he entered the house, walked across to add it to those already on the escritoire. With his back still towards her, he asked abruptly:

"Are you going to obey your father and accept young Vaine?" She uttered a little sound of query and dismay, and he added, still without turning: "Thaddeus has just told me."

"I—I suppose so!" Serena swallowed hard, her hands clenching tightly on the arms of the chair. "It is a good match. Mr. Vaine's home is close to Lord Avenhurst's, and when Lucy marries him we shall still be neighbors. Mama and Papa would come to live nearby, too."

"Very convenient!" Julian said savagely, and turned at last to face her, though since the escritoire stood beneath the window, his back was to the light and she could not clearly see his face. "It is settled, then? Lucilla and Avenhurst?"

"Not formally." She seized with relief upon the slight change of subject, for it was so much easier to talk to him about Lucilla than about herself. "But I feel sure they will be betrothed before the season ends."

"You may depend upon it. Avenhurst can give her everything she has ever wanted, and what Lucilla wants, she takes. You, of all people, should know that."

"Be fair with her, Julian! I am sure she cares for Lord Avenhurst."

"Perhaps! The question does not greatly concern me. What

does is the fact that, having told your father you do not want to marry Simon Vaine, you are now thinking of doing so. Do you not know your own mind?"

"I like him very well." Serena's head was bent, and she was carefully tracing with one fingertip the gilding on the arm of the chair. "I would like to live in the country, and since Lucilla—!"

"Confound Lucilla!" Julian said violently. "You have been obliged to play second fiddle to her all your life, but this is a matter in which you *must* put your own inclinations first. Don't sacrifice your whole future just to suit the convenience of your family."

"Why should you suppose it to be a sacrifice?" Quite suddenly, Serena was overwhelmed by bitterness and anger and a sort of desperate defiance. "I *want* to stay near Papa and Mama and Lucy! They will be all I have after—!" She bit back the words in the nick of time and jumped to her feet. "I am going to tell Papa I will do as he wishes."

She had reached the door and began to open it when Julian's hand came against it from behind her and slammed it shut again. As she stood frozen, staring in panic at its blank, polished panels, she heard him say unsteadily, in a tone he had never used to her before:

"Oh, my darling, I'll not let you do it!"

She was afraid to believe, afraid that she had misunderstood the emotion roughening his voice; not until his hand on her shoulder turned her towards him, and she looked up into his eyes, did she dare to accept the truth. Then she was in his arms, and he was searching her face with a gaze which was humble and yet demanding.

"Will you marry *me*, Serena, and come with me to Virginia?"

The need for pretense was past, the need to set a guard on word and glance and gesture. Now at last she could look at him with her love shining clear and unafraid in her eyes.

"Anywhere, Julian," she said simply, and lifted her face trustfully for his kiss. "Anywhere in the world, with you."

Thaddeus and Margaret received with astonishment the news that Serena and Julian wished to be married, and with fortitude the knowledge that this would mean parting with their elder daughter, possibly forever. Serena, secure now in the shelter and certainty of Julian's love, accepted this with

221

amused affection, knowing that while Lucilla was within reach, and they could watch her charmed and dazzling progress, it would not matter much to them that Lucilla's sister was on the other side of the world. They loved her in their way, but, as Margaret said complacently, they would know that Serena was safe and happy with Julian; she always was.

Lucilla herself was amused and indulgent—surely, she said, it would be rather like marrying one's elder brother—but a little put out that they would not be staying in England.

"It's such a *waste,* Serena!" she lamented. "Imagine marrying a man as rich as Julian, and then letting him bury you in the wilderness."

"Virginia isn't all wilderness, Lucy," Serena protested, laughing. "Remember how Julian described Williamsburg to us."

"It is a wilderness compared to London," Lucilla said with finality, "and not London only. Just think, Serena! You could go to Paris, Rome, Venice—all the famous cities we have heard of and read about. At least persuade Julian to take you on a tour of Europe before you go to America."

"I don't want a tour of Europe," Serena replied patiently. "I would have been quite happy to go straight to Virginia from Jamaica if Julian had asked me."

"You would be happy to go anywhere if Julian asked you," Lucilla said indulgently. "You always were. Now, when I marry Avenhurst, I shall insist that he takes me abroad."

"You *are* going to marry him, then?"

"When he proposes to me," Lucilla replied mischievously. "Serena, Prudence Rivers has been telling me about Avenhurst Place, his principal seat. It is huge, and a veritable palace! She was born there, you know, and lived there until her grandfather died."

"I thought her home was at Bath."

"It is now. Her mother would not stay anywhere near Avenhurst Place after the present viscount inherited. There was some ill feeling between his family and Prudence's grandfather, but the old man could not prevent him inheriting. I was not attending particularly, for you know how Prudence's tongue runs on, but there was some nonsense about a wicked uncle who fled the country and died abroad. That is why everything came to Avenhurst."

"Lucy," Serena said earnestly, "be serious for a moment. You do love Lord Avenhurst, don't you?"

"To be sure I do! He is rich and titled and handsome and young. Everything I have ever dreamed of."

"Yes, but would you still love him if he were not rich and a peer of the realm?"

"Of course I would." Lucilla paused, watching relief spread across her sister's face, and then added in a matter-of-fact tone: "But I would never marry him."

"Lucy!" Serena was shocked, for she had cherished the hope that Lucilla's feelings for the viscount had changed her. "How can you be so worldly?"

"Serena!" Lucilla mocked her, though not unkindly. "Just because *you* are lovesick, is there any reason why *I* should be? Avenhurst *is* rich and titled, and nothing can alter that, so stop fretting over me, and consider instead how you are going to tell that poor, dull Mr. Vaine that you have decided to marry Julian instead."

Serena, however, was spared that uncomfortable duty, for when Simon presented himself, it was her father and Julian who received him, and he left the house without seeing Serena herself. She was thankful to have escaped a difficult meeting, but later confessed to Julian that she feared she had treated Simon rather badly.

"Yes, you unconscionable flirt," Julian said comfortably, pressing a kiss into her palm and folding her fingers over it, "but stop worrying about Vaine's injured feelings, and tell me instead how soon you can be ready to marry me."

"I'm ready now," she said candidly. "I wish we could be married tomorrow."

The teasing look vanished from his eyes, and he caught her against him in a grip which seemed to crush all the breath from her body. Surrendering her lips to his, aware of the pounding of his heart against her own, she felt herself drowning in a torrent of unfamiliar sensations, at once ecstatic and alarming, and clutched at his shoulders as if to save herself from being submerged completely. When at last his hold slackened a little, she still leaned helplessly against him, her face, with closed eyes and slightly parted lips, upturned to his.

"Serena!" he said softly, and though he tried for a light tone, his voice was unsteady. "Oh, love, I have wasted so many years we might have shared! I will put up the banns at once. We can be married within a month, and if I can arrange passage for us, we'll reach Virginia before the au-

223

tumn is over." A thought occurred to him. "Or do you want to stay in England for Lucilla's wedding?"

She stirred in his arms, but only to nestle closer. "She won't miss me," she said philosophically, "and neither will Mama and Papa. Let us go home as soon as we can, Julian. I want so much to see Meadowsweet."

Above her head, Julian smiled to himself. He had not told her about the house, nor did he intend to. He would not deprive her of the delight of recognition, the discovery that the home to which he brought her was one such as she had always dreamed of. She would have familiar servants about her, too. The faces which greeted her when she entered her new domain would be those she had known since her childhood....

"I have just thought of something, though," she added suddenly. "Did you not tell Papa that you would not leave England until he had settled upon the house he wished to buy, so that you could deal with the business of purchasing it?"

"Avenhurst can undertake that responsibility instead." Julian's lips moved gently against her temple as he spoke. "Your father will be looking for a house in his part of the country, and meanwhile there is room and to spare at Avenhurst Place."

"Julian!" He was aware of her little movement of surprise. "I did not suppose *you* knew Avenhurst Place."

For a moment he was silent, cursing himself for that slip of the tongue; then he said as indifferently as he could: "Septimus lives within two or three miles of it, and has known the house for years."

The oblique answer had to satisfy her, and he gave her no chance to question it, capturing her lips again and kissing her into forgetfulness of so trivial a matter. Yet at the back of his mind the resolve was hardening to be done with England as soon as might be; to marry his love and carry her off to the home waiting for them on the other side of the world, far away from the risk of chance discovery or self-betrayal; to lay to rest forever the ghost of Jocelyn Rivers.

The news of the betrothal of Serena Loring to Julian Severn created something of a sensation in fashionable circles, and provoked in some hitherto hopeful quarters a feeling that it was gross selfishness on the part of two such matrimonial prizes to promise themselves to each other. Septimus Twigg was delighted. He had no liking for Lucilla and considered that she and Avenhurst were well matched, but Serena had quickly won a place in his affections. He still wished that his godson would claim his rights, but had resigned himself to the fact that the wish would never be granted, and accepted with sorrow but with resignation the information that Julian Severn and his bride would be sailing for Virginia soon after their wedding. It was something to have seen Julian again. To have known the man Julia's son had become.

The first time Lady Selford encountered the betrothed couple, at a drum given by Lady Atterbury, she formally offered them her warm good wishes, but later, buttonholing Julian on his own, said in her brusque way:

"Well, sir, you have rewritten my play for me! I should have known that life would not permit matters to be rounded off as neatly as in the theater."

He lifted a humorous eyebrow at her. "Less neatly, perhaps, madam, but from my point of view, far more satisfactorily."

"I don't doubt that. Let us hope it will prove as satisfactory from Miss Loring's point of view," she retorted, putting him in his place. "Septimus tells me you intend carrying the poor girl off to some outlandish spot on the other side of the world, among wild beasts and heathen savages."

"I cannot believe that Septimus told your ladyship anything of the kind," he replied with some amusement. "The frontier has moved westward, Lady Selford, and that part of Virginia in which my plantation lies is, I assure you, entirely civilized."

"H'm!" She studied him through her lorgnette. "Why Virginia, Mr. Severn?"

"Why not, madam? It is a new land, a land of great opportunity."

"And is England so barren of opportunity, sir? I would have supposed that for *you,* opportunity would not be far to seek."

Her choice of words startled him, and he gave her a hard look. She returned it blandly.

"None that appeal to me, Lady Selford," he replied with finality. "I can think of nothing which would persuade me to spend the rest of my life in England."

She gave her harsh chuckle. "You are frank, sir, if unflattering. I'll say no more!"

Meanwhile, in the adjoining salon, Serena, standing momentarily on her own, was dismayed to hear herself addressed by the light, bored voice of Sir Digby Vaine. She had not been aware that he was present.

"Alone, Miss Loring? Allow me to offer you my felicitations upon your betrothal, reserving until I encounter Mr. Severn the congratulations he undoubtedly deserves."

She had turned quickly at his first words. He was standing just behind her, supporting himself on the ebony crutch and regarding her with a faint smile. She said hurriedly:

"You are very kind, sir, and I am sorry—!" She broke off and impulsively held out her hand to him.

"That you felt yourself unable to accept my son's proposal?" he concluded, taking the hand in a light clasp. "So am I, dear lady! Such a marriage would, I fancy, have been the making of him." He kissed her hand with an air and then released it.

"Was he—?" She hesitated. "I trust, sir, that Mr. Vaine's disappointment was not too great?"

"He is desolate," Sir Digby admitted, "but you must not blame yourself, Miss Loring. Your affections are engaged elsewhere. I understand."

"Thank you," Serena replied, and then paused, wishing that someone else would join them. She was only slightly acquainted with Vaine, and never felt quite at ease in his company, distrusting the faint mockery which habitually lurked in his voice and his hooded eyes.

"I wonder, Miss Loring," Sir Digby said after a moment, "if you will accord me the privilege of a few minutes' private conversation? There is something I wish to say to you, but not here, where at any moment we may be interrupted." He saw her doubtful, puzzled look and added reassuringly: "I suggest only that we step on to the balcony yonder."

A nod indicated the spot close by where the heavy curtain was looped back from a long window which stood open to a small, balustraded balcony. It was scarcely less public than the room in which they stood, and though she had no desire to talk alone with Vaine, there seemed to be no harm in agreeing to his request. Perhaps, she thought with another twinge of guilt, it had something to do with his son.

She inclined her head and moved the few paces which took

226

her through the window and onto the balcony. It was flooded by the light of a full moon which dimmed the candles in the salon behind her, and she did not notice that as Vaine followed her, he paused and with a deft jerk released the cord holding the curtain, so that it swung down into place and shut them off from the crowded salon. Then he turned back to Serena, who stood looking down into the street below, where the light from the open front door and the flambeaux flanking it spilled across the steps, and a sedan chair preceded by a linkboy with his flaring torch was swaying past.

"Tell me, Miss Loring," he said softly, "are you really content to be plain Mrs. Julian Severn?"

"Sir!" The balcony was so narrow that the hoop of her pink tiffany gown brushed his leg as she turned indignantly to face him. "If you are seeking to plead your son's cause, I find it an intolerable insult. I am betrothed to Mr. Severn."

"No," Sir Digby said bluntly, "you are not. You are betrothed, Miss Loring, to Jocelyn Rivers, the rightful Viscount Avenhurst."

The moon seemed to spin like a silver coin down the sky; the lights in the street rushed up to meet it. Serena clutched at the balustrade to steady herself.

"What did you say?" she asked faintly.

"That the man you have always known as Julian Severn, the man you have promised to marry, is the only surviving son of the third Viscount Avenhurst. Jocelyn Rivers, the fourth viscount."

The stone of the balustrade was rough beneath Serena's hands, and the texture of it was the only thing that convinced her she was not dreaming. She said in that same faint voice:

"I do not understand. Lord Avenhurst—!"

"The young man you know by that title is Godfrey Rivers, head of the northern and junior branch of the family. He inherited only because the true heir could not be traced." Sir Digby paused, and though he was intently watching Serena's white face in the moonlight, his voice by contrast was sympathetic and reassuring. "This has been a shock to you, Miss Loring, but permit me to explain. When Jocelyn Rivers was eighteen, he quarreled violently with his father about the course his future was to take, left Avenhurst Place secretly by night and disappeared. All Lord Avenhurst's efforts to find him—and these never ceased until his lordship's death nine years later—met with no success. In the end his death was presumed, and Avenhurst passed to young Godfrey."

"No!" Serena's exclamation was a muted cry of denial. "You are mistaken—you must be! Others would have recognized him. Lady Avenhurst—!"

"But I did not recognize him," Vaine interrupted smoothly. "I doubt if anyone would, for except for his height and the color of his eyes, Severn bears little resemblance to Jocelyn Rivers at eighteen. But Septimus Twigg was Jocelyn's godfather and devoted friend, and I have learned from conversation with your mother that a few months after Jocelyn's disappearance, Julian Severn arrived in Jamaica, bearing a letter from Twigg entreating your father's good offices for a young man needing to make his way in the world. A young man with no family commitments whatsoever."

"That does not prove—!"

"True! It does not *prove* anything, but is it not a most singular coincidence? I have elicited from your mother the information that Severn was nineteen when you first met him. 'A lanky youth with black hair' is how she describes him, and *that* description, Miss Loring, exactly fits Jocelyn Rivers as I remember him."

Her surroundings had steadied themselves now that the first shock had been assimilated, and though her heart was thudding so violently that she could scarcely breathe, her wits were beginning to work again. Why was he telling her this? Was it true, or did he just believe it to be true? Or was it some colossal and incomprehensible hoax?

"If what you say is true"—she was feeling her way now, cautiously refusing to accept anything he said—"why is he keeping it secret now that he is in England again?"

"My dear Miss Loring, I am not omniscient! Perhaps he had some quaint notion of winning your hand while you were still in ignorance of his real identity. Perhaps—which is, if you will forgive me, more likely—he anticipates some difficulty in proving it. There is only his word, and Twigg's. No one, not even his own stepmother, has guessed who he is."

"No one, Sir Digby, save yourself. Or so you would have me believe."

"As you say, madam, none save myself. I need hardly say that he may depend upon me to uphold his claim."

"I am sure he would be grateful, sir, if what you suppose were true."

"It *is* true, Miss Loring. I do not ask you to accept my word for it. Seek corroboration from Septimus Twigg. He, I am sure, will be only too happy to give it."

"Why should he, Sir Digby?"

"My dear lady, you must have perceived that Twigg has no kindness for the supposed Lord Avenhurst, who now fills the place belonging rightfully to Twigg's beloved godson. He must have been sworn to secrecy, or he would have disclosed the truth when old Avenhurst died."

"In that event, sir, it is unlikely that Mr. Twigg will break his silence now."

"He would break it for you, ma'am, for you are in a uniquely privileged position. You are the future viscountess." Serena made no reply, and after a moment Vaine continued softly: "Think for a moment what that means. Your future husband, I understand, is already a very rich man, but not all his wealth can purchase the privileges which in his rightful guise he can bestow upon you. An ancient name, the rank of peeress, great estates which have belonged to his family for centuries. These are your right. He should claim them for you, and for the children with which I trust your union will be blessed. Apart from all this, think of your sister, who appears to be on the point of bestowing her hand upon the supposed viscount."

"Are you advising me, sir," Serena asked curiously, "to rob my sister to benefit myself?"

"My dear Miss Loring, you will not be robbing her! You will be saving her from a shocking *mésalliance*, for without the viscounty, young Godfrey Rivers is no more than a country squire of modest means. I am sure you need have no qualms on Miss Lucilla's behalf, since she has half a dozen titled suitors besides Avenhurst."

There was a pause. Serena's mind was a chaos of conflicting thoughts and emotions, and she did not know what to believe, even what she wanted to believe; but out of the confusion one question emerged, demanding an answer.

"Tell me one thing, Sir Digby," she said quietly. "Why come to me?"

"My dear young lady—!"

"Why not to Julian himself? Or even Mr. Twigg?"

"Miss Loring, Jocelyn Rivers and I were never closely acquainted, and it would be exceedingly embarrassing for both of us if I were to approach him directly to offer my support. However, in view of what I know—"

"What you suspect."

"Very well! What I *suspect*, I cannot bring myself to remain silent."

"I see! You conceive it to be your duty," she said softly.

There was the tiniest hesitation before he answered, and she saw his eyes flash in the moonlight as he bestowed on her one of his piercing looks. Then, apparently deciding that the remark was as guileless as on the surface it sounded, he said easily:

"You understand me precisely, ma'am. My duty, not least of all to you, who will, if I may be permitted to say so, grace the high position to which your marriage will raise you."

She did not believe him. Sir Digby Vaine, she thought, was a stranger to altruism, and so he must have some other reason, something he did not wish her to suspect. Julian would have to be told about this extraordinary conversation, yet how *could* she ask him if he had been deceiving her? Deceiving them all, ever since he arrived in Jamaica? Why, if this incredible thing were true, was he keeping it from her even now? Was it really just a quarrel with his father which had led him to abandon a great inheritance? Somehow Sir Digby's story had not rung true in that respect, and against her will Serena found herself remembering that Prudence Rivers had spoken of a "wicked" uncle. To be sure, Prudence tended to exaggerate, but why "wicked"? And Julian had spoken confidently of Avenhurst Place....

Suppose it were *not* true? Suppose Sir Digby were genuinely mistaken, or lying to serve some unfathomable purpose of his own? Would Julian ever forgive her for having doubted him? Question after question went spinning through her mind, and she felt sure of only one thing. Until she had a chance to talk to Julian, privately, without fear of interruption, she must make Vaine believe that he had convinced her.

"You are too kind, sir! I must think about what you have told me! Learn to accustom myself—it is scarcely believable—a viscount—!" She paused, as though recollecting herself, and then said hurriedly: "I must go back! If my absence were to be noticed—!" She left the sentence unfinished.

He bowed silent assent and turned to draw aside the curtain so that she could pass through, keeping himself discreetly hidden from view as he did so. Then he let the heavy fabric fall again, and stood staring thoughtfully at the houses on the other side of the street, a faint smile curving his thin lips.

She had risen to the bait, as he had been certain she would. As she could not fail to do, this little nobody from the colonies, who, too timid to take advantage of the opportunities London offered, had scuttled into the refuge of betrothal to a man she had known since her childhood. Who was dazzled by the glittering future now dangled before her and, probably even more enticing than that, by the prospect of equaling for once the achievements of her more beautiful and spirited sister.

Sir Digby, smiling quietly in the moonlight, felt very pleased with himself.

Septimus Twigg was troubled. He made another early call at the house in Arlington Street, and, alone with his godson in the back parlor, said abruptly:

"Julian, it's my belief that Vaine means mischief."

Julian frowned. "In what way?"

"In the way likely to hit you hardest of all," Septimus told him grimly. "Through Miss Serena. He was private with her for some ten minutes at the drum last night." He saw the change in Julian's expression and added hastily: "Now don't misunderstand me, lad! I'm not suggesting he means *her* any harm, for all that happened was that he persuaded her to step out onto the balcony with him. I'll wager no one else noticed, but I happened to be on my way to speak to her at the time. No, the thing that troubles me is what Vaine can have to say to your future wife which can't be said in public."

"She did seem to become very quiet last night," Julian agreed. He struck the arm of his chair with his clenched fist. "By God, if Vaine has said anything to distress or frighten her—!"

"You will have to find out," Septimus said urgently. "I don't trust him, Julian! If he has guessed who you are, he'll not hesitate to make it public to serve his own ends."

"To serve his own ends?" Julian repeated in astonishment. "Why the devil should it matter to Digby Vaine whether I am known as Julian Severn or Jocelyn Rivers?"

"It would not," Septimus agreed with a touch of grimness, "but it would matter a great deal if you were known to be Viscount Avenhurst."

"Confound it, Sep, if you are to become profound—!" Julian's words were checked suddenly, and he stared with narrowed eyes at his godfather. "You mean he has some grudge against young Godfrey?"

"Yes, he has." Mr. Twigg hesitated, seemed to hold a brief, silent argument with himself and then continued irritably: "Damn it all, there's no need for secrecy! It seems all London knew of it, for Augusta took the trouble to write and tell me, and it was even hinted at in the newspaper. Vaine hates Godfrey, Julian, because a year ago the young fool made a cuckold of him."

After one startled moment, Julian found that he was not surprised. Celia might have remained faithful to her husband until he was left maimed and crippled, but afterwards it was inevitable that, with her instinctive shuddering away from physical infirmity, she would seek consolation elsewhere; and Sir Digby was an intensely jealous man.

"Vaine discovered it, of course," Septimus was saying, "and brought her ladyship back to the country before the season was half over. She was ill, he said, and I know for a fact that she was confined to her rooms for a month and more, seeing no one but her waiting-woman and Vaine himself. He had dismissed her abigail in London, and replaced her with a tight-lipped harridan who looked more like a jailer than maid to a lady of quality." He paused, meeting Julian's incredulous look. "Digby Vaine is a man it's not prudent to injure. I fancy her ladyship will not stray again."

Julian thought of Celia as she now was. The fragile look of her; the brittle gaiety; the breathless anxiety to placate her husband which was implicit in every word and look and gesture. Septimus was right. Whatever punishment Vaine had inflicted upon her for her infidelity must have been severe.

"And I suppose if Vaine had been whole, he would have sent his friends to wait upon Avenhurst, and avenged his honor with sword or pistol," he said slowly, "but as it is—!"

"As it is," Mr. Twigg interrupted him, "he must be hankering for some other means of revenge, and if he has guessed who you really are, he will know he has found it. Godfrey Rivers has been Viscount Avenhurst for more than three years, long enough to grow accustomed to all the privileges that position bestows. What satisfaction for Vaine if he could condemn him to become again a mere country squire, particularly now, when he seems on the point of winning Miss

Lucilla's hand. Surely Thaddeus would forbid her to marry him in those circumstances?"

"He would not need to," Julian informed him drily. "God-frey would soon fall from Lucilla's favor if he were stripped of rank and fortune, and Vaine must realize that. He is shrewd enough to have taken her measure."

"I don't like it," Mr. Twigg said worriedly. "If Vaine has guessed the truth, the whole story will soon be out. Julian, you *must* find out how much he has told Miss Serena."

"I know, but how the devil am I to do that? Oh, damn Vaine to hell!" Julian sprang to his feet and began to pace restlessly about the room. "Sep, what can I say to her? How can I ask her whether or not she knows that the man she has promised to marry is branded in the eyes of the world as a child-murderer?"

He broke off, heeding too late his companion's quick warning gesture. Septimus was staring past him with a look of utter dismay, and Julian, swinging around, found that the door had opened quietly while he was speaking, and that Serena herself, wide-eyed with shock, was standing on the threshold.

He stared at her, numb with consternation, dreading to see her shrink from him, but instead she closed the door gently behind her and came across the room towards him. Came to him unfalteringly, with steadfast, trusting eyes, until she was close enough to reach up and set her hands on his shoulders and look into his face.

"It is not true," she said in a low voice, and the words were neither a blind protest nor a plea for reassurance, but the calm avowal of unshakable conviction. "It could not be. You are incapable of so vile a crime."

Julian's hands lifted to cover hers and gather them into his own. "No," he said simply, "it is not true, but there are many who believed it once, and would believe it again."

It was as though they were alone in the room. Looking into each other's eyes above their joined hands, they had forgotten Septimus Twigg, forgotten everything except their mutual need to comfort and reassure, and their thankfulness that not even this crisis had the power to come between them. After a moment he bent and kissed her, and Mr. Twigg, feeling as though he had suddenly become invisible, got up and tiptoed out of the room. Neither Julian nor Serena noticed him go.

"Julian," Serena asked after a while, "did Sir Digby tell me the truth last night? Are you really Viscount Avenhurst?"

"By right of birth, I am," he admitted. "What else did Vaine tell you?"

Briefly she told him, and as he listened, Julian realized how foolish he had been to underestimate the man, to let the fact that they had been only slightly acquainted blind him to the danger of Sir Digby's keen wits detecting the implications of Julian Severn's connection with Septimus Twigg. Once that link had been established, the rest had followed as naturally as night followed day.

Drawing Serena to sit with him on the sofa lately occupied by Mr. Twigg, Julian told her the whole story of his early life. He held nothing back, and perhaps revealed even more than he intended, for when he paused, Serena, who had been sitting with her hands in his, freed one of them and gently touched his cheek.

"I understand now what first drew me to you when I was a child," she said softly. "You knew I was lonely and unhappy because you had been unhappy in the same way."

He captured the hand again and bore it to his lips. "You were my salvation then, my darling, just as you are my hope of happiness today. Can you forgive me for deceiving you all these years?"

She brushed this aside as being of little importance. "What is there to forgive? You are my own dear love, and that is all that matters."

He caught her close again, and she curled herself happily, trustfully into his embrace, while Julian silently thanked God that discovery of his secret had cast no shadow between them. If Vaine's disclosures had robbed him of Serena, he thought, he would have killed him, cripple or no. Yet one thing Vaine had said to her had some justice in it. Serena did have the right to be Viscountess Avenhurst. No title in the land could adorn her as much as she would adorn it, but he would reclaim his birthright for her sake if that was what she wanted....

"Julian!" Serena spoke diffidently. "Can we not be married at once and go away from London? I cannot bear to think that anything may prevent us from going home to Meadowsweet. For it might do so, might it not, if the truth became known, even though you do not want to be Viscount Avenhurst?"

"It might," he admitted. "I would renounce the title, but God knows how long it might be before all was settled. Is that what you really want, Serena? To be a planter's wife in Virginia rather than a peeress in England?"

"More than anything in the world," she replied simply. "It was always Mama and Lucy who wanted to cut a dash in the world of fashion, not I. Lucy says I have no ambition."

"Well, *she* has more than enough for two!" Julian spoke absently; then, after a pause, added with sudden resolution: "I must see Vaine and try to convince him that he is mistaken. Or, failing that, that I have no intention of being forced into admitting my real identity."

"Forced into it?" Startled, Serena sat upright again. "Would he do that?"

"I fear so!" Julian hesitated, but then decided on a measure of frankness. "You see, sweetheart, it is Avenhurst he is seeking to injure. My young kinsman has wronged him, and nothing matters to Vaine but revenge."

"That is monstrous!" Serena said indignantly. "How dare he expose *you* to slander and gossip just to serve his own ends? I knew he had some wicked purpose in telling me what he did!"

IV

Sir Digby received Julian courteously, and without surprise. Begged him to be seated; to take a glass of wine. Julian declined both invitations and came straight to the point.

"I am informed, sir, that you harbor a curious delusion concerning me. Abandon it! It is quite erroneous."

"Indeed?" Vaine's head was thrown back, his veiled gaze intent upon the taller man's face. "I find that impossible to believe."

"I commiserate with you. The fact remains that you are mistaken."

There was a little silence. Vaine continued to study Julian, and Julian met his eyes unwaveringly, faintly disdainful. At length Vaine shook his head.

"I wonder," he remarked, "why your lordship is so reluctant to admit the truth. To reach out your hand and take what is rightfully yours."

Julian's brows lifted. "My dear sir, you have mistaken your man. I am not a needy adventurer, to be dazzled into gambling for a prize to which I have no right. On the other hand, if I *were* the man you suspect me to be, surely the fact that I make no attempt to prove it would indicate that I have no desire to resurrect my younger self."

"Not for your own sake, perhaps, my lord, but what of the lady you have asked to be your wife?"

"Another error, Sir Digby, which proves you to be a poor judge of character. You measure the elder sister by the younger."

Anger glinted for a moment in the sleepy hazel eyes. "And what of the younger sister, my lord? Will you stand by and permit your friend's daughter to commit herself to so disastrous a match?"

Julian shook his head. "If I believed, sir, that there were the slightest danger of Lord Avenhurst's position being seriously challenged, I would *not* permit it. Allow me to assure you that no such danger threatens."

Vaine's lips had tightened. He was preserving his customary air of mocking urbanity, but Julian observed with satisfaction that it was costing him a considerable effort.

"Let us understand each other, Sir Digby," he said quietly. "For reasons of your own, you have chosen to delude yourself into believing that I am the son of the late Lord Avenhurst. I assure you repeatedly that I am not, but you seem unable to accept my word. That is your misfortune, but remember this. Your differences with young Avenhurst are no concern of mine, and I will not be used as a stick with which to beat him."

Sir Digby's eyes were sleepy no longer. Fury fairly blazed in them.

"Do you seriously expect me to believe that you are *not* Jocelyn Rivers?"

"What you believe, sir, is your own concern. I give you facts. I am Julian Severn, a shipowner and planter, lately of Jamaica and now of Virginia. No more, no less—no matter how earnestly you may wish it were otherwise. So let this be the end of the matter. To persist in it can only bring ridicule upon you."

He paused, but Vaine, his thin, lined face white with anger, seemed unable to find words with which to reply. Julian bowed slightly and turned away, but paused with his hand on the door handle to look again at the older man.

"One thing more, Sir Digby! This curious obsession with my supposed identity has prompted you to distress Miss Loring. You would do well to remember that that is something I do not permit."

238

Still no reply. Julian went out and closed the door softly behind him.

He hoped that he had succeeded in convincing Vaine, if not of his identity, at least of the fact that he had no intention of making any claim to Avenhurst, but he knew he could place no dependence on this being the end of the matter. Sir Digby, possessed by jealousy and burning with the desire to revenge himself upon the man with whom his wife had betrayed him, was quite capable of making his belief public. Julian could persist in his denial and no one could compel him to admit that he was Jocelyn Rivers, but once the connection between Jocelyn-Julian and Septimus Twigg became common knowledge, no denials would be believed. The scandalmongers would make holiday. Not only would all the sordid details of Jocelyn's disgrace be resurrected and raked over, but Godfrey's present sure claim to the title would be called into question; and, through Godfrey and Lucilla, Thaddeus and Margaret would be subjected to worry and distress. A fine return for all that Julian Severn owed to them.

No, Serena was right. The sooner they were away from London, the better. Julian summoned a hackney carriage and had himself driven to Lloyd's Coffee House in Lombard Street, where the latest shipping news was always to be obtained.

Luck was with him. There was word of a ship leaving the Pool of London for Yorktown in ten days' time, and Julian, following this promising lead, discovered that she was a well-found vessel with suitable accommodation for passengers. He concluded the arrangements then and there, bespeaking passage for himself and Serena and their two personal servants. It would mean obtaining a license so that they could be married before leaving England, but he anticipated no difficulty in that direction.

The day was well advanced by the time he returned to Arlington Street, and Serena was keeping anxious watch for him from the window of the drawing room on the first floor. She came to the head of the stairs as he was admitted to the house, and he took the flight two at a time and caught her hands in his.

"We sail for Virginia in ten days, sweetheart," he told her. "Can you be ready?"

"Oh, Julian, yes!" Her eyes were shining; her fingers clung to his. "But is it possible to be married in so short a time?"

"Yes, by special license." He kissed her hands and then,

239

with an arm about her, swept her back into the drawing room, where her parents and Lucilla were sitting. "Thaddeus, I have found a ship bound for Yorktown. Have I your permission to marry Serena immediately?"

Thaddeus Loring looked at him, catching in voice and manner a glimpse of the Julian of five years ago; and Seena—! The girl seemed positively to glow with happiness.

"Would it make any difference if I said no?" he asked humorously. "How soon do you put to sea?"

"In ten days, from the Pool," Julian was beginning, but Margaret interrupted with an exclamation of dismay.

"Ten days? Julian, have you taken leave of your senses? I cannot possibly make all the arrangements in so short a time."

"Oh, Mama, we do not want a great fuss, or a crowd of guests," Serena protested before Julian could reply. "Just you and Papa and Lucy and Mr. Twigg, and perhaps Lady Selford, since she has been so kind to us."

"What, and have it said you were married in a hole-and-corner fashion, as though we have something to be ashamed of?" Margaret, usually so placid, was for once seriously put out. "I cannot see any necessity for such unseemly haste. You have been betrothed only a few days."

"There will not even be time," added Lucilla, stating what, for her, would have been an insuperable objection, "for you to have a bridal gown made."

"Lucy, I have a dozen pretty dresses to choose from," Seena said impatiently. "I have told you, I do not want a great fuss!"

She should have guessed, she was thinking with angry self-reproach, what Mama's reaction would be. London had gone to her head, so that even her elder daughter's wedding had been looked forward to as an important social event, and it would not be easy to persuade her to forego her triumph. She said earnestly:

"Mama, it is *my* wedding, so may I not have the sort of quiet, simple ceremony I would prefer? Indeed, there will not be time for anything else, since we are to leave England so soon."

"But *why* must you leave so soon?" Margaret demanded irritably. "Yes, Julian, I know you have found a ship, but it is not, I presume, the *only* vessel which plies between London and Yorktown!" She turned to her husband. "Thaddeus—!"

Loring had been watching Julian, seeing the scarcely curbed impatience in the strong, dark face, an impatience which went beyond even that of a man as deeply in love as Julian undoubtedly was with Serena. He is not only eager to claim his bride, Thaddeus thought suddenly. He wants to be done with England; to put the past behind him once and for all, and what right have we to deny that to him; to either of them? Let them go, with our blessing, to the life they are to share.

"I fear there is no stopping them, my dear," he told Margaret, and though he spoke quietly, even with a touch of humor, she recognized the finality of the words. "If I do not give my consent, I suspect we may find ourselves with an elopement on our hands. You will have to resign yourself to a private ceremony."

This, however, she refused to do, and, while Julian attended to the formalities of obtaining the license and arranging for the ceremony to take place, plunged into a whirl of preparation, determined to do the best she could with the limited time at her disposal. As a bride, Serena held the center of the family stage for the first and last time in her life, and Lucilla was cast into the shade, but, being Lucilla, was not content to remain there. Within twenty-four hours she had accepted a proposal of marriage from Godfrey, and stepped into prominence again as the future Viscountess Avenhurst.

Julian felt profoundly uneasy. He had hoped to marry Serena and embark for America before news of the wedding became known, though he realized now that this had never been possible without the very explanations he was so anxious to avoid, but, thanks to Margaret, the wedding was as much a matter of comment and gossip as Lucilla's betrothal. It seemed too much to hope that Sir Digby Vaine would not seek to take advantage of the situation.

Two days later Julian's misgivings were justified. An anxious Serena waylaid him as he entered the house and led him off to the back parlor.

"Julian, Lady Vaine has been here. We are all bidden to dine with her and Sir Digby tomorrow. I know! I know!" she added as she saw his expression. "I would have declined if I could, but I was out shopping with Lucy when her ladyship arrived, and by the time we returned, she and Mama had it all settled. As it happened, none of us had any engagements for tomorrow."

"I don't like it!" Julian was frowning. "Vaine would not invite us to dine with him unless he means mischief."

"Her ladyship *said* he wishes to hold a little gathering for some of our particular friends to bid us Godspeed," Serena offered doubtfully, "though that does not seem to me very likely."

"Nor to me, my love! *She* may believe it to be no more than that, but I'll wager Vaine himself has some other purpose in mind."

"I am not sure Lady Vaine does believe it," Serena said thoughtfully. "I have the impression that she cares for it as little as we do."

"Very likely," Julian agreed. "Did she give you any idea who the other guests will be?"

"No, but Avenhurst arrived just before you came in, and he has received an invitation."

"Then we may be sure some devilry is planned. A man of Vaine's nature does not invite his wife's former lover to his table without some very pressing reason. Yes," he added grimly as he encountered her started look, "that is the source of Vaine's enmity. The affair is over now and there is no need for Lucilla or your parents to know of it, but apparently it was the talk of the town a year ago." He frowned. "Does Avenhurst intend to accept?"

"Yes, for I heard him tell Lucy that he would come here and escort her to Sir Digby's house. I suppose he could not well refuse without displeasing her."

"He probably feels there will be less awkwardness if he arrives with us instead of alone. I'll wager he is on tenterhooks, wondering what Vaine intends."

Her troubled gaze searched his face. "What do *you* think he intends?"

He shrugged. "To try to force me into admitting that I am Jocelyn Rivers. How he proposes to do it I cannot guess, but whatever means he uses, it is bound to be damnably unpleasant." He took her hands in his and stood looking gravely down at her. "Will you ever be able to forgive me, my darling, for exposing you to it?"

"Oh, Julian, what a foolish question!" She smiled lovingly up at him, her fingers entwined with his. "*You* are not to blame! Besides, how can he force you to admit anything of the kind?"

"He cannot, of course, but he does not need to. Once the link with Septimus is established—and you have seen how convincingly he can do that—no denials of mine will be believed. The stumbling block, you see, is that I *am* Jocelyn Rivers, and have no way of proving that I am not, for Sep's word will not be accepted, any more than my own."

"This has happened because Mama insists upon making such an occasion of our wedding," Serena said bitterly. "If Sir Digby had known nothing about that—! We should have been married secretly, Julian, and not told anyone until the very day we were to embark. Or eloped, as Papa said. I am sure I have heard that one can be married at sea, by the ship's captain."

"Serena!" Julian caught her to him, laughing a little yet deeply touched. "Would you really have done that?"

"I would do anything to make sure that we sail for home next week, as we have planned." She laid her hands up at him. "Nothing will prevent that, will it, no matter what Sir Digby may do?"

"No," he said recklessly. "No, by God, nothing shall prevent it!"

Yet, even as he spoke, he wondered if he would be able to make good that promise. If the threatened storm broke, could he, even for Serena's sake, sail away and leave others to bear the brunt of it? Oh, damn Vaine, and Avenhurst, and Celia, too, for creating between them this intolerable situation!

"I suppose," Serena said diffidently after a moment, "that it would do no good if we made some excuse not to go to Sir Digby's house after all? Would that spoil his plans, do you think?"

Julian shook his head. "We could place no dependence on that, sweetheart, and if there is to be any hope at all of refuting his allegations, I must be there to meet face to face whatever challenge he chooses to throw down."

"*We* will meet it face to face," Serena corrected softly, clasping her arms about his neck. "You and I, Julian. Together. Now and always."

The composition of the party which assembled in Celia's drawing room the following afternoon immediately confirmed Julians' suspicions. Simon Vaine was there (under constraint, to judge from his expression), and also Celia's father, William Croyde, a widower now and apparently making an annual visit to his daughter and son-in-law, while Lady Avenhurst and Prudence arrived just ahead of Julian's party. Lady Selford, escorted by Septimus, joined them soon afterwards. The company was completed by Major Martin Ashe, a neighbor of Vaine's who had been a boyhood crony of Jocelyn Rivers, and his wife; and Lord and Lady Atterbury. The latter, Julian reflected grimly, were the only guests present who had no connection with Jocelyn, but as her ladyship was notorious as the most avid gossip in London, the reason for their inclusion was not far to seek.

Celia, flitting from one guest to another, seemed unable to be still. She was painted more heavily than usual, but this served only to emphasize a pallor against which the rouge and carmine showed harshly on cheeks and lips, and did nothing to disguise the haunted, haggard expression in her beautiful eyes. Julian wondered whether she had any idea of what Vaine intended, or whether her agitation was due solely to Avenhurst's presence. The viscount himself was palpably uneasy.

Simon, poker-faced, offered Serena and Julian his felicitations and then rather ostentatiously devoted all his attention to Prudence Rivers, while in Mr. Twigg, anxiety took the form of a testiness and gruffness which more than once caused Lady Selford to look very hard at him. Julian himself preserved his usual assured bearing but was conscious of tension within him like a coiled spring, and he knew that Serena's grave composure was a mask for similarly taut and jangled nerves. Sir Digby, smiling and urbane, regarded the company with veiled, secret eyes, and bided his time.

When they moved from drawing room to dining room, it was seen that Lady Vaine followed the new fashion of seating ladies and gentlemen alternately at her table instead of facing each other across it. This was considered rather daring by the older generation, and Lady Selford put up her lorgnette to regard the arrangement with disapproval, but, most uncharacteristically, refrained from comment. Perhaps, Julian thought with a flicker of wry humor, even the redoubtable Augusta was subdued by a sense of things impending.

The meal was long, elaborate and, to some of the guests at least, almost unbearable in its very normality. It lasted for more than two hours, but at last the cloth was removed and wine brought and poured for the whole company, for it was still the custom for the ladies to take one glass with the gentlemen before retiring to the drawing room. When all had been served, Sir Digby signaled to a footman, who immediately came forward to help him to rise and to hand him his crutch. With his free hand Vaine picked up his glass.

"My friends," he said, and all other talk died away as his guests turned expectantly towards him, "let us drink a toast to the future Viscountess Avenhurst," and with the utmost deliberation he raised the glass, not to Lucilla, but to Serena on the opposite side of the table.

There was a moment of stunned, bewildered silence. In Lucilla's face the beginnings of a complacent smile vanished, and she flushed scarlet to the roots of her powdered hair. Serena, white-faced, flashed a look of frantic appeal towards Julian, but it was Godfrey who first recovered his voice.

"If this is meant for a jest, Sir Digby," he said indignantly, "the point of it escapes me. Nor do I greatly care for your humor."

"I am not jesting, *Mr. Rivers!*" Sir Digby's eyes, gleaming with malice, never wavered from the young man's face. "Miss Serena Loring is very shortly to be married to your kinsman. To Jocelyn Rivers, the fourth Viscount Avenhurst."

A little sound, half gasp and half whimper, broke from Celia's lips, but otherwise the silence remained complete. Godfrey went white, and cast an angry, uncomprehending look at Julian, and the eyes of the whole company turned in the same direction.

He had not moved. Leaning back a little in his chair, one hand in its wealth of fine lace resting on the polished table, he bore that sustained regard with no change of expression. Almost he seemed amused, and only Serena and Mr. Twigg guessed how great an effort was needed to retain that pose.

"My dear sir," he said, and somehow managed to infuse the same sort of tolerant amusement into his voice, "pray recollect that when you confided to me your incomprehensible conviction that I am someone I am not, I advised you against repeating it for fear of ridicule. What a pity you did not heed that excellent advice." He turned to Lady Avenhurst. "Madam, Sir Digby implies, I believe, that I am your stepson. Would it help to convince him, do you suppose, if you assured him that I am not?"

His tone invited her to share his own amusement at an

245

absurdity. She smiled uncertainly but continued to stare at him, her gaze searching the lean, tanned face with lines etched deeply about the eyes and the stern mouth, framed by the formally dressed, snow-white hair. He lowered his eyes, and with a steady hand raised his glass of wine to his lips.

"Of course he is not! Jocelyn Rivers is dead—has been dead for years!" Godfrey's voice was a shade too loud and too belligerent, with a ragged edge of alarm. Then, with sudden inspiration: "If Severn *were* Jocelyn Rivers, Mr. Twigg would have recognized him!"

Vaine smiled unpleasantly. "I am sure that Mr. Twigg is very well aware of our friend's real identity. That he has always known the whereabouts of Jocelyn Rivers, for the simple reason that he himself sent Jocelyn to Jamaica." He looked at Septimus. "Well, Twigg? Can you in honesty deny it?"

"Neither Mr. Twigg nor I," Julian put in smoothly before Septimus could reply, "has ever sought to conceal the fact that it was upon his advice, and with his introduction to Mr. Loring, that I first went to Jamaica. I, Sir Digby. Julian Severn."

"And Julian Severn appeared in Jamaica only a few months after Jocelyn Rivers vanished from England," Vaine retorted sneeringly. "We are to believe, are we, that that is mere coincidence?"

"What *I* believe," Septimus said explosively, "is that you, sir, have taken leave of your senses! You ask us to accept that you alone have recognized Julian Severn as Jocelyn Rivers! You, who were scarcely acquainted with the boy! What of those of us who knew him well? Lady Avenhurst? Major Ashe?" He paused, but neither made any response beyond a doubtful, embarrassed exchange of glances. Septimus smote the table with his open palm. "I tell you, the suggestion is absurd!"

"I observe, Twigg," Sir Digby replied silkily, "that you take care not to enquire of my wife. Yet she, too, knew Jocelyn Rivers. Knew him well." There was mockery in his voice, and in the look he bestowed upon Celia at the other end of the table. "Come, my dear, what do *you* say? Now that I have opened your eyes, do you not recognize in Mr. Severn an old—friend?"

Everyone looked towards Celia, but she was staring at Julian. Across the table, across the polished wood and the glasses of wine that glowed like jewels in the candlelight, their glances met and held. It seemed inconceivable that now she would not know him, and he braced himself for the words which would defeat him utterly. They did not come. Instead she dragged her gaze away, cast one anguished, despairing glance at Godfrey, and then with a great sob buried her face in her hands.

"Scarcely conclusive!" Vaine's voice was smooth, but his wife flinched as though a lash had curled itself searingly about her body. "Too invidious a choice to make, no doubt."

A little stir of acute embarrassment, sensed rather than heard or seen, passed round the table, and Julian felt a tentative flicker of hope. Perhaps Vaine had overreached himself by so blatantly demonstrating the jealous motive behind his actions. Trying to take advantage of this, Julian turned to Godfrey.

"My lord, Sir Digby seems determined to wrest your honors from you and bestow them upon me, and though I cannot suppose that you, any more than I, take that determination seriously, pray let me assure you that I have no more claim to those honors than I have desire to assume them. I am *not* Jocelyn Rivers. My name, as I have repeatedly assured him, is Julian Severn."

"Ah, yes! From Northumberland!" Sir Digby's voice was still as smooth as silk. "Well, Mr. Severn from Northumberland, since you are *not* Jocelyn Rivers, perhaps you will tell us *who* you are." He paused as though for a reply, but Julian made no response. Vaine's brows lifted. "Come, sir, you are eager to prove me wrong, and you may do so very easily. A few simple facts about your home and family. Is that too much to ask?"

It was not, and they all knew it. Julian, glancing swiftly round the table, saw expectancy in the faces turned towards him, and silently cursed himself for not having invented the facts Vaine was demanding, and fabricated some sort of evidence to support them. Now it was too late. Whatever he said would be doubted and questioned, and since it could not be proved, would make matters worse than before.

He was intensely aware of the faces around the table. Godfrey, white as death, with beads of sweat on his brow, and beside him, Lucilla's stricken look. The Lorings, alarmed and bewildered, aghast at this threat to their darling's happiness; Septimus looking desperately worried; Augusta like a jeweled and watchful hawk; and Serena—most of all, he was aware of Serena, of her loving, pleading, trustful gaze. He was going to fail her. All their hopes and plans hung in the balance, yet he could not keep his promise. His mind seemed numb, and he could think of nothing to say.

"No?" Vaine's hateful, mocking voice sounded triumphant. "You are strangely reluctant, sir, and I would be willing to wager that is because no one in Northumberland has ever heard the name of Severn, or could claim acquaintance with you or any other member of that family."

"You would lose your wager, Sir Digby!"

It was Lady Selford who had spoken, and the intervention was as startling to the company as a trumpet call, commanding everyone's attention. Her voice was arctic, and so was the look she bent upon Vaine.

"I am shocked!" she stated in measured tones. "Shocked beyond measure! Never have I experienced so gross an abuse of the duty owed by a host to his guests. It passes all belief! As for Mr. Severn—'fore Gad, sir! Do you dare to suppose that *I* would sponsor anyone of whose antecedents I knew nothing? I am wholly familiar with his family background. I knew his late mother when she was a child, I was a guest at her wedding and I remember him well when he was a little boy." She paused, lifted her lorgnette and through it surveyed Sir Digby with haughty challenge. "You do not, I trust, presume to question *my* veracity?"

This, as Vaine well knew, was more than he dare do, for Augusta Selford wielded a power few would venture to challenge. Her influence reached far beyond the fashionable world of which she was the acknowledged doyenne. Through her large family she could bring pressure to bear upon many Government and diplomatic circles where Sir Digby's political interests also lay, and though a staunch friend, she could be an implacable enemy. If she chose to marshal her forces against him, he could well find himself facing a future in obscurity, and that was too high a price to pay even for revenge upon Avenhurst. Whether or not she was speaking the truth was immaterial; her word would be accepted everywhere in preference to his.

"I would not be guilty, Lady Selford, of such discourtesy," he said with savage politeness. "I was not aware that you are so intimately acquainted with Mr. Severn's family, but ob-

248

viously I must accept your ladyship's assurance and acknowledge myself mistaken."

It was an ambiguous reply, admitting defeat but nothing more, and for a moment she continued to survey him as though considering whether to demand a more complete recantation. Eventually she decided merely to twist the knife a little.

"It is always rash, Sir Digby, to make wild allegations without being certain of one's facts. Had you applied to me, I would have pointed out your error and so spared all of us a great deal of unnecessary embarrassment. Only a very foolish person, or a very malicious one, would have failed to take so elementary a precaution." Without pausing to see the effect of this withering rebuke, she turned to Celia. "In the circumstances, Lady Vaine, you will forgive me, I am sure, for asking you to have my carriage summoned immediately."

Celia, who by this time looked ready to faint, cast a glance of frantic inquiry at her husband, but receiving no help there, gave the necessary orders in a failing voice. It was clear that Lady Selford had expressed the feelings of all the guests, and that everyone was anxious to escape as quickly as possible from the hideously embarrassing situation created by their host. There was a general rising from chairs; an awkward exchange of banalities to fill the uncomfortable pause; sidelong glances at Julian, at Avenhurst, at Vaine himself, who had sunk down into his seat again and sat with bowed head, chin buried in the lace at his breast and hands clenched hard on the arms of the chair.

A servant announced that Lady Selford's carriage was at the door. Augusta inclined her head frigidly to Celia and then looked around.

"Julian!" It was the first time she had ever addressed him by his first name. "You will escort me, if you please."

It startled him, but he had the presence of mind to respond without hesitation. "It will be a privilege, madam." He bowed to Celia. "Lady Vaine."

The hand she extended to him seemed cold and lifeless in his. The beautiful, haggard eyes lifted to search his face with questioning and doubt, and he knew that she was asking herself if it could possibly be true; if this could indeed be Jocelyn Rivers, whom she had fancied she loved, a lifetime ago. He kept his own expression deliberately impersonal, kissed the cold fingers before releasing them, and turned to offer his arm to Lady Selford. She set a jeweled claw on it and, with a gracious inclination of her head to the rest of the company, went with him out of the room.

"Until today," she observed dispassionately as they slowly descended the stairs, "I had always supposed Digby Vaine to be reasonably adroit. One can only suppose that the desire for revenge has deprived him of his wits."

"Will any harm come of it, ma'am?" Julian asked bluntly. "For myself it does not matter, since I am leaving England for good, but what of Avenhurst? Will there be talk?"

"Undoubtedly there will be talk. Maria Atterbury will see to that, but I can assure you that *my* word carries far more weight than hers. Vaine will find that it is he who comes off worst from this affair, which is no more than he deserves. To invite guests to his table, and then do his best to set them at each other's throats—'fore Gad! I have never heard the like."

"I will admit," Julian remarked drily, "that the prospect of Vaine's falling into his own snares affords me considerable satisfaction. I'll warrant, though, that it will be a long time before he forgives himself for inviting your ladyship to witness his expected triumph."

She gave her harsh cackle of laughter and paused in the hall to let a deferential footman lay her velvet wrap about her shoulders. Then, placing her hand on Julian's arm again, she said as they went out into the street:

"He had the impertinence to try to make use of me. I would have been obliged to punish him for that, even had I not been concerned to assist you and your charming bride."

He smiled, but when he spoke his voice was serious. "I shall be eternally grateful to you, Lady Selford. It would have been impossible for me to disprove Vaine's assertions, and I was growing desperate when it occurred to you to inform him that you had known my mother. I cannot imagine why you should go to such lengths on my behalf."

They had reached the carriage by this time. Augusta let him help her up into it, and when she was seated and had arranged her spreading satin skirts to her satisfaction, extended a beringed hand for him to kiss. He did so, but when he would have released it, the jeweled fingers tightened suddenly on his, holding him prisoner. Startled, he looked up into the painted hawk-face and saw the faded but compelling eyes glinting with impish amusement.

"Why I should lie for you, you mean," she said with un-disguised relish; "but you see, my dear boy, I did know your mother. I remember her very well. She had brown eyes, like yours, and her name was Julia."

It was autumn again when Julian brought Serena to Mea-dowsweet. They had stayed for a time in Williamsburg, where, renewing acquaintances made a year ago, he was struck afresh by the friendliness of the Virginians. They seemed genuinely pleased to see him again, and with one accord took Serena to their hearts. Julian, looking on with love and pride, saw her bloom with new assurance, watched her take, with sweet serenity, her place in the world which was to be theirs henceforth. Freed from the shadow of Lucilla, she had come at last into her own.

She had not yet seen the plantation, though Julian had ridden out there soon after their arrival. There would be a great deal to do. Some furniture he had bought along with the house, books and silver and porcelain and glass from Verwood's Kingdom had come north aboard the *Merry Venture*, while during his first weeks in London he had bought lavishly of the best the master craftsmen of England could provide. These goods had been shipped to Virginia ahead of him, and now the house slaves worked with a will, unpacking the innumerable crates and boxes, cleaning and polishing, so that all would be in readiness for the mistress of the house to arrange as she chose. Already touchingly grateful to Julian for buying them from Thaddeus Loring, their delight when he told them that "Miss Rena" was now his wife knew no bounds.

Now the day for which he had been waiting so long had come at last, and he was bringing home his bride. In a bor-rowed coach—for their own was still being built—behind some of their newly acquired horses, they were traversing the long plantation drive, and the moment he had first en-visaged more than a year ago was close at hand.

Serena, sitting with one hand in Julian's and the other grasping the strap which hung beside the window, looked out contentedly at the passing scene. Already she was enchanted by this land. The vastness of it, the thousands of miles of almost unexplored wilderness to westward, awed her but did not make her afraid; she could feel the power of it like a challenge. Boundless land, boundless opportunity. That was what Julian had said, and she knew he had been thinking not only of themselves, but of generations yet unborn. Gazing out across the well-tended fields, Serena smiled a small, secret smile. She was quite certain now, but she was waiting to tell him until they were together under their own roof-tree....

"Only a few minutes longer, sweetheart!" Julian lifted her fingers to his lips. "Then you will see your new home."

She turned to him, smiling, moving her hand in his so that she could lay the palm against his cheek. She had no idea what the house would be like, for he had refused to describe it, saying that she must wait to see it for herself. Of course she was eager to reach it, but this was of far less importance to her than the fact that Julian was beside her, that they would be together for the rest of their lives.

The coach halted. Reuben, who had ridden beside the coachman, came to let down the step. Julian jumped down and turned to take her hand, watching her face as she emerged.

She paused on the step to look eagerly about her. Saw the wide lawns and the rose beds and the soaring trees, the house of rose red brick with its tall windows and the graceful white pillars flanking the door. Incredulously, with dawning wonder and delight, her gaze passed over it all and finally came to rest on her husband's face.

"Julian!" she whispered. "Oh, Julian!"

Marshaled by Samuel, the house slaves had assembled outside the front door, beaming their delight at this reunion. With Julian beside her, Serena went from one to the other, greeting them like the old friends they were, and so at last they passed into the house. He led her straight to the drawing room, to the window where he had stood the previous year, but now it was her face he studied, and not the scene outside. He was reaping to the full the harvest of his long patience.

"I still cannot believe it!" she whispered at last. "It is here, just as I have always imagined it. Oh, I am so glad you did not tell me."

"I would not for the world have missed this moment," he said with a smile. "I wanted to see your face as you recognized your house."

"*Our* house," she corrected him softly. "Julian, how in the world did you find it?"

"I wish I could claim credit for doing so, but until I came

to inspect the estate, I had no idea what the house was like." He moved close behind her where she stood looking from the window, and put his arms around her so that she leaned back against him. "But when I stood here, as we are standing now, I knew that I had found the fulfillment of your dream." His arms tightened round her, and he bent his head to brush his lips against her temple. "I found something else that day, my darling! I found that it was Serena I loved. Had always loved, ever since she took possession of my heart when she was a little girl."

That is the truth, he thought. The only truth, the only reality. Celia was a boy's romantic dream, a dream as fragile and bright as a bubble, vanishing at the first breath of adversity; Alathea, with her doomed, golden beauty, was a brief fever in my blood; but Serena is companion and friend as well as my one true love. She is the other part of myself.

The sky was overcast, and a sudden gust of wind sent the last leaves racing and rustling across the grass; the rose beds were bare of blossom. Julian said ruefully:

"I planned to bring you here in summer, when all the roses are in bloom."

"They will bloom again next summer, and through all the summers we shall share." Serena drew a long breath of utter happiness, and then stirred and turned in her husband's embrace and clasped her arms around his neck. "My own dear love, I have something to tell you."

ABOUT THE AUTHOR

Sylvia Thorpe was born and educated in London and on leaving school, studied for three years at the Slade School of Fine Art, first at the Ashmolean Museum, Oxford, and later at University College, London. These studies helped to increase her already deep interest in the past, particularly in the seventeenth and eighteenth centuries. She now lives in Herefordshire, in the beautiful countryside—the Welsh Marches—that provided the setting for her Gothic romance, *Tarrington Chase*, and the opening chapters of *Three Loves*.

Writing has always been a favorite pastime and, while still a student, she wrote two historical romances. *The Scandalous Lady Robin* was accepted for publication, and since then she has written twenty-five novels, set in periods ranging from the seventeenth century to the Regency. In 1972, one of them, *The Scapegrace*, won the Elizabeth Goudge Historical Award.

Sylvia Thorpe is a founder member and former chairman of the Romantic Novelists' Association, and her other interests include period costume, amateur theatricals, the countryside, and dogs. Especially boxers, of which breed she owns a large and handsome specimen of great character.

Let COVENTRY Give You
A Little Old-Fashioned Romance